S. SEBASTIAN

CLAUDIA

THE GIRL WHO WENT IN SEARCH OF HAPPINESS

KNIGHT SWORD
PUBLICATION®

For inquiries or permissions, contact - admin@knightswordpublication.com

First edition

ISBN (paperback): 978-1-0681516-0-6
ISBN (hardcover): 978-1-0681516-1-3

Proofreading by Hugh B.
Cover art by Rafal Kucharczuk

This book was professionally typeset on Reedsy.
Find out more at reedsy.com

To my little boy, Ryan

At just three years old, you've already filled my world with more wonder, joy, and love than a lifetime ever could.
One day, when you're older, I hope you'll know:
Everything I do, I do with you in my heart.
I love you, always.

Contents

1

ITS COLD OUT HERE

The alarm clock rang sharply on the bedside table. The glowing red digits read 7:00 am—18 December 2002. Emmanuel lay still beneath the heavy duvet, unmoving. For a long moment, he didn't stir, his breath slow and steady. Then, reluctantly, his left hand reached out and silenced the ringing.

He didn't open his eyes straight away. He waited, as if expecting something—a voice, a touch. But the room remained silent. His right hand reached instinctively across the bed, finding only cool sheets. The emptiness hit him like a slow wave. With a heavy breath, Emmanuel pushed the duvet from his face and blinked into the dim morning light. Realisation settled over him with a quiet weight.

Sitting up with a weary sigh, he rubbed his face roughly, trying to chase away the sleep. His arms stretched wide, with his bones cracking in protest, before his hands dropped to the mattress. He sat still for a moment, staring absently towards the window, where heavy snow was falling in soft, endless silence.

He rose from the bed and padded across the room to the small bed tucked in the corner. Luca, his six-year-old son, was curled beneath his blanket, sound asleep. Emmanuel gently adjusted the covers, tucking them around Luca with quiet care. A flicker of tenderness softened his features as he watched the boy. Then, without a word, he turned and slipped out of the room.

The kitchen greeted him with cold stillness. He stopped at the doorway, frowning slightly. The kitchen door leading to the courtyard was ajar, letting in a thread of icy wind. Laura was standing outside, leaning against the brick wall. A cigarette smouldered between her fingers. She wore her worn coat, with lakes of snow clinging to her shoulders. Her posture was rigid, and distant.

Without a word, Emmanuel stepped outside and wrapped his arms gently around her from behind. He leaned in close, with his breath visible in the frosty air.

"What are you doing out here?" he murmured in his thick Italian accent. "It's cold out here."

Laura didn't answer. She took another long drag from her cigarette, exhaling slowly, with her eyes fixed on the white falling snow. He pressed a kiss to the back of her neck.

"Come inside, please," he whispered. "Let's shut the door."

She shifted slightly, just enough to glance back at him. Irritation flickered in her eyes.

"And do what?" she asked coolly.

He pulled back a little.

"What's wrong with you? You didn't even give me a morning kiss when you got up…"

Laura said nothing. The silence between them deepened as she continued to smoke. Emmanuel pressed on: "Are you still angry about last night? I'll figure something out, Laura. Just give me some time."

She turned more fully towards him now, with the cigarette hanging loosely between her fingers. Her voice was bitter. "Figure something out? You've been 'figuring it out' for a long time, Emmanuel. Exactly how long do you need?"

Frustration bubbled in his chest. He rubbed his forehead, trying to stay calm.

"Why are you always angry with me?" he asked. "I lost my job because I broke my leg. My leg's better now. I'll get another job. It might just take some time—that's all I'm saying."

Laura spun on him; her expression fierce.

"It might take time? Yeah…" she said sharply, shaking her head. She took another drag from her cigarette.

His voice faltered now, and his eyes were glistening.

"Before the accident, I was taking care of this family, Laura. I know things are tough now, but at least I was working—not like you."

Her body stiffened, as her eyes ignited with fury. Without a word, she brushed past him, storming inside and leaving the door open behind her. Emmanuel followed quickly, with anxiety gripping him.

Inside, Laura turned to face him. Her voice was low, and trembling with restrained rage.

"I never worked? Oh, really?" she whispered. "It's a man's responsibility to run the house, not mine? You need to understand that…"

She paused, inhaling deeply. Then, with her eyes locked onto his, she added, "Listen to me, Emmanuel. I've got a Christmas gift for you. I'm pregnant."

He froze.

The room fell completely silent, save for the faint ticking of the kitchen clock. His heart thundered in his chest. In one swift motion, he lunged forward and yanked the cigarette from her fingers, tossing it outside into the snow. Then he slammed the door shut with a noise that echoed through the house.

Grabbing two chairs from the kitchen table, he placed one firmly behind Laura and guided her into it. Then he sank into the other chair, facing her, the anger in his face melting into something closer to desperation.

"Laura, you're pregnant," he said, voice shaking. "Every action you take affects our baby. But you're acting as if you don't care."

"I don't," she said flatly.

He flinched. The coldness in her voice chilled him more than the snow ever could.

"How can you be so cold?" he asked. "You're talking about a life, Laura."

She looked away, with her eyes somewhere far beyond the kitchen.

"This is a life?" she said. "We've been living in my parents' house for how long now? Surviving off my benefits, barely getting by... and now another one is coming. What exactly do you want me to say?"

He leaned closer, with his hand brushing her shoulder, and a plea in his voice.

"I know you're angry. And I'm sorry—I shouldn't have said what I did. Look, I will find a job soon, I promise. I'll make things better. If I have to go back to the shop, I'll do it. I know it'll be tough finding something better later, but... please, Laura. Just believe me. I'll fix this."

Her gaze sharpened.

"I've been believing you all this time, Emmanuel. I just... I can't anymore." Her voice turned to steel. "Let me be very clear: I can't go through this again. We're not having this child. I want an abortion."

Emmanuel shot up from his seat and dropped to his knees beside her, with his hand resting gently on her thigh.

"Laura, I understand you're upset, but this is our baby," he said. "We need this child. I'll take any job—anything. Just please, reconsider..."

She stared down at him, with her voice steady and cold.

"This isn't about emotion. It's my decision."

His breathing quickened.

"Laura, please don't say that," he whispered. "I'll do anything—I swear. I'll work any job. Just don't…"

Footsteps interrupted him.

Harry, Laura's father, stepped quietly into the kitchen, heading towards the coffee machine. Emmanuel rose awkwardly, retreating to his chair. A tense silence followed.

Harry sighed as he turned towards them.

"I overheard your conversation from my room," he said. "I shouldn't interfere, I know… but Laura, please. Do not make this decision."

Laura looked up slowly. Her expression was unreadable. The silence stretched out, before she finally answered, voice subdued yet resolute.

"Fine, I won't," she said. "But understand one thing clearly—I won't be able to love it."

Harry's face twisted.

"'It'?" he echoed, disbelief coloring his tone.

Emmanuel, sensing the moment spiralling out of control, forced a fragile smile.

"Alright, let's not complicate things more than they already are," he said gently. "Harry, what do you think? Do you think it'll be a boy or a girl?"

Harry stirred sugar into his coffee, with his expression still tight. But after a beat, a faint smile cracked through.

"I think it'll be a baby girl," he said. "And if it is, maybe we could call her Claudia."

Silence returned, but now it carried a different weight. Outside, the snow continued to fall, whispering against the window as Emmanuel glanced towards Laura. She said nothing. Her gaze was distant.

2

22 YEARS LATER

Claudia stood before the mirror, droplets of water still clinging to her face. Her reflection stared back at her—eyes rimmed with exhaustion, jaw clenched, lips pressed into a thin, unyielding line. The cold morning air crawled over her damp skin. She wiped her face briskly with a towel.

With quick, practiced fingers, she pulled her vivid purple hair into a ponytail. She looked like someone in a hurry. She was.

She turned without a second glance and stepped out of the bathroom. Her bare foot struck an empty bottle lying near the doorway. It rattled across the floorboards and hit the wall with a dull thud.

The room was its usual wreck. Clothes spilled over the arm of a chair, some draped across the heater. Bottles stood in corners like silent witnesses to sleepless nights.

She rifled through a pile on the floor, pulling on a pair of jeans and a sweater. She snatched up a leather jacket, her constant companion, and stepped out of her room. As she descended the staircase, the jaunty melody of a Christmas song filled the chilly air, drifting from the cosy living room below.

Sitting by the glowing fireplace Janet, her landlord—a kind-hearted woman in her 70s wrapped in layers of warm clothing. She cradled a steaming cup of tea, staring quietly into the flickering flames.

Claudia's face warmed into a smile as she approached.

"Good morning, Janet. Up early as usual, I see."

Janet turned her head slowly, a knowing smile playing across her lips.

"And you're late, as usual."

Claudia chuckled, moving towards the kitchen. "Well, you know me..."

Janet followed behind her—slower, but steady. As Claudia poured herself a mug of tea and grabbed a piece of toast, Janet's voice turned softer, tinged with melancholy.

"I saw my son last night, in my dream."

Claudia paused mid-bite and glanced up, her tone gentle. "Oh? What was the dream about?"

Janet's eyes shimmered with memory. Her voice, wistful and light, carried a warmth that filled the space between them.

"He was dressed as Santa Claus," she said. "He ran towards me, holding a present and a bouquet of flowers. He looked... so happy."

"That sounds lovely," Claudia said, a soft smile curling her lips. "Did you see what the present was?"

But Janet's face changed. Her smile vanished. Tears brimmed in her eyes, and her voice began to tremble.

"As he was running towards me, smiling... he was shot. By another soldier." She swallowed. "And I just stood there, unable to move... unable to do anything at all."

Claudia set her tea down immediately, stepping forward to wrap Janet in a warm, steadying embrace. She held her, rubbing her back in slow, soothing motions.

"Oh, Janet," she murmured. "It's okay. You know he's in a better place now."

Janet leaned into her, her voice cracking as she continued.

"My boy loved this country more than anything. So patriotic, so brave. But they sent him off to fight in a land he'd never known, to die for reasons none of us understood. And he died alone, Claudia—surrounded by strangers who celebrated his death."

Claudia held her tighter, her own throat tightening with unspoken grief. There were no words to fix what was broken. Janet, sensing her silence, gently pulled away and dabbed at her tears.

"Oh dear, I'm sorry, love. I didn't mean to upset you. Go on—you'll be late for school."

Claudia hesitated; concern written plainly on her face. "Are you sure you're okay? I could stay back if you need some company…"

"No, no." Janet gave her hand a soft squeeze. "You go ahead, sweetheart. I'm alright now. I'll see you this evening, alright?"

"I'll come home early," Claudia promised, giving her one last hug before heading out into the crisp winter morning.

Outside, She approached her battered old Volkswagen Polo, with the faded paint and rusty edges testament to years of wear. Sliding into the cold seat, she started the engine, glancing back toward the window. Janet stood watching, waving gently. Claudia waved back warmly, then drove off into the cold December mist.

* * *

Dressed in grease-streaked mechanic overalls, Andrew stepped into the coffee shop. The faint jingling of the bell above the door announced his arrival. The warm aroma of freshly brewed coffee filled the air as he walked toward the counter.

Behind the counter, Sofi, the young barista, immediately noticed him. Her face lit up with a smile, her eyes lingering on him for a moment longer than necessary.

"Hey, Andrew," she said playfully. "How do you want your coffee today?" She leaned slightly forward, giving him a once-over.

Andrew returned her smile with a subtle smirk. "You know how I like my coffee," he replied, his tone smooth yet warm.

She chuckled softly, brushing a strand of hair behind her ear. "Strong and sweet, just like you?"

Andrew laughed lightly, his rugged charm apparent as he leaned on the counter. "You've got me all figured out."

She turned to prepare his usual order, but the air between them was still charged with unspoken chemistry.

As Andrew waited, his gaze shifted to the window. Something outside caught his attention. His smile dimmed, becoming more thoughtful. "Make it two," he said casually, with his voice calm but deliberate.

The barista paused mid-motion, glancing over her shoulder toward the window. Her smile faltered as her eyes followed his line of sight. Whatever—or whoever—she saw changed her demeanor instantly. Without a word, she turned back to the counter, her movements brisk as she prepared the two coffees.

Moments later, Claudia walked into the shop, moving with purpose. She headed straight for Andrew, her face a mix of urgency and frustration. She pulled her purse from her bag, rummaging through it until she found what she was looking for. She handed it to him.

"It's £600. That's all I have," she said. "Do you even know how much I've given you? Because I don't."

Andrew's expression shifted to disappointment. He held the money briefly before handing it back to her. "Thank you," he said softly. "I'm sorry. I thought I was doing everything for us. That's why I never kept track of it. I'll figure something out."

Claudia sighed, her tone softening but still impatient. "Don't try to play tricks on me, Andrew. I don't have time for this." She shoved the money back into his pocket.

Sofi, now standing at the counter with their drinks, called out, "Coffee's ready!" She offered Claudia a polite smile. "Good morning, Claudia."

Claudia turned briefly toward Sofi; her tone distracted but polite. "Good morning, Sofi. I'll see you later. I'm already late for school."

Andrew grabbed the coffees, handing one to Claudia as they walked out of the shop.

"Are you sure about the money?" Andrew asked as they headed to her car.

Claudia shot him a look. "Andrew, if this were the first time, I'd try to make you feel better. But it's not. So just shut up and get in the car. I'll drop you at the shop, then go. I'm already late to clock in. If I keep this up, I won't have a job—then you'll have no one to ask for money."

They exchanged tired smiles, as a hint of humour broke through the tension. They climbed into the car and drove off.

3

THE OUTSIDER'S SMILE

As Claudia arrived at the school, her nearly broken Volkswagen Polo sputtered to a stop in the car park. She gathered her belongings from the passenger seat, stepped out, and attempted to shut the door. It wouldn't close.

Frowning, she tried again. And again. Finally, on the third attempt, the door slammed shut with a reluctant click.

In the distance, she spotted two other teachers, Tara and Rachel, walking toward the school together. Claudia waved and smiled. The two teachers returned polite smiles, but their stiff posture and the way they leaned into each other, whispering, betrayed their true feelings. Claudia could tell they didn't particularly like her. She wasn't sure why.

As she approached, she caught fragments of their hushed conversation punctuated by occasional laughter, followed by quick glances in her direction. Choosing to ignore them, Claudia maintained her warm demeanour.

"Good morning, Tara. Good morning, Rachel. How are you both today?" she asked, in a bright and cheerful voice.

With less warmth, they responded in unison, "Good morning, Claudia."

Tara glanced at her watch, clearly searching for an excuse to end the interaction. "I'm late for my class. I need to get started," she said quickly, turning to Rachel. "What time's your class?"

Rachel flipped through her schedule absentmindedly. "Ten o'clock."

Tara sighed. "Better get moving and prepare the materials for class," she said, then gave Rachel a quick nod. "Alright then, I'll see you in the afternoon."

Finally turning back to Claudia, Tara flashed a playful grin. "Anyway, no music class in the morning, right? So you'll just be hanging around, pretending to be busy. Catch you later!" Without waiting for a response, Tara strode off briskly toward her classroom. Rachel lingered for a moment, giving Claudia a fleeting glance before heading off in the opposite direction.

Claudia stood there for a beat, watching them disappear down the hallway. Their dismissive attitudes no longer stung the way they once had. She had grown used to being treated like an outsider.

With a deep breath, she straightened her posture, adjusted the strap of her bag, and walked on. Her steps were steady, and her expression calm, as she readied herself the day.

* * *

As she stepped into the staff room, the door creaked slightly as it closed behind her. The smell of freshly brewed coffee and faint hints of chalk dust lingered in the air. Around the long wooden table in the centre of the room, a few teachers sat chatting in low voices, with mugs of coffee in hand. The chatter subsided for a brief moment as Claudia walked in.

"Good morning, everyone," she said, with her tone bright but measured.

A few teachers murmured a half-hearted "morning" in return. Most avoided eye contact, returning their attention to their conversations or the papers they were marking. She didn't linger—just brewed a cup of coffee and headed to the music room.

The music room carried the gentle scent of polished wood and old sheet music. Morning light poured through tall windows, casting soft rectangles on the floor. Three pianos stood at the far end, each with its own bench, slightly worn from years of use. Along the walls, shelves were stacked with tambourines, guitars, and small violins, all ready for the children's eager hands. A few colourful posters of composers and musical scales decorated the walls, faded slightly at the edges.

Claudia stepped inside quietly, coffee in hand. The room felt still, like it was holding its breath.

"Good morning, Claudia," said Mr. Greene, the history teacher, adjusting the cuffs of his tweed jacket. "You're in early."

"Morning," she smiled. "Needed a quiet moment."

He nodded knowingly. "Right. Well, don't let me interrupt. Just wanted to say hello."

And with that, Mr. Greene gave a quick wave and moved on down the corridor.

Claudia sank into the bench beside the piano, letting her shoulders relax She wrapped both hands around the coffee cup, took a slow sip, then reached into her pocket for her phone.

* * *

The dimly lit betting shop buzzed with the low murmur of voices, the occasional clatter of keyboards, and the rhythmic shuffle of bets being placed. Andrew sat hunched over a terminal, his fingers drumming anxiously against the counter as numbers flickered across the screen. His heart pounded. He had placed a few bets—nothing too crazy, just a calculated risk. A chance to turn things around.

His eyes darted over the screen, following the shifting odds. Then—suddenly—the numbers aligned. His bet had won.

For a second, he just stared, not quite believing it. Then a slow grin spread across his face, his pulse surging as he saw how much he had won.

"Yes!" he whispered, exhilarated. His hands trembled slightly as he leaned back in his chair, sucking in a deep breath. He had done it. He had actually done it.

His phone buzzed in his pocket. Still riding the high, he fumbled for it, barely glancing at the screen before answering — Claudia.

"Hey, babe, guess what?" he said, his voice brimming with excitement.

Claudia sat alone in the music room, coffee cooling in her hands. The room was silent, except for the distant hum of a vacuum down the hall and the occasional creak of wood settling. She didn't move, her fingers resting lightly on the warm ceramic mug.

"What?" she asked, distracted, eyes fixed on the dust motes floating in the sunbeam.

Andrew stepped outside, holding the winning receipt and lighting a cigarette with shaky hands. "Come on, take a wild guess. Feel the energy, babe. Feel what I'm feeling right now."

Claudia leaned back slightly, staring at the worn bench across from her. "Hmm... you lost again?"

Andrew exhaled sharply, shaking his head. "Come on, Claudia! I won! I actually won this time!"

Claudia paused, her expression unreadable. "Wow. That's... new."

Andrew's grin faltered at her tone. "See? This is why I hate sharing good news with you. You never believe in me."

Claudia set her coffee aside on the piano's edge. "It's not that I'm not happy for you, Andrew. I'm just tired. We've lost so much money gambling, and you promised me you were done with it. And now—here we are again."

Andrew flicked his cigarette away as his excitement dimmed. He turned and walked back inside, lowering his voice. "I was happy, Claudia. I wanted to celebrate with you. But you just killed the moment."

Claudia stood and walked slowly between the pianos, her fingertips brushing one of the keys. "I'm not trying to ruin anything, Andrew. I just want you to be careful. You know I love you, but we can't keep living like this."

Andrew slumped into a chair, shoving a hand into his pocket. He sighed. "I get it. Anyway, I stopped playing. I'm cashing out now. That's it."

Claudia let her hand rest gently on the piano, her voice softening. "If that's true, please—just take the money and go to your shop."

Andrew pulled the winning receipt from his pocket, staring at it. His fingers traced the edges as he thought for a moment. Then he smirked. "You know what? Let's celebrate tonight. It's on me."

Claudia glanced at the clock on the wall, her voice quiet. "Not tonight. After I visit my dad, I need to be home early. Janet needs me." She turned toward the door. "Tomorrow, though—we'll go all out."

Andrew chuckled, shaking his head. "Alright, alright. Tomorrow it is."

"I gotta go, babe. Love you. Bye."

Andrew stared at the receipt as the call ended. He took a step toward the cash counter—then hesitated.

His eyes flicked toward the roulette betting machine.

Just one more round.

His grip on the receipt tightened. Then, with a slow breath, he turned back toward the machine.

4

WHEN MEMORY BECOMES A DOORWAY

The soft hum of the air conditioner filled the quiet care home room. Emmanuel sat in an armchair by the window, with his gaze fixed on the garden outside. His expression was distant, and his hands were resting on his lap, with the fingers occasionally twitching. Luca sat beside him, leaning forward with his elbows on his knees, watching his father closely.

"Beautiful day out there, isn't it, Papa?" Luca asked, in a calm voice, tinged with sadness.

Emmanuel turned his head slightly, his cloudy eyes struggling to focus on Luca. "Ah, yes… beautiful." A small smile flickered across his lips, but it was fleeting, before disappearing into the haze of his thoughts.

The door opened, and a nurse entered with a clipboard in hand. She was young, with a warm smile and a kind demeanour. "Good morning, Emmanuel. How are we feeling today?"

Emmanuel's eyes lit up as he saw her.

"Claudia!" Emmanuel exclaimed, his voice filled with sudden joy. "Oh, Claudia, my little girl. You've come to see me."

The nurse paused, exchanging a glance with Luca, who offered an apologetic smile.

"Papa," Luca began gently, "this is Nurse Annie. Claudia isn't here right now."

But Emmanuel waved him off, his focus entirely on the nurse. "Don't be silly, Luca. I know my daughter. Claudia, come here, come to Papa." He reached out his hand, beckoning the nurse closer.

Annie hesitated, then stepped forward, her professional demeanour unshaken. "Hello, Emmanuel. I'm happy to see you too."

Emmanuel took her hand in his trembling but, surprisingly firm grip. "You've always been so good to me, Claudia. Even when you were a little girl, you'd bring me tea in the garden. Do you remember? You'd laugh when I told you stories about the stars."

Annie smiled softly, her heart aching as she played along. "Yes, I remember."

Luca stood and placed a hand on Emmanuel's shoulder. "Papa, that's not Claudia. She's coming later today. This is Nurse Annie."

Emmanuel frowned, his expression clouding with confusion. "Not Claudia? But..." He looked back at Annie, his brow furrowed. "No, no. This is my Claudia. She even smells like her... lavender and... roses."

Luca crouched down to meet his father's gaze. "It's okay, Papa. I promise Claudia will be here soon. She'll be so happy to see you."

Emmanuel's eyes flickered, as uncertainty took hold. He looked back at Annie, then at Luca. "Claudia... or... no, I don't..." His voice trailed off, and he sank back into his chair.

Annie stepped away, her professional mask slipping for a moment as she exchanged a sympathetic look with Luca. "He's having a good day, considering," she said quietly.

Luca nodded, his hand still on Emmanuel's shoulder. "Thank you for being kind about it. He gets confused a lot lately."

Annie gave him a reassuring smile. "It's all part of the job. I'll check in later." She slipped out of the room, leaving Luca alone with his father.

Emmanuel sat silently for a while before speaking again, his voice soft. "She'll come, won't she?"

Luca's throat tightened, but he forced a smile. "Yeah, Papa. She'll come. She always does."

Emmanuel sat back in the armchair, and his hands clutched the blanket around him. Luca grabbed a magazine next to him and started flipping through its pages, though his mind wasn't really on the words.

Emmanuel began to speak again, with his voice low and strained. "Claudia... my sweet little girl." His words were pulled from a deep well of memories. "She always tried so hard. So hard to make her mother see her..." He trailed off, shaking his head slowly, lost in thought.

Luca set the magazine aside and leaned forward, focusing on his father's words.

"She'd draw pictures, you know. Beautiful pictures of flowers and sunshine. She'd leave them on Laura's bedside table, hoping—hoping Laura would say something." Emmanuel's voice faltered, and his eyes narrowed, as if he could see a long-past scene unfold before him. "But Laura... she wouldn't even look. Just brushed them aside like they were nothing."

Luca's chest tightened, hearing the pain in his father's voice. He held his breath, letting the moment pass before he responded.

"She'd sit by the window," Emmanuel continued, his voice barely above a whisper. "Watching Laura leave the house without a word. I could see it in her eyes, that question she never asked—'Why doesn't she love me?'" His hands tightened around the blanket, the tremors in his fingers growing more pronounced.

Luca's throat constricted, but he stayed silent, giving his father the space to speak his heart.

Emmanuel let out a shaky sigh, shaking his head slowly. "I tried, I really did. Tried to fill the space Laura left behind. But it wasn't enough. A child needs her mother. And Laura... she just... she couldn't give her that."

Luca's gaze softened. The silence between them stretched on for a moment, thick with things unsaid.

"And Claudia," Emmanuel murmured, his voice breaking slightly. "She grew up thinking she wasn't enough. Always trying to please everyone, always bending over backward. As if earning everyone's approval could fill that hole Laura left in her heart." A deep sigh escaped him, and he closed his eyes, as though the weight of those memories was too much to bear. "It breaks me, Luca. It breaks me that she had to carry that pain."

Luca blinked rapidly, trying to hold back the tears. His voice was thick when he spoke. "She's a strong woman, Papa. But she's not alone. We see her. We love her."

Emmanuel's eyes opened, the cloudiness of his vision seeming to clear for a moment. He looked at Luca, his gaze searching. "Yes... yes, we do. But I wish I could've done more. I wish I could've made her feel... whole."

Luca reached out, placing a hand on his father's shoulder, squeezing gently. "You did, Papa. You did everything you could."

Emmanuel gave a small, sad smile, but his eyes soon drifted back to the window. The silence between them deepened, but this time, it was comforting—an unspoken bond that neither needed to put into words.

"She deserved so much more... my Claudia," Emmanuel whispered one last time, as if releasing a long-held sorrow.

And in that room, amid the quiet and the fading light, his love for

Claudia echoed through the words of the man who once could have done everything for her, if only time hadn't slipped so far from his grasp.

* * *

The door swung open, and three students entered the music room—Amira, Jacob, and Max. Amira gave Claudia a bright smile, Jacob offered a polite nod, but Max lingered near the door, arms crossed and gaze downcast.

"Good morning," Claudia said, clapping her hands gently. "Let's start with a simple scale warm-up."

Amira and Jacob headed straight to their keyboards, fingers already hovering over the keys. Max stayed put, unmoving.

Claudia walked over, her voice soft. "Max, everything okay?"

He shrugged. "I don't like piano."

"That's alright," she said, crouching slightly to meet his eyes. "You don't have to like it today. But how about trying it your way? Just sit down and press a few keys. No rules. No sheet music. Just… explore."

Max hesitated. Then, without a word, he shuffled over to an empty keyboard. He poked at a few keys—awkward, unsure, but playing.

Claudia gave him a small nod. "That's it. That's music too."

As the lesson went on, Max's shoulders loosened, and he began mimicking the notes of the simple tune Claudia played for the group. Amira was already humming along, and Jacob tapped a steady rhythm.

When the session ended, Amira and Jacob packed up and left chatting. Max lingered.

At the doorway, he paused. "Miss Claudia?"

She turned. "Yes?"

He looked up briefly. "Thanks," he mumbled, then slipped out into the hall.

Claudia smiled after him

Claudia remained in the music room, gathering sheet music into a neat pile on her desk. The soft clatter of chairs and faint hallway footsteps filtered in from outside.

The door swung open again.

Tara stepped in, her heels clicking sharply on the wooden floor as she crossed the room with purpose.

"Claudia, hi!" Tara said, sounding unexpectedly cheerful.

Claudia looked up, startled but pleased. "Oh, hi, Tara! How are you?"

Tara placed a hand on the back of a student chair and let out a dramatic sigh. "I'm okay, but honestly, I'm swamped. My history class is doing this big project, and I'm supposed to run this after-school workshop for them today. But I just found out I have this last-minute meeting I absolutely cannot miss."

"Oh, that sounds stressful," Claudia said, furrowing her brow with sympathy.

Tara leaned in slightly, lowering her voice. "It's a nightmare. I was thinking… you're so good with the kids, and they really like you. Maybe you could cover for me? Just for today? It's just an hour or so, and it's nothing complicated—just keeping them on track with their project research."

Claudia blinked. "Oh, I don't know, Tara. I don't know much about history, and I already have my piano lessons this afternoon."

Tara waved a dismissive hand, her smile sweet but calculated. "Oh, come on, it's not about the subject. They just need some supervision and a friendly face. And honestly, you're such a lifesaver—I can't think of anyone better for the job."

Claudia hesitated, her fingers fidgeting with the edge of a music folder. Tara pressed on, her tone softening.

"You know, I've always admired how you're so willing to help. It's one of the things that makes you so special around here."

Claudia's cheeks flushed at the compliment. She smiled shyly, fiddling with her pen. "Well... if you really think I can handle it, I guess I could rearrange my lessons for later."

Tara clapped her hands together with a grin. "You're the best, Claudia! Seriously, I owe you one. Thank you so much."

Before Claudia could respond, Tara was already halfway to the door, tossing a quick, "I'll send you the details!" over her shoulder.

Left alone in the quiet of the room, Claudia sat down slowly behind her desk. She knew she'd only agreed because she wanted people to like her. She felt a mix of pride and unease at the thought.

* * *

Emmanuel's face twisted with frustration as he glared at the care staff standing beside him. His wrinkled hands clenched the edge of the table; his body was tense with resistance.

"Why are you blocking me?" he snapped, his voice thick with irritation. "I told you—I need to go to the shop!"

The carer, a weary-looking woman in her forties, sighed and shook her head. She had been standing close, ready to catch him if he wobbled.

"Mr. Emmanuel, I'm not stopping you," she explained, her tone patient but strained. "I'm just here to make sure you don't fall."

"I don't need help," Emmanuel huffed. "I can manage just fine on my own!"

"Please, you're not steady on your feet today," the carer insisted, with concern in her voice. "If you take a wrong step, you could hurt yourself."

But Emmanuel wasn't listening. Frustrated, he took a bold step forward—and instantly, his knee buckled. A sharp gasp left his lips as his body swayed dangerously.

Before he could crash to the floor, the carer lunged forward, grabbing him firmly by the arm. "I've got you!" she said quickly, tightening her grip as she steadied him.

Emmanuel's breath came in short, startled bursts. His fingers clutched her arm as he regained his balance, his face momentarily betraying his fear before he masked it with irritation.

"See? That's exactly why I was standing next to you," the carer said, guiding him gently but firmly back to stability. "You need to sit down before you hurt yourself."

Emmanuel muttered under his breath, but he allowed her help lower him into the armchair.

The carer crouched beside him. "I know you want to go to the shop, but right now, you need to rest. If you fall, you'll end up in the hospital. And then you really won't be able to go anywhere."

Emmanuel exhaled sharply, still frustrated, but unable to argue. He sank deeper into the chair, rubbing his forehead.

The carer straightened, clearly relieved that—for now—he was safe. "Let's just take a minute, alright?" she said gently. "You can try again later."

Emmanuel huffed but didn't respond. He simply looked away, staring out of the window, as the carer stood by his side—watchful, exhausted, but unwavering.

After ensuring he was comfortably seated, the carer stayed with him for a few minutes, watching as his breathing steadied and his restless energy faded. Once she was certain he had settled, she quietly stepped out of the room.

As she turned to leave, she spotted Claudia walking toward Emmanuel's room. Claudia slowed when she saw the carer standing just outside, giving her a small, tired smile. The carer smiled back, with a hint of relief on her face.

"Hi," Claudia greeted softly. "How is he today? The usual?"

The carer exhaled, nodding. "You know him... A sweetheart during the day, always asking for his children. But in the evenings, it's like he becomes someone else."

Claudia sighed, with an expression of sadness and guilt. "I know... I'm really sorry."

The carer shook her head. "It's not your fault. He's strong, Claudia. And sometimes... he lashes out."

Claudia's face fell. "I don't even know what to say except... thank you. Really. For everything you do for him. I know it's not easy."

The carer reached out and squeezed Claudia's hand. "We all feel for you and Luca. Emmanuel is so young to have dementia. I've never come across someone his age with it—it's rare."

Claudia nodded, her voice barely above a whisper. "He's only 65... I don't know what went wrong. It's been four years, and it's only getting worse. Never better."

Before the carer could respond, a sudden thud echoed from Emmanuel's room. Both women froze, then rushed inside.

Emmanuel lay sprawled on the floor, his face dazed and confused. The carer immediately pressed the emergency call bell.

Within seconds, Nurse Annie came running in. At the same time, Claudia knelt beside Emmanuel, struggling to lift him; but he was too heavy.

"What happened?" Annie asked urgently as she crouched next to them.

The carer, still catching her breath, answered, "We were talking outside when we heard the noise. When we came in, we found him like this."

Annie nodded; her expression was sharp and focussed. "Claudia, step back for a moment."

Claudia hesitated but moved aside as Annie quickly checked Emmanuel for any bleeding or fractures. Two more carers entered the room, ready to assist.

After a thorough check, Annie looked up. "No visible injuries, but we need to be careful. Let's get him onto the bed."

With practiced coordination, the carers gently lifted Emmanuel and settled him onto the bed. He seemed exhausted, with his eyelids fluttering as he let out a soft sigh.

Stepping outside the room, Annie turned to Claudia. "This is the third time this week he's been found on the floor," she said, with her voice firm but understanding. "After the leg fracture and surgery last month, he's not steady on his feet. But he doesn't understand that, and it makes things dangerous for him. He needs constant supervision."

Claudia's jaw tightened. "What happened to the one-to-one care you promised?"

Annie let out a slow breath. "We're still waiting for the assessment. And you know, with Christmas in a week, things are moving even slower. But the good news is—we have a date. January 6."

Claudia's expression flickered between frustration and relief. "At least there's a date," she murmured.

Just then, the carers stepped out of the room. One of them gave a small nod to Claudia. "He's on the bed now, comfortable. He seems really tired."

Annie placed a reassuring hand on Claudia's arm. "Alright, I'll see you later," she said before walking off with the carers.

Claudia took a deep breath, then turned back toward Emmanuel's room, bracing herself for whatever came next.

Claudia walked quietly into Emmanuel's room. He was lying on the bed, with his breathing steady, and his face calm for the first time in hours. His eyes were closed, and, for a brief moment, he looked at peace.

She pulled a chair closer and sat quietly beside him. Gently, she reached for his hand, holding it softly, as if trying to connect with the man he used to be.

Emmanuel stirred at her touch. His eyelids fluttered open, and, for a fleeting second, his gaze met hers. But then, his face twisted with anger.

"You bitch," he spat, his voice sharp and accusing. "You think you won? I'll see you in court!"

Claudia's stomach dropped. "Papa, stop," she said, trying to keep her voice steady. "It's me... Claudia."

But Emmanuel's agitation only grew. His body tensed as he tried to sit up, his voice rising. "What the fuck did you think? That you could hit my car and just drive away?" His breathing grew heavy, and his eyes were wild with confusion.

Claudia's chest tightened. She had seen him like this before—trapped in a past that never happened, fighting battles that weren't real. No matter how many times it happened, it still hurt just the same.

She swallowed hard and slowly stood up from the chair, taking careful steps toward the door. Without saying another word, she turned the lock, shutting it gently so no one outside could hear his shouting.

As she stood there, her fingers still gripping the handle, her eyes filled with tears. She took a deep breath, forcing herself to stay composed, but the ache in her heart was undeniable.

For a moment, she simply stood there, listening to Emmanuel's rambling fade into murmurs. Then, after quickly wiping her face, she turned back toward him, ready to face whatever came next.

* * *

Claudia pulled into the driveway, parked her car, and made her way to the front door. She pressed the doorbell, and within moments, Janet opened it with a warm smile.

"Hey, you're back," Janet said, stepping aside to let Claudia in. "How was your day?"

Claudia returned the smile, though it didn't quite reach her eyes. "Just like any other day," she replied.

Janet chuckled at the familiar response. "Figures. How was yours?" Claudia asked as they walked toward the lounge.

"Same as always," Janet shrugged.

Claudia unwound the scarf from around her neck, tossing it carelessly onto the sofa before collapsing onto another. Janet, following behind, picked up the scarf, folded it neatly, and placed it on the armrest.

Noticing the gesture, Claudia sighed. "Sorry."

Janet waved it off with a small smile. "No worries. You've always been like this—why start apologizing now?"

Claudia smiled, then shifted to get more comfortable. She stretched out, resting her legs on the armrest, her body sinking into the cushions.

After a brief silence, she turned to Janet. "You've always treated me like a daughter. Why?"

Janet sat down on the opposite sofa. She gave Claudia a knowing smile—the kind that spoke volumes.

Instead of answering directly, she changed the subject. "Did you eat anything?"

Claudia sat up, tilting her head. "Is your daughter coming for Christmas?"

Janet sighed as she stood up, her tone neutral. "I don't know. Maybe. You know we don't exactly get along." She paused for a moment, then added, "I guess I'm just an old-school woman. I can't always understand the way people do things nowadays." She let out a dry chuckle. "But I've learned how to pretend when I have to."

Claudia studied her for a moment, then grinned as she sprang up from the couch. As Janet started walking toward the kitchen, Claudia hugged her from behind.

"Well, lucky for you, you've already got a daughter right here," she said.

Janet laughed, shaking her head. "Yeah, yeah. Let's eat."

Still laughing, they made their way to the kitchen together.

5

ALONE IN THE CROWD

The school hallways buzzed with the usual morning chatter Claudia adjusted the strap of her bag and made her way to the staffroom, her mind already cluttered with the tasks ahead.

Inside, a few teachers sat around the table, sipping coffee and flipping through lesson plans. Claudia grabbed a mug from the cupboard and poured herself some coffee before turning to Sarah, one of her colleagues.

"Hey, Sarah," Claudia started, keeping her voice light. "I was wondering if you could help me supervise the Year 9s during lunch. I've got a pile of paperwork I need to catch up on, and it'd really save me some time."

Sarah hesitated, stirring her tea a little too intently. "Oh, I'd love to, Claudia, but I actually promised Mr. Patel I'd cover his duty today," she said with an apologetic smile. "Maybe ask Lisa?"

Claudia turned toward Lisa, who had been listening while scrolling through emails on her laptop. Before Claudia could even speak, Lisa let out a sigh.

"Ugh, I wish I could," she said, shaking her head. "But I've got a meeting with the head right after lunch. It's about the new curriculum changes. You know how that goes."

Claudia forced a smile. "Of course. No worries."

She glanced across the room at David, who was flipping through a stack of worksheets.

"David, any chance you could..."

"Ah, Claudia, you wouldn't believe the mountain of marking I have to get through today," he cut in quickly, not even looking up. "Absolute nightmare. I barely have time to breathe."

Claudia's smile tightened. "Right. Got it."

She took a sip of her coffee, suddenly finding the taste bitter. It wasn't the first time this had happened—she knew how it worked. People had their own struggles, their own workload. But it was hard not to notice the way they always seemed so busy when she needed a favour.

Taking a deep breath, she forced her shoulders to relax.

Trying to shake off the disappointment, she turned back to the coffee pot and lifted it slightly. "Anyone want a refill?" she said, in a casual voice.

Sarah smiled politely but shook her head. "No, I'm good, thanks."

Lisa waved a hand dismissively. "Already had too much caffeine today."

David didn't even look up from his marking. "Nah, I'm fine."

Claudia nodded, pouring herself another splash before setting the pot down. She lingered for a moment, hoping for some warmth, or acknowledgment—but none came.

Grabbing her planner, she headed toward the door. Another day, another battle to be fought alone.

* * *

The garage was filled with the usual sounds of clanking tools, the hum of an engine idling in the background, and the faint buzz of a radio playing some old rock song. Andrew was hunched over the open hood of a car, his gloved hands deep in the engine, trying to loosen a stubborn bolt.

Then—"Shit!"

He yanked his hand back, shaking it off as pain shot through his fingers. Ripping off his glove, he inspected his hand, cursing under his breath.

"I'm so tired of this," he grumbled, tossing the glove onto the workbench. "This is not what I should be doing. I should be a millionaire by now, partying on a yacht, not fixing some broke-ass car that's older than my grandma."

His colleague, Jake, who was working on another car, chuckled as he wiped grease off his hands. "Oh yeah? And what's a yacht without some fine-ass women?"

Andrew smirked, flexing his sore fingers. "You already know—big booty bitches, man. Nothing but curves and champagne."

Jake laughed, shaking his head. "Damn, how many are you planning to have?"

Andrew shot him a mock-serious look. "All of them. Every single one. Maybe—maybe—after I'm done, I'll let you have what's left." He laughed.

Jake shook his head, grinning. "Selfish bastard."

Andrew shrugged. "Gotta live the dream, man."

A loud growl interrupted their banter—Andrew's stomach. He patted his stomach and sighed. "Anyway, enough about my billionaire lifestyle. It's lunchtime. Let's eat before we pass out from hunger."

Jake tossed his wrench onto the workbench and pulled off his gloves. "Hell yeah, I'm starving."

As they started walking toward the back room, gloves folded in their hands, still laughing, Jake asked, "Hey, you up for a beer later this evening?"

Andrew shook his head. "Can't, man. I'm going out with Claudia tonight."

Jake raised an eyebrow. "Ooh, fancy. Alright, tomorrow then?"

Andrew grinned. "Yeah, tomorrow sounds good."

The two of them disappeared into the back room, still trading jabs and jokes as the garage hummed on without them.

* * *

The soft glow of the vanity mirror illuminated Claudia's face as she carefully applied a deep red lipstick, pressing her lips together to even it out. She was almost done getting ready when her phone rang. She glanced at the screen—Andrew.

With a knowing smile, she picked up. "I'll come and pick you up in half an hour," she said casually.

Andrew's voice came through the line, slightly agitated. "That's what you said half an hour ago."

Claudia rolled her eyes and changed her tone, letting her voice drip with seduction. "Don't you want your girlfriend to look hot and sexy? If I show up looking like a mess, what will people think of you, my love?"

There was a pause, followed by the sound of Andrew exhaling sharply. Then, without another word, he hung up.

Claudia smiled, staring at her phone for a second before setting it down. She grabbed a tissue and dabbed away the excess lipstick, tilting her head as she admired herself in the mirror. Running a hand through her hair, she whispered to her reflection, "Oh, what a lovely, sexy babe you are," before chuckling to herself.

She grabbed her jacket from a pile of clothes, slipped it on, and rushed out of the room.

In the lounge, Janet was reclining on the couch, watching TV. Claudia walked up behind her and wrapped her arms around her in a warm hug. "See you later. Good night!" she said cheerfully.

Janet turned her head slightly, smiling. "Have fun, but be careful out there," she said in a motherly tone.

Claudia winked and, with a playful twirl, headed for the door, with excitement bubbling in her chest.

* * *

Claudia pulled up to Andrew's place, parked the car, and stepped out with deliberate confidence. She adjusted her tight, flashy dress, striking a subtly seductive pose as she leaned against the car, waiting for him to notice.

However, he barely glanced at her. He walked straight past, opened the car door, and got in without a word.

Claudia's smile faltered slightly. She had dressed to impress, but it was clear he wasn't in the mood to appreciate it. She knew why—he was still annoyed that she was late. With a small sigh, she slid into the driver's seat and shut the door behind her.

As she buckled her seatbelt, she turned to him "I know, I know—I'm too hot to handle," she said with a mock sigh, flashing him a grin. "But lucky for you, I'm still in love with your broke ass. So relax and enjoy the ride."

Andrew remained silent, staring straight ahead, his expression unreadable.

Not one to let the mood stay sour, Claudia leaned in and pressed a quick kiss to his cheek. "Let's party," she said, revving the engine with a playful glint in her eyes.

Andrew exhaled, shaking his head slightly, but a small smile played at his lips as Claudia drove away.

The club was alive with pulsing lights and heavy bass, the kind of energy that made it impossible not to move. Claudia and Andrew were in the middle of it all, dancing close, laughing, and drinking. Claudia swayed her hips, throwing in a few teasing, sexy moves just for Andrew. He grinned, loving the attention, and joined in, matching her rhythm.

They were completely caught up in the moment, letting the music and alcohol wash everything else away.

Later, they sat near the bar, with drinks in hand, catching their breath. The music was still pounding, making conversation difficult, but Claudia leaned in with a wide smile. "You know what? This…" she gestured around them, "the music, the lights, the drinks—you. It all makes me so happy. I don't feel anything bad at all. What about you?"

Andrew took a sip of his drink, nodding. "Same," he said, though his voice barely carried over the noise.

Claudia kept moving her head to the beat, her eyes wandering over the dance floor. Then she turned back to the bar, catching the bartender's attention. "Another one," she called, tapping her empty glass on the counter. As the bartender prepared her drink, she turned back to Andrew with a playful smile.

Feeling bold, she leaned in, rubbing the back of his neck as she inhaled his scent. "Just let me know when you want me to stop," she murmured, her lips brushing his ear. "I don't want to break your bank."

Andrew suddenly pulled back, his expression shifting. "I don't have any money on me," he admitted. "You need to pay for me too."

Claudia froze. She sat back, staring at him. "Wait… what? Yesterday you said you won. What happened to that?"

Andrew hesitated, rubbing the back of his neck. "I... I tried to double it." He exhaled. "And I lost it all."

Claudia didn't say anything. She just kept looking at him, with her face unreadable.

Andrew tried to brush it off, flashing a quick grin. "Don't worry. I'll win it back. Just like last time. I got this."

The bartender arrived with Claudia's drink. She glanced up and gestured for the bill. The bartender nodded and walked away as she rummaged through her bag, searching for her phone.

Andrew reached out, gently holding her wrist. "You know how this works," he said, his voice smooth but insistent. "Losing happens, but you know I'm good at this. I'll win it back—maybe even double what I lost."

Claudia froze for a moment, then lifted her head, giving him a sharp look.

Andrew hesitated, then forced a weak chuckle. "Okay... maybe not double."

Without responding, Claudia continued searching through her bag as the bartender returned, placing the bill on the table. She pulled out her phone, tapped to pay, and watched as the transaction went through.

Then, without hesitation, she picked up her drink and downed it in one go. The glass hit the table with a clink as she exhaled sharply.

Grabbing her jacket, she stood up.

Without a word, she turned and walked out of the club.

Andrew watched her go, but she didn't look back.

6

THE LAST SCHOOL DAY BEFORE CHRISTMAS

The coffee shop had a cosy morning buzz, as the hum of quiet conversations blended with the sound of steaming milk and clinking cups. Behind the counter, Sofi glanced up just as Andrew walked in. She greeted him with a warm smile, raising an eyebrow as if silently asking, "The usual?"

Andrew gave a small nod as he made his way to the counter.

"How was it last night?" Sofi asked casually, reaching for the coffee beans.

Andrew sighed. "Oh, not that great."

Just then, his phone chimed with a notification. He slipped a hand into his pocket, pulled it out, and scanned the screen.

Sofi noticed and smirked. "Want me to make it two?"

Still looking at his phone, Andrew replied without much thought. "If it's for yourself, sure, make it two."

Sofi chuckled softly as she prepared the drinks, setting cups on the counter. Leaning slightly toward him, she asked, "That bad, huh?"

Andrew grabbed his cup and exhaled. "I don't know... but one thing's for sure—she wants everything her way and doesn't understand anyone else's situation." He took a sip. "What can you do about that?"

Sofi opened her mouth to reply, but another customer walked in. She glanced over and instinctively moved to the register.

Andrew reached into his pocket, pulled out some coins, and placed them on the counter. As he turned to leave, he called over his shoulder, "See you later."

Sofi, still mid-order, looked up. "Wait—I didn't get the whole story!"

Andrew smirked, already heading for the door. "Maybe later, not now."

And with that, he was gone.

* * *

Claudia sat in the staff room, unwrapping her sandwich as she scrolled through her phone. The hum of distant chatter from the hallway filled the air, but she was too lost in thought to notice.

The door swung open, and Mr. Greene walked in with his lunchbox in hand. He greeted her with a nod as he sat across from her, opening his container of pasta.

"You're here early," he noted, stabbing his fork into the meal.

Claudia sighed, setting her phone down. "Yeah, I was starving, so I figured I'd eat before the rush."

Mr. Greene smirked. "So... how was last night? Did you have fun?"

Claudia groaned, rolling her eyes. "Ugh, don't even remind me."

Mr. Greene chuckled. "Looks like it didn't go your way."

She shook her head, taking a bite of her sandwich. "It started off fine, you know? Music, drinks, dancing—felt like a good time. But then, as always, Andrew had to ruin it."

Mr. Greene raised an eyebrow. "What did he do this time?"

Claudia leaned back in her chair. "Lost all his money trying to 'double it' or whatever nonsense he always says. And guess who had to pay for the drinks?"

"Oof." Mr. Greene winced. "Let me guess—he didn't even seem sorry?"

Claudia scoffed. "Of course not. He acted like it was no big deal. Just brushed it off, saying he'd win it all back soon. Meanwhile, I'm the one stuck footing the bill."

Before Mr. Greene could respond, the door opened again, and another teacher walked in, heading straight for the kettle. Claudia lowered her voice, but there was a sharpness in her tone.

"Anyway," she said, brushing invisible crumbs off her lap. "He hasn't even called today, and you know what? I'm not going to contact him for a whole week. Let's see how that goes."

Mr. Greene chuckled. "Bold move. Think he'll last a week without reaching out?"

Claudia smirked. "If he does, then I have my answer, don't I?"

She took another bite of her sandwich, pretending not to care.

Her phone started ringing. She picked it up, glanced at the screen, and answered.

"Hello?"

On the other end, Luca was sitting in a police car, dressed in his uniform. His colleague, sitting beside him, was unwrapping a burger as they monitored the busy road with their mobile speed camera.

"You busy?" Luca asked.

"No, I'm on my lunch break," Claudia replied, stretching her legs out under the table.

Luca's tone turned slightly reproachful. "I called you twice last night. Why didn't you pick up?"

Claudia sighed. "I had a bad day, wasn't in the mood to talk. But funnily enough, I just picked up my phone to call you, and here you are. It's almost like we've got twin telepathy—except you got all the bad fashion sense."

Luca scoffed. "Excuse me, this uniform is iconic."

"Yeah, for ruining people's day with speeding tickets."

She twirled her fork between her fingers, then said, "You visited Dad two days ago, didn't you? The carers mentioned it."

Luca exhaled. "Yeah, I did. He was talking a lot about you, you know? Always thinking about you."

Claudia smiled faintly but then shook her head. "That's nice, but every time I see him after work, he's a completely different person— swearing, moody..."

Luca's voice softened. "You know his memory's declining fast. It's heart-breaking to see."

Claudia picked at her lunch. "I have such a great time with him at the weekends, but during the week, it's like I'm meeting a stranger. He's not even a bit like my dad."

Luca sighed. "That's why I only visit during the day."

There was a pause before Claudia asked, "How are Rose and little Luca?"

Luca stayed silent for a moment before answering, "It's getting more complicated... You know that already, so why do you keep asking?" He groaned. "Anyway, I didn't call to be attacked, I called to ask about your Christmas plans."

Claudia shrugged. "Nothing special. Spending time with Dad, celebrating like always."

Luca exhaled. "Just wanted to confirm, that's all. Thought maybe you'd finally found someone desperate enough to invite you for a romantic Christmas dinner."

"Oh, ha-ha," Claudia deadpanned. "If that's your way of hinting I should settle down, I'd like to remind you that your love life is the equivalent of a reality TV show—entertaining, dramatic, and occasionally tragic."

Luca chuckled. "Fair enough."

Just then, Claudia's phone buzzed with another incoming call. She glanced at the screen—it was Andrew.

"Luca, I've gotta go. I'll call you later."

"Hold on," Luca interrupted. "Before you go, do you need any money or anything?"

Claudia laughed. "Oh, I'm alright, Mr. Millionaire. I don't need any money—I'm not like before. I've got a job, I make my own money now," she said playfully. "Do you want some?"

Luca chuckled. "So we've got two millionaires in the family now?"

"Yeah, but only one of us knows how to spend it wisely," Claudia said.

They both laughed before Claudia glanced back at her phone—Andrew's call was still ringing.

"I really have to go, I'll call you later."

She hung up and quickly tried to answer Andrew's call, but by the time she pressed the button, the line had already gone dead.

With a sigh, she got up and walked over to the sink, rinsing out her lunch container. She kept glancing at her phone, but it stayed silent.

* * *

The winter sky outside was already darkening, streaked with the last hints of daylight as the school day wound to a close. The hallways, usually filled with the noise of students, had quieted down as the last few stragglers grabbed their coats and backpacks, eager to start their Christmas break.

Inside the staff room, Claudia dropped into a chair, rubbing her temples. The day had been exhausting—students too excited to focus, teachers barely holding everything together, and an endless stream of last-minute requests before the school shut its doors for the holidays.

She had just wrapped her hands around a much-needed cup of tea when the door swung open.

"Tara," Claudia muttered, seeing the familiar grin on her colleague's face. "Why do I feel like you're about to make my life difficult?"

Tara let out a dramatic gasp, placing a hand over her heart. "Excuse me! Can't a friend simply enjoy your company on the last day before Christmas break?"

Claudia arched an eyebrow. "Tara."

Tara laughed, sliding into the seat beside her. "Alright, alright. Maybe I do need a little favour. But, Claudia, this could be huge for you."

Claudia exhaled, setting down her tea. "Go on…"

Tara leaned in, lowering her voice like she was sharing a state secret. "You know how the principal's been talking about recognising staff who go the extra mile? The ones who show real dedication?"

Claudia frowned. "I've heard a few things."

Tara nodded eagerly. "Well, I may have dropped your name in conversation the other day. Just saying how reliable you are, how people really appreciate you, and how much you deserve to be noticed."

Claudia crossed her arms. "Uh-huh. And what exactly have you signed me up for?"

Tara placed a hand on her arm, her expression all sincerity. "It's nothing major—just a tiny thing that could make a huge impression. My sister's coming over for Christmas, and today I was supposed to pick her up from the station. But…" She let out an exaggerated sigh. "I've just been asked to attend this important school networking event. The kind where the principal really sees who's committed."

Claudia gave her a flat look. "You want me to pick up your sister. And how exactly does that help my career?"

Tara gasped, as if Claudia had missed something obvious. "Oh, Claudia, it's not about the pick-up. It's about being a team player. You know how the principal values that. These little things add up."

Claudia hesitated. The last thing she wanted after such a long day was another responsibility. But at the same time, she had been trying to stand out more at work, and Tara was good at making things happen.

Tara gave her a knowing look, sensing her indecision. "Look, you do this for me, and I guarantee the principal will remember your name. Who knows? Next time there's a leadership opportunity, a project, maybe even a pay rise—guess whose name will be fresh in their mind?"

Claudia groaned, rubbing her forehead. "Fine. I'll do it. And this is the last time—"

Tara beamed, clapping her hands together. "You are the best, Claudia. Honestly, this is why people love you. You're so dependable."

Before Claudia could respond, Tara was already gathering her things, throwing a cheerful "You're a lifesaver! I owe you!" over her shoulder as she breezed out of the staff room.

Claudia let out a long breath and reached for her phone.

She tapped the screen, scrolling through her notifications. No more missed calls. No messages.

Her brows knitted together as she checked again.

With a sigh, she locked the phone and set it down on the table.

Suddenly, the door creaked open again. Tara stepped back in, a slight crease between her brows.

"You haven't seen my sister, have you?" she asked, walking over quickly. She held out her phone, showing Claudia a photo of a smiling young woman with dark hair and a bright scarf. "This is her."

Claudia leaned forward, squinting at the screen. "Ah, now I know who I'm supposed to pick up."

Tara grinned, relief flashing across her face. "You're a star, Claudia. I love you!" she said dramatically, then turned and walked away, her voice echoing faintly down the hallway.

Another favour. Another thing people expected from her.

She didn't mind helping. She really didn't.

The last of the daylight faded, and the school halls emptied for the holidays.

And yet, Claudia couldn't shake the feeling that she wasn't going anywhere at all.

* * *

The evening air was crisp, carrying the scent of roasted chestnuts from a nearby street vendor. Claudia stood outside the station, shifting her weight from one foot to the other, her breath visible in the cold. Christmas lights twinkled above the entrance, casting a festive glow on the damp pavement.

She scanned the crowd spilling out of the station, waiting for Tara's sister. People rushed past her, dragging suitcases, and greeting loved ones with tight hugs. The station buzzed with excitement— homecomings, reunions, and last-minute holiday plans.

Her eyes landed on a striking young woman standing near one of the station pillars, with her arms crossed as she stared at her phone. She had electric blue hair, shaved on one side, with a nose piercing and large bangles hanging from both ears. More piercings decorated her tongue, which caught the light as she spoke quietly to herself. Tattoos peeked from beneath the collar of her leather jacket, stretching up her neck and covering her hands where her fingers tapped against her phone screen.

Claudia blinked in recognition. Janet's daughter.

Taking a breath, she walked over, hesitating for a brief moment before speaking.

"Lena?"

The young woman looked up, with her brows furrowing, before her face shifted into mild surprise. "Claudia?"

Claudia offered a small smile. "It's been a long time."

Lena returned the smile. "Yeah, I guess it has." She shoved her hands into her jacket pockets. "What are you doing here?"

"Picking up one of my colleague's sisters. And you?"

"Waiting for my partner." Lena's voice was casual, but nonetheless guarded.

Claudia hesitated for a second, then decided to get straight to the point. "Have you thought about visiting your mum for Christmas?"

Lena's jaw tightened, and she rolled her eyes. "She wouldn't want me there."

"That's not true," Claudia said gently. "She misses you. She talks about you all the time. She's lonely, Lena."

Lena gave a humourless laugh. "Yeah? She misses the daughter she wants me to be. Not this." She gestured vaguely to herself—the piercings and the tattoos. "She can't accept who I am."

Claudia crossed her arms, nodding slowly. "I get it. And you have every right to feel that way. But you don't have to change who you are to show up for Christmas. Just being there... that would mean everything to her."

Lena sighed, kicking at the pavement with her boot. "She's the one who pushed me away."

"I know," Claudia admitted. "And I know it's not fair. But… maybe this is a chance for her to realise she doesn't want to lose you."

Lena chewed her lip ring for a moment, then exhaled. "I don't know."

Before Claudia could say more, a woman emerged from the station, pulling a suitcase behind her. She was tall, dressed in a fitted black coat, with dark curly hair and an effortless confidence. Her eyes immediately sought out Lena.

Lena's face brightened as she walked toward her. The woman leaned in, pressing a quick kiss to Lena's cheek before glancing curiously at Claudia.

Lena smirked and said, "This is Claudia—Mum's new daughter."

Claudia chuckled and shook her head. "Come on."

They both smiled before Lena's partner extended a polite nod.

"Ready to go?" she asked.

Lena looked at Claudia one last time, with something unreadable in her expression. "I'll think about it."

Claudia smiled. "That's all I ask."

Lena nodded, then followed her partner toward a car parked nearby. Claudia watched as they got in and drove off into the night.

She let out a slow breath, unsure whether she had truly made a difference.

Before she could dwell on it, she heard her name.

"Claudia!"

She turned to see Tara's sister approaching, suitcase rolling behind her.

"You must be Claudia," she said, a little out of breath. "Tara told me you'd be here."

Claudia pushed aside her thoughts about Lena and smiled. "That's me. Welcome. Long journey?"

The girl shrugged, pulling her scarf tighter around her neck. "Not too bad. The train was packed, though. Christmas rush, I guess."

Claudia nodded, reaching for the handle of her suitcase. "Come on, let's get you out of the cold."

As they made their way to the car, Claudia couldn't stop wondering why everyone was always asking her for favours. Maybe it was because people liked her.

* * *

The drive from the station was quiet at first, Tara's sister, Emily, stared out the window, watching the city lights blur past. Christmas decorations twinkled from shop windows, and the streets were still bustling, despite the late hour.

"So, first time back home in a while?" Claudia asked, breaking the silence.

Emily sighed, stretching her legs. "Yeah. Work's kept me busy. And Tara's been hounding me about making time to visit, so... here I am."

Claudia chuckled. "That sounds like her."

Emily smiled. "She can be persuasive, huh?"

"You have no idea."

They shared a knowing laugh before Emily turned serious. "You seem... nice. Tara talks about you like you're some kind of saint."

Claudia scoffed. "Not quite. I just have a hard time saying no."

Emily grinned. "Well, good luck surviving Christmas with her. She'll probably rope you into something else before the week's over."

"No doubt."

Soon, they pulled into Tara's driveway. The house was lit up, with a warm glow spilling from the windows. As soon as Emily stepped out of the car, the front door flew open, and Tara rushed out, arms wide.

"Finally!" Tara called. "I was starting to think you'd changed your mind."

Emily groaned. "I almost did."

Claudia smiled, watching the sisters reunite.

Tara turned to her. "Thank you, Claudia. Seriously."

Claudia just waved it off. "Go enjoy your family time."

As she got back into the car and drove away, she finally let out a deep breath.

Home was only a short drive away, and the thought of unwinding for the evening was more than welcome.

* * *

When Claudia stepped inside, warmth wrapped around her. The soft hum of classical music floated from the lounge, and the scent of Janet's lavender-scented candles filled the air.

Janet was sitting in her favourite chair, with a cup of tea balanced on the armrest, and her eyes closed, as if she was savouring the melody. When she opened them and spotted Claudia, her face lit up.

"There you are," Janet said, turning down the music. "I was beginning to think you got kidnapped by Tara."

Claudia laughed as she dropped her bag by the door. "Almost. But I made it out alive." She plopped onto the couch with a sigh. "And from today onwards, Christmas leave has officially begun. I'm free."

Janet's eyes twinkled. "Well then, how about we go out tomorrow? Do a little Christmas shopping?"

Claudia tilted her head. "You sure you want to deal with the madness?"

Janet waved a hand dismissively. "I've handled worse. Besides, it's tradition. When I was younger, Christmas was the highlight of the year. We'd count down the days, sneaking peeks at presents under the tree, waiting for the big day. The excitement, the music, the food... it was magical."

Claudia smiled, picturing Janet as a young girl, wide-eyed with Christmas joy. "Sounds wonderful."

"It was," Janet said softly. "Things were simpler back then. Anyway, let's have a cosy night in, a warm cup of tea, and a classic movie.

"Great," said Claudia, "That sounds like what we both need."

She leaned back, pulling out her phone. She glanced at the screen, checking her notifications. No messages. No missed calls.

Her smile faltered for a second, before she shook it off.

"Right, I'm going to change into something comfortable," she said, standing up.

Janet watched her carefully but didn't comment. "I'll make us some tea."

Claudia nodded and disappeared into her room, while Janet made her way to the kitchen, and started setting out the mugs.

7

A SEASON FOR SECOND CHANCES

The high street was alive with festive cheer. Twinkling fairy lights adorned the trees, shop windows sparkled with Christmas displays, and the air was filled with the warm aroma of roasted chestnuts and cinnamon-scented drinks. Janet and Claudia strolled through the bustling crowd, as they admired the festive decorations.

They wandered into different shops, browsing through shelves of winter clothes, Christmas decorations, and gift sets. It felt simple yet special—the kind of day Claudia had always loved.

After a while, they decided to take a break in a cosy coffee shop, and settled into a cosy table by the window. Janet sighed as she pulled off her gloves and unzipped her jacket. That's when she noticed it—a small hole on the sleeve.

"Well, that's it," she said, inspecting it closely. "This jacket's been with me for ages. I suppose it's time for a new one."

Claudia smiled, taking a sip of her coffee. "We'll find you a good one before we head home."

However, Janet wasn't paying attention to her. She was gazing out of the window, watching the people pass by—the shoppers, the street musicians, and the Christmas stalls selling handcrafted gifts. But instead of wonder, there was something else in her expression.

"This isn't the England I knew," Janet murmured, almost to herself.

Claudia frowned. "What do you mean?"

Janet shook her head, her lips pressing into a thin line. "It's changed so much. Too many foreigners everywhere. Sometimes I don't even feel like I'm in my own country anymore." She glanced at Claudia. "Do you watch the news? There's crime everywhere. It's not safe anymore."

Claudia sighed, setting down her cup. "I get why you feel that way, but people need somewhere to live too, don't they? It's not easy for anyone."

Janet gave a dry laugh. "You say that because you're too young. You never saw England the way it was before." She shook her head again and looked back outside, disappointment settling in her features.

Claudia could see that nothing she said would change Janet's mind, so she decided to steer the conversation elsewhere.

"Did you buy anything for Lena?" she asked casually, watching for Janet's reaction.

For a moment, Janet didn't answer. She just stared at her coffee cup.

Claudia leaned forward. "I have a feeling she might come visit you this Christmas."

Janet scoffed. "She won't."

"She might," Claudia pressed. "And if she does, wouldn't it be nice if you had something for her?"

Janet exhaled slowly, her expression unreadable. "Did you convince her to come?"

Claudia raised her eyebrows. "Maybe."

Janet's jaw tightened slightly, but there was something softer in her eyes—something that gave her away. She clearly wanted to believe it.

"If she's coming," Janet muttered, "she'd better come alone."

Claudia didn't argue. She just nodded, letting the moment settle between them.

Finally, Janet picked up her bag. "Alright, let's go buy something, then."

Claudia grinned. "Now you're talking."

* * *

They stepped into a grand shopping mall, the entrance framed by giant golden reindeer and shimmering Christmas trees. Inside, festive music played overhead, and shoppers hurried around, their arms full of bags.

They decided to split up, agreeing to meet by the entrance half an hour later.

Claudia made her way to a clothing store first. She picked out three Christmas jumpers—one for Luca, one for Emmanuel, and one for herself. They were thick, cosy, and had a fun but stylish pattern, perfect for Christmas morning.

Then, she wandered into a luxury watch store. Her eyes landed on a Tissot watch—sleek, elegant, and timeless. It cost £1,000, which was a lot more than she could afford. But still, she imagined Andrew's face when he opened it. She only hesitated for a second before pulling out her card.

As she walked out with the carefully wrapped box in her bag, she spotted a warm, high-quality jacket—the perfect one for Janet. Without thinking twice, she bought it.

Meanwhile, Janet had made her way into a designer store. She stood in front of a display of handbags, her fingers running over the fine leather. After a long moment, she selected one that was expensive, but beautiful.

As she walked toward the counter, she spotted Claudia approaching. Without hesitation, Janet grabbed another bag before stepping up to pay.

When Claudia reached her, Janet turned to her with a casual smile. "All sorted?"

Claudia nodded, lifting her shopping bags. "Yep. You?"

Janet just hummed in response, accepting the wrapped gifts from the cashier.

Neither of them said anything as they stepped out of the store together, but there was an unspoken understanding between them.

As they walked toward the exit, Claudia glanced at Janet's shopping bag. She didn't say anything, but she knew—Janet had bought something for Lena, after all.

Maybe, just maybe, this Christmas wouldn't be so bad.

* * *

That night, Claudia lay in bed, staring at the ceiling, with a restless mind. The day had been long, yet sleep refused to come. With a sigh, she reached for her phone, hesitating for a moment before dialing Andrew's number.

After a few rings, his deep, familiar voice answered. "Claudia?"

"Why didn't you call me?" she asked, in a voice softer than she had intended.

Andrew exhaled. "I did. But you didn't call me back, so I thought you were still upset. I figured I should give you some space."

Claudia closed her eyes, guilt creeping in. "I was upset... I still am.

Your gambling, Andrew—it's a real problem. That night at the club, I just—I couldn't take it anymore."

"I know," Andrew admitted. "I messed up, Claudia. I hate that I disappointed you. But I swear, I'm done with it. No more gambling."

There was a beat of silence before Claudia spoke. "Promise me."

"I promise," he said; the sincerity in his tone made her chest tighten. She sighed. "I'm sorry, too... for how I reacted. I just—"

"No, don't apologize," Andrew interrupted. "You were right to be mad. I needed to hear it."

Another moment of quiet settled between them before Claudia shifted under the covers, biting her lip. "I miss you..."

Andrew chuckled. "Oh yeah? You should've thought about that before giving me the cold shoulder."

She smirked. "I know... but right now, I can't stop thinking about you."

His breath hitched slightly. "Yeah?"

"Mm-hmm." Her voice dropped into a sultry whisper. "I wish you were here."

Andrew groaned. "You're killing me, Claudia."

She giggled. "Am I?"

"You have no idea," he muttered.

They exchanged flirtatious, heated words, teasing each other until the tension between them felt almost unbearable.

"Now I really regret not coming over," Andrew murmured, his voice thick with longing.

Claudia smiled, feeling a warmth spread through her. "Maybe next time, you won't make me wait so long."

He chuckled. "Oh, I'll make it up to you, trust me."

Feeling a little more at peace, Claudia curled up under her blankets. "Goodnight, Andrew."

"Goodnight, beautiful."

As she ended the call, a small smile lingered on her lips. The day had been long and complicated, but at least now, she could fall asleep with the sound of his voice still echoing in her mind.

* * *

8

CHRISTMAS DAY

On Christmas Day, Claudia woke up to the soft glow of morning light streaming through her curtains, with a rare cheerfulness bubbling inside her. The world outside was blanketed in frost, but inside, everything felt warm and bright. Humming to herself, she slipped out of bed, headed straight for the shower, and let the hot water wash over her, refreshing and invigorating.

After drying off, she pulled on the Christmas jumper she had bought just a few days earlier. It was cosy and festive; as she caught a glimpse of herself in the mirror, she couldn't help but smile—she looked beautiful, radiant even. For once, it felt like the day held promise.

Picking up her phone from the nightstand, she dialled Andrew's number. He answered after a couple of rings.

"Hey, babe," he said, his voice still thick with sleep.

"Happy Christmas!" she said.

"Happy Christmas to you too," he replied, seeming to perk up. "What's the plan for today?"

"I'll visit Dad this morning, but I thought we could meet in the evening and go out for dinner."

Andrew's tone lifted with enthusiasm. "Sounds perfect. I can't wait." They exchanged a few more sweet words before hanging up. Claudia, still smiling, tucked her phone away and headed downstairs, with a light heart.

As she walked toward the lounge, the familiar notes of Christmas songs drifted through the house, adding to the festive atmosphere. The scent of cinnamon and fresh pine mingled in the air. She followed the music to the kitchen, where she found Janet bustling about, making tea.

Without hesitation, Claudia wrapped her arms around Janet from behind and planted a soft kiss on her cheek. "Happy Christmas, Janet," she whispered, her voice filled with genuine affection. She handed over a carefully wrapped gift, the paper adorned with tiny gold stars.

Janet turned, as her face lit up with surprise. "Oh, my love," she murmured, pulling Claudia into a warm hug. "Happy Christmas to you too." There was a tenderness in her voice that wrapped itself around Claudia like a blanket.

Janet disappeared for a moment, before returning with a small, beautifully wrapped gift of her own. She placed it gently in Claudia's hands.

Claudia stared at the gift, her heart swelling unexpectedly. She hadn't expected this—not because Janet wasn't thoughtful, but because being treated with this kind of maternal warmth was something she wasn't used to. Memories of her own mother's cold indifference flickered in her mind. Her throat tightened, and, before she could stop herself, tears welled in her eyes.

She opened her mouth to speak, to say thank you, or this means so much, but no words came out. Instead, she looked down and carefully peeled back the wrapping. Inside was a beautiful bag—sleek, elegant, and unmistakably her style. Claudia's eyes lit up, and a bright smile broke through the emotion clouding her face. She held the bag like it was something precious, her joy shining through.

"Janet, it's perfect," she finally whispered, voice trembling. "Thank you... so much."

Janet, sensing the flood of feelings, pulled Claudia close, holding her tight. "It's alright, my darling." She gently rubbed Claudia's back. They stood there for a while, wrapped in the quiet comfort of each other's presence, until Janet pulled back slightly, cupping Claudia's face in her hands.

"Go see your father, love. Spend time with him," Janet said gently, brushing a stray tear from Claudia's cheek. "And when you come back, we'll have tea and watch a film together, alright?"

Claudia nodded, with her voice still caught in her throat, and gave Janet one last squeeze before grabbing her coat.

As Claudia stepped outside, Janet followed her to the door. "Have a good visit, love," she called, waving with a smile. But as Claudia walked down the path, Janet's smile faltered slightly. She lingered in the doorway, watching until Claudia's car disappeared down the street.

Behind her warm expression, worry and anxiety tugged at her heart. Will Lena come? The question echoed in her mind, the uncertainty weighing heavy on her chest. She closed the door softly, with the festive music still playing in the background, but her thoughts were far from the holiday cheer.

* * *

Claudia arrived at the care home, the festive decorations catching her eye as soon as she stepped inside. Twinkling lights framed the doorways, garlands adorned the walls, and the soft sound of

Christmas carols played from a nearby speaker. The warm scent of spiced oranges and clove filled the air, mingling with the familiar, comforting smell of the home. A few residents sat in armchairs in the lounge, their eyes bright with anticipation.

Claudia made her way down the corridor, with her footsteps soft on the polished floor. When she reached Emmanuel's room, the door was closed. She knocked gently, and after a moment, a carer opened the door slightly, peeking out.

"Personal care," the carer explained politely.

Claudia smiled and handed over a carefully wrapped gift. "This is a Christmas jumper for him. Could you help him put it on, please?"

The carer nodded warmly, taking the gift. "Of course," she said before closing the door softly.

Claudia turned and walked toward the nurses' station. She greeted the nurse on duty with a bright smile. "Good morning, and happy Christmas!"

The nurse looked up from her paperwork, returning the smile. "Good morning, Claudia. Happy Christmas to you too."

Claudia glanced around, noticing the hum of activity in the home. "Is something happening today? It looks like everyone's waiting for something."

The nurse nodded, her face lighting up. "Yes, children from the local church are coming to sing carols. It's a bit of a tradition here."

Claudia's eyes brightened. "Oh, that sounds lovely. Do you think I could bring my dad out to listen?"

"That should be fine," the nurse replied, "but he'll need to be in a wheelchair." She stood up from her chair. "I'll let the carers know they should help transfer him."

"They're actually with him now. I just came from his room."

The nurse nodded and walked down the corridor to Emmanuel's room. Claudia waited by the nurses' station, glancing around at the cheerful decorations. A few moments later, the nurse returned.

"We're keeping a closer eye on him these days," she said softly. "Even though he doesn't have one-to-one care, we're treating him as if he does."

Claudia's heart swelled with gratitude. "Thank you. That means a lot."

The nurse added gently, "Just be careful when you're with him. He can't weight-bear properly anymore, but he doesn't realise it."

Claudia nodded. "Don't worry, I'll be very careful. And my brother Luca will be here shortly, so I'll have help."

Just then, the carers opened Emmanuel's door. Claudia's heart lifted as she saw her father dressed neatly in the Christmas jumper she'd brought. His hair was combed, and he looked peaceful, more like himself than he had in a long time.

Claudia smiled, feeling a wave of warmth wash over her.

As she walked into the room, his face lit up with joy.

"Happy Christmas, Papa," she said.

Emmanuel's eyes sparkled as he realized his daughter had come to visit. His face, which was so often clouded with confusion, was now filled with pure happiness. Claudia walked over to him, gently pushing his wheelchair closer to the window, where the winter sunlight streamed in. She pulled a chair next to him and sat down.

"It's Christmas today, Papa," she said softly. "And it's really cold out there."

At the mention of the cold, Emmanuel's expression shifted. His eyes grew distant, as if he were being pulled back into a memory. He reached out, grasping Claudia's hand tightly.

"Laura," he whispered. "Don't do this… we need this child. I'll get a job soon. Children are God's gift."

Claudia's eyes filled with tears, as the words cut deep into her heart. She took a shaky breath, willing herself to stay strong. After a brief pause, she gave his hand a gentle squeeze and reached into her bag for her phone.

"Hey, Papa," she said softly, trying to shift the moment. "Let's take a picture together. I want to remember today."

She switched on the camera and leaned in close, with her face next to his. Emmanuel smiled, his eyes lighting up again. Claudia snapped the selfie, capturing a rare, beautiful moment of connection between them.

Before she could admire the photo, the door creaked open, and Luca walked in, with his police uniform crisp against the festive backdrop.

"Luca!" Emmanuel called out, snapping out of his memory. "You're here!"

"Happy Christmas, Dad," Luca said, stepping forward and giving Emmanuel a gentle pat on the shoulder. As he passed Claudia, he playfully bumped her shoulder but then paused, noticing the tears still lingering in her eyes.

"Hey, why are you crying?" he asked softly.

Emmanuel noticed too, his brows knitting with concern.

Claudia quickly wiped her eyes and forced a smile. "Something just got in my eye, that's all."

They shifted the mood, diving into a joyful conversation. Emmanuel began sharing stories from past Christmases, his voice animated as he recounted a particularly special moment he had spent with Claudia. The warmth of his anecdotes brought genuine smiles to both their faces.

After a while, Emmanuel looked at his children hopefully. "Please, take me outside. It's been so long since I've had fresh air."

Claudia and Luca exchanged a glance and nodded. "Of course, Papa," she said.

They informed a nearby carer, who helped them bundle Emmanuel in a thick jacket to protect him from the cold. As they wheeled him into the corridor, Luca leaned in toward her.

"You know," he whispered, "if he starts singing Christmas carols out there, I'm blaming you."

"Oh, come on, Luca. You love a good sing-along. Maybe you can finally hit those high notes you always miss."

Luca snorted. "I'll leave the high notes to you, Mariah Carey."

As they wheeled Emmanuel into the garden, the crisp winter air greeted them. They positioned themselves near the lounge window, where other residents were gathered, waiting for the children's carol performance.

Luca grabbed two chairs, placing them in an arc around Emmanuel's wheelchair. Once seated, he handed Claudia and Emmanuel their wrapped gifts.

Claudia chuckled, shaking her head as she examined her gift. "If this is some shampoo or shower gel, you can give it to Rosie," she said.

Luca laughed. "At least I got you something. You didn't bring me anything!"

Claudia gasped, feigning shock. "Oh, I forgot! I left it in the room. Go and get it!"

Luca rolled his eyes. "Yeah, sure, I'll grab it on the way."

"It's a jumper," Claudia added, grinning. "Same as mine and Dad's. Go get it and put it on so we can take a nice family picture."

Groaning but clearly secretly pleased, Luca got up and walked back towards the building.

"Don't forget to model it on the runway when you come back," Claudia called after him.

"Yeah, yeah," Luca muttered, waving her off.

As he disappeared, the children from the church began setting up their microphones and speakers, preparing for the performance.

Claudia and Emmanuel watched through the glass, their faces lighting up as the children started to sing. Despite being outside, they could clearly hear the sweet voices carrying through the chilly air.

Emmanuel began singing along, with his voice soft

"I'm enjoying this moment," Emmanuel said, turning to Claudia. "I feel completely happy… you, me, Luca… Oh my God, thank you."

Claudia squeezed his hand gently. "We're happy too, Papa."

After the first carol, Emmanuel looked at Claudia with a hopeful smile. "Can I have a cup of tea?"

"Of course," Claudia replied, standing up. "I'll be right back."

As she walked back inside, she spotted Luca near Emmanuel's room, looking puzzled.

"Where did you leave the jumper?" he called out.

Claudia laughed, shaking her head. "You can't even find a jumper in a room and you call yourself a bloody policeman?"

Luca scowled playfully. "Oh, piss off. I'm not wearing anything. If you want a picture, take it as I am."

Claudia smirked. "Come on, Luca. Save that manliness for Rosie, not me. Now shut up and get the present. It's on the side table, under my handbag."

Luca muttered under his breath but turned back to the room, while Claudia headed towards the kitchen to fetch Emmanuel's tea, her heart light and full from the warmth of family.

9

THE DAY THAT CHANGED EVERY THING

Claudia walked back towards the garden, balancing a tray with three cups of tea, her cheeks still warm. As she passed, she spotted Luca stepping out of Emmanuel's room, now wearing the bright Christmas jumper she'd bought him. The festive pattern clashed hilariously with his serious police demeanour, making her chuckle.

Luca noticed her and spun around like he was on a catwalk. "Well? How do I look?"

Claudia raised an eyebrow. "Honestly? I thought we'd have a cute family photo in matching jumpers... but now I'm not so sure."

Luca rolled his eyes dramatically. "Oi, shut it, you muppet. You're just jealous I look better in mine."

"Better? You look like a Christmas turkey wrapped in tinsel." Claudia snorted, adjusting the tray in her hands.

Luca laughed, shaking his head. "Yeah, yeah."

They were still grinning when they turned the corner, but then they froze. A group of carers were huddled around something—or someone—on the ground. The children, who had been singing carols, had stopped mid-song. Their wide eyes were staring, watching the scene unfold in eerie silence.

Claudia felt the tray slip slightly in her grip, as her stomach knotted. Luca's smile vanished. "Shit."

He sprinted ahead, his boots thudding against the pavement. Claudia set the tray down on the nearest table with trembling hands and followed, with her heart hammering in her chest.

As she got closer, the awful reality hit her like a punch to the gut.

Emmanuel was sprawled on the ground next to a large potted plant, with his head cradled in a carer's lap. Blood was pooling beneath him, bright and terrifying against the cold stone. A carer pressed a wad of gauze against his head, but it was already soaked through.

Claudia felt the breath leave her body. "No, no, no..." Her legs felt like lead as she staggered forward.

Luca was already kneeling by Emmanuel. "What happened?"

Before anyone could respond, a carer turned sharply towards Luca and Claudia, her voice trembling with frustration and fear. "Didn't we tell you he shouldn't be left alone?"

Claudia's heart sank deeper. The words felt like a slap. She opened her mouth, but no words came out. The guilt gnawed at her chest, leaving her breathless.

Another carer, trying to stay calm, added, "One of the kids said he got excited hearing the carols... he tried to stand up, maybe dance, and just lost his balance. Then he fell and hit his head on the planter."

Luca clenched his jaw, but his focus stayed on Emmanuel. "What do we do now?"

"The nurse is on the phone with the ambulance," another carer replied quickly. "He's lost a lot of blood, and it's still coming. They'll take him to the hospital as soon as they get here."

Claudia's legs gave out, and she sank into a chair nearby, her vision blurring with tears. She stared at her father's pale face, and the blood seeping through the gauze, and all she could think was, "This is my fault. I shouldn't have left him."

Luca noticed her crumbling and rushed over, crouching beside her. "Claudia. Hey. Look at me."

She couldn't. The guilt was too heavy.

"It's going to be okay," he whispered, pulling her into a hug. "They're taking care of him. This isn't your fault."

But Claudia barely heard him. The weight of the moment pressed down, suffocating her.

Minutes later, the ambulance arrived, with its lights flashing in the cold winter air. The paramedics moved quickly, lifting Emmanuel onto a stretcher.

Luca followed the stretcher out, his hand resting protectively on their father's arm. Claudia remained frozen in her chair, with her body numb as the world moved around her in a blur of flashing lights and hushed voices.

When Luca returned, he knelt in front of her, his eyes soft but urgent.

"Claudia, we need to go. We'll follow the ambulance to the hospital."

She blinked, her breath shaky. "I… I shouldn't have left him. I just wanted to get tea…"

Luca's grip on her hands tightened, his voice firm. "Claudia, stop. This wasn't your fault. It was an accident. You hear me? An accident."

But the words felt hollow. Claudia let him pull her to her feet, as her mind stayed trapped in that awful moment. She followed him to his car, her movements stiff and mechanical.

Once inside, as Luca started the engine, Claudia whispered, almost to herself, "I'm the reason this happened."

Luca's jaw clenched, his voice low but steady. "No, you're not. Don't do this to yourself."

Claudia didn't respond. She stared out the window, as the flashing lights of the care home faded into the distance, with the weight of guilt heavy in the silence between them.

* * *

The drive to the hospital felt like it took forever. The car was silent except for the rhythmic sound of the wipers brushing away the light drizzle on the windshield. Claudia sat motionless in the passenger seat, with her eyes fixed on the flashing red and blue lights of the ambulance ahead of them.

When they finally pulled into the hospital car park, Luca killed the engine and turned to Claudia. "You ready?"

Claudia didn't respond; she just nodded slightly, with a pale, strained face. They both climbed out, with their breath visible in the cold air as they hurried toward the entrance.

Inside, the fluorescent lights of the A&E waiting room felt harsh against the sterile white walls. The faint buzz of conversations, beeping monitors, and the shuffle of hurried footsteps echoed around them. Claudia felt overwhelmed; her heart was pounding in her chest as they approached the reception desk.

Luca stepped forward, with his badge, which was clipped to his belt, catching the light. "Emmanuel Rossi. He was just brought in—head injury."

The receptionist checked the system, then gave a polite, but rehearsed smile. "He's with the trauma team now. Someone will come out to update you shortly."

They thanked her and moved to the waiting area, settling into two plastic chairs that felt colder than the air outside. Claudia stared at the linoleum floor.

The minutes felt like hours.

Finally, a doctor in scrubs approached, with his face calm but serious.

"Family of Emmanuel Rossi?" he asked, glancing between them.

Luca stood quickly; Claudia followed suit, though her legs felt weak beneath her. "Yes, we're his children."

The doctor gave a nod. "Your father is stable for now, but he's sustained a significant head injury. We've controlled the bleeding, but he'll need a CT scan to check for internal damage or swelling." He paused, with his eyes softening. "It's going to take some time. These things can't be rushed, but we'll do everything we can."

Claudia swallowed hard, trying to find her voice. "Can we see him?"

"Not just yet," the doctor replied gently. "We need to get the scan done first. But I promise, as soon as it's safe, we'll let you know."

Luca nodded. "Thank you, doctor."

The doctor disappeared down the corridor, leaving them standing there.

Claudia sank back into her chair, with her head in her hands. "I can't believe this is happening."

Luca sat beside her, his hand resting on her shoulder. "He's tough, Claudia. You know Dad. He'll pull through."

But Claudia wasn't sure if she believed it. All she could see was the blood, and the carer's words were echoing in her mind.

"I shouldn't have left him..." she whispered again.

Luca's grip tightened slightly, his voice steady but firm. "Stop. You need to stop blaming yourself. It was an accident."

Claudia didn't answer. She leaned back against the hard plastic chair, staring at the ceiling tiles, praying for good news.

And so, they waited.

* * *

After what felt like an eternity of sitting in the sterile waiting room, Luca glanced at the clock on the wall and let out a heavy sigh. Claudia's eyes were red and tired, and her body was slumped in the uncomfortable plastic chair. The hospital's fluorescent lights made everything feel even more exhausting.

Luca nudged her gently. "Come on, let's get some coffee. We'll go mad just sitting here."

Claudia hesitated, staring down the corridor as if she was expecting the doctor to reappear at any moment. But finally, she nodded; her body was too drained to argue. They stood up and made their way to the small coffee shop tucked into the corner of the hospital's main lobby.

The café was quiet, a stark contrast to the beeping monitors and distant chatter of the A&E. The faint smell of burnt coffee and antiseptic lingered in the air. Luca ordered two coffees and a couple of biscuits, before sliding into a booth near the window from which they could still see the entrance to the emergency department.

Claudia wrapped her hands around the warm cup, letting the heat seep into her cold fingers. She stared into the dark liquid for a moment before finally breaking the silence.

"Luca… I think I'm going to go home for a bit," she said quietly; her voice was hoarse from hours of holding back tears.

Luca looked up, with a frown. "What? You sure?"

Claudia nodded, her eyes still fixed on her coffee. "Yeah… I just need to grab a few things. If they keep Dad here overnight—which they probably will—I want to stay with him. I can't leave him alone like that again."

Luca reached across the table, squeezing her hand gently. "You are there for him. We both are. But don't burn yourself out, alright? We'll take turns. I'll stay tonight if you need a break."

Claudia managed a small smile, grateful for her brother's support. "Thanks, Luca. But I want to be here tonight. I'll just grab some clothes, my charger... and maybe a book."

Luca nodded, finishing the last sip of his coffee. "Alright. I'll stay here and wait for any updates. Just... don't rush, okay?"

Claudia stood up, grabbing her coat. "I will. I'll be back soon."

As she walked out of the coffee shop and into the cold night air, Luca watched her go, with a heavy heart. He knew how much their father's condition weighed on Claudia, and he could only hope that they'd get some good news soon.

* * *

10

THE DAY STILL HOLDS ITS SECRETS

Claudia stepped out of the Uber in front of the care home, with the cold air biting at her cheeks as she wrapped her coat tighter around herself. The events of the day swirled in her mind like a storm. She hurried around the corner to where her car was parked, with her breath visible in the icy air. Sliding into the driver's seat, she let out a shaky sigh, gripping the steering wheel tightly. Just breathe, Claudia. You need to get through this.

Before starting the engine, she pulled out her phone and stared at the screen for a moment. Her thumb hovered over Andrew's name in her contacts. She knew she had to let him know. With a deep breath, she tapped the call button and held the phone to her ear.

It only rang twice before Andrew picked up: "Hey, babe! You on your way?"

Claudia swallowed hard, with her throat tight. "Hey, Andrew. Listen… I…" Her voice cracked, and she took a moment to steady it. "I'm really sorry, but I can't meet you tonight."

There was a pause on the other end, then Andrew's voice softened. "What's wrong? Are you okay?"

Claudia closed her eyes, leaning her head back against the headrest. "It's my dad. He... he had a bad fall at the care home. We had to rush him to the hospital. There was so much blood, Andrew." Her voice wavered; the memory was too fresh, too vivid. "I just... I can't leave him right now."

Andrew was quiet for a moment, then his voice came through, gentle but insistent. "Do you want me to come to the hospital? I can be there in like, 20 minutes. Whatever you need, Claudia."

Claudia felt a pang of gratitude, but she knew she couldn't handle anyone else right now—not even Andrew. She needed space to process everything. "No, it's okay," she whispered. "I just... I need to focus on him right now. I'll call you when I'm ready, I promise."

Andrew sighed on the other end, clearly wanting to do more. "Are you sure? I hate the thought of you dealing with this alone."

Claudia forced a small, appreciative smile, even though he couldn't see it. "I'm not alone. Luca's with me, and... I'll be okay. I just need some time."

There was a pause, then Andrew spoke again, more softly. "Alright. But you better call me when you're ready. I'm here whenever you need me, okay?"

"I know," Claudia whispered. "Thank you, Andrew. I'll talk to you soon."

She ended the call before her emotions could overwhelm her again, staring at the phone in her lap for a moment. Then, with a deep breath, she tucked it away, started the car, and pulled onto the road. The drive home felt like a blur, with the streets blending together in a grey smear of headlights and damp pavement. She hadn't want to leave her dad, but she had no choice. Just grab your things, Claudia, and get back.

But when she pulled up to her house, another wave of tension hit her. Lena's car was parked outside; her partner was sitting alone in the driver's seat, which sent a ripple of unease through her. The bright green hair was unmistakable, but her expression was tight and distant, as if she was bracing for something. When she spotted Claudia approaching, she gave a strained, polite smile.

Claudia gave her a slight nod, but didn't linger. Her stomach was already twisting into knots, and now there was a new tension settling in her chest. As she neared the front door, muffled voices seeped through the walls—sharp, raised voices.

Her heart sank. Janet and Lena.

She paused, with her hand hovering over the doorknob. The last thing she needed was to walk into the middle of one of their arguments. But she didn't have time to stand there debating. Get in, grab your stuff, get out. She turned the key in the lock, pushing the door open as quietly as possible, and then slipping inside like a ghost.

She closed the door behind her without a sound, but their voices hit her like a slap.

"You never tried to understand me!" Lena's voice cracked through the house, sharp and raw.

"I did try, Lena," Janet shot back. "But you changed so much, I didn't know how to handle it!"

Claudia froze in the entryway, as her breath caught in her throat. She didn't want to hear this. She couldn't hear this. But there was no avoiding it—the words echoed down the hallway, each one cutting deeper.

She crept towards her room, grateful for the wall that separated the kitchen from the lounge. They wouldn't see her, but their voices followed her like shadows, refusing to be shut out.

It's not about handling me, Mum," Lena's voice wavered, but the anger held strong. "It's about accepting me. You made me feel like I wasn't good enough because I didn't fit into your perfect little box."

Claudia reached her room and closed the door behind her with trembling fingers, but even the barrier of wood couldn't muffle their words. She moved quickly, grabbing clothes and toiletries, but her heart was pounding too loudly in her ears to focus.

"I never asked you to be perfect, Lena," Janet hissed, her words like ice. "I just expected you to be normal. Look at yourself—do you even recognise who you are in the mirror?"

"This is exactly why I don't visit you," Lena snapped; her voice was shaking with anger.

There was a heavy pause before Janet's next words, but when they came, they felt like a slap.

"I had two kids. God took one, and the devil took the other. Now I'm all alone."

Claudia froze, with her hands resting on the edge of her dresser. Those words cut deeper than she expected. Claudia closed her eyes, trying to block out the words. But they kept coming.

Lena's voice broke through, raw and shaking. "How dare you?" she whispered. "I will never visit you again."

"If you'd come alone, this wouldn't have happened," Janet spat back. "But no, you had to bring your girlfriend. Do you even realise what a sin that is?"

Claudia clenched her fists at her sides, with her nails digging into her palms. The words were like poison, seeping into every corner of the house.

"You know why I came here?" Lena's voice was hoarse, but steady. "Because Claudia asked me to. Otherwise, I wouldn't even have called to wish you a miserable Christmas."

Janet's response came like a dagger. "Claudia? She's no better. Always a mess, no discipline, purple hair like some kind of rebellious teenager. I've never liked her."

Claudia's breath hitched in her throat. What? The words echoed in her head, louder than any argument, any insult. She's been pretending all along…

Lena's voice rose, trembling with disbelief. "You're pure evil. Claudia sees you like a mother. She trusted you."

There was a bitter, hateful laugh from Janet. "I only like having her around because she is normal; she is more like proper British person, not some… freak…"

Claudia's knees nearly buckled. Who is this woman? She felt like the ground beneath her was crumbling. Everything she'd believed about Janet—her kindness, her warmth, and the support she'd offered—it was all a lie. Just another mask.

She zipped up her bag, with her hands shaking violently. She needed to get out. Now.

She crept back down the hallway, with her heart pounding so loudly she was sure they could hear it. As she slipped out the front door, the cold night air hit her like a slap, but it was nothing compared to the chill settling in her chest.

She spotted Lena's partner still sitting in the car, her bright green hair catching the glow of the streetlights. Their eyes met through the glass, and in that moment, Claudia saw it—the understanding. The exhaustion. The same pain mirrored in someone else.

Claudia forced a shaky smile, with her voice barely above a whisper. "Take care of her, yeah?"

Lena's partner nodded, her expression softening with quiet solidarity.

Claudia didn't wait for more. She climbed into her car, with her hands trembling on the steering wheel. She sat there for a long, heavy moment, staring at the dark road ahead. Her heart was pounding, and her thoughts racing, but all she could hear were Janet's words echoing in her mind.

With a deep, shuddering breath, she started the engine and drove off into the night—back towards the hospital

As Claudia drove through the quiet, dimly lit streets toward the hospital, her mind replayed Janet's words over and over. "I only like having her around because she is normal; she is more like proper British person, not some… freak…"I never liked her." The sting of those words settled deep in her chest, heavier than the cold winter air pressing against her car windows. She had trusted Janet, and let her into the vulnerable parts of her life. Janet had filled the space her mother had left hollow, or so Claudia had thought. But now, all those shared cups of tea, the laughter in the living room, the warm hugs—they felt tainted, like a lie wrapped in kindness.

Is this the person I felt safe around? Claudia wondered, with her grip tightening on the steering wheel. She had never expected those words, not from Janet. It wasn't just the betrayal of hearing her true thoughts—it was the realisation that maybe Claudia had been fooling herself all along, desperate for approval from someone who never truly cared.

When she finally pulled into the hospital parking lot, with the fluorescent lights reflecting off the wet pavement, Claudia took a deep breath, and forced herself to push Janet out of her mind. Focus on Dad. He's what matters now.

* * *

Inside the hospital, the sterile smell and quiet hum of machines greeted her like an old, unwelcome friend. She found Luca sitting in one of the stiff plastic chairs outside Emmanuel's room; his head was tilted back against the wall, and he had his eyes closed.

"Hey," Claudia whispered, as she approached.

Luca opened his eyes and sat up straighter, with a weary look. "Hey. No changes so far," he said; his voice was tinged with exhaustion.

Claudia placed a comforting hand on his shoulder. "You should go home, Luca. Little Pete will be waiting for you, and Rosie probably needs a break from child-minding."

Luca shook his head, rubbing his eyes. "I don't want to leave you here alone."

"I'll be fine," Claudia assured him, offering a small, tired smile. "I just need some time with Dad. Go home, get some rest, and come back tomorrow."

Luca hesitated for a moment, then nodded. "Alright. But call me if anything changes, yeah?"

"I will," Claudia promised.

Luca stood, pulling her into a quick, tight hug. "Hang in there, Claud."

"You too," she whispered.

As Luca disappeared down the corridor, Claudia pushed open the door to Emmanuel's room. The steady beep of the heart monitor was the only sound that greeted her. Her father lay motionless, with his face pale but peaceful, a stark contrast to the chaos of the day. Claudia pulled a chair next to his bed and sank into it, finally succumbing to the exhaustion she'd been holding at bay.

She pulled out her phone, scrolling through photos of her and Emmanuel—laughing in the park, and sitting at the piano, with their faces lit with genuine joy. The images felt like fragments of a different life, one that was slipping further away with each passing day.

A tear rolled down her cheek as she gently touched the screen, her heart aching. I'm here, Papa, she thought. I'm not going anywhere.

And as the night stretched on, Claudia sat in the small hospital room, surrounded by the fading echoes of the past, holding onto the hope that some part of her father was still holding on too.

11

FLICKER OF HOPE

The next morning, Luca walked into Emmanuel's room, carrying two coffees—one of which he handed to Claudia, who was slouched in the chair beside their father's bed. The beeping of machines was the only sound in the sterile room. Claudia had dark circles under her eyes from the sleepless nights.

Luca settled into the chair next to her, taking a sip of his coffee before glancing her way. "Hey, uh... Janet called me yesterday."

Claudia stiffened slightly but didn't respond.

"She was asking about you," Luca continued. "I told her what happened with Dad, so she knows. But..." he trailed off, giving her a pointed look. "Why haven't you picked up her calls?"

Claudia sighed, staring into her cup. "I just... haven't felt like talking to anyone."

Luca raised an eyebrow but didn't push further. He could tell there was more to the story, but if Claudia wasn't ready to share, he respected that.

After a few moments of silence, Luca glanced at the time and let out a sigh. "I should probably head back. Pete is with the childminder, but she needs to leave soon, and Rosie's working late." He stood, squeezing Claudia's shoulder gently. "I'll be back tomorrow, alright?" Claudia nodded, offering a small, grateful smile. "Thanks, Luca."

As he left, Claudia remained seated, with her eyes drifting back to Emmanuel. She swallowed the lump in her throat, feeling the weight of the past few days settle over her.

She didn't go back to the house. The thought of facing Janet after everything she'd overheard was too much. Instead, she spent the following days at the hospital, buying a few clothes from a nearby shop to get by. The sterile hospital room became her temporary home, with the steady rhythm of her father's heartbeat on the monitor the only sound that offered her any comfort.

As the days crawled towards the end of the year, Claudia still sat by Emmanuel's side, holding his hand, unsure of what the new year would bring but knowing she wasn't ready to face anything beyond this room just yet.

* * *

On the afternoon of December 31st, Claudia sat quietly beside Emmanuel's bed, her fingers lightly tracing the wrinkles on his hand. The rhythmic beep of the heart monitor filled the otherwise silent room. She had grown used to the stillness, to the unpredictability of his consciousness flickering in and out. But nothing had prepared her for what happened next.

Emmanuel's eyes fluttered open, clear and focused in a way Claudia hadn't seen in months.

"Papa?" Claudia whispered, as her heart skipped a beat.

Emmanuel's gaze settled on her, soft and full of recognition. His lips trembled slightly before he spoke.

"Claudia," he whispered, his voice weak but steady. "I'm... really sorry for how your mother treated you." His eyes glistened with emotion. "I tried my best to make it better for you... I'm sorry if it wasn't enough."

Tears welled in Claudia's eyes as she gripped his hand tighter. Before she could respond, the door creaked open, and Luca stepped into the room. He eyes widened as he saw his father awake and lucid.

"Papa?" Luca breathed, stepping closer.

Emmanuel turned his head towards Luca, with a proud smile spreading across his face. "My son... I feel so proud looking at you." His voice wavered, but the warmth in his words was undeniable. "Please... take care of your sister."

Claudia and Luca exchanged a look, their hearts swelling with joy and relief. For the first time in what felt like forever, their father was here—not lost in the fog of dementia, but fully present, the man they remembered.

Emmanuel gave a soft sigh, his eyes fluttering shut again. "I'm at peace now," he murmured. "But I feel so sleepy... can I go back to sleep?"

Claudia choked back a sob, brushing a gentle hand over his forehead. "Of course, Papa. Rest."

As Emmanuel drifted back into sleep, his breathing steady and calm, Claudia and Luca sat in stunned silence, with tears streaming down their faces—but this time, they were tears of happiness. Their father had come back to them, even if just for a fleeting moment. And in that moment, everything felt whole again.

Once their father was asleep, Claudia and Luca stepped out of the hospital room, with their hearts still racing. They found the doctor, checking his chart in the corridor.

"How is he, doctor?" Claudia asked, her voice filled with cautious hope. "He just spoke to us, and he seemed to know exactly what was going on."

The doctor offered them a reassuring smile. "That's a very good sign. Moments of clarity like this often indicate stabilization. You both can relax a little now."

Relief washed over them. Claudia exhaled deeply, feeling like she could finally breathe again. Luca clapped her on the back. "Come on, let's grab something to eat. You need it."

They walked to Claudia's car, and as soon as they slid into their seats, Luca glanced around the interior with a teasing grin.

"This car still holding together, or are we going to have to push it to the restaurant?" he joked, tapping the dashboard like it might fall apart any second.

Claudia rolled her eyes, starting the engine with a mock flourish. "Hey, don't disrespect the Polo. She's got character."

As they pulled out of the parking lot, Luca's eyes landed on a neatly wrapped gift sitting on the passenger seat. He picked it up with a mischievous smirk. "What's this? A late Christmas present for your favourite brother?"

Claudia snatched it back, grinning. "In your dreams. Ask Rosie to buy you one like this."

Luca chuckled, shaking his head. "Yeah, right. She's more likely to throw something at me than buy me gifts these days."

They shared a laugh as Claudia drove them to a nearby restaurant. The meal was filled with light hearted banter and a sense of relief neither of them had felt in weeks. For the first time in a long while, things felt normal.

After they finished eating, Claudia dropped Luca back at the hospital.

"You sure you don't want me to stay?" she asked as he stepped out of the car.

Luca waved her off. "Go on, enjoy yourself for once. I'll keep an eye on Dad. Just come back later."

Claudia smiled; her heart felt lighter than it had in days. As she drove off, she felt an excitement bubbling inside her. Her father was stable, and she wanted to share the good news. Without thinking twice, she headed toward Andrew's place, eager to see him, give him the gift she'd bought, and finally enjoy a moment of happiness together.

* * *

Claudia pulled up to Andrew's garage, filled with thoughts of the good news about her father. She stepped out of the car, with the wrapped gift tucked under her arm, ready to share both her excitement and the present she'd picked out for him. But as she walked toward the entrance, she noticed something unusual—the garage was quiet—too quiet. There was no loud clanging of tools, and no muffled curses from under a car hood. One of Andrew's co-workers, leaning against a car with a wrench in hand, glanced up when he saw her.

"He's off today," he said casually, wiping his hands on a rag.

Claudia's smile didn't falter. She shrugged, thinking nothing of it. It's the last day of the year, she reminded herself. Maybe he decided to take the day off, hit up the pub, or… she rolled her eyes, maybe he's at the betting shop, thinking he'll hit it big before midnight.

She thanked the man and headed back to her car. As she started the engine, she pulled out her phone and dialled Andrew's number, balancing it between her ear and shoulder. It rang and rang, but there was no answer. She tried again, a little slower this time, but still, nothing. No response.

Probably drinking already, she thought with a smirk, tossing the phone onto the passenger seat. But still... she found herself driving toward his flat. Just to surprise him, she told herself. He'll be thrilled when he sees me.

As she turned onto his street, her heart lifted a little at the sight of his scooter parked out front. So, he's home. She parked behind it, grabbed the gift from the passenger seat, and headed to the front door.

The key he'd given her long ago felt cool and familiar in her hand as she slid it into the lock. She pushed the door open quietly, eager to surprise him, and to see the look on his face when she told him about her dad.

But as she stepped into the living room, the air seemed to thicken.

There, on the couch, was Andrew... He was fast asleep, with Sofi curled up next to him. Their bodies were too close, the kind of closeness that didn't need explaining. Claudia stood frozen, with her heart pounding in her ears, louder than any noise around her.

The gift slipped from her hands, hitting the floor with a soft thud. The sound stirred Andrew. His eyes fluttered open, bleary and unfocused. He glanced around, but his gaze didn't register anything amiss. Too tired—or maybe too comfortable—he let his eyes close again, sinking back into sleep.

Claudia didn't wait for more. She turned and walked out, each step feeling heavier than the last. She made it to her car, but when she tried to slam the door shut, it wouldn't catch. She yanked it open and slammed it again. Nothing. The third time, it finally clicked shut.

Her breath came out in ragged gasps as she started the engine. She cranked the radio up, letting the music fill the space in which her thoughts were starting to spiral. But it wasn't enough. The tears came hot and fast, blurring her vision as she pulled away from the curb.

She didn't know where she was going, but anywhere was better than where she was. The music blasted in the background, but it couldn't drown out the weight pressing down on her chest. Her sobs matched the rhythm of the tires on the road, the betrayal echoing louder than any song ever could.

12

THE MOMENTS BEFORE FALL

C laudia gripped the steering wheel as she drove through the bustling streets, her heart pounding with a different rhythm to the world around her. The city was alive—vibrant and electric—as people flooded the streets, laughing, cheering, and ready to welcome the new year. Strings of lights were wrapped around lamp posts, casting a festive glow, and shop windows were adorned with glittering decorations. Horns honked, not out of frustration, but celebration, as groups of friends leaned out of car windows, waving sparklers and shouting greetings to strangers.

Couples strolled hand in hand along the pavements, with their faces glowing under the fairy lights, while children pointed excitedly at fireworks that were already starting to light up the evening sky. Music spilled out from open windows and bars, each beat a reminder that life was moving forward—joyfully, unapologetically.

But inside Claudia's car, it was a different world. The pounding bass of the radio was too loud, drowning out the city's celebrations, yet it couldn't quiet the storm raging inside her. Her chest felt tight; the betrayal she had just witnessed was clinging to her like a second skin. Every laugh, every sparkle, and every sound of celebration outside felt like a cruel joke, a reminder of everything she wasn't feeling.

She wiped at her face, only to realize more tears had replaced the ones she'd just brushed away. Her car rattled as she drove over uneven cobblestones, with the door rattling after her earlier struggle with it. It matched her mood perfectly—broken, but stubbornly holding on.

As she left the city centre behind, the bright lights faded into the distance, but the sound of fireworks continued to crackle in the night sky. She turned off the main road, with her headlights casting long shadows across empty streets until she finally pulled into the quiet, empty parking lot of a small park.

She killed the engine, and the sudden silence was deafening.

Leaning back in her seat, Claudia glanced out at the playground, where children were still playing, with their laughter echoing across the park. Parents sat on benches, chatting, and sipping hot drinks from paper cups, completely oblivious of the storm inside her car.

Is this what life is? she wondered bitterly. Everyone laughing, moving on, pretending everything's fine. But it's all a lie, isn't it? And no one even notices. That's it.

Her eyes lingered on the kids, and their bright and carefree faces under the soft glow of the streetlights.

"Enjoy it while you can," she whispered, her voice thick with bitterness. She knew better than anyone—life didn't send warnings before it knocked you down. And right now, it felt like it had knocked her flat again, leaving her gasping while the rest of the world danced into the new year without her.

Her phone rang, cutting through the heavy silence. She glanced at the screen—Andrew. Without hesitation, she hung up, her jaw tightening. But the phone rang again. And again.

With an irritated sigh, she silenced the phone and tossed it onto the passenger seat, face down. She let her body sink into the seat, extending it back as far as it would go. The exhaustion from days at the hospital finally weighed her down; before she knew it, her eyes fluttered shut. The hum of the world outside faded as sleep took over, and her mind briefly escaped the whirlwind of emotions.

* * *

Claudia stirred from her restless sleep, disoriented by the muffled sounds of laughter and shouting outside her car. Her eyes fluttered open just as a sharp tap-tap-tap echoed against her window. She jolted upright, with her heart pounding in her chest.

A group of young people, cheeks flushed from the cold and maybe a little too much champagne, were gathered around her car. One of them, a guy with a glittery party hat tilted on his head, leaned down and knocked again, grinning from ear to ear.

"Happy New Year!" he shouted through the glass. His friends echoed him with cheers and whoops.

Claudia blinked, as her mind struggled to catch up with the noise and flashing lights in the distance. Fireworks crackled faintly in the sky, with their colours reflecting off the car's windshield. For a split second, she was caught between the surreal celebration outside and the heavy weight of everything inside her.

She managed a weak smile and raised her hand in a small wave. The group laughed and moved on; their voices faded into the night as they disappeared down the street.

The car fell silent again, but Claudia's pulse was still racing. She reached for her phone on the passenger seat, flipping it over. The screen lit up—10:30 PM. Her breath caught when she saw 30 missed calls. Without thinking much of it, she sighed heavily and tossed the phone back onto the seat, ignoring the gnawing feeling in her gut.

She started the car, and gripped the steering wheel. But as she was about to pull away from the curb, a sudden thought struck her—Papa.

Her chest tightened. She hadn't checked on Emmanuel since earlier, and guilt surged through her. She reached over, grabbed the phone again, and unlocked it, with her thumb hovering over Luca's contact. But her heart dropped when she realized the 30 missed calls weren't all from Andrew as she'd assumed. The last 15 were from Luca.

A cold, sinking feeling spread through her chest as she quickly hit the call button, with her hands trembling as she brought the phone to her ear.

Her heart was pounding so hard she could hear it in her temples. The second the call connected, Luca picked up.

"Claudia..." He said her name as if it hurt to speak. There was a pause, heavy and unnatural, the kind of silence that screamed something was terribly wrong.

"What? Luca, what is it?" Her voice cracked, as panic rose in her chest.

"Papa's gone." The words came out flat, as if he'd been trying to prepare himself to say them, but no amount of practice could soften them.

Claudia felt the world tilt beneath her. Gone? Her mind scrambled to understand, but the words just echoed in her head, over and over, refusing to make sense.

"He passed away after you left," Luca continued; his voice was quieter now, almost a whisper, like saying it out loud made it more real. "I tried to call you. Over and over. He... he woke up before he passed, Claudia. He asked for you."

Her breath caught in her throat, a sharp, painful gasp like she'd been punched in the chest. He asked for me.

"But you weren't there," Luca's voice broke, and the weight of his words crushed her.

A sob burst from Claudia's lips, raw and uncontrollable, like it had been waiting just beneath the surface. Her vision blurred as hot tears streamed down her face. She could barely form words, her heart shattering with each beat.

"I wasn't there..." she whispered, the guilt gripping her like a vice. She could hear Luca trying to speak, but his words were muffled by the roaring in her ears, the rush of blood and grief overwhelming everything else.

"He left in peace," Luca tried again, his voice gentle, like he was trying to offer her something—anything—to hold onto. "He wasn't in pain."

But it didn't matter. None of it mattered. She hadn't been there. She hadn't been there when he needed her most.

"I need to go," she croaked; her voice was barely recognizable even to herself.

"Claudia, please don't..."

But she didn't let him finish. She pressed end call with trembling fingers, staring at the screen for a moment before she switched the phone off completely. The black screen stared back at her, offering no comfort, and no answers.

She dropped the phone onto the passenger seat like it was something toxic that she couldn't bear to hold any longer. Then, slowly, she leaned forward, resting her forehead against the cold steering wheel. For a moment, there was nothing—just the hollow echo of Luca's words in her mind.

Then the grief hit her, hard and fast, like a tidal wave crashing over her. She sobbed, the deep and guttural kind of crying that comes from a place so raw it feels like it's tearing you apart from the inside. Her shoulders shook violently as she clutched the wheel, with her knuckles white from the grip. She cried for her father, for the moments they'd lost, and for the years dementia had stolen from them. But most of all, she cried for herself—for not being there, for failing him.

The minutes stretched on endlessly, as her cries eventually faded into quiet, exhausted sniffles. She sat there, slumped against the steering wheel, with her body drained, and her soul hollow. The night outside continued, indifferent to her pain. She could hear distant fireworks now, faint pops and bursts in the sky as the city celebrated the arrival of a new year.

She slowly sat back in her seat, wiping at her tear-streaked face with the sleeve of her jumper. Her eyes were red and swollen, and her heart was still aching, but something else flickered beneath the grief. A quiet, simmering resolve. The pain hadn't lessened, but there was a sharp clarity in its wake.

Without thinking, she turned the key in the ignition. The engine roared to life. She gripped the steering wheel tightly, with her knuckles still trembling, and pulled out onto the road.

She didn't know exactly where she was going, but she knew one thing for certain: nothing would ever be the same again.

Claudia's grip on the steering wheel tightened as she sped through the city, with her foot heavy on the accelerator; the familiar streets blurred past her in a haze of neon lights and smudged reflections. The city was alive—more alive than she'd ever felt. Laughter spilled from packed bars, fireworks crackled in the distance, and crowds filled the streets, cheering in the new year with oblivious joy. But inside her car, it was suffocatingly silent, except for the rhythmic pounding of her heart.

The speed cameras flashed behind her like mocking strobe lights, capturing her recklessness, but she didn't slow down. She blasted through red lights and wrong turns, even barrelling down a one-way street, with her headlights cutting through the oncoming darkness like she didn't belong in this world anymore—and maybe she didn't.

She didn't even flinch when a horn blared, or when a pedestrian yelled something she couldn't hear. None of it mattered.

Bridge after bridge, she drove along the Thames, each one crowded with people celebrating the turn of the year. Couples kissed under streetlights, families gathered to watch the fireworks burst into colour above the river, and friends shouted and sang together. She hated them all in that moment.

Finally, after weaving through winding streets, she found it—the fifth bridge. It was quiet, and empty. A forgotten stretch of concrete, far enough from the crowds, from the life she couldn't touch.

A "No Parking" sign glared at her from the side of the road. She slammed the car into gear and, with a jolt of anger she didn't fully understand, drove straight into it. The metal crumpled under the force of the impact, as the sound echoed sharply in the stillness. It felt good—like hitting back at a world that had been punching her for far too long.

She killed the engine and stepped out of the car, as the door slammed shut behind her. The bitter, icy air hit her like a slap, but it didn't compare to the cold settling in her chest. She didn't bother locking the car or even glancing back. Let the world take what it wanted—everything else had already been stolen from her.

She walked toward the edge of the bridge, with her boots clicking softly against the concrete, the sound strangely loud in the emptiness. The wind whipped around her, tugging at her hair and biting through her clothes, but she didn't care. The cold wasn't nearly as sharp as the weight pressing down on her heart.

Reaching the ledge, she placed her hands on the cold metal railing and stared into the dark, churning waters below. The river looked endless, a black void stretching out beneath her, swallowing the faint reflections of the city lights. She felt like that river—vast, empty, and invisible beneath the surface.

Her mind spun with many things—the avalanche of grief, betrayal, and loneliness crashing over her all at once.

Her mother's face flashed in her mind, sharper than all the rest. The cold, distant eyes that always seemed to look through her rather than at her. The constant disapproval in every glance, and every word. Claudia could still hear her voice—clipped, impatient, and always finding fault. "Why can't you be more like Luca?" Her mother had made her feel like an inconvenience, a mistake she couldn't wait to correct.

People using her for favours, always making Claudia feel like helping was a path to approval. But it wasn't. No one cared unless they needed something from her.

Janet pretending to care, and pretending to be a mother figure, while hiding her bitterness and judgment behind fake smiles. Claudia had wanted to believe in that connection so badly, but it had been a lie.

Andrew cheating. His face flashed in her mind—his laughter, the empty promises, and the way he'd held her like she mattered. And Sofi, curled up beside him in bed, like Claudia was nothing more than a forgotten footnote in his life.

And then… Papa. The memory of his hand in hers, his smile that day in the garden. And she hadn't even been there when he'd needed her most. She had abandoned him. She would never hear his voice again—she would never see him smile.

The tears blurred her vision as she stared into the abyss below. The world felt too heavy, and too sharp. The air felt too cold, pressing against her chest like it wanted to squeeze the life out of her.

Is this all there is? she thought. Pain, disappointment, and pretending?

She closed her eyes, letting the tears roll down her cheeks unchecked, as the sound of distant fireworks was muffled by the roar of the river beneath her. The wind howled in her ears, but it wasn't enough to drown out the voices in her head—the echoes of loss, of betrayal, of loneliness.

For a moment, it felt like the river was calling her—whispering promises of quiet, stillness, and finally letting go.

She stood on the ledge, her hands gripping the cold, rough iron beam beneath her. The icy wind whipped against her face, biting through her skin, but the weight in her chest felt heavier than the cold ever could. She stared down into the dark water below, with her tears blurring the already shadowed ripples. The river looked endless, like it could swallow her whole, take everything—the pain, the loneliness, and the exhaustion—and finally give her peace.

But as she took a shaky breath, a sudden flash of light hit her face. Headlights. A car was approaching from the distance, its beams cutting through the darkness like an accusation. Panic surged in her chest. She wasn't ready to be seen. Not like this.

Quickly, she ducked beneath the thick iron beam of the bridge, pressing herself against the cold metal, with her breath shallow. She waited, as the car rolled across the bridge above her, its tires humming over the asphalt. The noise grew louder, and closer, until the car passed by, and its rear lights faded into the night.

Claudia exhaled; her body was trembling—not from the cold, but from the sheer force of her despair. She stood back up on the beam, on unsteady feet, and stared back down at the river. This is it, she told herself. No more pretending. No more hoping.

13

THE LIGHT ON THE BRIDGE

As she leaned forward, with her heart racing, something inside her hesitated. She wasn't sure if it was fear, sorrow, or just the ghost of the little girl who still wished someone would stop her, tell her she mattered.

The wind howled around her, and the darkness felt endless. She closed her eyes, trying to push past the fear, and to just let go.

Then a voice came from behind her—clear, unexpected, and jarringly ordinary.

"Wait five more minutes—the fireworks are about to start!"

Claudia froze, her heart hammering in her chest. She snapped her head around, scanning the darkness, but saw no one. The bridge stretched out in both directions, empty and silent, except for the distant hum of the city celebrating a new year she wanted no part of.

Then the voice came again; it was steady and calm, but with a hint of amusement.

"On your right. It's dark—you probably can't see me."

Claudia's breath caught in her throat. She squinted into the shadows on her right, but the darkness was too thick. The cold iron beneath her feet felt even more unforgiving now.

"You can't make me change my decision," she snapped, with her voice trembling as much from the cold as from the surge of anger in her chest.

"I never asked you to," he replied, in a tone as smooth as silk. "All I suggested was for you to wait five more minutes. After that, you won't see lights like this again. You might as well enjoy them while you still can."

Claudia stared out into the void, with her heart pounding in her ears. She stood there, trying to hold on to the anger, but something about the calm, casual tone gnawed at her. After a moment, curiosity got the better of her.

"I can't see you," she muttered, her voice softer this time. "Where are you?"

In the distance, a faint glow flickered—a mobile screen, lighting up just enough to reveal the shape of someone sitting near the center of the bridge.

Her pulse quickened, but not with fear. She stepped down from the ledge, her feet crunching softly against the gravel as she walked toward the light.

"Don't even think about trying to talk me out of this," she warned as she approached.

The voice chuckled, low and unbothered.

"Why would I?" he said, sounding almost amused. "But just so you know, you're heading toward the centre of the bridge now. The drop's higher there. Better odds of success, if that's what you're after. "Claudia stopped for a heartbeat, the words hanging in the air like fog. But then she kept walking, her eyes locked on that faint glow. The absurdity of it all twisted in her chest—was this some kind of joke?

As she was a few steps away, the first burst of fireworks exploded in the sky, casting brilliant flashes of red and gold across the dark river.

In that fleeting, brilliant light, she finally saw him.

He was young—mid-20s, maybe 27 at most. His face was sharp, with high cheekbones and piercing eyes that seemed to catch even the dimmest light. His hair was dark and slightly messy, and he sat casually on the railing, with one leg dangling over the edge like he didn't have a care in the world. The fireworks lit up only half of his face, leaving the other side shrouded in shadow.

And then the light faded.

Claudia's breath hitched as the world plunged back into darkness. She blinked into the void. She tried to work out what she was feeling. Not fear, but something else. Curiosity, maybe. Or the strange comfort of having someone—anyone—there.

She found herself holding her breath, waiting for the next firework, just to see him again. Just to make sure he was real.

Her footsteps were slow and hesitant on the cold iron beam. As she drew closer, a faint scent drifted toward her—a clean, sharp mix of body spray and winter air. It was oddly comforting, like an unexpected tether pulling her back, and anchoring her to something she couldn't yet name.

He didn't look up right away. Instead, he patted the spot beside him, with his eyes fixed on the dark sky as if waiting for it to offer him something. Another firework exploded in the distance, lighting up the night in bursts of red and gold.

Claudia hesitated. But something in his calm, steady presence made her sit down beside him. She stole a glance at his face now that she was close enough to see him, trying to read him, to understand what kind of person sat alone on a bridge on the cusp of a new year. But his expression was serene, as if he belonged there—not just another lost soul, but someone who had made peace with the night in a way she couldn't comprehend.

Claudia opened her mouth to speak, but before any words could escape, he raised his hand, palm facing her, silently asking her to wait then very slowly, pointed his finger to the sky . She turned her gaze toward the sky, more out of curiosity than compliance, just as another firework burst into a thousand shimmering sparks. The colours were reflected in the dark water below, fleeting and beautiful.

For a long moment, they sat in silence. A brilliant firework burst overhead, casting streaks of gold and crimson across the night sky. The river below caught the reflection, shimmering for a fleeting moment before darkness reclaimed it. The soft echo of the explosion rolled across the bridge, fading into the silence that stretched between them.

The man, still perched casually on the railing, let out a slow breath, his gaze fixed on the sky. Then, almost as if speaking to himself, he murmured,

"Beautiful, isn't it?"

Claudia didn't answer. She pulled her knees close to her chest, staring straight ahead, refusing to meet his eyes.

The man remained unbothered by her silence. Instead, he reached for the bottle wrapped in its crumpled paper, took an unhurried sip, and let the moment stretch before speaking again.

"Do you know why I chose this spot?"

Claudia's fingers curled around the edge of the railing, cold against her skin. Still, she didn't answer.

The man exhaled softly, as if content to fill the silence himself.

"It's quiet," he continued. "Not many people come here. And from this spot, you get the perfect view of the fireworks."

He swirled the bottle absently in his hand before glancing at her.

"I imagine you had your own reasons for choosing it as well."

Claudia turned her head slightly toward him. The flickering light from the fireworks caught in her dark eyes, but she remained wordless.

The man let the thought linger, tapping his fingers idly against his bottle. The distant cheers from the city felt like ghosts against the vastness of the night. Then, in that same effortless, measured tone, he said, "Everyone is given the same life, but it is how one chooses to see it, and what one chooses to do with it, that truly makes the difference."

He turned his head slightly then, finally meeting her gaze—not with pity, nor judgment, just an unsettling certainty.

"Just as I was here to admire the fireworks, and you... you were here to bring your story to an end. Same place, but used for entirely different purposes."

His words landed with a quiet finality, like a stone dropping into still water.

Claudia's breath hitched. Something about the way he said it—so plainly, as if it was merely a fact—sent a ripple of unease through her. She turned away sharply, eyes locking onto the dark water below.

The weight in her chest grew heavier. A part of her knew—had known for a while—that she wasn't entirely sure of her decision. And yet... the pain still clung to her, wrapping around her ribs like iron chains.

Her voice, when it finally came, was quieter than she expected, yet laced with something bitter.

"Not all lives are the same, you know," she muttered, her grip tightening on the railing. "Some people carry pain so deep it swallows them whole. Just like the night."

The man didn't answer immediately. He took another sip from his bottle, with his fingers relaxed around its neck.

A hush fell between them, stretching long enough that Claudia almost thought he wouldn't reply at all.

Then, as another firework bloomed in the sky—a cascade of silver that illuminated the entire bridge for a fleeting moment—he finally spoke.

"You know... fireworks wouldn't be nearly as beautiful in the daylight."

His voice was low, steady—like something he had long made peace with.

"It is the darkness that makes them brilliant."

He tilted his head slightly, as if considering his own words. Then, after a beat, he added,

"Just like life."

The firework faded, plunging them into darkness once more.

Claudia sat frozen, her breath caught in her throat. Something inside her wavered, a fragile thread pulling tight. She turned her gaze back to the water, but for the first time that night, she didn't feel so sure of what she was supposed to do.

The wind whispered around them, carrying the scent of cold iron and distant smoke. The city behind them kept celebrating, unaware of the two souls sitting on the edge of the world—one at peace, and the other at war with herself.

And in the silence, the man simply took another sip,

They sat there in silence, with the space between them filled with the distant echoes of the city's celebration and the intermittent bursts of fireworks.

Every explosion lit up the night for mere seconds—streaks of gold, silver, crimson, and blue painting the sky before fading into darkness again. The river mirrored them in broken, shimmering fragments, reflecting their fleeting brilliance.

The man remained still, with one arm resting loosely on his knee, the other occasionally lifting the bottle to his lips. Claudia sat beside him, motionless, though her mind was tangled in a war she wasn't sure how to win.

Each firework seemed to stretch time, as if the universe was granting her these last moments to reconsider. And yet, the weight of everything she'd been carrying still pressed down on her.

When the final firework fizzled out, leaving only the vast, endless dark in its place, the silence became heavier. The absence of light, of colour, and of sound—it was as if the world had returned to its natural state, uncaring and indifferent.

And then, without a word, the man reached out and tapped her shoulder.

Claudia flinched slightly, as if she had been pulled from a trance.

"It's finished," he said simply.

She blinked, her throat tightening as she turned to him. The dim glow of the distant streetlights barely outlined his form, but she could still make out the unreadable expression on his face.

A strange, hollow feeling settled in her chest. She wasn't sure what she had expected him to say, but somehow, the finality in his voice made something inside her ache.

She remained still, searching his face as if waiting for him to continue speaking. To stay. To give her something—anything—to hold on to.

But he only rose to his feet, stretching slightly as he exhaled into the cold air.

"Good luck with what you came to do."

And with that, he turned and began to walk away.

Claudia's lips parted, but no words came. A storm raged inside her—a desperate pull between the pain that had brought her here and the strange, unsettling shift his presence had caused.

She should have felt relief that he was leaving.

But instead, she felt like she was unravelling.

She watched his retreating figure, silhouetted against the dim city lights, and something inside her clenched.

She didn't want him to go. Not like this. Not without... her.

"Stop!" Claudia's voice cut through the stillness of the night, urgent and raw. "Where are you going? Why... why did you do this to me?"

The man paused mid-step, with his back still to her. For a long moment, he remained motionless, as if he was weighing up whether to respond. Then, slowly, he glanced over his shoulder, the faintest hint of a smile tugging at the corner of his lips—subtle, unreadable.

"I didn't do anything." His voice was calm, almost indifferent.

He turned away again, but before he could take another step, Claudia took a half-step forward, with the words tumbling out before she could stop them. "Wait. Please." Her voice was quieter now, but no less desperate. "Can I ask for just a little more of your time?"

This time, he turned fully, facing her. The dim streetlights illuminated just the edge of his sharp features, casting shadows that made it impossible to tell what he was thinking. But there was something in his eyes—something knowing, and almost sad.

Claudia felt frustration rising in her chest, and tightening her throat. Her fingers curled into fists at her sides. "If I told you what I'm going through, you'd laugh at me."

The man arched an eyebrow but said nothing. He simply waited.

The silence stretched out, thick and expectant, until finally, Claudia broke it. The words poured out of her in a rush, her voice cracking under the weight of emotions she had tried so hard to bury.

"People use friendship for their own advantage. My landlord—who I thought was like a mother to me—she doesn't even see me as a person. She was pretending the whole time." She swallowed hard, pushing forward. "My boyfriend cheated on me. And the only person who ever truly loved me—my father—he died today... because of me. Because of my carelessness."

Her voice wavered. The tears that had been threatening finally spilled over, carving silent paths down her cheeks. She dropped her gaze to the pavement. "Nobody loves me. Nobody cares about me."

101

The man stood there, silently absorbing her words. He sighed, the sound soft against the crisp night air.

Then, finally, he spoke. "I don't know much about you," he said, his voice steady but gentle. "But one thing I can tell you for certain—you won't find happiness by pouring all of yourself into others and waiting for them to return what you've given."

Claudia swallowed hard, but she said nothing.

"Real happiness," he continued, "isn't something you borrow from others. It's not something they can give you. The only place you'll ever truly find it..." His eyes locked onto hers, quiet and unwavering, "...is inside you."

She blinked, as his words settled into her, like stones thrown into still water.

"The most important person who should fall in love with you... and care for you... is you."

Claudia's breath hitched. The words felt foreign—like an idea she had never considered before. She opened her mouth, about to argue, but he raised a hand, stopping her.

"If you don't love yourself," he said, with his voice softer now, but no less firm, "how do you expect anyone else to?"

Claudia flinched. The truth in his words struck harder than she had anticipated, deeper than anything she had told herself in the darkest corners of her mind.

"I do love myself," she insisted, though the words came out weaker than she intended. "I respect myself."

He shook his head slowly, his expression unreadable.

"You never did," he murmured. "If you did... you wouldn't be here."

She inhaled sharply, with her chest tightening. A part of her wanted to snap back, to argue, and to prove him wrong. But another part of her—the part that had led her here tonight—knew he wasn't wrong at all.

The man turned again, his figure slipping into the quiet darkness of the bridge.

Claudia stood frozen in place, with her mind spinning, and her heartbeat loud in her ears. The silence was heavy and suffocating.

And then, before she even realized she was moving, she took a step forward.

"Wait." Her voice was softer this time, hesitant, but certain. "I know we're strangers, but... can I ask for a few more minutes of your time?"

He exhaled, amused, then gestured with a small nod. "Walk with me."

She fell into step beside him. The night air was biting against her skin, but she barely felt it.

"I don't know what's wrong with me," she admitted finally, her voice small. "I don't know why I feel this way. Why I always end up feeling... like I'm never enough."

The man took a slow sip from the bottle in his hand; his footsteps were steady on the pavement.

"Tell me something," he said, his tone thoughtful. "What have you done with your time that makes you proud of yourself?"

Claudia hesitated.

His voice remained calm, but firm. "And I don't mean things you've done for other people. I mean just for yourself."

She stopped walking. Her eyes darted to the river below, avoiding his gaze. "I'm not special," she muttered. "I don't have any real talent. Nothing about me is remarkable."

A beat of silence passed between them.

"How much time do you actually give to yourself?" he asked.

She blinked, startled by the question. "Not much," she admitted. "I'm always... busy. With people, with work, with everything else."

The man exhaled, nodding knowingly. "It's not just you. Most people are like that. They're too busy with everyone else—or buried in their phones. They don't even realize they're neglecting themselves." Claudia bit her lip, with her breath fogging in the cold air. "How do I start?" she asked, almost in a whisper. "How do I change?" The man tilted his head slightly, considering her. "You start," he said simply, "by giving yourself time. And then, little by little, you'll figure out how to spend it in a way that actually matters to you." He took another sip from his drink before continuing.

"I'm not talking about going out, drinking, or trying to distract yourself. I'm talking about something meaningful. Something that makes you feel like you're building something, even if it's just for yourself. Try that. You might not understand it today or tomorrow... but eventually, you'll find it."

Claudia inhaled, her mind turning over his words. "I'll try," she murmured. But then she hesitated.

He noticed. "What?"

She struggled for a moment before asking, "But what if I don't know where to start?"

A serene smile tugged at the corner of his mouth. "Start by running."

Claudia frowned, confusion flickering across her features. "Running?" she echoed. "How is that supposed to help?"

His eyes glinted with something unreadable. "Just try it," he said simply. "You'll understand soon enough."

She narrowed her eyes at him, half skeptical, and half intrigued. But deep down, she knew she would try to take his advice.

The man gave her one last glance, with a small, knowing smile playing on his lips. "So. What's next?"

Claudia exhaled. "I'm going home."

But it wasn't just about going home anymore. Something had shifted. She no longer felt the emptiness clawing at her, no longer felt trapped in the weight of everything she'd lost. For the first time in a long time, she felt like there was something to figure out—something worth finding.

She didn't have all the answers. But she had something.

And maybe, just maybe, that was enough to start with.

The man nodded approvingly. "Good. Then book an Uber, get home safe. Happy New Year."

"Happy New Year," Claudia echoed, her voice softer now, carrying a warmth she hadn't expected to feel tonight. She reached for her phone, patting the pockets of her jeans—only to realize they were empty. A sudden memory flashed: tossing it onto the car seat after switching it off.

She let out a sigh. "I, uh... left my phone in the car," she admitted, gesturing toward her battered vehicle, which was slouched awkwardly against a bent no-parking sign. "Do you mind coming with me to find it?"

He followed her gaze, taking in the haphazard parking job and the unfortunate sign. One brow lifted in quiet amusement.

"Judging by your parking skills, I'd say you might need a new car."

Claudia huffed a small laugh. "At the time, I thought it was my last drive. Honestly, with the way I handled it tonight, they might just revoke my license."

They walked toward the car, with their footsteps slow against the gravel. The city behind them was quieter now, but distant echoes of celebration still lingered in the air. Claudia reached into the open door, spotting her phone and purse on the seat. She grabbed them, and pressing the power button—nothing. The screen remained stubbornly dark.

The man leaned against the side of the car, watching her struggle. "Want me to book you an Uber?"

She exhaled, slipping the lifeless phone into her bag. "I guess I don't have a choice."

He pulled out his phone, tapping the screen. "What's the address?"

She gave it to him, and as they stood there waiting, he cast another glance at her car, shaking his head slightly.

"I'm honestly surprised this thing made it here in one piece. It looks like it's held together by sheer willpower."

Claudia smirked. "It gets the job done... most of the time."

But just as the lightness of the moment settled, a sudden thought cut through it. Her expression darkened, the weight creeping back into her voice.

"I don't want to go back," she blurted out.

The man turned to her, his amusement fading into quiet curiosity. "Why not?"

She hesitated, trying to find the right words. "Janet... she was pretending to care about me. I believed her, but I realized it wasn't real."

He studied her for a moment, then asked, "Can I ask you something?"

Claudia nodded hesitantly. "Yeah."

"As a house... were you comfortable there?"

She frowned slightly, considering it. "Yeah. It's a good house. It has everything I need. It's convenient for work." She hesitated before adding, "But Janet's there all the time."

He nodded. "And as a landlord... did she ever cause you trouble?"

Claudia thought about it. "No. Even when I was late on rent once, she never made a fuss."

"But you thought she loved you like a daughter?" he pressed gently.

Claudia's lips pressed into a thin line. "I... I thought so."

He raised an eyebrow, his voice calm but firm. "Did she ever call you her daughter? Or did you just assume she saw you that way?"

Claudia looked down at the pavement, as the truth settled uncomfortably in her chest. "She never called me that."

He nodded slowly. "Then don't give up your comfort over an

illusion. You moved in because it was practical and convenient—not because you were looking for a mother."

His words hit harder than she expected, but instead of breaking her, they steadied her. It was like someone had finally spoken a truth she had been too afraid to admit.

The Uber pulled up to the curb, with its headlights sweeping over the quiet street.

"Go back," he said, his voice softer now. "Play along if you have to. But don't walk away from something good just because it wasn't what you imagined it to be."

Claudia stared at him, the weight on her shoulders suddenly felt lighter. Not gone, but bearable. She let out a slow breath, then gave him a small, grateful smile.

"Thank you," she said quietly.

She hesitated, as if searching for something more to say, then looked at him, scanning his face. "Anyway... I'm Claudia. I never asked your name." She shifted slightly. "Or your number. I'd like to meet you again."

He took a slow step closer, his expression was unreadable, with his gaze steady. "You came here tonight with no intention of meeting anyone ever again," he said quietly. "Because you were giving too much of yourself to others. But look at you now... you're a different person. You don't need me."

Claudia opened her mouth to argue, but the words never came. She simply stared at him, feeling both exposed and strangely understood.

"I wish you all the luck," he added, with a small, knowing smile tugging at the corner of his lips. "And happy New Year."

As he turned to leave, he glanced back over his shoulder. "By the way... my name is Mr. Nobody."

Claudia blinked, with a strange mix of amusement and disbelief crossing her face. She had never met anyone like him before, and the surreal nature of the encounter made her feel slightly off balance—in the best way.

Before she could stop herself, she blurted out, "Okay, Mr. Nobody— can I at least know what you were drinking?" She gestured toward the bottle still wrapped in its crumpled paper bag.

The man glanced down at it, then back at her with a mischievous glint in his eye. "Oh, this?" He gave it a small shake. "That's called Business."

Claudia raised an eyebrow, smirking. "Business? What kind of business?"

He chuckled, the sound low and effortless, drifting into the cold night air. "None of your business."

Claudia let out a small laugh, half-humiliated, but half-entertained. She shook her head, unable to decide if he was the most frustrating or the most fascinating person she'd ever met.

The Uber's headlights flickered as the driver honked softly. Claudia pressed the power button on her phone one more time. This time, the screen lit up. She quickly snapped a picture of the car's number plate.

The man's voice drifted over her shoulder, teasing. "Why do you need a picture of the number plate?"

She turned to him, a playful glint in her eyes. "It's for business."

They shared one last look, as a brief, unspoken moment of understanding hung in the air between them.

Then, without another word, Claudia climbed into the Uber, the door clicked shut behind her, and the car pulled away into the night.

14

LIGHT ENOUGH TO RETURN

As the Uber rolled down the quiet streets, Claudia leaned her forehead against the cold glass of the window, with her breath fogging up the surface. The city lights flicked past her, but she barely noticed them. Her mind was tangled in the night's events—the bridge, the fireworks, and the stranger who called himself Mr. Nobody.

His words echoed in her head.

"You won't find happiness by pouring all of yourself into others. The only place you'll truly find it... is inside you."

She exhaled, closing her eyes for a brief moment, trying to hold onto the weight of everything he'd said before it slipped away.

Instinctively, she pulled out her phone and tapped on the screen, her thumb hovering over the picture she'd taken of the number plate. Without overthinking, she sent it to Luca.

But as soon as the message went through, she hesitated.

The dim glow of the phone screen flickered against her fingertips, but her mind had already moved elsewhere.

She shouldn't be going home.

Her heart clenched with a quiet realization, but before she could talk herself out of it, she leaned forward, tapping the driver's shoulder. "Change of destination," she said, with her voice firmer this time.

The driver glanced at her in the mirror, and waiting.

Claudia inhaled deeply, steadying herself.

"The hospital on the Fulham Road.'"

As the Uber pulled up to the hospital entrance, Claudia stepped out; the air was cool rather than cold now. She exhaled deeply, as if shedding the intensity of the bridge, of the stranger, and of everything that had nearly swallowed her whole.

She pulled out her phone and dialled Luca. The phone rang only once before he answered.

"I'm outside," she said softly.

"Give me a second," he replied.

A moment later, Luca emerged from the hospital doors, with his hands tucked into the pockets of his jacket. The moment he saw her, something in his expression shifted—relief, and maybe even quiet happiness. She looked different. She wasn't carrying the same crushing weight in her posture, or the same hopelessness in her eyes.

She met his gaze briefly before looking away. "Let's go inside."

Luca didn't say anything, just gave a small nod and walked beside her through the quiet corridors.

When they reached Emmanuel's room, the sight of him was like a punch to the gut. He looked peaceful and still—as if he was merely asleep. Claudia swallowed, stepping closer to him. The beeping monitors were gone. The hum of machines was replaced by silence.

She leaned down, brushing a soft kiss against his forehead. Her lips barely moved as she whispered, "You don't have to worry about me, Papa. You can rest now."

Luca, standing a few steps behind her, caught the way her lips moved but didn't ask what she said. He simply watched, taking in the moment, feeling the solemnity of it in his own quiet way.

After a long beat, Claudia straightened. She didn't cry. Not now. She just exhaled, touching his hand one last time before turning back toward the door.

They walked out of the hospital together. Once they reached the parking lot, Luca pulled out a cigarette, lighting it with a slow flick of his lighter. The flame illuminated his face for a second before flickering out.

He took a slow drag, staring into the distance. "The undertakers have been informed," he said, in a steady voice. "They'll come and collect him tomorrow."

Claudia swallowed hard, letting the words settle. It still felt surreal, too sudden—too final.

"Did you... arrange everything?" she asked after a moment.

Luca nodded. "Mostly. I thought you'd want to decide the details." She exhaled slowly, glancing up at the sky. "Yeah. I do."

Silence stretched between them, not heavy, not awkward—just there. A quiet acceptance of everything they couldn't change. Standing there, talking about logistics instead of drowning in the emotions behind them, felt oddly grounding.

Luca took another drag from his cigarette before flicking it to the ground, crushing the embers beneath his shoe. Then, without another word, he pulled open the car door.

"Come on. I'll drive you home."

Claudia nodded, slipping into the passenger seat. The soft hum of the engine filled the quiet as they pulled away from the hospital, with the city stretching out before them.

Neither of them spoke much during the drive, but the silence no longer felt heavy to Claudia.

As Luca pulled up in front of Janet's house, the car idled in the quiet of the night. The soft hum of the engine was the only sound between them.

Just as she reached for the door handle, Luca spoke.

"Goodnight, Claudia."

She paused for a moment, with her fingers resting on the handle. A small, almost imperceptible smile flickered across her lips, but she didn't let it linger.

"Goodnight, Luca," she said softly.

He gave her a slight nod, and without another word, she stepped out and closed the door behind her. As she walked toward the entrance, she didn't look back—but she could feel Luca's gaze following her for a moment before he drove away into the night.

* * *

Claudia stood in front of Janet's house, with her fingers tightening around the strap of her bag. The place looked the same as always— the warm porch light was casting a soft glow, and the curtains were drawn just enough to shield the inside from prying eyes. It felt strange, standing here now, after everything.

Taking a deep breath, she stepped up to the door and unlocked it. The familiar creak of the hinges filled the quiet. As she stepped inside, the soft flicker of the television cast restless shadows across the dimly lit living room. The screen glowed with muted colours, but no sound filled the space—only the faint hum of static before the next scene shifted.

Janet was asleep on the couch, with her head tilted back against the cushions, and one arm draped over her stomach. In her other hand, a half-empty glass of wine rested precariously against her leg, dangerously close to slipping from her fingers. It was a sight Claudia had seen countless times before, one that once stirred emotions she couldn't quite name—loneliness, resentment, or maybe even yearning.

But now, she simply felt... nothing.

She paused in the doorway, staring at the woman who had once felt like a mother figure, and occupied so much of her heart. Now, Janet was just another person—imperfect, distant, and tangled in her own world.

Claudia waited for a moment, as if expecting something inside her to shift, to crack open and let in the hurt again. But nothing came. No bitterness. No anger. Just quiet acceptance.

Without a word, she turned away, walking toward her room. The wooden floor creaked beneath her steps, but Janet didn't stir.

Inside her room, the air was still, the familiar walls enclosing her in a silence that felt different tonight. It wasn't heavy, nor suffocating—it was simply there.

She dropped her bag onto the chair and pulled off her jacket, moving on autopilot. The exhaustion that had clung to her for days seemed to settle deeper, but for once, it wasn't the kind that clawed at her with restless thoughts.

Claudia slipped into bed, with the sheets cool against her skin. As she closed her eyes, she expected the usual tug of regret, the echo of everything she'd been running from.

But sleep came quickly.

15

THE FORGOTTEN GIFT

The next morning, the air was crisp, carrying the last remnants of the night's cold as Claudia stepped outside. The quiet hum of the sleeping city surrounded her, with the streetlights still flickering softly as dawn approached. She pulled the hood of her sweatshirt over her head, adjusting her earbuds before taking a deep breath.

And then, she ran.

Her feet hit the pavement in a steady rhythm, the sound merging with the distant rustle of trees and the occasional car rolling down the street. The world felt empty, and peaceful—just her, the road, and the quiet thud of her heartbeat keeping pace with her steps.

At first, it felt unnatural; her body was resisting, as her muscles protested with every movement. But as she kept going, something inside her shifted. The weight in her chest, the heaviness she had carried for so long, loosened—if only a little. The cold air stung her lungs, but it made her feel awake, alive in a way she hadn't felt in a long time.

By the time she reached home, her breath was ragged, and her legs were aching, but there was a strange satisfaction coursing through her. She slowed to a walk as she reached the front door, pulling her hood down, her skin damp with sweat.

Stepping inside, warmth wrapped around her, was a stark contrast to the biting morning air outside. The house was quiet, except for the low hum of the television in the living room. Janet was awake; her eyes flicked toward Claudia as she entered.

Janet raised an eyebrow, taking in her flushed face and heaving breaths. "You're up early," she remarked, sipping her coffee. "And running, of all things? What a change."

Claudia grabbed a bottle of water from the fridge, twisting the cap off as she met Janet's gaze. She took a long sip before answering, her voice steady.

"Yeah," she said simply. "Everything changed."

Janet's expression shifted, softening. She set her coffee down and stepped forward. "Claudia, I heard about Emmanuel. I'm so sorry. I know how much he meant to you." Her voice carried a note of sympathy, the kind that might have once made Claudia's chest tighten with doubt, with longing for something real between them.

But not anymore.

Claudia met Janet's gaze, offering a small, polite nod. "Thank you," she said, her tone composed, almost unreadable.

She had spent too long hoping for something genuine from people who only saw her as convenient. And now, she had no desire to pick apart Janet's intentions, or to wonder if her concern was real or just another performance.

So she played along, offering the responses expected of her.

"It's been... difficult," she added with a carefully placed sigh, glancing down and holding back the emotion.

Janet nodded, placing a gentle hand on her arm. "I can imagine. If you ever need anything, you know I'm here, right?"

Claudia forced a small smile, one that didn't quite reach her eyes.

"Yeah. I know."

Claudia took another slow sip of water as she walked down the hallway, with her breathing still settling from the run. Muscles she hadn't noticed in years were aching, but it wasn't an unpleasant feeling. It was proof—proof that she had moved, that she had done something for herself.

She pushed open her door and stepped into her room. The air was stale, heavy, as if it had been trapped in time. Letting out a slow breath, she closed the door behind her and turned, letting her gaze sweep across the room.

It was a mess. Clothes were piled haphazardly on the chair, books stacked in teetering towers on the floor, and empty cups littered the nightstand. A life left on pause.

She sighed, rubbing the back of her neck, and turned toward the table in the corner. A pile of clothes sat there, half-forgotten, draped over something solid. Something that had been there for years, untouched.

Claudia hesitated. Then, with slow hands, she started pulling the fabric away, one piece at a time.

And there it was.

A piano.

Her piano.

Her breath caught in her throat. The once-pristine surface was coated in dust, and the edges dulled by neglect. She traced her fingertips lightly over the keys.

It had been a gift. From her father.

She remembered the day he had given it to her—how his eyes had shone with quiet pride as he watched her touch the keys for the first time

Her fingers hovered over the keys, as if expecting them to whisper something back to her. But she didn't play. Not yet.

Instead, she grabbed a cloth and began wiping away the dust, slowly, and carefully, as if peeling away layers of herself in the process.

When she was done, she stepped back, staring at it.

It still looked the same.

But somehow, it felt different.

Turning away, she glanced back at the mess in her room. She exhaled deeply, then rolled up her sleeves. One by one, she picked up the scattered clothes, folded them, or tossed what she no longer needed into a pile to be taken away. The books found their place on the shelf. The empty takeaway cups were thrown away.

By the time she was done, the space felt lighter. She felt she could finally breathe.

With a deep inhale, she grabbed fresh clothes and made her way to the bathroom.

The hot water cascaded over her, washing away the sweat and the exhaustion—everything she had carried for so long. She closed her eyes, tilting her face up to the stream, letting the warmth seep into her bones.

When she stepped out, wrapped in a towel, she felt something strange. Fresh. Awake.

Still damp, she walked to the window and hesitated. The curtains had been shut for as long as she could remember, blocking out the world, while keeping everything closed in.

She reached for them, paused, then, in one swift motion, she pulled them open.

Golden morning sunlight poured in, chasing away the shadows, stretching across the floor, and warming her skin.

Claudia stood in front of the mirror, brushing her fingers through her still-damp hair. The morning light filtered through the window, illuminating her freshly cleaned room. The scent of her shower gel lingered in the air, mixing with the faint, nostalgic smell of the piano wood.

She pulled a light sweater over her t-shirt, laced up her sneakers, and grabbed her water bottle. It had been a long time since she'd gone to the park—really gone, not just passed by in a hurry. Today, she wanted to sit, breathe, and just exist without the weight of everything pressing down on her.

Just as she was about to step out, her phone buzzed.

Luca.

A part of her hesitated before answering. It was early, and Luca wasn't the type to call without a reason.

She picked up, pressing the phone to her ear. "Hey."

"Hey," Luca's voice came through, steady but quieter than usual. "You busy?"

Claudia frowned slightly. "Not really. I was about to go for a walk—maybe sit in the park for a while."

A short pause. Then, his voice, careful but firm, "Can I meet you?"

Something about the way he said it made her sit up straighter.

"Is everything okay?" she asked, trying to keep her tone light, but a sliver of tension crept in.

"Yeah, yeah. Nothing bad. I just… need to talk to you," he said, keeping his voice even. "I didn't want to text it."

Claudia narrowed her eyes slightly.

She exhaled, running a hand through her hair. "Alright. I'll be at the park near my place."

"Which spot?"

"The old wooden bench by the lake," she replied.

"I'll be there soon."

She hesitated, then asked, "Luca, are you sure everything's okay?"

There was a moment of silence. Then, with a reassuring note in his voice, he replied, "It will be. Just wait for me."

Claudia exhaled and nodded, even though he couldn't see her.

"Okay."

The call ended, but the feeling lingered.

She slipped her phone into her jacket pocket, as a slight unease settled in her stomach. Luca wasn't pushing, but he clearly wasn't being entirely open either.

She stepped outside, with the morning air biting at her skin as she made her way toward the park.

Whatever he wanted to say, it mattered.

The morning air carried the sound of rustling leaves and the occasional chirp of birds as Claudia sat on the weathered wooden bench, her gaze skimming over the still lake. A soft breeze brushed past her, carrying the scent of damp earth and pine. She exhaled, stretching her legs out as she waited.

Luca's footsteps were quiet but firm as he approached. He didn't call out—just walked over and stood beside the bench for a moment before finally speaking.

"I didn't even realize," he started, his tone controlled but edged with something unreadable. "Not until my colleague called me this morning, saying there was a car near the bridge—smashed up, parked over a no-parking sign." He exhaled sharply, running a hand through his hair. "Your car."

Claudia glanced up at him, with a small smile tugging at the corner of her lips, as if she'd already made peace with the situation.

"Yeah," she admitted, leaning back against the bench. "Guess I left it there."

Luca sighed, shaking his head. "And I should have asked you about it when I dropped you home. But honestly? I was too stressed to even think straight."

Claudia chuckled, though there was no humour in it. "I was too angry to care. Too frustrated. Everything felt like it was crumbling, so I just..." She hesitated, then smirked, her tone light but holding a weight beneath it. "I let myself be reckless for a while."

Luca folded his arms, his expression tightening. "You don't care. Right now. But the police will. You're gonna get a notice, Claudia. You might even lose your license."

She shrugged. "Not 'might.' I will lose it. I ran some lights on the way there."

Luca's brows furrowed. "What the hell did you actually do?"

Claudia held his gaze for a moment, then looked away, watching the ripples on the water. "Doesn't matter now, does it? What's done is done. I'll pay the fine, go through whatever I have to. I'll deal with it."

Luca let out a slow breath, with his eyes scanning her face, searching for something—anger, regret, or anything. But she was calm. Not careless, but... settled.

After a moment, he sat down beside her. His voice was quieter now, less sharp. "Alright. As long as you know what's coming."

They sat there for a moment. Neither of them spoke; they just listened to the wind threading through the trees. Finally, Luca cleared his throat.

"I called everyone who mattered to Papa," he said. "They all agreed— we should hold the funeral next week." Claudia turned to him, her expression unreadable. "What do you think?" he asked.

She swallowed, then nodded. "Yeah. That sounds right."

Luca exhaled. "January 9?"

Claudia hesitated for a second, then nodded again. "January 9."

He glanced at her once more, as if trying to read between the lines, but he didn't press further. Instead, he pushed himself up from the bench, brushing off his jeans.

"Well, I should go," he said simply.

Claudia nodded, watching as he took a step away.

But then, just before he left, he paused. He turned back to her, his

120

expression softer than before. "You look different," he said quietly. "In a good way."

Claudia blinked, momentarily caught off guard. Then she smiled— it was not forced, and not empty, but real.

"Maybe I am," she admitted.

Luca gave her a small nod before walking away, disappearing into the winding paths of the park.

Claudia sat there for a while longer, staring at the lake, and letting everything sink in. The funeral, the car, and the countless questions.

"What do I do now?"

The thought circled in her mind, not with dread, but with a quiet curiosity she hadn't felt in a long time.

16

BETWEEN GRIEF AND REBIRTH

The morning air carried the scent of damp pavement as Claudia walked through the school gates. The familiar surroundings felt strangely distant, like she was stepping into a place where she no longer belonged. Yet, the routine of it—students rushing past, the murmur of conversations, and the occasional ring of laughter—grounded her in a way she hadn't expected.

As she entered the main hallway, a few staff members noticed her almost instantly. Their faces softened with sympathy.

"Claudia," Mrs. Emerson, the history teacher, said gently, placing a hand on her arm. "I'm so sorry for your loss."

Claudia gave a small nod, offering a polite but measured smile. "Thank you."

Mr. Hayes, one of the senior teachers, approached next. "If you ever need anything, we're here for you."

"I appreciate that," she replied, keeping her voice steady.

Similar sentiments followed as she made her way toward the staff room—colleagues pausing to acknowledge her, offering condolences, and quiet reassurances. She responded with grace, thanking them each time, but their words pressed against her. It was kindness, but also a reminder.

By the time she reached the staff room, she exhaled slowly, as if shedding the tension that had built with each interaction. It was strange—how grief made people tiptoe around her, and how their voices softened as if afraid she might break.

But she wasn't going to break.

Not anymore.

She straightened her shoulders and stepped inside, ready to take on the day.

* * *

The days passed in quiet transformation. Claudia ran every morning, feeling the cold air burn in her lungs, as the steady rhythm of her feet against the pavement grounded her in a way she couldn't explain. At first, she ran to escape—to silence the thoughts that clawed at the edges of her mind. But as time went on, she realized it wasn't just an escape anymore. Something was shifting inside her. She couldn't name it, but she could feel it, like the first crack of light breaking through a long, dark tunnel.

At home, she continued the charade with Janet.

She still smiled, still nodded at all the right moments, and still played the role of the grateful, affectionate tenant who looked up to Janet like a mother. She told herself it was easier this way—to let Janet believe the illusion rather than disrupt whatever fragile peace existed between them. But deep down, she felt nothing. No warmth, no attachment.

Janet was just Janet.

She had never been a mother to Claudia, and Claudia had finally stopped wishing she would be.

Yet, she continued to let Janet think otherwise.

She relished in Claudia's seemingly unwavering affection, unaware that every word, every touch, every act of care was nothing more than a performance.

However, at school, the shift in Claudia did not go unnoticed.

She had spent years being the agreeable one—the one people could talk at without expecting resistance, the one who bent herself into whatever shape made others comfortable. But now, things were different. There was something about the way she carried herself that made people pause. A quiet authority in her posture, a certainty in her voice.

She was no longer the girl people dismissed.

People started looking at her differently. They started listening when she spoke. They no longer assumed she would agree to every little thing without question. Instead, they included her—not out of pity, and not out of obligation, but because they recognized that she had a place among them.

And then, January 9th arrived.

The weight of the day settled on her chest the moment she opened her eyes.

The funeral was today.

Claudia sat on the edge of her bed, staring at the floor, with her fingers pressing into the mattress as she tried to steady herself.

This wasn't just about saying goodbye to her father.

It was about deciding, once and for all, who she was going to be from now on.

She laced up her running shoes with the same quiet determination she had built over the past days. The cold morning air nipped at her skin as she stepped outside, with her breath clouding the air. She took a deep breath, shaking off the unease creeping up her spine, and started running.

But something felt off.

With every step, something pressed down on her chest—heavy, and suffocating. It wasn't physical exhaustion; it was something deeper, something she couldn't shake. She pushed forward, with her feet striking the pavement harder, and faster, as if outrunning the feeling would make it disappear.

The ache only grew.

Each breath felt tighter. Each stride felt heavier.

She had been running every day, building endurance, finding a strange kind of solace in the rhythm of it—but today, five minutes in, it felt like it had been an hour. Her lungs burned, her legs ached, but it wasn't just the strain of running.

It was knowing what day it was.

She wanted to stop. She wanted to turn back, crawl under her blankets, and pretend the day didn't exist.

But she forced herself forward.

One more step.

Then another.

And another.

Until she couldn't anymore.

Her body gave in before her mind did, and she slowed to a walk, then stopped altogether, with her hands on her knees as she tried to catch her breath. The cold air stung her throat, her pulse drumming in her ears.

She had never struggled like this before.

Claudia clenched her jaw, swallowing the frustration, but she knew she couldn't push herself any further. Not today.

Without another thought, she turned around and gingerly made her way home.

By the time she stepped inside, with sweat clinging to her skin, she felt no relief. She grabbed a bottle of water from the kitchen and drank it in slow gulps as she leaned against the counter.

The heaviness in her chest hadn't faded. If anything, it had settled deeper.

She exhaled sharply and made her way to her room, closing the door behind her.

There, in the quiet of her own space, she let herself feel it—the weight of the day, the exhaustion, the grief.

She sat on the bed, staring at nothing, breathing through the emotions she had been trying to outrun.

Claudia barely realized when she drifted into sleep. The exhaustion from her failed run, and the intensity of the day pressing against her chest—it had all caught up with her. But the moment she heard the knock on her door, her eyes snapped open.

A second knock followed, lighter this time.

"Claudia?" Janet's voice was gentle but firm. "Are you getting ready?"

Claudia sat up slowly, rubbing her face. The feeling hadn't left her—it had settled, deeper now, like something permanent. She took a deep breath before pulling herself up and opening the door.

Janet stood there, already dressed in a modest black dress, with her graying hair pinned neatly back. There was something careful about the way she looked at Claudia, as if she were searching for something in her expression.

"I'm going to be ready soon," Janet said, studying her for a moment longer before adding, "I didn't hear anything from your room, so I wanted to check. We'll leave together?"

Claudia swallowed hard and nodded. "Yeah. Okay."

Janet gave her a small nod before turning away, and heading back to her own room.

Claudia closed the door and leaned against it for a second, pressing her palm to her forehead. Everything inside her felt slow, and sluggish, as if she were moving through water.

But she didn't have time to fall apart.

She pushed open the door and went straight to the bathroom. The cold shower did little to shake off the feeling, but at least it forced her awake. When she stepped out, with the steam curling around her, she felt a little more steady—just enough to get through the day.

Back in her room, she pulled out the black dress she had laid out the night before. She had always hated it. It fit well, and looked appropriate, but it had a way of making her feel even smaller inside it. As she zipped it up, she glanced at her reflection in the mirror.

She barely recognized herself.

For so long, she had been defined by what others needed from her. The people who used her kindness. The relationships that drained her. The version of herself that she had built for the world.

But this person? The one staring back at her?

She wasn't sure who she was becoming yet—but she knew she was changing.

Claudia exhaled and turned away from the mirror.

By the time she stepped out of her room, Janet was waiting near the door, holding her small black clutch. She didn't say anything—just gave a small nod before leading the way outside.

The taxi ride was silent, with the city passing by in muted colors.

And then, before she was ready for it, the church came into view.

17

THE SPACE HE LEFT BEHIND

The air was thick with the scent of damp earth and incense as Claudia stood beside Luca, her fingers unconsciously gripping the fabric of his sleeve. She was finding it hard to breathe. The priest's voice droned on in steady, solemn tones, leading the prayers, and the murmured responses of those gathered blended into a low hum.

Her father's coffin was slowly lowered into the grave. The finality of it struck her like a cold wave, and she clenched her jaw, trying to keep the emotions at bay. But when the first shovelful of dirt hit the polished wood with a dull thud, something inside her cracked.

Her grip on Luca tightened.

He didn't say anything—didn't look at her, and didn't try to comfort her with words. He simply let her hold on, anchoring her in a moment that felt too vast, too unbearable to face alone.

People from the school were there, even Tara, standing a few feet away, her hands clasped together in a display of solemn respect. Claudia's family, distant relatives, and old friends she barely remembered had gathered, their hushed condolences blurring into one another.

Janet stood near Rosie, watching Claudia with the perfect balance of concern and restraint. She stepped forward at one point, placing a hand on Claudia's shoulder, murmuring, "I'm so sorry for your loss, love."

Claudia nodded, offering Janet a small, tight smile in return. She had spent so long pretending Janet was like a mother to her—today was no different.

One by one, people approached, whispering their sympathies before stepping back, giving her space. Claudia barely heard them. Her world had shrunk to the rectangle of earth before her, and the stone in her chest that no words could ease.

The priest said his final words. The last prayers were spoken. And then, silence. The kind that settled deep, that intensified the grief.

Luca's hand brushed against her back, a quiet reminder that she wasn't alone. But it didn't change the reality before her. Emmanuel was gone. And all she could do now was stand there and watch as the earth swallowed what was left of him.

Claudia stood frozen, with everything she had built over the past few days threatening to crumble beneath her. She could feel it—the unraveling. It started as a tremor deep within, the same rumbling she had heard on the bridge that night. That slow, creeping collapse of control.

She tried to suppress it, to push back against the tide rising inside her, but the cracks were widening, and no amount of willpower could hold them together.

People were beginning to drift away, murmuring their final condolences before walking off in quiet pairs or small groups. Some gave her lingering glances, as if they were waiting to see if she needed anything, but she remained still, letting them pass her like distant echoes.

Then, just as the last figures faded into the background, she sensed someone approaching. A presence that sent a ripple through her chest before she even lifted her gaze.

Two feet stopped in front of her.

She looked up—her breath catching in her throat as her eyes locked onto something painfully familiar.

The watch.

The watch.

Not just any watch.

A Tissot watch.

The one she had bought for him.

For Christmas.

The one she had spent hours choosing, imagining how he would react when he unwrapped it. And he was still wearing it.

The sight of it sent something visceral through her, a shock of emotion so sharp it nearly stole the breath from her lungs.

She followed the watch—her watch—up to the man wearing it.

Andrew.

Her heart lurched violently, a storm surging inside her. The unraveling turned into freefall, and for a brief, terrifying moment, she thought she might actually fall apart right there, in front of him.

But she didn't.

She forced herself to stay composed, to push every emotion back into the pit of her stomach.

Andrew hesitated, as if searching for the right words. His face was tense, and careful, lined with something raw.

"Claudia… I—I just wanted to say I'm sorry," he began, his hands tensing at his sides. "I didn't know how to come to you, how you'd react if I reached out sooner, but I couldn't just stay away today. I need you to know that… that I regret everything. I hurt you, and I hate myself for it." His voice wavered slightly. "I don't expect anything from you. I just… I just want you to know you're not alone. I'm here for you. Always."

Claudia clenched her jaw, feeling her nails dig into the fabric of her coat. Inside, she was breaking apart, fragments of every emotion colliding violently within her—anger, grief, betrayal, exhaustion. But on the outside, she remained eerily calm.

Her voice, when it finally came, was quiet but sharp, cutting through the cold air like a blade.

"Today is my father's funeral," she said, deliberately choosing her words. "Right after my boyfriend funeral on the 31st."

Andrew flinched, his face shifting as if she had struck him.

She lifted her gaze, locking eyes with him fully for the first time. Her stare was dark, intense, and unwavering. Her next words came out like steel. "So, please," she said, "leave me alone."

Andrew's throat bobbed as he swallowed, his breath leaving him in a slow exhale.

He looked at her for a moment longer, maybe searching for something in her face—an opening, or a softening—but there was none.

He nodded, barely, just enough to acknowledge that he understood. And then he turned and walked away.

Claudia remained standing, with her body rigid, and her breathing shallow. She felt like she should collapse, like she should break apart completely now that he was gone.

But she didn't.

She just stood there. Still. Silent. Holding on to the last, fragile pieces of herself.

Luca stood by the cemetery gate, with his hands tucked into the pockets of his coat as he watched the last of the mourners filter out. He had been waiting for Claudia, but she hadn't moved. She stood there, frozen in place, staring at the freshly covered grave, lost in something he couldn't see.

His brows knitted together. Something was off.

He lifted his hand and signed from the distance: "You're not coming?"

Claudia blinked as if snapping back to the present. She met his gaze and, after a brief pause, signed back: "You go. I'll come in a while."

Luca didn't move.

He could have left her alone, to respect her space. But something about the way she was standing there—so still, so rigid—clearly didn't sit right with him.

So instead of walking away, he turned back.

He approached her carefully, with his voice low but firm. "You okay?"

Claudia exhaled slowly, forcing a small nod. "I'm fine. Just... need some time."

Luca studied her for a moment, his eyes scanning her face.

Just as he was about to say something else, his phone buzzed in his pocket. Rosie.

He pulled it out, glancing at the screen.

With one last glance at Claudia, he sighed. "Alright," he said finally. "Catch up soon."

She nodded, but she didn't watch him leave.

She just stood there, hands clenched at her sides, staring at the grave.

And in that quiet moment, she let herself feel the full weight of everything.

She lowered herself onto a cold bench, her body feeling heavier than it should. The distant murmur of voices, the rhythmic thud of shovels packing earth over the grave, and the rustling of the wind through the trees all blurred together, distant and unreal.

But inside her, something real was unraveling.

The noise—the same unbearable rumbling she had heard on the bridge that night—was back. She had silenced it for days, drowned it out with routine, with running, with pretending. But now, standing in front of this undeniable, irreversible loss, it surged through her, like a storm she could no longer hold back.

She pulled out her phone with unsteady hands, tapping on the screen.

The gallery opened.

A familiar image stared back at her—the last picture she had taken with her father. The two of them were sitting in the care home, his smile warm but tired, her own face shadowed with unspoken things.

Her thumb hovered over the screen, tracing the edges of the image as if she could reach through it, and hold onto something that was already gone.

A tear traced her cheek and fell onto the glass. She reached out, gently wiping the screen — as if that single gesture could undo everything.

The screen responded to the touch, with the image sliding away.

A different picture took its place.

A number plate.

Her breath hitched. The cold night, the bridge, and him.

She wished she could talk to him again. Not forever—just one more time.

It was not because she missed him, but because she wanted to hold on to the person she had been becoming these past few days. The person she was trying so hard to be. And she was afraid—so afraid— that without something to anchor her, she would slip right back into the version of herself who had stood on that bridge.

Her fingers curled around the phone.

Where was he now? Would she ever see him again?

Would he even care if she did?

She inhaled deeply, pushing herself up from the bench. "You don't need him, Claudia," she told herself.

But her heart disagreed.
One more time.
Just once.
And then she'd let him go.

18

BACK TO THE BRIDGE

Claudia stepped out of the cemetery, her feet moving with a purpose she couldn't quite justify. She wasn't sure what she was hoping for—if she was hoping at all. But as she walked toward the main road, one thought gripped her mind.

The bridge.

Would he be there?

It made no sense. He had no reason to go back there, and no obligation to show up. But that night had changed something in her, and right now, with everything crashing down, she felt an inexplicable pull toward that place.

Without hesitating, she pulled out her phone and booked an Uber.

The ride was silent. Claudia watched the city pass by in streaks of vibrant lights and headlights, but she wasn't really seeing anything. Her fingers tapped absently against her knee, her pulse quickening the closer they got. It wasn't fear. It wasn't regret. It was something she couldn't name.

When the car pulled up near the bridge, she hesitated before stepping out.

But the moment she stepped out, she knew it wasn't the same.

There were no fireworks this time. No chilling wind biting through her coat. Just an eerie stillness, the bridge stretching out in front of her, as empty as she had worried it might be.

Still, she didn't leave.

Instead, she crossed the street, stepping into a small coffee shop facing the bridge. The scent of roasted beans and warm pastries greeting her as she walked in, shaking off the chill.

A barista, a girl with a tired but friendly face, asked, "What can I get you?"

"Just a flat white," Claudia murmured.

She took a seat by the window, with her eyes fixed on the bridge as she sipped her drink.

Time slipped by unnoticed. Customers came and went, with laughter and soft chatter filling the café, but Claudia remained frozen in place. She ordered another coffee. Then another.

And she waited.

The afternoon faded into evening. The streetlights flickered on. People hurried past the bridge, oblivious to the fact that she was sitting there, hoping for something—or someone—she couldn't even name.

By the time she was halfway through her fourth cup, a voice pulled her from her thoughts.

"This will be your last one," the barista said gently. "We're closing in twenty minutes."

Claudia blinked, glancing at the clock. 6:40 PM.

She had been sitting there for hours.

The barista hesitated, wiping her hands on her apron. "Were you waiting for someone?"

Claudia let out a small, breathy chuckle. "I think so."

"Did he stand you up?"

Claudia stared down at her coffee. "No. He never even promised to meet me."

The barista frowned. "Then... give him a call?"

Claudia shook her head. "I don't have his number."

A flicker of confusion passed over the girl's face. "Then maybe call someone who knows him? Someone you both have in common?"

That was the problem. There was no one. No connection. No thread to pull.

Claudia exhaled, staring out the window at the empty bridge. "This was a waste of time," she muttered, mostly to herself.

The barista didn't argue.

Claudia sighed and pulled out her phone, booking an Uber.

As she stepped outside, waiting for the car, she cast one last look at the bridge.

Empty.

Of course it was.

She swallowed hard and climbed into the car, with her fingers tightening around her phone. Maybe she was never meant to see him again.

Disappointment pressed down on her chest. She had wanted to meet him—needed to, even—but she had been foolish to think it would just happen.

She exhaled sharply, rubbing her temple as the car began to move. Her reflection in the window was looking just as lost as she felt.

Then, her phone rang. She glanced at the screen. It was Luca.

For a moment, she considered ignoring it. But something in her—maybe exhaustion, maybe the familiar comfort of his voice—made her answer. "Hey," she said, trying to sound normal.

"I didn't see you after the funeral," Luca said, with concern in his voice. "You alright?"

Claudia hesitated, fingers tightening around her phone. "Yeah. I'm fine."

"You sure?"

She swallowed. "I... I went to see someone. But it didn't happen."

Luca was silent for a second, then he sighed. "It's okay," he said, with his tone softer now. "I just called to check on you. You looked really sad earlier."

Claudia pressed her forehead against the cool window glass, closing her eyes briefly. "Yeah... it was hard."

"I know."

Silence lingered between them, but it wasn't uncomfortable.

"If you need anything, just call me, alright? I'll come see you," Luca added. Then, with a small chuckle, "I wish I could just call you over to my place, but, you know... Rosie."

Claudia let out a small breath of amusement, though it barely reached her eyes. "Yeah. I know."

As they spoke, her gaze drifted to her phone screen, where the last image still lingered—the picture of the Uber's number plate.

Something twisted inside her. Before she could overthink it, she blurted out, "Luca, can you help me find the owner of a number plate?"

Luca frowned on the other end. "What? Why? Who?"

Claudia hesitated. "The last Uber I took that night... the number plate I sent you. I need to find out who owns it."

"Why?"

She scrambled for an excuse. "I— I think I left my wallet in the car that night."

Luca didn't sound convinced. "Claudia, seriously?"

"Please, Luca," she pressed, sounding almost desperate now. "It's important."

He sighed heavily. "This is not exactly legal, you know."

"Please," she begged.

There was another pause, longer this time. Then finally, Luca exhaled.

"Fine," he muttered. "When I go in for my shift tomorrow, I'll find out what I can."

Relief washed over her, as her grip on the phone loosened. "Thank you, Luca. Really."

"Yeah, yeah," he said, but there was warmth in his voice. "I'll let you know."

The call ended.

Claudia let out a slow breath, staring down at her phone. She felt a flicker of hope.

She didn't know why she needed to find him. She only knew that she had to.

As Claudia stepped into the house, before she could even take off her shoes, Janet was there, arms open, pulling her into a hug. "I'm so sorry, sweetheart," Janet murmured, rubbing Claudia's back in slow, soothing circles. "I know today was hard."

Claudia stiffened for a brief second before forcing herself to relax into the embrace.

"Thank you," she said, in a measured voice. "I think I just need to be alone for a bit. Get some rest."

Janet pulled back, studying her with concern. "Of course. I understand. Take all the time you need, love."

Claudia nodded, offering a small, tired smile before heading to her room. As soon as the door clicked shut behind her, she exhaled sharply, pressing her back against it.

She wasn't grieving anymore. Not in the way people expected her to.

She just wanted this night to end—so tomorrow could begin. So she could find him.

Kicking off her shoes, she climbed into bed, lying flat on her back, and staring at the ceiling. Her mind raced—turning over every possibility, every scenario, and every way she could track down the Uber driver and, somehow, find Mr. Nobody.

Would Luca actually pull through?

Would she even see him again?

Did he even exist beyond that night?

Her thoughts blurred together, as exhaustion started pulling her under. And then—darkness.

Sleep came quickly, but even in her dreams, she was searching.

Tracking Mr. Nobody

19

IN PURSUIT OF MR. NOBODY

The next morning, Claudia woke to a dull, gray light filtering through her curtains. She lay still for a moment, staring at the ceiling, her mind already set on the day ahead.

Before she could spiral into overthinking, she grabbed her phone and dialed the school.

"Hello, this is Claudia," she said, keeping her voice steady. "I'd like to request ten days off. I'm... not in the right headspace to return just yet."

The administrator on the other end didn't hesitate. "Of course, Claudia. Take all the time you need. Let us know when you're ready."

Claudia exhaled, as a quiet relief washed over her. She knew she wasn't ready—not yet. Not until she found him.

At exactly 12 p.m., her phone rang. Luca. She snatched it up before the first ring even finished.

"I got it," Luca said without preamble. "The driver's name is Suhail Khan. I've sent you the address."

Claudia pulled up the text, scanning the location. It was a quiet street on the outskirts of the city.

"Thank you," she said.

"Claudia," Luca's voice softened, "are you sure this is worth it?"

She hesitated, then gave the only answer that felt right. "I have to do this."

Luca sighed but didn't push further. "Alright. Be careful."

She hung up, grabbed her coat, and left.

* * *

The house was modest, with a small front yard, littered with children's toys. Claudia hesitated for a moment, adjusting her expression, then knocked on the door.

A woman in her late 30s answered, wearing a simple shawl over her shoulders. She looked at Claudia with curiosity, rather than suspicion. "Yes?"

Claudia gave a polite, slightly flustered smile. "I took a ride in your husband's car a few nights ago—on New Year's Eve. I lost my wallet in his car, and I really need to get in touch with him. Would it be possible to have his number?"

Suhail's wife frowned. "He's out working. Let me call him."

Claudia nodded, heart pounding as the woman dialed.

"Suhail, there's a woman here saying she lost her wallet in your car on New Year's Eve."

A pause. Claudia held her breath.

"No wallet?" The woman repeated Suhail's words before turning back to Claudia. "He says he doesn't have it."

Claudia forced a disappointed expression. "Could I maybe speak to him? It's really important."

The woman's demeanor changed instantly. Her lips pressed into a thin line. "If he doesn't have it, there's nothing else to talk about. Sorry."

She shut the door.

Claudia stood there for a moment, swallowing her frustration. This wasn't over.

She didn't leave. Instead, she waited.

Two hours turned into three.

The sky had darkened slightly when she finally spotted Suhail's car rolling down the street.

She didn't wait for him to park. Instead, she ran towards the vehicle, waving him down.

Suhail braked abruptly, rolling down the window, and looking at her in confusion. "Are you the woman from earlier?"

"Yes," Claudia said quickly. "Please, I need your help. I took a ride in your Uber on New Year's Eve. I need to know who booked the trip for me."

Suhail's expression turned wary. "I can't give out passenger details. It's against Uber policy."

Claudia clenched her fists. "Please. I'll pay you."

He shook his head. "Even if I wanted to, Uber drivers don't have full passenger information. We only see the first name."

Claudia exhaled sharply, thinking fast. "Fine. Just the name. Anything."

Suhail hesitated, then let out a sigh. "One hundred pounds."

Claudia didn't hesitate. She pulled out her wallet and counted the cash.

Suhail took the money, pulled out his phone, and scrolled through his trip history. After a moment, he nodded.

"The name was Sewell."

Claudia froze.

She handed over the money, muttered a quiet "thank you," and walked away

* * *

Claudia was in a small café near the street corner, the warmth inside wrapping around her like a blanket against the cold. The air was thick with the scent of fresh coffee but she barely noticed.

"One black coffee, please."

The barista nodded, tapping in the order. Claudia paid and took a seat near the window, staring blankly outside as she pulled out her phone.

Sewell.

She typed the name into the search bar, with her fingers tense. The screen loaded—pages upon pages of random results, but nothing useful. No clear leads. No connection.

She tried again. Different keywords. Variations. Still nothing.

The longer she stared at the screen, the more the frustration settled in her chest. Who the hell was he?

A small clink snapped her from her thoughts.

"Your coffee," the barista said, placing the cup on the table before walking away.

Claudia exhaled, wrapping her fingers around the warm ceramic. She took a sip, hoping it would clear her mind. It didn't.

She let out a sigh and picked up her phone again. There was only one person who could help her.

She scrolled to Luca's name and hit call.

The phone rang twice before he picked up.

"What now?" Luca's voice held an edge of impatience.

Claudia hesitated, suddenly unsure if she should ask. "I need your help again," she finally said.

A pause. Then, a sigh. "Claudia, what are you into?"

She swallowed, gripping the coffee cup tighter, wondering how much she should tell him.

"I... I just need to find someone."

Luca scoffed. "That's vague. Who?"

She took a deep breath. "His name is Sewell."

Luca's silence stretched for a moment too long. "And why, exactly, are you looking for this guy?"

Claudia ran her fingers over the rim of the coffee cup. "Because... that night, when Papa died, I didn't know what to do. And I met this person." She paused, choosing her words carefully. "Talking to him... it helped. More than I expected."

She heard Luca shift on the other end. "And now you think you need to talk to him again?"

Claudia hesitated. "Yes."

Luca didn't respond immediately. When he finally spoke, his voice was quieter, and more serious. "Claudia, just a name isn't much to go on."

"I know," she admitted. "But can you try?"

There was a pause. Then Luca asked, "where did you meet him?"

Claudia looked down, her voice almost a whisper. "On the bridge... where my car was found.

Luca sighed. "I'll see what I can do. No promises."

Relief flooded through her. "Thank you."

"Yeah, yeah," Luca muttered. "I'll call you if I find anything."

The line went dead.

Claudia sat there, staring at her coffee. Her heart was still restless, but at least now, there was hope.

She finished the last sip and stood up, pulling her coat around her as she stepped back into the cold.

Without a second thought, she hailed an Uber, sliding into the backseat.

Even as the car pulled away, she knew—this wasn't over

Claudia lay in bed, staring at the ceiling; her mind was restless despite the exhaustion. The room was silent except for the faint hum of the city outside. Then her phone rang.

She jolted slightly before grabbing it; it was Luca.

She answered immediately. "Hello?"

"Come outside," Luca's voice came through, steady but firm.

Claudia blinked. "Now?"

"Now."

She hesitated for only a second before throwing her gown over her pajamas and slipping on her slippers. The cold air hit her as she stepped outside, and she pulled the fabric tighter around her body.

A police car was parked by the curb. Luca was sitting inside, leaning back in the driver's seat, with one arm resting on the wheel. As soon as he spotted her, he stepped out, shoving his hands into his jacket pockets.

Even under the dim streetlight, she could see the concern on his face.

"Are you okay?" he asked, his voice softer than usual. "I know you're going through a lot, and I know you're not handling it well." His words weren't harsh—just honest.

Claudia exhaled, tucking a strand of hair behind her ear. "Luca..."

He kept going, his brows furrowing. "I get it, alright? I do. But whatever you're chasing—"

"Did you find him?" she interrupted, her voice cutting through the night air.

Luca paused. He studied her for a second, then sighed.

"Yeah," he said. "I think I did."

Her breath hitched.

Luca pulled a folded piece of paper from his jacket pocket and handed it to her.

Claudia took it, with her hands trembling slightly as she unfolded the paper, scanning the words with wide eyes. She had it. An address. A name.

"I had to go through a lot to get this," Luca muttered, rubbing the back of his neck. "I had to check CCTV footage from that night on the bridge just to match his face. Now I owe a hell of a lot of favors."

Before he could say another word, Claudia threw her arms around him.

It caught him off guard.

Luca stiffened for a brief second, then exhaled. He couldn't know exactly what was going on, but this was clearly important to her.

She whispered, "Thank you."

Luca didn't say anything. He just stood there, letting her hold onto him for a moment longer before she pulled away.

Then, clearing his throat, he stepped back, and his usual smirk returned.

"Alright," he said. "I gotta go. But if you need anything—real help, not this kind of mess—call me."

Claudia chuckled, shaking her head.

Luca shot her one last look before getting into the car. The engine rumbled to life, and as he pulled away, she stood there, gripping the paper like it was the most important thing in the world.

Just as she was about to unfold it, Luca rolled down the window and called out, "By the way, that's his office address. His house is out in the countryside, so if you want to find him in the city, that's your best shot."

Claudia nodded, as she tightly gripped the slip of paper.

As the tail-lights disappeared into the night, she whispered to herself, her breath barely audible in the cool air...

"Antony Sewell."

A small smile tugged at her lips.

Then, with a quiet exhale, she turned and walked back into her house.

* * *

As the morning light filtered through her curtains, Claudia moved with a rare sense of excitement. Her hands skimmed through the clothes in her wardrobe, searching for the right one. Not just any dress—the dress. The one that made her feel confident, and that she always thought brought out the best in her.

After a few moments of searching, she found it—a simple yet elegant dress that fit her just right. She slipped it on, smoothing the fabric over her frame before stepping to the mirror.

Next, she reached for her hairdryer, letting the warm air run through her strands until they fell into place. With careful precision, she tied it up in a style that framed her face just the way she liked. It looked effortless, yet polished.

She opened her vanity drawer, selecting a soft, fresh fragrance and dabbing it gently onto her wrists and neck. The scent lingered in the air, giving her a final touch of confidence.

She couldn't even remember the last time she dressed up for something—no, for someone.

Once she was ready, she grabbed the slip of paper Luca had given her the night before, holding it in her hands for a moment before taking a quick picture of it on her phone. Just in case.

With a deep breath, she booked an Uber.

20

THE CHASE ENDS HERE

The ride felt strangely quick, or maybe she was too preoccupied to notice. When the car finally pulled up, Claudia stepped out onto the pavement, with her heels clicking against the concrete.

She glanced up at the towering skyline, the sleek glass buildings reflecting the morning sun. Canary Wharf: the heart of business and finance—an entirely different world from the places she usually found herself.

Clutching her bag, she took another deep breath and scanned the area, searching for the building number.

And then, she found it: a massive corporate building, with its entrance lined with polished steel and revolving doors. It was intimidating, impressive, and exactly what she had expected.

She hesitated for a second before stepping forward.

She had come this far. Now, all that was left was to walk inside.

As Claudia stepped through the revolving glass doors, she was immediately engulfed by the overwhelming grandeur of the building. The air carried a distinct scent—an expensive mix of fresh-cut flowers, polished wood, and something crisp, like new paper. The high ceilings, gleaming marble floors, and modern, gold-accented decor radiated an air of exclusivity. Everything about the place felt intimidating, refined—a world that didn't quite belong to her.

Her heels clicked against the polished floor as she made her way toward the reception desk, feeling the weight of every gaze in the room. The people around her looked effortlessly polished—tailored suits, expensive watches, whispered conversations about numbers and deals she didn't understand. For a fleeting moment, doubt crept in. She felt out of place.

But she pushed through it.

She reached the desk, where a blonde receptionist, sharp in both appearance and demeanor, looked up from her screen with a professional, indifferent smile.

"Good morning. How can I help you?"

Claudia returned the greeting with a polite nod. "I'm here to meet Mr. Antony Sewell."

The receptionist's expression faltered for a fraction of a second—a barely noticeable flicker of surprise, maybe even suspicion. Claudia felt it immediately. The woman straightened slightly, as if reassessing her.

"Do you have an appointment?" she asked, her voice smooth but laced with an undercurrent of formality.

Claudia swallowed, keeping her composure. "No, I don't. But he knows me very well."

The receptionist's lips pressed into a tight smile—a rehearsed, professional dismissal. Claudia could feel the subtle wall being built between them.

"I'm sorry," the woman said, her fingers poised over the keyboard, "but Mr. Sewell only sees visitors by appointment. I'm afraid I can't let you through without one."

Claudia exhaled slowly, choosing her words carefully. "Can I book an appointment with him?"

The woman hesitated, studying Claudia as though searching for any sign of deception. "Yes, of course," she replied. "What is the meeting regarding?"

Claudia forced a small smile. "It's something personal."

The receptionist didn't break eye contact. "I understand, but I'll need a reason to process the request."

Claudia held her breath, feeling cornered. If she was too vague, she'd be dismissed. If she revealed too much, she might risk ruining her only chance to meet him.

"It's just... private," she finally said, lowering her voice slightly. "Could you at least pass on my request? It's important."

The woman gave a slow nod. "I can try," she said, though her tone didn't sound hopeful. She slid a notepad toward Claudia. "Please write down your full name, contact details, and any additional information you'd like him to know."

As Claudia took the pen and filled out the sheet, she couldn't help but ask—curiosity pushing past caution:

"He works here as what, exactly?"

The receptionist's eyes flickered up sharply, her professional demeanor faltering for just a second.

"I thought you said you knew him?"

Claudia's heart skipped. She had slipped. She shouldn't have asked. Recovering quickly, she gave a small, easy laugh. "I do," she lied. "I just... forgot what he does, that's all." She placed the pen down carefully, offering the woman her best attempt at a nonchalant smile. "Never mind, it's not important."

The receptionist remained unreadable, her eyes scanning Claudia for a moment longer. Then, without another word, she picked up the note, glanced over it briefly, and placed it to the side.

"I'm afraid I won't be able to book an appointment for you," she said finally, her voice cool. "For security reasons."

Claudia felt the ground shift beneath her feet. Security reasons? Her stomach twisted—she had made a mistake.

Her mind raced for a way to salvage the situation. "Look, I—"

"I'm sorry," the woman cut in, polite but firm. "But there's nothing I can do."

Claudia clenched her jaw, trying to suppress the frustration building inside her. She had ruined it.

After a long pause, she inhaled sharply and forced her voice to remain steady.

"Can I wait in the lounge?"

The receptionist hesitated, then gave a small nod. "Of course. As long as you like."

Claudia walked slowly to the corner of the high-ceilinged lounge, each step heavy with the weight of her thoughts. She lowered herself into one of the sleek, leather chairs, tension still coiling tight in her chest. She had come so far.

And just like that, she had lost her only lead.

As Claudia sat in the lounge, she kept her gaze low, fingers lightly tracing the edge of her handbag. The atmosphere around her was polished and refined.. Every passing second made her feel more like an outsider.

She lifted her eyes, scanning the room. People came and went, with heels clicking on the marble floors, having conversations that sounded hushed yet laced with purpose. Some were dressed in sharp suits, others in elegant business attire—looking powerful, and self-assured.

Claudia couldn't shake the feeling that she didn't belong here.

Then, the elevator doors slid open.

The moment he stepped out, something thundered inside her chest. Mr. Nobody.

His presence seemed to shift the energy in the room. His tailored suit, dark and impossibly expensive, fit him like a second skin. The crisp white shirt beneath contrasted perfectly with his tanned complexion. He carried himself with a quiet confidence, a man who knew exactly who he was.

And then there was his scent.

The same one from that night—a blend of something deep, rich, and unforgettable. It curled into the air, reaching her before he even saw her.

Claudia sat frozen as he walked toward the receptionist, engaging in a brief exchange. But he wasn't alone.

Four people—two men and two women—approached him immediately.

One of the women, who was tall, and striking, with long waves of caramel-colored hair, was staring at him like he was the only thing in the world worth looking at. The other woman, a sleek brunette, spoke to him with intense focus, with her expression flickering between admiration and urgency.

The two men with them—also dressed impeccably, and looking serious—entered the conversation.

As Claudia observed the scene, a sinking feeling creeping up her spine.

This was his world. And she didn't belong in it.

She finally understood why he hadn't given her his contact. He wasn't just some guy sitting on a bridge that night—he was someone important, someone unreachable.

The insecurity hit fast and sharp. Her grip on her handbag tightened, and her breath became shallow. She needed to leave. Without a second thought, she pushed herself up from the chair, moving quickly, trying to slip out unnoticed.

She reached the entrance, and was pushing open the heavy glass door when she heard his voice: "Claudia."

She froze, with her pulse roaring in her ears.

Slowly, she turned her head back, with her breath catching in her throat.

Mr. Nobody.

And he was smiling.

That same effortless, elegant smile, but now, there was something different. He looked... happy to see her.

She saw it in his face before he even said a word.

Antony murmured something to the receptionist before walking toward her; every step was measured, unrushed, and completely in control. The moment felt surreal—as if the world had shifted slightly off its axis.

And then there were the stares.

People were looking at her.

She could feel them. Silent questions hanging in the air—who was she? Why was Antony Sewell calling out to her?

Claudia wanted to disappear.

But Antony was walking toward her as if she was the only person in the room.

"What are you doing here?" His voice was warm, as his eyes scanned her face. "How did you manage to find me?"

She opened her mouth, but nothing came out.

Her body wouldn't move, and her lips wouldn't form words. She was frozen.

Antony chuckled softly, reaching out and giving her a gentle shake. "Hello?"

Claudia blinked, snapping out of her daze.

He's real. And he's right here.

Antony tilted his head slightly, watching her with quiet amusement. "You came all this way to see me and you were just going to leave without saying hi?" His voice softened, but there was something playful beneath it. "Come on, let's have a seat."

Before she could even process what he was saying, he turned slightly to the group of people waiting for him.

"You guys go ahead. I'll catch up soon."

The brunette hesitated; it looked like she was about to say something, but the words died on her lips. She gave a brief nod, exchanged a glance with the others, and then they all made their way out of the building.

Claudia, still dazed, let Antony lead her back into the lounge.

As they settled into two seats, she struggled to find the right words. across from him, in a place where he clearly belonged, and she didn't.

She glanced at him—he was watching her, waiting.

Finally, she let her breath out. She hadn't realized, but she had been holding it.

She instinctively reached for the hem of her dress, smoothing it out as if something was wrong with it. It wasn't. But, as she was surrounded by people who looked like they had stepped out of glossy magazines, she couldn't help but feel out of place. Too plain. Too underdressed. Too... ordinary.

She swallowed, glancing at Antony before quickly lowering her gaze.

"I'm sorry," she murmured, her voice almost hesitant. "I know I shouldn't have come."

Antony leaned back, the corner of his lips curling into that same effortless smile—one that made it seem like nothing in the world could shake him.

"Come on, don't be silly," he said, his voice smooth and amused. "But I'll admit, I'm impressed. You actually managed to track me down." He tilted his head slightly, studying her with curiosity. "And considering I don't have social media, I have to ask—how did you do it?"

Before Claudia could answer, the receptionist approached, her demeanor completely different this time. Gone was the cold, questioning look from earlier—now, she was professional, almost accommodating.

"What can I bring for you to drink?" the receptionist asked, her tone polite, almost... respectful.

Claudia hesitated, as her mind still caught up with everything happening around her. "Just a glass of water," she finally said.

The receptionist nodded, then turned to Antony, with an expectant expression.

Antony simply gave a small gesture—a slight wave of his hand; it looked casual, and effortless. "I'm fine," he said, not breaking eye contact with Claudia.

Antony watched her for a moment, then leaned forward slightly, a playful glint in his eye. "So?" he prompted. "Come on, I'm curious."

Claudia exhaled, knowing she'd have to explain sooner or later.

"My brother is a policeman," she admitted after a moment.

Antony raised an eyebrow, clearly intrigued. "Still," he mused, "that doesn't explain much."

Claudia bit her lip, hesitating for a second before continuing.

"I... usually take a picture of my cab's number plate before I get in and send it to my brother. For safety. You saw me do it."

Antony's expression didn't change, but there was a flicker of something he was suppressing.

"With that number, I found the driver. And then, well..." Claudia hesitated, watching his reaction. "I paid to get the passenger details." She exhaled, glancing away before adding, "And my brother helped me with the rest."

Antony's eyebrows lifted slightly, as amusement flickered in his eyes. For a moment, he just stared at her.

Then, he let out a soft chuckle, shaking his head.

"You really went through all that... just to find me?" His tone wasn't mocking, just genuinely intrigued.

Claudia swallowed, suddenly feeling ridiculous.

"I—" she started, but words failed her. She had no real explanation that didn't make her sound crazy.

But he didn't look angry. If anything, he looked entertained.

Antony, leaning back in his chair. "Well," he mused, "I can't decide if that's flattering... or mildly alarming."

Claudia sighed, rubbing her temples. "I know it sounds bad. It is bad. I'm sorry. But..." she trailed off, struggling to find the right words.

Antony watched her for a beat, then leaned forward, resting his elbows on the table.

"Go on," he said, his voice softer now. "Tell me why you did it."

Claudia took a slow breath, steadying herself. "Since that night on the bridge... I've changed," she said, her voice quieter than before. "I even started running." A small, almost self-deprecating smile played on her lips. "But yesterday... was my father's funeral. And I felt like I was losing everything I'd built up. I just... I felt like I needed to see you, to talk to you. One more time."

Her fingers curled slightly around the hem of her dress, as nerves crept in. "I know I shouldn't have done it like this. I'm sorry."

In the background, the phone at the reception desk rang, and the receptionist picked it up, speaking in hushed tones.

Antony sighed, shaking his head slightly. "Stop saying sorry," he said, his tone light but firm. "I'm actually glad you found me."

Claudia blinked, surprised. "You are?"

He smiled. "Yeah. Two days ago, I found myself thinking about you."

Her curiosity piqued. "Really? What were you thinking?"

157

Before Antony could respond, the receptionist approached their table, with her expression poised but professional. "Mr. Sewell, the team you were speaking with earlier just called. It's time for the flight." Antony exhaled, standing up and reaching for his jacket. "Right," he muttered, sliding his arms through the sleeves before turning back to Claudia. "I have to go. But... I'd like to see you again." He paused. "Are you free this Saturday or Sunday?"

Claudia, still caught in the surprise of the moment, quickly nodded. "For the next nine days, actually," she admitted.

A flicker of amusement crossed his face. Without another word, he pulled out his phone and handed it to her. "Save your number."

She only hesitated for a second before taking the phone and typing it in. As she handed it back, she debated for a brief moment—should she call her own phone? Just to have his number?

But she didn't. Instead, she simply returned the device with a polite smile.

Antony glanced at the screen, then at her. "I'll contact you when I'm back. We'll definitely meet."

With that, he turned and walked with a confident stride toward the entrance, drawing the attention of people around him. The receptionist, now back at her desk, watched with renewed interest. Claudia remained seated for a moment, watching him go, and processing everything that had just happened.

Then, slowly, she stood up and walked out of the building, stepping back into the city, feeling... different.

21

THE RECOIL

The three days of waiting were filled with anticipation. Claudia found herself checking her phone more often than she wanted to admit. Each time it buzzed, her heart leaped, only to sink when it wasn't the message she was hoping for.

She tried to distract herself—running longer than usual, cleaning the apartment until there was nothing left to straighten, even sitting at the piano, letting her fingers hover over the keys. But the silence of her phone loomed over her, making her wonder if she had misread everything.

By Friday evening, the excitement had started to wane, replaced by creeping doubt.

Was he just being polite? Does he regret offering to meet? Is this his way of quietly avoiding me?

The thoughts tumbled in, one after another, twisting in her chest.

Then, just as she was about to accept that maybe she'd been too hopeful, her phone lit up with a message from an unknown number.

"You free tomorrow?"

Her breath caught.

She stared at the words for a moment before quickly typing back.

"Yes, I'm free."

No hesitation. No overthinking.

Seconds later, another message popped up—just a location and a time.

She tapped the link, expecting a café, maybe a quiet park— somewhere simple. But as the screen loaded, her stomach tightened.

A clay pigeon shooting range in Kent.

She stared at the name for a long moment, then opened the map. It wasn't just any shooting range—it was a high-end, exclusive club. The kind of place where people wore tailored sports jackets and leather gloves just to fire a shotgun.

Her fingers hovered over the screen as a wave of doubt crashed over her.

Why would he pick this place?

Does he think I know how to shoot?

What if I completely embarrass myself?

What kind of people even go to these places?

Is this some sort of test?

She had never touched a gun in her life. She had never even seen one outside of movies. The idea of standing in a field, holding a shotgun, surrounded by people who probably grew up doing this— felt ridiculous.

For a brief moment, she considered cancelling it.

Maybe I should text him and say something came up…

But another voice in her head cut through the overthinking.

It's not about the place. It's about seeing him again.

That was the only reason she had been waiting, checking her phone more times than she cared to admit.

And now, here it was.

No "see you there", no "looking forward to it". Just a name, a time— 11 am—and a place that made her feel like she had stepped into someone else's world.

Claudia put her phone down and exhaled.

She had no idea what tomorrow would bring.

But one thing was certain—she was going.

* * *

Claudia arrived at the range just before 11 am, stepping out of the Uber onto a long gravel driveway leading to the grand entrance of the club. The building was a mix of old-world charm and modern luxury—a stately lodge with towering windows, polished wood, and an air of exclusivity that made her stomach tighten.

She had spent the entire ride convincing herself that this wasn't a mistake. That it didn't matter she had never held a gun before. That Antony wouldn't have invited her if he thought she didn't belong here.

But as she walked through the entrance, her confidence wavered.

The interior was immaculate—dark oak, leather chairs, and a roaring fireplace in the lounge area where people in fitted tweed jackets and high boots sipped espresso while discussing their morning rounds. She could hear the sharp pops of gunfire from outside, echoing across the open fields behind the building.

She swallowed hard.

Antony had chosen this place?

A young man in uniform, clearly a staff member, greeted her at the reception.

"Good morning, ma'am. Do you have a booking?"

Claudia hesitated before replying. "I'm meeting someone. Antony Sewell?"

The man immediately nodded. "Ah, Mr. Sewell. He's already outside. Follow me."

She nodded and followed him through a hallway leading to a private outdoor range.

The second she stepped outside, the cold morning air hit her, crisp and fresh. The view was breath-taking—vast open fields stretching toward the horizon, the sky a pale winter blue. A few groups were scattered across the range, their voices mixing with the occasional boom of a fired shot.

Then, she saw him.

He was standing a few meters away, dressed in a plain white t-shirt, with the sleeves hugging his arms, paired with dark trousers. His stance was relaxed yet composed; his hands were resting lightly on a sleek, polished shotgun, which was slung effortlessly over his shoulder.

He was mid-conversation with an instructor, nodding at something the man had said before turning, as if sensing her presence.

When his eyes met hers, that same knowing smile crossed his face. She felt her heartbeat pick up.

"You came," he said, his voice carrying effortlessly over the space between them.

Claudia pulled her coat tighter around her. "Of course I did. You asked me to."

He chuckled and walked toward her; his presence was commanding without effort. As he got closer, she caught that familiar scent—the same one she had noticed the night on the bridge.

"I wasn't sure if you'd like the idea," he admitted, scanning her face. "Shooting isn't for everyone."

Claudia let out a small, nervous laugh. "That's one way to put it. I've never even touched a gun before."

Antony smirked, tilting his head slightly. "I figured."

Her eyes narrowed playfully. "Did you invite me here to humiliate me?"

He laughed—a smooth, low sound. "Not at all. I just thought it'd be… different. A way to get out of your head for a while."

Something about the way he said it made her pause.

Had he chosen this place because he knew she'd never done it before? Because he wanted her to try something new?

She exhaled. "Well, I guess I'm here. What now?"

Antony held up a pair of protective earplugs and glasses, extending them toward her.

"Now," he said, amusement dancing in his eyes, "I teach you how to shoot."

Claudia adjusted the earplugs Antony had handed her, with her fingers fumbling slightly. The weight of the shotgun felt alien in her hands—solid, cold, and heavier than she expected. She shifted uncomfortably, watching as Antony loaded shells into his own gun with effortless ease.

"Alright," he said, glancing at her. "Ready?"

Claudia inhaled, tightening her grip around the weapon. Her eyes flicked toward the clay pigeon launcher, a sleek, mechanical contraption standing about 50 meters away.

"Not really," she admitted.

Antony with a serene smile. "Good."

He turned to the instructor, giving a short nod. With a mechanical click, the machine whirred to life, launching the first clay into the air with incredible speed.

With a fluid, practiced motion, Antony raised his shotgun, tracking the target for a split second before pulling the trigger.

Boom.

The air cracked with the sound, sending a vibration through her chest. In the distance, the clay shattered into a dozen pieces, vanishing mid-flight as if it had never existed.

Before she could react, another clay was sent flying.

Antony fired again.

It was another perfect hit.

Claudia barely had time to process it before he smoothly lowered the gun, turning back to her with an expectant look.

"Your turn."

She tensed, gripping the gun tighter. "I don't think so."

Antony arched an eyebrow. "Why not?"

She exhaled sharply. "Because I'm going to miss. And it's going to be embarrassing."

With a tranquil smile he said. "That's a terrible reason not to try."

She glared at him, but he continued, in a light but firm tone.

"You're not here to impress anyone, Claudia. You're here to shoot."

She let out a shaky breath. "And if I miss?"

Antony shrugged, setting his gun down. "Then you miss. But if you keep standing there refusing to shoot, I'll have to assume you came all the way here just to watch me look good."

Claudia rolled her eyes. "Arrogant much?"

He chuckled. "Come on, I'll walk you through it."

He stepped closer, adjusting her stance with gentle precision, guiding her feet into position, and giving her safety advice. The proximity made her hyper-aware of him—the warmth of his hand grazing her wrist as he adjusted her grip, and the faint scent of leather and cologne lingering around him.

"Relax your shoulders," he instructed, tapping them lightly. "You're stiff."

Claudia tried, but her heart was racing.

"Keep both eyes open," he added. "Don't focus on the barrel, focus on the target. Trust your instinct."

She took a breath and nodded.

"Ready?"

No.

"Yeah."

"Call for it."

She hesitated, then muttered, "Pull."

The clay launched into the air. She swung the barrel, trying to track it.

Then she pulled the trigger.

Boom.

The shot went wide, nowhere near the target.

Her stomach twisted.

However, Antony looked completely unbothered. "Again."

Claudia clenched her jaw.

She called for another.

And missed.

Then another.

And missed again.

She lowered the gun, as frustration crept in. "I told you I'd be terrible at this."

Antony chuckled, leaning casually against the stand. "You're not terrible. You just keep hesitating."

Claudia turned to him, exasperated. "I'm literally pulling the trigger. How is that hesitating?"

"You're overthinking." He took the gun from her, inspecting it lazily. "The trick is, you don't aim—you follow. The second you try to force it, you're already too late. Just track the clay and shoot. Trust your instinct."

She exhaled. "Trust my instinct. Right."

Antony handed the gun back, locking eyes with her.

"One more time."

Claudia hesitated. Then, gripping the shotgun tighter, she stepped back into position.

She focused, took a breath, and called, "Pull."

The clay soared into the air.

This time, she didn't overthink.

She moved, let her body take over—and fired.

Boom.

The clay exploded into fragments, scattering in the sky like fireworks.

For a moment, she stood frozen, almost unsure whether what she had just done was real.

Then, slowly, she turned to Antony.

His grin was instant. "Told you so."

Before she could stop it, broad smile spread across her face—a real smile.

"That felt..." She searched for the right word.

"Good?" Antony offered.

Claudia let out a breathless laugh. "Yeah. Really good."

She squared her shoulders, as newfound confidence settled in.

"Alright. Let's do it again."

Antony chuckled, handing her another shell.

"Now you're getting it."

As the session continued, Claudia found herself loosening up. She had started as a bundle of nerves and hesitation, but it was now turning into something unexpected—fun.

The instructor, noticing their growing ease, decided to make things more interesting. With an amused smile, he set up a small competition between them. "Alright," he said, adjusting the clay targets. "Let's see who's got the better aim."

Antony smirked, glancing at Claudia. "Feeling competitive?"

She scoffed playfully, shouldering the gun. "I should warn you, I'm naturally talented at things I've never tried before."

"Is that so?" he mused, loading his shotgun. "Let's test that theory."

The game began. Claudia's first few shots were off, but she quickly adjusted, getting the hang of the movement, the weight of the gun, and the rhythm of the trigger pull. Her confidence grew with every target she hit, and soon enough, she was laughing at Antony's mock frustration when she finally caught up to his score.

When she struck three in a row, she gasped and turned to him with wide, excited eyes. "Did you see that?"

Antony chuckled, lowering his gun. "Not bad. You might have some hidden talent after all."

By the time the session wrapped up, Claudia was grinning from ear to ear. Her shoulders, which had been tense, were now relaxed. She felt a kind of lightness she hadn't in a long time. The instructor tallied up their scores and, with a teasing grin, declared Antony the winner—but only by two points.

Claudia rolled her eyes. "Fine. But next time, I'll beat you."

Antony , collecting their gear. "Next time?"

She hesitated, realizing what she'd just said, but then shrugged. "Yeah, next time."

They handed in their equipment and made their way back toward the main building. The sky had shifted from bright afternoon sun to the golden hues of late evening, casting long shadows over the manicured landscape of the range.

* * *

Inside, the air was warm, carrying the scent of coffee and pastries from the in-house café. Antony gestured toward a table near the window, and they took a seat.

Claudia leaned back, stretching slightly. "I can't believe I actually enjoyed that."

Antony tilted his head. "Why not?"

She chuckled. "Well, for one, I never imagined holding a gun, let alone shooting one. And two... I just assumed I'd be terrible at it."

He leaned forward, resting his arms on the table. "Tell me something—do you always doubt yourself this much?"

Claudia raised an eyebrow. "Excuse me?"

He smiled slightly. "You walked in here convinced you'd fail. And now, you're sitting across from me, after nearly beating me. So, was it luck, or do you just not realize what you're capable of?"

She just looked at him.

Antony leaned back in his chair, a knowing glint in his eyes. "Exactly. So maybe, just once, you should consider the possibility that things might actually work out."

Claudia exhaled, leaning back in her chair. "Easier said than done."

She tried to lighten the moment, forcing a small chuckle. "I was joking," she said, nudging her cup slightly. "I am changing—I've noticed it myself. I came here with a head full of questions, but look at me now... sitting here, feeling proud of myself, and already looking forward to next time."

She glanced at him, hoping to read his reaction, then added, "See? I know I have to change. And I am changing." She flashed a small smile. "It was a joke, but... you get what I mean."

Antony studied her for a moment, with his expression softening slightly. He didn't smile, but there was something in his eyes—approval, maybe. Or understanding.

Antony set his cup down, tapping his fingers lightly against the ceramic. "You know," he said, his tone thoughtful, "the biggest difference between humans and animals is communication."

Claudia tilted her head slightly, intrigued but unsure where he was going with this.

He leaned forward, with his gaze steady. "But just because you can speak... doesn't mean you should speak carelessly." His voice was calm but firm. "Words are powerful, Claudia. What you say, even as a joke, matters. Who you are... is reflected in what comes out of your mouth."

She blinked, caught off guard by the weight of his words. He wasn't scolding her, but there was something about the way he said it that made her sit up a little straighter.

"So please," he added, his voice softening just a little, "don't downplay yourself. Not even for fun."

The air between them settled into something quieter, and more reflective. Without realizing, Claudia tapped her fingers lightly against the rim of her own coffee cup, absorbing what he had just said.

She had spent so much of her life making light of her own abilities, brushing off her worth as if it was something negligible. But now, sitting here with him, hearing those words, she realized how carelessly she had done it—how easy it had been to belittle herself, even in jest.

Antony wasn't laughing. He wasn't rolling his eyes or shrugging off the conversation. He was looking at her like her words mattered. Like she mattered.

She swallowed, nodding slightly. "Okay," she murmured. "I get it."

Wanting to shift the conversation to something lighter, she tilted her head and smirked slightly. "By the way… in your office building, when I was leaving, I made sure you wouldn't see me. But somehow, you called my name so loud that half the room heard. How did you even notice me?"

Antony set his cup down, amusement flickering across his face. "Your hair," he said simply, then let out a small laugh.

Claudia narrowed her eyes. "You think my hair is funny?"

He shrugged, looking entirely unbothered. "Yeah. It reminds me of a traffic light."

Her mouth fell open. "Excuse me?! How dare you insult me like that?" she shot back, still half in disbelief.

Antony took a slow sip of his coffee, completely unphased by her outrage. He raised an eyebrow. "I wasn't insulting you. You asked how I noticed you, and I gave you my honest answer."

"So you think you can be rude just because I asked for your opinion?"

"If you find it rude, that's your problem, not mine," he said smoothly. "You asked, and I answered. If you wanted me to say something nice, you should've asked me to compliment your hair instead."

Claudia crossed her arms, glaring at him. "So you don't think it was rude?"

"My opinion is my own," he replied, his voice calm but firm. "I can't change it for someone else's convenience. If I did, I'd just be lying, and that's not something I'm interested in."

She scoffed. "But you could have just kept that opinion to yourself."

Antony gave a serene smile. "In this case, I only answered because you asked. If I'd said it on my own, just to tease you, that would be rude. But there's a difference."

Claudia narrowed her eyes at him, trying to decide if she was actually offended or just enjoying the argument. "So, what's wrong with my hair, exactly?"

"There's nothing natural about it," he said easily.

She blinked. "What do you mean?"

He gestured vaguely toward her. "Look at the colour."

She let out an exaggerated sigh. "A lot of people dye their hair. It's normal."

"A lot of people do, sure," Antony said. "But people like you tend to go for bright colours like that."

Her eyes narrowed further. "And what do you mean by people like me?"

He leaned back, as he took another sip of coffee. "People who like all the attention."

Claudia felt a wave of humiliation wash over her. Heat crawled up her neck, and her chest tightened. Without another word, she grabbed her handbag and abruptly stood up. The chair scraped against the floor, sharp and grating, as she turned on her heel and stormed out of the café.

Antony didn't move. He remained seated, watching her leave as he took another slow sip of his coffee—he was clearly unbothered, and unshaken.

Claudia didn't look back though. She pushed through the entrance, stepping outside into the crisp afternoon air. Her breath came out uneven, and frustration was curling in her stomach as she yanked out her phone and quickly booked an Uber.

The minutes seemed unbearably long. Each passing second only made her more irritated. With her arms crossed, she stared down the road, willing her ride to come faster.

Then, behind her, the glass door swung open. She didn't have to turn to know who it was.

Antony strolled out, moving with his usual unhurried grace. He finished the last sip of his coffee and tossed the empty cup into a nearby bin, before stepping up beside her, with his expression calm, and unreadable.

"You said you're off for nine days," he said smoothly, as if nothing had happened. "Shall we meet tomorrow?"

Claudia turned sharply, her glare sharp as a blade. She couldn't believe what she was hearing.

"I came here thinking I'd have a good time," she said; her voice was tight with restrained anger. "And now I'm standing here, feeling humiliated and insulted, waiting to go home."

Antony exhaled, tilting his head slightly. "We did have a good time," he said. "But now, you feel insulted and humiliated." His tone remained unwavering. "Why? Because nobody told you before? Because you've just now realized how others might see you?"

Her fingers curled into a fist at her side. A thought gnawed at her—is this really the person I thought would make me feel better?

"Claudia," he continued, his voice calm but deliberate, "you asked me for my opinion, and I gave it to you. That's all." He shrugged slightly. "The truth is, most people probably see you the same way I do. They just don't say it to your face."

A cold wave passed through her, sinking deep.

"I would have respected it," he added, his gaze steady, "if you had simply said, 'I like this colour, so I have this colour.' That would've been enough. But instead, you're upset—not because of what I said, but because now you know how others might see you."

Claudia opened her mouth to argue, but he didn't give her the chance.

"You think altering something about yourself—something artificial—and pretending that's who you are will bring you value or happiness?" His voice didn't waver, not even for a second. "Let me tell you—it won't."

His words landed with a quiet, unsettling weight.

"It only destroys you," he continued. "So stop acting like you're the last resistance against the natural order, and start loving yourself for who you are. Add value to yourself by learning, and by growing—not by changing things that were never broken in the first place."

As the Uber pulled up, its headlights briefly flashed over them.

Claudia swallowed, with her throat dry. Every part of her wanted to snap back, to say something sharp enough to cut through his certainty.

But she couldn't.

Because deep down, some part of her—however small—knew that he wasn't trying to hurt her. He was just telling her what he believed to be true.

And somehow, that made it worse.

Without another word, she pulled open the car door and stepped inside.

As the Uber rolled away, Antony stood where he was, with his hands in his pockets, watching her go. He made no attempt to stop her.

But for the first time, Claudia wasn't sure if she wanted to leave his words behind.

She just didn't know what to do with them yet.

* * *

As the car pulled away from the curb, Claudia let out a slow, unsteady breath. The countryside streamed past her with the greens, browns and yellows bleeding into each other, but her mind was elsewhere— still stuck back at the shooting range, still stuck on him.

Her fingers tightened around the strap of her bag, pressing into the fabric as if grounding herself.

"You think altering something about yourself—something artificial—and pretending that's who you are will bring you value or happiness?"

Antony's voice echoed in her head, steady and deliberate, refusing to fade, no matter how hard she tried to push it away.

She hated the way his words lingered, and wormed their way under her skin, making her question things she'd never doubted before.

Have I really been pretending?

The thought left an uncomfortable weight in her chest.

For so long, she had been reshaping herself, tweaking parts of who she was—her hair, her attitude, the way she carried herself—believing that, with each change, she was moving closer to the version of herself she wanted to be.

And yet, with just a few sentences, he had made her feel like it was all an illusion.

Like she was just a collection of choices she'd made to be seen in a certain way, rather than someone who was truly herself.

She swallowed hard, staring at her reflection in the dark window. The vibrant streaks in her hair stood out against the dimly lit cityscape, suddenly feeling out of place—too loud, and too deliberate.

Is that really how people see me? Someone desperate for attention? Her stomach twisted.

She didn't think that was why she had dyed it.

But what if it was?

What if, deep down, she had been seeking validation in ways she hadn't even realized?

She exhaled sharply, shifting in her seat.

It wasn't just the words that unsettled her—it was how effortlessly he had delivered them, as if they were an undeniable truth, stripped of sugar-coating or false comfort.

Antony had never been cruel, not once. But he was honest. And that was what made it sting the most.

She closed her eyes for a moment, willing herself to let it go, to push it into the part of her mind she didn't have to deal with right now.

The Uber as it approached her neighbourhood, and the familiar streets started to ground her slightly.

She told herself she would think about it tomorrow.

Tonight, she just needed sleep.

* * *

The room was quiet—too quiet. The kind of silence that made thoughts louder.

Claudia sat in front of the mirror, with her elbows resting on the vanity, and her fingers lightly tracing the edge of a hairbrush she wasn't even aware she had picked up. The dim glow of the bedside lamp cast soft shadows on her face, highlighting the tension in her expression.

Her gaze flickered over her own reflection, studying herself as if she were a stranger.

The bright streaks in her hair, the carefully curated image she had built—was it all just a mask?

Her chest felt tight as she replayed Antony's words in her head.

A part of her wanted to be angry, and to dismiss it as nothing more than his opinion.

But deep down, wasn't this the very reason she had felt so out of place that day at Canary Wharf?

She had walked into that building full of poised, confident people and instantly felt like she didn't belong—as if she were an imposter in her own skin.

Why?

Had she always felt this way, or had she been too busy reinventing herself to notice?

A hollow feeling opened up inside her.

If she had truly been happy, and content with who she was becoming... why had she stood on the bridge that night?

Her breath hitched slightly. The realization unsettled her more than anything else.

She needed answers. But where could she even find them?

A sudden pang of longing pulled at her chest. She missed her father. Desperation clawed at her as she reached for her phone. She scrolled through old photos—pictures of them together, of birthdays, and of ordinary afternoons spent laughing.

And then, she found her.

The girl before it all.

Before the colours. Before the persona. Before the constant, exhausting effort to shape herself into something else.

She looked at the girl on the screen—the wide, genuine smile, and the ease in her posture. There was no pretence in her expression, no calculated angles. Just happiness.

Her thumb swiped to a recent picture.

There, she was posing, with a practiced smile, and her expression sculpted into something pleasing.

And suddenly, she saw the difference.

The girl in the old photo wasn't trying to be anything.

The girl in the new one... was playing a part.

Her throat tightened.

Who was she now?

And more importantly... had she lost something in trying to become someone else?

A deep, aching confusion settled inside her. She didn't have the answers. But for once, she knew she needed to start looking for them.

With a quiet breath ,Claudia picked up her phone, her fingers hovering over the screen as she typed out a message.

"Tomorrow—where? What time?"

She stared at it for a moment, debating whether to send it. But then she did.

The screen remained silent: no typing bubbles, and no response. The seconds stretched into minutes, as the quiet of her room amplified her restlessness.

Then, her phone buzzed.

For a brief second, her heart leapt—but when she looked at the screen, it wasn't Antony.

It was Luca.

Without thinking, she declined the call and set the phone down.

Her reflection stared back at her, but something was shifting in her mind.

She leaned forward, studying the girl in the mirror. The streaks of bright colour in her hair suddenly felt loud—like they belonged to someone she wasn't sure she was anymore.

Antony's words echoed in her mind.

"Stop acting like you're the last resistance against nature and start loving yourself as who you are."

She exhaled deeply, running a hand through her hair. Then, in a quiet, resolute motion, she stood up, walked into the bathroom, and pulled out a box of hair dye from the cabinet—the one she had bought a long time ago but never touched.

It was a more natural colour.

She wasn't sure if this decision was about Antony, about the people at Canary Wharf, or about herself. Maybe it was a mix of everything.

But for the first time in a while, it wasn't about proving something. She applied the dye, carefully covering the strands, watching the artificial brightness disappear under the new colour. When she rinsed it out and blow-dried her hair, she felt an odd sense of relief—as if a weight had been lifted off her.

Finally, she stepped back and looked at herself in the mirror. She looked… different.

Not better necessarily, just… more her.

She lay back on her bed, staring at the ceiling. The room was dark except for the soft glow of her phone screen beside her.

She reached for it, half out of habit, and half out of restless curiosity.

There was a message from Antony.

She clicked on it.

"11 am. Location: Sterling Aerodrome, Dartford , Kent."

Her eyes lingered on the words.

She put the phone down on her chest, exhaling slowly. She didn't know how to feel about it.

Excitement? Anxiety?

Maybe both.

But somehow, despite the uncertainty, a small, amused smile crept onto her face.

She switched off the light, turned onto her side, and closed her eyes, before drifting to sleep feeling something other than lost.

22

WINGS OF HER OWN

C laudia moved through her morning routine with quiet purpose, dressing without hesitation—a black crew-neck jumper, black skinny jeans, and black boots. She pulled her hair into a neat ponytail and slipped her sunglasses into her bag.

When she stepped into the living room, Janet was lounging on the couch, with her eyes on the TV but clearly not paying much attention. As Claudia passed by, Janet glanced up—and for a brief moment, her expression shifted. Surprise flickered across her face, followed by something softer.

"You look really good."

Claudia stopped, blinking in mild surprise. Janet had never commented on her appearance before—not like this, not in a way that felt so sincere.

She hesitated for a moment before saying, "Thank you."

But curiosity got the better of her, and before she could stop herself, she added, "You never said that before. What made you say it now?"

Janet tilted her head slightly, studying her. Then, with an easy shrug, she said, "You never looked like that before."

The words weren't meant as an insult. They were said in a way that was almost kind.

Claudia held Janet's gaze for a moment, then let out a small, genuine smile. "I see." She didn't push for more. And for once, she didn't need to.

With that, she grabbed her bag and stepped outside, sliding into the waiting Uber.

As the car pulled away, she watched the city flow past, her thoughts steady, focused.

Sterling Aerodrome: that was where she was headed. An airfield. A private one.

The Sterling Aerodrome was just outside the city, a private airfield known for catering to the elite—discreet, exclusive, and always impeccably maintained.

As Claudia's Uber pulled up to the entrance, she glanced out the window, taking in the sight of sleek private jets lined up along the runway, with their polished surfaces gleaming under the late morning sun. The airfield wasn't crowded; a few luxury cars were parked near the hangars, and the occasional distant hum of an aircraft taking off filled the otherwise quiet space.

She exhaled, adjusting her sunglasses as the car slowed to a stop.

This was definitely not the kind of place she had ever expected to find herself.

And yet—here she was.

As Claudia stepped out of the Uber, the sun cast a golden sheen over the airfield. The morning air smelled of fuel and fresh tarmac, as the quiet hum of a distant jet taking off blended with the sound of her own heartbeat.

She barely had a moment to take it all in before the building doors swung open and Antony stepped out. His usual effortless confidence was on full display as he walked toward her, but midway, he suddenly paused. His gaze swept over her—taking in the ponytail, the understated black outfit, and the sunglasses perched on her nose. For a second, she thought she saw something flicker in his eyes— approval? Surprise? But before she could figure it out, the moment passed. He continued walking, with the usual good-natured composed smile at the edges of his lips.

"Good morning." His voice was light and easy. Then, after a small pause, he added, "You look..." He trailed off, watching her reaction.

Claudia narrowed her eyes. "Look what?" she pressed.

Antony's smile deepened as he slipped his hands into his pockets. "Different." Then, after a beat, he added, "But nice."

Claudia pushed her sunglasses to the top of her head. "I'll take that as a compliment."

He nodded toward the airfield. "Welcome to one of my favorite places."

She glanced around, noting the high-end private jets parked across the strip and the polished hangars that gleamed under the sun. It was obvious this wasn't a place that just anyone could walk into.

"So, where are we going?" she asked.

Antony's smile widened. "I'll tell you. Just follow me."

She did.

Inside the main building, he had a brief conversation with one of the staff members before stepping back out. Without much explanation, he motioned for her to follow again.

"Let's go," he said casually, leading her straight onto the airfield.

As they walked across the tarmac, Claudia's steps slowed when Antony veered toward a small aircraft parked nearby—a sleek red-and-white plane that looked alarmingly tiny.

Antony placed a hand on the aircraft and turned to her, with his voice filled with casual amusement. "This is a Tecnam P2002 Sierra Mk II." He patted the side of the fuselage. "And this... is what you're going to fly today."

Claudia's entire body stiffened.

She ripped the sunglasses off her face, staring at him in absolute disbelief. "Excuse me?!"

Antony barely held back a chuckle. "You heard me."

"I…" She gestured wildly at the plane. "I've never flown anything in my life."

"I guessed that."

"And I don't think I can do this." Her voice had an edge of panic now. "This is insane. I'm scared."

Antony's expression changed ever so slightly, as if she had just disappointed him. With a small shrug, he turned away.

"Oh. I thought you said you'd changed." His tone was light, but there was an unmistakable challenge in it. He sighed dramatically. "That's okay. Let's drop the plan. Come on, let's go back in." Without waiting for a response, he started walking toward the building.

Claudia blinked, completely thrown off.

What the hell was that?

"Stop. Stop!" she called out, utterly confused.

Antony turned back, raising an eyebrow, and waiting.

"Do you know how normal human beings have conversations?" she said.

His lips twitched. "Why? You're not able to understand me?"

She let out a sharp breath, as if trying to clear the frustration out of her system.

"Let's fly," she finally said, throwing her hands up in defeat.

That pleased him. A small smile crept onto his face. He lifted a hand, shaped his fingers like a gun, and playfully "shot" at her. Then, without another word, he turned and walked back to the plane.

* * *

Inside the cockpit, Claudia strapped herself in, feeling a strange mix of nerves and anticipation.

Antony handed her a headset, putting his on as well. His voice came through the intercom, cool and steady. "Alright, listen up." He gestured toward the controls in front of them. "That's the yoke."

"The what?"

"The yoke—this thing." He tapped on it. "It controls the airplane's ailerons. In simple terms, it lets you move the plane 'up,' 'down,' 'left,' and 'right.' Twisting it controls roll and pitch."

She nodded slowly, with her fingers gripping the seatbelt strapped across her chest. "Right. Up, down, left, right. Got it."

He pointed at another dial. "This is the altitude indicator. It shows our relation to the horizon. If we're level, if the nose is too high or too low—this keeps us oriented."

"Okay..."

Then, he tapped the altimeter. "This tells us how high we are above sea level."

Claudia nodded, pretending to absorb all the information, but her brain was already spiraling into panic.

The engine roared to life, and her grip on the seat tightened. Her heart pounded against her ribs. The vibrations of the aircraft felt amplified, thrumming through her body like an alarm she couldn't switch off.

She wanted to tell Antony that she felt panic creeping up her throat, that her hands were clammy against the seatbelt strap, and that she wasn't sure she could go through with this.

But she kept quiet.

She didn't know how he would respond—would he be irritated? Disappointed? Would he turn the plane around and say it wasn't worth the effort?

She stole a glance at him.

He looked completely at ease, flicking switches, checking dials, and speaking into the radio as if he'd done this 1,000 times before.

She exhaled slowly.

Maybe it was too late to back out now.

Maybe she didn't want to.

Then, without another word, the aircraft began to move forward. Claudia's stomach flipped as the earth dropped away beneath them, but before she could panic, she realized something.

She was flying.

As they ascended, the earth shrank beneath them, its vast sprawl reduced to a patchwork of fields, roads, and rivers. The sun hung above the clouds like a golden crown, casting soft beams that scattered across the misty horizon. The sky stretched endlessly before them, an open canvas of blue and white.

Claudia was still gripping the seat but with slightly more ease; she felt something shift inside her. The world below—its noise, its chaos, and its endless complications—seemed so different from this angle.

Antony glanced at her. "How's the view? You enjoying it?"

With a nervous but genuine smile, she exhaled. "Beautiful."

He smiled, with his eyes still on the sky.

She turned her gaze downward, marvelling at how distant everything looked from up here. "It's strange," she murmured, "everything seems so... small. As if nothing is actually happening down there."

Antony chuckled. "Yeah. True."

Then, after a moment of silence, he added, "I really want to say something about life that fits this situation perfectly... but I won't."

Claudia looked at him, intrigued. "Please," she pressed, eager to hear his thoughts.

He shook his head. "No."

She insisted. "Come on. You've already started."

Antony sighed, still focused on the sky ahead. "Alright. Consider your problems as the ground… and where we're sitting right now as your point of view."

Claudia frowned slightly. "Explain."

He simply smiled. "You already understand. And if you don't… you will."

She stared at him for a second longer before letting the words sink in.

After a moment, she shifted in her seat. "How long have you been flying?"

"Four years."

She nodded thoughtfully. "Mmm."

Antony turned toward her, adjusting the flight path. "Alright. Now, you fly."

Claudia's head snapped toward him. "Wait, what?"

"Take the yoke. Make sure the horizon stays level."

Her pulse spiked. "I… what if I mess up?"

Antony grinned. "Then we crash."

Her eyes widened, but he laughed. "Relax. I've got control too. Just hold it steady."

Hesitantly, she placed her hands on the yoke. The cool metal felt unfamiliar beneath her fingers. However, as she focused, she felt something else—excitement.

The plane responded to her movements, gently and smoothly. She felt a rush of exhilaration unlike anything she had ever experienced before.

Antony watched her, nodding. "Good. Keep it steady."

As they glided through the air, he said, "I'm turning left."

"Okay," she replied, fully immersed in the moment.

The plane tilted slightly to the left.

And then—gravity pulled at them.

Claudia felt her stomach drop, and before she could stop herself, she grabbed Antony's thigh tightly, with her fingers digging into the fabric of his pants.

"Make it straight! Make it straight!" she yelled, with her eyes wide with fear.

Antony, unbothered, smoothly leveled the aircraft. His expression remained unreadable as he glanced at her. "Are you okay?"

She exhaled, trying to steady her breath. "Yeah... I just didn't expect that."

He raised his eyebrows. "Maintain the level flight now."

Claudia hesitated, then steadied herself and resumed control. But an idea popped into her head.

Slowly, she tilted the plane to the right.

Antony barely reacted. "Why are you turning?"

She smirked. "Because you made me feel scared, so now I want you to feel the same."

He glanced at her, clearly unimpressed. "You realize I've been flying for years, right?"

Claudia blinked, then let out a defeated sigh, leveling the plane once more. "Yeah... I forgot."

A few moments later, Antony pointed ahead. "Look at that."

She followed his gaze, and her breath hitched.

Beneath them, stretching across the horizon, was a breath-taking landscape—a vast coastline wrapping around the land, with cliffs standing tall against the sea, and, at the heart of it all, a castle perched on a hill. It looked like something out of a fairy tale.

"This," Antony said, "is the Isle of Wight."

Claudia's lips parted slightly as she took in the sight. The golden light from the sun shimmered on the water's surface, and waves crashing silently against the shore. The castle, with its ancient stone walls and towering turrets, looked like it had been pulled straight from history. A winding path led from the castle down to the sea, disappearing into the trees below.

"It's... unreal," she breathed.

Antony nodded, with his voice softer now. "Yeah. It is."

For a moment, neither of them spoke. They just cruised along, floating between the sky and the sea, watching the world from above.

Then, Antony adjusted their course. "Time to head back."

Claudia nodded, still mesmerized by the view as they turned back toward the airfield.

As they flew back toward the airfield, Claudia felt something different. This time, the fear was gone, replaced by a strange exhilaration. It wasn't just the thrill of flying—it was the realization that she had done something she had never thought she would.

Antony landed the plane smoothly, before guiding it back to the base. As the engine powered down, Claudia let out a breath she hadn't realized she was holding.

"That was..." she trailed off, searching for the right word.

Antony glanced at her, "Different?"

She nodded, still processing everything. "Yeah... different."

They climbed out of the cockpit, and Antony disappeared into the building for a few minutes. Claudia stood outside, stretching her arms, as her mind replayed the flight over and over.

When he returned, he walked toward her with a casual ease, spinning his car keys between his fingers. "Come on," he said, nodding toward the parking area.

Claudia followed him, expecting to see a normal car—but the moment she spotted the sleek, gleaming red Ferrari Purosangue, she caught her breath.

"Seriously?" she asked, staring at the car.

Antony unlocking it with a single click. "Why? You don't like it?"

Claudia shook her head. "I don't even know if I should sit in something this expensive."

"Well," he said, opening the passenger door for her, "you just flew a plane, so I'd say you can handle sitting in a Ferrari."

She rolled her eyes but climbed in. The interior smelled of leather and something else—something crisp and expensive, just like everything else about him.

Antony slid into the driver's seat, pressed the ignition, and the engine purred to life, a deep, resonant sound that sent a small thrill through her.

As they pulled out of the airfield, the roads stretched wide and open ahead of them. The sun was still shining, casting a golden glow over the countryside. The car moved effortlessly, its speed smooth but powerful.

Claudia turned to him. "So, where are we going?"

Antony's eyes were fixed on the road. "Somewhere that serves good coffee."

She leaned back, watching the world go by. Today had been unlike anything she had ever experienced. And somehow, she had a feeling—it wasn't over yet.

As they sped down the open road, Claudia let herself sink into the plush leather seat, with her fingers lightly tracing the stitching along the door panel. The hum of the engine filled the cabin, low and powerful, making her stomach flutter—not from fear, but from something else entirely.

Antony didn't speak much, but he didn't need to. He drove with the same effortless confidence he had in everything he did, with his hands relaxed on the wheel, and his gaze steady on the road ahead.

Claudia finally turned to him. "So… where exactly are we going?"

Without taking his eyes off the road, Antony . "A place I think you'll like."

She raised an eyebrow. "That's vague."

"That's intentional."

Claudia rolled her eyes, but she didn't press further. Instead, she watched the scenery change—as the open countryside gave way to small villages, then to orchards.

Fifteen minutes later, Antony pulled into a long, private driveway lined with trees, leading to a grand restaurant overlooking a lake. The building was modern yet elegant, with its floor-to-ceiling glass windows reflecting the setting sun. It wasn't just a restaurant—it was the kind of place people came to for celebrations, business meetings, or to impress someone.

Claudia's fingers twitched slightly. "You know, when you said 'coffee,' I wasn't expecting... this."

Antony put the car in park and turned to her. "I never said coffee. I said somewhere that serves good coffee." His lips quirked up at her unimpressed expression. "Besides, I was starving."

Claudia exhaled, shaking her head with a small smile. "Of course you were."

They stepped out of the Ferrari, and Claudia followed him through the grand entrance.

* * *

23

A DIFFERENT KIND OF MIRROR

Inside, the restaurant exuded understated luxury—with soft golden lighting, crisp white tablecloths, and waiters in sharp black suits moving gracefully between tables. A faint melody played in the background, blending seamlessly into the atmosphere. The hostess, an elegantly dressed woman with a polished smile, greeted them immediately. "Mr. Sewell," she said, in a smooth voice. "Your table is ready."

Claudia glanced at Antony, raising an eyebrow. "You planned this?"

"I don't do waiting in lines."

She sighed but followed him to a table near the window, where the view of the lake shimmered under the last light of the day. As they settled in, a waiter appeared, placing two leather-bound menus in front of them.

Antony didn't bother looking at his. "I'll have the steak, medium rare," he said casually, before glancing at Claudia. "And you?"

Claudia opened the menu, scanning the options. Everything looked expensive, but she wasn't about to let that intimidate her. She tapped her finger on a dish. "The sea bass."

"Excellent choice," the waiter said, taking their menus before gliding away.

Claudia leaned back in her chair, looking across the table at Antony. "So… flying, shooting, now a fancy dinner. Is this just a normal Sunday for you?"

Antony picked up his glass of water. "More or less."

She shook her head with a soft laugh. "Of course it is."

Then, after a brief pause, she leaned forward slightly. "Can I ask you something?"

Antony glanced up from his glass, nodding. "Yeah."

She hesitated for a second before speaking. "Who are you exactly?"

Antony offered a serene smile as he set his glass down. "You came looking for me—not for who I am, but for what I am. So, just leave it as it is."

Claudia frowned slightly. "I just thought…" but she didn't finish the sentence. She wasn't even sure how to. Instead, she exhaled and decided to shift the conversation.

"You know… you really made me upset yesterday," she said, in a casual tone, though there was a flicker of something else in her voice. "But you haven't asked anything about it at all today."

Antony took a sip of water before replying, with his expression calm. "Are you upset now?"

Claudia blinked, caught off guard by the question. "No… I'm not."

"Then why waste time?" he said simply, picking up his fork.

Claudia stared at him for a second before shaking her head, half amused, and half exasperated. "Where do you even get these kinds of answers?"

Antony only smiled, saying nothing.

The waiter arrived at that moment, placing their meals in front of them. Claudia glanced down at her plate before looking back up at him.

"I don't know much about you," she admitted, "but I do know you're really rich. And yet... I've never seen you wearing anything obviously expensive. No big brands, no flashy logos. Why is that? You don't like fashion?"

Antony tilted his head slightly, as if considering her words. Then he pursed his lips. "Why? Do I not look good in what I wear? Is that what you're saying?"

Claudia rolled her eyes. "That's not what I meant. I mean, when you walk down the street, you see a certain type of people wearing big brands—celebrities, businesspeople, and influencers. It's common among the rich. So I was just curious."

Antony wiped his mouth with his napkin before answering. "When celebrities wear brands, they get paid to do it. That's why they wear them. Apart from that, the only people who buy these things just to show them off are the ones who want validation—not the ones who are actually rich."

Claudia frowned, intrigued. "What do you mean by that?"

Antony leaned back slightly, studying her before responding. "Look around. The ones flashing brands—where do you usually see them? Malls? Streets? Workplaces?"

Claudia thought for a second, then nodded. "Yeah... I guess so."

"Exactly," he continued. "People don't buy these things because they love them. They buy them because they want other people to see them in them. They need the validation, the approval. But the irony is, the people they're trying to impress are the ones in the same financial bracket as them."

Claudia sat there, absorbing his words.

Antony leaned back slightly, studying her before responding. "Take your workplace as an example," he said, then paused, tilting his head. "Do you work?"

Claudia nodded. "Yeah, I do. I'm a music teacher."

A flicker of interest passed through his eyes. "Music teacher," he repeated, as if testing the words. "Alright, so let's take your school, then. Imagine one of the teachers walks in with an LV bag. Maybe she feels proud when she shows it off at that moment. But the reality is, the people she's targeting for validation—her colleagues—are all earning around the same salary. Nobody is really impressed. It's a cycle of people trying to convince each other they have more than they actually do."

Claudia sat there, absorbing his words.

"If you don't believe me, think about your own life," Antony continued. "Say you walk into a store, see an expensive pair of shoes, and buy them out of excitement. That excitement fades the moment you're alone in your room. Because deep down, you know it wasn't necessary. And eventually... you regret it."

Claudia leaned back in her chair, staring at him. She'd never really thought about it like that before.

Antony continued, his voice calm but firm. "All I'm saying is— buy things because they're good for you. Not for someone else's validation."

Claudia picked up her glass, processing his words. It wasn't the first time she had heard something like this, but coming from him, it carried a different weight—like it wasn't just an opinion, but something he lived by.

"So, you never buy anything just because it's trendy?" she asked, half-curious, but half-challenging.

Antony took a sip of his drink. "Trends come and go. I don't let people decide what I should wear, drive, or own."

She exhaled, nodding slowly, thinking about all the times she had bought things just because they were in fashion or because she wanted to fit in.

Antony leaned back in his chair, watching her reaction. "Validation is addictive, Claudia. Once you start dressing, speaking, or even thinking in ways that are meant to impress others, you stop being yourself."

Claudia pressed her lips together. "I guess that makes sense."

Antony gestured toward her plate with his fork. "Good. Now eat before you start overthinking again."

She let out a small laugh, shaking her head as she picked up her fork. For the first time in a while, she felt like she was actually learning something—something that wasn't just interesting, but that could actually change the way she saw herself.

Antony's fork paused mid-air as Claudia ate. His gaze held steady on her, unreadable but attentive.

"You said you're a music teacher," he noted casually before taking another bite of his meal. "Which instrument do you teach?"

"Piano," Claudia answered, stirring her fork idly through her plate. "But I play the guitar and violin as well."

Antony raised an eyebrow, with a flicker of something close to admiration crossing his face. "Impressive. What made you choose to learn those instruments?"

Claudia hesitated for a moment, with her fingers tightening slightly around her fork. She wasn't sure why, but answering that question felt... heavier than she expected.

"When I was young," she began slowly, "my mother didn't like me much. Or at least, that's how it felt. It affected me—more than I realized at the time." She exhaled softly, with her eyes momentarily distant. "But my father... he loved me. A lot. And to distract me, to make me feel better, he bought me a piano. A really good one."

She paused, with a small, almost wistful smile playing at her lips. "With that piano, I spent hours—days—just playing, learning. I got good at it, and my father saw that. So he bought me more instruments to learn."

Antony leaned back slightly, watching her. "And you loved it?"

Claudia nodded, then let out a small chuckle, though there was little humor in it. "At the time, my biggest dream was to become a famous musician. I thought… maybe if I became successful, my mother would finally love me." She shook her head, with a hint of self-mockery in her smile. "But before that could happen, my mother got sick. Cancer. She died when she was 40."

Antony didn't speak or move. He simply listened.

"After that," Claudia continued, in a quieter voice, "all the drive I had to be a musician just disappeared. It was like, what was the point anymore?" She let out a breath, setting her fork down on the table. "I still played. I still learned. But it was different."

For a moment, silence stretched between them, not awkward, but full of something unspoken.

Antony finally spoke. His voice was calm and measured. "And now?"

Claudia blinked at him. "What?"

"You said you lost your drive to be a musician." He tilted his head slightly. "But you still play. You still teach. So… why?"

Claudia thought about that for a second, then shrugged. "I guess… I don't know. Habit, maybe. Comfort." She looked down at her plate, poking at her food. "Maybe I'm just scared to admit that I don't really know what I want anymore."

Antony didn't reply right away. Instead, he simply watched her, with his expression unreadable, but somehow knowing. Then he leaned forward, resting his elbows on the table.

"You know," he said casually, "that night on the bridge, you told me you didn't have any real talent. That nothing about you was remarkable."

Claudia stiffened. She hadn't expected him to bring that up.

"And now," he continued, setting his glass down, "you're sitting here telling me you play three different instruments. And that you once dreamed of being a musician."

She lowered her gaze, feeling something settle in her chest. She had no defense.

Antony exhaled, shaking his head slightly. "This is what happens when people spend all their time trying to please others," he said, speaking calmly but firmly. "They neglect themselves. They forget who they are."

Claudia swallowed, gripping the edge of the table.

Antony took a slow sip of his drink; his gaze was unwavering. Then, as if recalling something distant yet precise, he set the glass down and met her eyes.

"You asked me that night," he said, evenly, "where do I start?"

Claudia held her breath.

"If I were you," he continued, leaning forward slightly, "this is where I'd start."

The words struck her harder than she had expected—not because they were some grand revelation, but because they were so simple—so obvious.

She sat there, unmoving, with her fingers tracing the rim of her glass. The air between them settled into something quieter.

For so long, she had been searching for answers in all the wrong places, chasing after people, after validation, and after anything that could fill the silence inside her. But now...

Now, she realized, she had always known where to start. She had just been too lost to see it.

As they sat in silence, Antony's words settled deep within Claudia's mind. The importance of what he had just said pressed against something inside her, something she had ignored for too long.

She shifted in her seat, suddenly needing a moment to breathe. "Excuse me," she murmured, pushing her chair back and standing up.

Without waiting for a response, she turned and made her way toward the restroom.

Claudia leaned against the sink, gripping its cold edges as she stared at her reflection. The dim glow of the restroom lights cast a soft halo around her face, but it couldn't disguise the truth in her eyes.

She looked... different. Not just because of the hair colour she had changed or the way she was dressed. It was something deeper, something unsettling.

"You told me that night on the bridge that you don't have any real talent. Nothing about you is remarkable."

Antony's words echoed in her head.

"And now you say you play three different instruments... And that you once dreamed of being a musician."

Her breath caught in her throat.

All this time, she had convinced herself that she was empty—that she had nothing to offer, and nothing worth holding on to. But had she been lying to herself?

She thought back to the little girl sitting at the piano, pressing her fingers against the keys for the first time. The sound had fascinated her, the way a simple movement could create something so... alive.

And her father—he had been there, watching, encouraging, and believing in her.

Somewhere along the way, she had stopped believing in herself.

Her entire life had been spent trying to be what others needed. A daughter her mother would love. A girlfriend worthy of loyalty. A friend people could depend on. But had she ever asked herself what she needed?

She had spent so much time giving pieces of herself away that she had nothing left for herself.

Claudia swallowed hard, gripping the sink tighter.

If I were you, this is where I'd start.

Music. It had always been music.

It was the one thing that was truly hers, untouched by expectations, untouched by anyone else's approval or validation.

And she had abandoned it.

She turned on the faucet, letting the water rush over her hands, feeling cool and grounding. Then she dried her hands under the air dryer, its hum filling the silence.

She had been so desperate to escape the version of herself she hated that she had buried the part of her that had always been enough.

Her reflection didn't change.

But something inside her did.

Claudia straightened herself up, smoothing her hands over her jumper before lifting her chin slightly.

She knew now.

She wasn't lost.

She had just been ignoring the road that had always been right in front of her.

With a final glance at her reflection, she turned and walked out of the restroom, feeling like she was finally walking toward something real.

As they finished their meal, Antony signalled for the bill. The quiet murmur of the restaurant surrounded them, but Claudia felt an unusual sense of stillness between them—like something had shifted.

The server placed the check on the table, and Antony reached for it without hesitation. As he settled the payment, he glanced at her.

"Would you like to meet again?" he asked, with his voice calm, and almost casual.

Claudia looked at him for a brief second before nodding. "Yes."

The response was simple, but she meant it.

He leaned back slightly. "I know you're free for four more days," he continued, slipping his card back into his wallet. "But I won't be able to meet you again during that time. After that... I don't know when you'll be free."

She tilted her head. "I'm always free on weekends."

Antony gave a small nod, as if making a mental note. "Alright. I'll text you then."

She was reaching for her handbag, preparing to leave, when his voice stopped her.

"Claudia."

She looked up.

"Please don't invest your emotions in me," he said, with his tone steady but kind. "I'm not your next destination for happiness. You need to find that inside yourself."

For a moment, she just stared at him.

If he had said that weeks ago, it would have hurt. It would have felt like rejection, or abandonment. But now, it didn't. Because she understood.

A small, knowing smile twitched on her lips. She didn't argue, and didn't try to deny it. Instead, she nodded—just slightly—and got up from her seat.

Antony watched her as she walked toward the exit, walking steadily, with her expression unreadable.

But as she stepped outside, into the cool night air, something felt... different.

For once, she wasn't in search of something—validation, escape, or purpose.

She already knew where to find it.

With that quiet certainty settling in her chest, Claudia pulled out her phone, and booked an Uber to take her home.

24

A CONVERSATION THAT NEED TO HAPPEN

Claudia woke with a rare sense of clarity. She laced up her running shoes and stepped outside, inhaling the crisp morning air as she started her run. Her body still wasn't used to it—her muscles ached, and her breath came short—but something about the steady rhythm of her feet hitting the pavement felt solid, almost like she was piecing herself back together.

By the time she returned home, her skin was damp with sweat, and her chest was rising and falling in deep, satisfied breaths. A long, hot shower washed away the exhaustion, leaving her awake, and refreshed.

As she stepped into her room, her gaze landed on the piano.

Gently, she lifted the lid, and her fingers brushed against something wedged inside.

A notebook.

She pulled it out, flipping through the pages. Her old music notebook. The ink had faded slightly, but the handwriting was hers—lyrics scribbled in the margins, half-written chords, unfinished melodies waiting for completion.

Her fingers hovered over the keys before pressing down softly, playing the fragmented tune she had once started. The notes were hesitant at first, slow and uncertain. But with each repetition, she remembered more. The melody, once buried, started resurfacing.

A soft knock on the door made Claudia pause. She turned to see Janet standing in the doorway, with her arms crossed loosely, and her expression softer than usual.

"I didn't know you still played," she said.

Claudia blinked, with her fingers still resting on the keys. "It's been a while."

Janet stepped inside, looking around before settling her gaze back on the piano. "Even though you were only playing pieces of it... it's beautiful."

Claudia hesitated, then gestured toward the chair near her bed. "Come in."

Janet nodded and sat down, watching her intently.

After a brief silence, she asked, "What piece is that? I don't think I've heard it before."

Claudia traced the edge of the music notebook. "You wouldn't have. I wrote it."

Janet's eyebrows lifted. "You wrote that?"

Claudia nodded.

Janet let out a quiet chuckle, shaking her head in disbelief. "You're telling me you can compose something like this, and you just kept it to yourself?"

Claudia exhaled through her nose, brushing her thumb over the worn notebook. "I wrote it a long time ago. I never finished it."

Janet's expression softened. "Why not?"

Claudia hesitated before answering. "I wrote it for my mother. I called it 'Mother's Love.' I wanted to finish it and play it for her one day... but she never got to hear it."

For a moment, Janet didn't say anything. Then, without warning, she reached forward and pulled Claudia into a hug.

Claudia stiffened slightly—this was unexpected. But after a second, she let herself lean into it.

When Janet pulled back, her hands still rested lightly on Claudia's arms. "Claudia... I had no idea."

Claudia gave a small shrug. "Not something I really talk about."

Janet exhaled, glancing down before meeting Claudia's eyes again. "There's something I need to tell you."

Claudia tilted her head, waiting.

Janet gave a small, almost self-conscious chuckle. "You know... after my husband and son passed, I held myself together. It hurt, but I managed. But my daughter..." Her smile faded. "When she left the way she did, that was different. That kind of loneliness... I wasn't ready for it."

She paused, with her voice quieter now. "That's why I opened my home to someone else. I thought... maybe it would help."

Claudia listened in silence.

Janet smiled slightly. "I didn't like the way you lived when you first moved in. You were all over the place—exhausted, constantly giving yourself away to everyone, but never keeping anything for yourself. It frustrated me."

Claudia pressed one key softly, letting the note linger.

"But now," Janet continued, "I see something different. You're starting to carry yourself in a way that makes sense. There's balance. And I like that."

Claudia tilted her head slightly. "So... what? You like me better now?"

Janet chuckled. "No. I liked you as a housemate back then. But now... I like you as Claudia."

Claudia blinked, processing the words.

Janet leaned back, with her voice softer. "I don't expect my daughter to love me again. But if I could ask for one thing… I'd want her to have a life like yours."

Claudia swallowed. Something about those words settled differently in her chest.

Janet gave her a small pat on the shoulder as she stood up. "I'll let you be."

Then, she left the room, closing the door softly behind her.

Claudia hesitated for a moment before following Janet into the lounge. She found her sitting on the sofa, and gazing out the window, apparently lost in thought. The soft afternoon light projected long shadows across the room, wrapping everything in a quiet stillness.

Without a word, Claudia sat down beside her. After a moment, she reached over and gave Janet a gentle squeeze on the shoulder.

"You'll be alright," she murmured.

Janet let out a slow breath but didn't take her eyes off the window. "You know, my mum and dad used to tell me stories about the war," she said finally. "Back then, kids as young as 14 or 15 were already working. They had proper responsibilities. Some were out in the fields, some in factories, some in offices—doing real jobs, helping to support their families. Can you imagine that?"

Claudia stayed quiet, sensing there was more Janet wanted to say.

"And back then, you made do with what you had," Janet went on. "Food was rationed. Clothes were rationed. You couldn't just nip out and buy something whenever you fancied. You had to plan ahead, be careful, and be sensible." She shook her head slightly. "This country didn't get where it is now by chance—it took graft, discipline, and a sense of duty."

She paused, letting out a short, dry laugh. "Even if you didn't have much, you made sure you looked presentable before stepping outside. Nowadays? I see people strolling around in their pyjamas—at the shops, at the airport, you name it. And somehow, that's called progress?"

Claudia frowned slightly, unsure how to respond.

Janet sighed, rubbing her hands together. "Maybe I sound like a dinosaur to you. Maybe I've not kept up with the modern world. But I don't care how modern things get—if you stop having self-respect, if you stop taking pride in yourself, then what's left?"

She finally turned to Claudia, her voice quieter but steady.

Janet exhaled, her gaze still distant. "You talk to young people these days, and what do you hear? They're not happy. They're anxious, lost. They feel like nothing's ever enough, like they're always chasing something just out of reach." She shook her head. "And it's everywhere you look."

Claudia listened, picking up on the weariness in Janet's voice.

"People choosing not to work, sitting around living off benefits and calling that a life." Janet's tone carried quiet frustration. "If everything's handed to you, if you've got all the free time in the world and no real responsibilities... then what are you?" She exhaled again. "Just... wasting space."

Claudia blinked, taken aback by the bluntness of it. But she could hear the weariness behind the words—the tiredness of someone who'd watched the world change in ways she didn't always recognise.

"You never truly value anything unless you've worked for it," Janet added, with her tone softening.

After a beat, Claudia spoke. "So... you reckon this whole generation's just lost?"

Janet sighed, leaning back slightly. "Not all of them. But far too many, yeah."

She gestured vaguely around the room. "Look at all this—mobiles, massive telly, and music on tap instead of cassette tapes or old radios.

None of this existed when I was your age. It's the younger lot who've built it. People with ideas and purpose made this world."

Claudia considered that, then shook her head gently. "But you can't lay all the blame at young people's feet."

Janet exhaled, tilting her head, thinking it over. Then, she gave a small nod. "You've got a point. It's not just them. Parenting's changed too. Back in the day, parents guided their kids, and prepared them for real life. Now, half of them seem more interested in showing off on social media than raising proper adults."

She leaned back into the sofa, eyes distant again. "But I do believe this—if you've nothing to get out of bed for, nothing you're striving towards, that's when you lose your way. And the longer you stay lost, the harder it is to find your way back."

Claudia nodded slowly. The words hit somewhere deep inside.

After a pause, she asked, "What was your purpose?"

Janet's face softened. A faint smile appeared, distant but warm. "I was a mum. A wife. A daughter. A physics teacher." She paused, with her eyes drifting as if she was looking for something in her memories. "And I loved every bit of it."

Claudia swallowed. Janet had lived with clarity—with roles, and with purpose. But what about her? Once, she'd dreamt of being a musician. She'd lived for validation, for a love that never came.

And now?

She wasn't sure.

But something about this conversation made her feel like it was time to find out.

Claudia let out a breath, eyes on Janet. "So... what do you think can actually fix all this? The way people are now?"

Janet shook her head slowly. "I don't know if it can be fixed, love. But I know this..." Claudia leaned in. "A person who wakes up excited about their day—excited about what they're building, about who

205

they're becoming—that person's got a shot at happiness." Janet looked her in the eye. "That much, I'm sure of."

Claudia let the words sit with her.

Janet leaned back, exhaling. "And you know," she added, "you're living in the best time. It doesn't matter if you're tucked away in some little village—you're still connected to the world. You've got access to more than we ever dreamed of." She gave Claudia a small smile. "You can do whatever you set your mind to."

Claudia sat there, quiet and thoughtful. Something had shifted.

Then, after a long pause, she looked up. "Why are you telling me all this now?" she asked. "You've never spoken to me like this before."

Janet studied her for a moment, then let out a soft laugh. "Because over the past couple of weeks, I've seen a change in you," she said simply. "I wouldn't have said any of this to the old Claudia."

Claudia blinked.

She realised someone else had noticed her change—not just on the outside, but deep down.

And for some reason, that stuck with her.

Claudia hesitated before speaking again. "Can I ask you something?"

Janet turned to her. "Of course you can."

Claudia took a breath. "I always felt like... you didn't really like foreigners. Sometimes, I even thought you were..." She paused. "A bit racist."

Janet let out a long breath but didn't look offended. "You're entitled to feel that way," she said. "But I grew up surrounded by people from all sorts of backgrounds. That was never the issue."

Claudia frowned. "Then what is it?"

Janet turned back to the window, picking her words. "It's not about individuals," she said finally. "But when too much changes too quickly—when there's no sense of balance, you lose the soul of a place. The character of a town. And that's hard. It affects people—

even if they can't quite say why."

Claudia listened, processing her words.

"But," Janet continued, "it's not just about them either. We can't place all the blame there. When people here refuse to work—when they choose to live off benefits instead of contributing—who's going to fill those vacancies? Someone has to. And that's how things shift."

Claudia sat with that for a moment. It wasn't the black-and-white answer she had expected.

Then, finally, she said, "Thank you... for talking to me like this."

Janet turned her head, and looked at her closely. Then, with a small smile, she said, "This is how a mother shows her daughter the ways of the world."

A pause.

Then Claudia smiled "Fancy making me a proper Janet-special cup of tea?"

Janet chuckled. "Come on, I'll show you the recipe."

Something inside Claudia loosened, as if a weight she'd carried had quietly slipped away

25

THE SHIFT

For the next week, Claudia found herself settling into a rhythm—one that felt surprisingly natural.

Every morning, she laced up her running shoes and hit the pavement. The steady rhythm of her breath and footsteps just felt right. It was different from before. She wasn't running to escape her thoughts anymore; she was running because it felt good. Because it was hers.

She also joined a local gym, something she had never considered before. The first few days were awkward—figuring out the machines, and feeling out of place—but soon, she found comfort in the routine. The burn in her muscles after a session felt like proof she was moving forward, and shaping herself into someone stronger.

In the evenings, Janet sometimes asked if they could go for walks together. At first, Claudia unsure of why Janet suddenly wanted to spend this time with her, but then she agreed.

Their walks became something she looked forward to. The air was crisp, and the streets quieter as the sun dipped below the horizon. Sometimes they talked, sometimes they didn't. And the silence between them wasn't uncomfortable. It was peaceful.

At home, she spent more time at her piano than she had in years. The half-finished melody that had once been abandoned was now something she worked on every day, shaping it, and filling in the gaps. She didn't know what had changed, but the notes felt clearer now, as if she was finally hearing them properly.

When she went to school, the days felt different too. The exhaustion that had once weighed on her shoulders wasn't there anymore. She still had work and responsibilities, but she didn't feel drained by them. Instead, she felt balanced.

And in the middle of it all, she found herself often glancing at her phone. Checking for messages that weren't there, from him.

She wasn't sure what she was expecting. He had said he would text when he was free, so every time she unlocked her phone, a tiny hope would flicker—only to disappear when there was nothing.

But as the days passed, she noticed something else.

She wasn't reacting to things the way she once had.

Situations that would once have overwhelmed her, and sent her spiralling into overthinking or self-doubt, no longer had the same hold on her. She stopped reacting emotionally and started responding calmly.

When things at school got hectic, she handled them without letting the stress consume her. When colleague said something blunt or challenging, she didn't take it personally. When she thought about Antony and the silence that had followed their last meeting, she didn't let it unravel her.

She just accepted things as they came, took a breath, and responded with clarity.

She was still the same Claudia. But something in her was changing.

And little by little, life was starting to feel like her own again.

* * *

The afternoon light slanted through the window of the school staff room, throwing long shadows across Claudia's desk. The day had been a blur of routine conversations. She was halfway through a cup of now-lukewarm tea when Tara walked in.

Tara never hesitated. She moved with the kind of certainty that made everything she said sound like a given. Before Claudia could say anything, she pulled out the chair across from her and sat down, resting her arms on the table like she belonged there.

"I need a favour," she said; her voice sounded smooth, almost casual. Claudia set her cup down, tilting her head slightly. "I'm listening."

Tara launched into an explanation—fast, direct, and layered with just enough charm to make it seem less like a request and more like an expectation. She had plans, she had obligations, and apparently Claudia was the only one who could help.

Claudia listened, but she didn't rush to respond.

When Tara finally finished, she leaned forward, with her smile widening. "So, you'll do it, right?"

Claudia let the silence stretch between them. She studied Tara's face—the slight tilt of her head, the easy confidence, the way she was already waiting for a yes, as if it was inevitable.

With a small, polite smile, Claudia said, "I'm actually free at that time. No plans so far."

Tara exhaled in relief, with her shoulders dropping slightly. "Great—"

"But," Claudia continued calmly, "I'm on anti-parasitic medication, so I don't think I should be feeding any parasites around me."

Initially, Tara just blinked.

Then the shift happened—the flicker of realization, and the way her expression tightened just slightly before she recovered.

"Wow," Tara said, sitting back, her voice losing its charm. "So that's how it is now?"

Claudia didn't flinch. She just tilted her head slightly, waiting.

Tara scoffed, shoving her chair back as she stood. "Unbelievable," she muttered before turning on her heel and walking out of the room.

Claudia picked up her tea again. It had gone completely cold, but she took a sip anyway.

After Tara left, Claudia leaned back in her chair, exhaling through her nose. The silence that followed was almost amusing. There was no arguing, no guilt, and no exhaustion—just peace.

She absent-mindedly picked up her phone, checking for notifications. Nothing.

With a small sigh, she scrolled through her contacts and pressed Luca's name.

The phone rang twice before he picked up. "What's up?"

"You free on Saturday?" she asked, already knowing the answer.

"Why?" His voice was cautious, but she could hear the curiosity underneath.

"Let's take Pete out," she said. "Movie, bowling—make a day of it."

Luca let out a breath. "Claudia... I'm off this weekend, but money's a little tight. I don't want to promise him something and then..."

"Oh, my God." She rolled her eyes dramatically, even though he couldn't see it. "Are you ever not broke?"

He snorted. "I have a family to feed. Not like you, Miss Independent."

"Excuses," she teased. "You're just bad with money."

"Right. Because working for the government pays millions."

She laughed. "Don't worry, I got it. Just say yes."

There was a pause, then a sigh of relief. "You sure? Because if you say it and then cancel, Pete's gonna be crushed."

"I'm sure," she reassured him. "Besides, I want to go. It'll be fun."

Luca chuckled. "Alright, then. Movie and bowling it is. You might regret this when Pete decides to challenge you at everything."

She grinned. "Oh, I plan on destroying him at bowling."

"Yeah, good luck with that," Luca said. "He's ruthless."

"Bring it on."

Ten minutes later, Claudia was still sitting at her desk, scrolling through her phone when it rang. Expecting it to be Luca, she casually reached for her earphones, plugged them in, and glanced at the screen.

Mr. Nobody.

She caught her breath.

Antony never called. He always texted.

Without hesitating, she answered. "Hello?"

His voice was as smooth and composed as ever. "Are you free on Saturday and Sunday?"

Her mind instantly flicked to her promise to Luca—the day out with Pete. But before she could think it through, a stronger thought crashed through her hesitation.

I can't miss this chance.

"Yes," she said, but there was a slight pause before the word left her lips.

Antony must have noticed because his response was instant. "Are you sure?" His tone was unreadable. "If you have plans, we can meet another time."

"No," she said quickly. "I don't." She took a breath, trying to sound casual. "I was just surprised you called instead of texting."

There was a brief pause before he responded. "I needed to ask something before making plans."

Claudia felt her stomach tighten with curiosity. "Okay... What is it?"

"Do you have a passport?"

She blinked, caught completely off guard. "My passport?"

"Yes."

She hesitated for a second, trying to piece together why he would ask that. "Yeah... I do."

"Good," he said simply. "Tomorrow, at 6:30 pm, someone will pick you up. I'll see you in Puglia."

She sat up straighter. "Wait... Where?"

"Puglia."

She tried to process the name, flipping through mental maps, but before she could ask another question, Antony said, "See you in the morning. And don't forget to bring your passport with you."

Then there was a click as he hung up.

Claudia sat there, staring at her screen, with her thoughts racing.

As soon as the call with Antony ended, Claudia quickly opened her browser and began typing Puglia. Before she could finish, her phone buzzed—Luca was calling. She rejected the call without thinking and refocused on typing.

Before the page could load, Luca called again. She sighed, answering this time while keeping her eyes on the screen.

"Claudia," Luca's voice came through, "I'll pick you up at 10:30 in the morning."

The search results popped up—Puglia, Italy. Her fingers hovered over the screen as the realization hit.

Luca kept talking. "I had a rough conversation with Rosie when she found out she's not coming with us."

Claudia barely heard him. Italy? The last time she had been there had been with her father when she was a kid. And now, suddenly, she was supposed to be there the next day?

"Pete's really excited too," Luca added.

There was silence on Claudia's end.

"You there?" Luca asked, more sharply.

She blinked, snapping out of her thoughts. "Yeah. Yeah, I'm here."

"Did you even hear what I just said?"

She hesitated. "Uh... say it again?"

Luca exhaled, clearly irritated. "I said I'll pick you up at 10:30 in the morning."

Before she could respond, he hung up.

Claudia stared at her phone, with her mind racing.

After a few seconds, she called him back.

"I can't come on Saturday," she said quickly.

There was silence on the other end before Luca's frustrated voice cut through. "Are you joking? I asked you twice before telling Pete. Now you're backing out?"

Claudia exhaled. "I know, I know. I planned to, but can we do it next weekend?"

Luca let out a bitter laugh. "Yeah, we can go next weekend or the week after. But I can't break my promise to Pete. So, if you're not coming, you're sending me £200 so I can still take him out."

Claudia rubbed her temple. She couldn't even argue—he was right.

"I'll transfer it when I get home," she said.

There was a pause before she added, "I just... I forgot I had something planned."

Luca scoffed. "Right. It must be important, then."

She sighed. "I'm really sorry, Luca."

"Yeah, whatever," he muttered. "I'll see you whenever." Then, he hung up.

Claudia lowered the phone, staring at the screen where Puglia, Italy was still staring back at her.

26

PUGLIA

Claudia sat on the edge of her bed, dressed in an oversized T-shirt, with her bare feet resting on the cool wooden floor. The dim glow of her bedside lamp cast soft shadows across the room, making everything feel quieter, and more intimate. She should've been getting into bed, letting exhaustion take over, but her mind wouldn't settle.

Her phone lay beside her, with the screen dark, but it felt like it was watching her—waiting for her to make a decision.

She exhaled, running a hand through her hair. Should I call him?

The thought had been circling her mind since the moment Antony hung up. She wasn't even sure why she wanted to. Maybe she was hoping for some reassurance—something that would make her feel less like she was walking into the unknown.

But what would she even say?

Hey, so… what exactly is the plan?

She could already imagine his response.

"Do you trust me?" He would ask it so casually, as if it was the simplest thing in the world.

And then what? If she said yes, he'd probably reply with, "Then why ask more questions?"

And if she said no? She could already picture him shrugging, his voice just as calm. "That's alright. Don't come."

And that would be it. No argument, no convincing her otherwise. Just a quiet door closing in front of her.

Would she even see him again if she chose not to go?

Claudia bit her lip, staring at the ceiling. The way Antony spoke—it was always with such certainty, as if he didn't need to explain himself to anyone. As if people would either walk beside him or not, but he wouldn't wait for them to decide.

And yet... he had called this time, instead of texting.

That alone made her hesitate.

After a moment, she sighed and leaned back against the pillows.

I'll go, she told herself.

There was no reason not to. And if she didn't, she knew she'd regret it.

With that decision made, she reached over, switched off the lamp, and pulled the covers over herself.

But even as she closed her eyes, sleep didn't come right away.

Her mind was still playing through the possibilities, the questions she wouldn't ask, and the answers she might never get.

* * *

The clock on Claudia's bedside table read 6:30 am, but she had been awake a long time. Dressed and ready, she sat on the edge of her bed, with her foot tapping softly against the floor. A faint morning chill lingered in the air, but she barely felt it—her mind was occupied elsewhere.

She was wearing a blue knit jumper, the soft fabric of which hugged her comfortably, paired with black slim-fit jeans and black boots. Her glasses sat tucked into her jeans pocket, though she wasn't sure she'd need them. She had checked her phone at least five times in the last ten minutes, waiting—for a call, a text, something from Antony.

Nothing.

She exhaled, pushing a hand through her hair. He said 6:30. What if I misunderstood? What if I was supposed to message him first? What if—

Her phone rang.

Claudia started, then fumbled to pick it up. An **unknown number**. She hesitated, then answered. "Hello?"

"Good morning, Miss Claudia," a polite male voice greeted her. "I'm your driver. I'll be there in five minutes."

She blinked, taken aback by the formality. "Oh—okay. I'll be waiting outside."

"See you shortly."

The call ended before she could ask anything else.

She grabbed her small black travel bag, took one last glance around the room, and stepped out into the crisp morning air.

The street was quiet at this hour, as the world was still waking up. A light breeze rustled the trees as she stood by the pavement, rubbing her hands together.

Then, from down the road, she saw it—a Mercedes-Maybach.

The sleek, black luxury car glided to a smooth stop in front of her. Too expensive. Too polished. It was the kind of car that turned heads, and yet, in this early morning stillness, it felt almost surreal.

The driver stepped out, a man in his mid-forties, dressed in a dark suit. His expression was warm and professional, but not overly formal. With a pleasant smile, he greeted her, "Good morning, Miss Claudia."

"Good morning," she replied, still trying to process everything.

He reached for her bag. "Allow me."

Before she could protest, he had already taken it from her, walking over to the trunk and placing it inside with practiced ease.

Then, he moved to the rear door, holding it open for her.

Claudia hesitated for a split second before stepping forward and sliding into the plush leather seat. The interior smelled of rich leather and a faint hint of cologne, the kind that belonged in places she never frequented.

The door shut gently behind her.

A moment later, the car pulled smoothly away from the curb.

Claudia exhaled slowly, with her fingers pressing against her lap.

The drive to the airport was silent, apart from the soft hum of the Mercedes Maybach's engine. Claudia sat back, with her fingers idly tracing the smooth leather seat beneath her, her eyes flickering between the cityscape outside and the immaculate interior. Everything about this felt foreign to her—too polished, and too effortless.

She had never been picked up by a private driver before, let alone driven in a car like this.

As they neared the airport, she expected to see the usual busy terminals and long security lines. Instead, the car veered off towards a separate entrance, more discreet and secluded. A private hangar stood at the far end, its massive doors open, revealing something she'd never thought she'd see in real life—a private jet.

It was sleek, silver with navy-blue accents, standing in perfect contrast against the pale morning sky. The polished exterior gleamed under the sunlight, looking untouched by the chaos of the outside world.

The Maybach slowed to a stop, and, before Claudia could even reach for the door handle, it swung open.

A uniformed airport attendant greeted her with a polite smile. "Miss

Claudia, welcome."

She barely had time to react before another staff member smoothly collected her luggage from the trunk.

A neatly dressed flight attendant in a tailored navy-blue uniform with gold accents approached. "Right this way, Miss Claudia."

Claudia only hesitated for a second before following. As she climbed the plush navy-carpeted steps, she couldn't shake the feeling that she was stepping into someone else's life.

And that feeling only deepened as she climbed through the door of the jet.

This wasn't anything like the cramped, noisy commercial flights she had taken before. The space was open, airy, and designed with understated elegance.

Instead of rows of seats, there were spacious cream-colored leather armchairs, positioned around polished walnut wood tables set with crystal glasses and fresh orchids. The walls were lined with large oval windows, letting in soft, natural light.

A soft, almost invisible hum from the engines filled the cabin— powerful, but far from overwhelming.

Claudia barely had time to process it all before a flight attendant stepped forward, with a warm, professional smile on her face.

"Please, make yourself comfortable, Miss Claudia. May I offer you a warm towel before take-off?"

Claudia nodded, still absorbing her surroundings. The attendant handed her a soft, lavender-scented towel, folded neatly on a silver tray.

As she wiped her fingers, she noticed a small monogrammed envelope resting on the tray beside her seat.

She picked it up, and unfolded the thick, expensive paper.

"Welcome aboard. Wishing you a pleasant journey. - A.S."

Antony.

Her lips curled slightly at the initials. He had thought about everything.

Just as she was beginning to process it all, a flight attendant reappeared beside her, holding a polished menu folder.

"Miss Claudia, may I offer you breakfast? Our in-flight chef has prepared a selection for today."

Claudia blinked. "You have a chef?"

The attendant's smile didn't waver. "Of course, Miss. Would you like to meet him?"

She let out a quiet, astonished laugh. "No, no. I was just… surprised."

The attendant nodded, as if she had heard this reaction before. "Would you like any recommendations?"

Claudia exhaled, still wrapping her head around everything, then nodded. "Yes… please."

The attendant opened the menu smoothly and read from it as if it were poetry:

- Truffle Scrambled Eggs with Brioche Toast
- Smoked Salmon & Caviar on Mini Blinis
- Greek Yogurt with Fresh Berries & Manuka Honey
- A Selection of Freshly Baked Pastries
- Cold-Pressed Juices, Specialty Coffee, or a Bellini

Claudia felt a strange thrill at the elegance of it all.

"I'll have the truffle scrambled eggs," she decided, then hesitated. "…And maybe the smoked salmon too?"

The attendant gave a pleased nod. "Excellent choice. Would you like fresh fruit as well?"

"Yes, please."

"And to drink?"

Claudia smirked slightly. "A Bellini. Why not?"

The attendant gave a slight bow. "Of course, Miss Claudia. I'll have everything brought out shortly."

She disappeared into the galley, leaving Claudia to sit in a quiet haze of disbelief.

As the jet ascended smoothly, Claudia peered out the window. The world below shrank, disappearing into nothing but soft blue and white.

For the first time in weeks, she felt untethered—floating, and free.

Not long after, another attendant appeared, setting down a beautifully plated breakfast on fine porcelain.

The aroma of truffle and warm, buttery brioche filled the air, making her mouth water.

The fruit platter—arranged like a piece of art—was made up of mango, dragon fruit, kiwi, raspberries, lychee, and pineapple, garnished with edible flowers and mint leaves.

The truffle scrambled eggs were creamy, rich, and perfectly folded on top of a golden brioche slice, with the delicate taste of truffle filling every bite.

The smoked salmon blinis sat neatly beside it, topped with a delicate dollop of black caviar that glistened under the light.

Her Bellini, perfectly chilled, sparkled in a fine crystal flute, with light condensation forming on the glass.

The eggs melted on her tongue, smooth, indulgent, with just the right hint of earthy truffle.

She exhaled slowly, closing her eyes for a brief second.

This wasn't just breakfast.

This was an experience.

As she ate, she noticed something—the crew knew exactly when to check in and when to step back.

They made sure she had everything she needed without ever making her feel watched.

It was seamless.

Claudia couldn't remember the last time she felt completely taken care of.

The three-hour flight passed in a blur of indulgence and quiet disbelief.

Between the decadent breakfast, the effortless comfort, and the weightless feeling of cruising above the world, Claudia found herself in awe of everything.

When the captain's voice finally announced their descent into Brindisi's Salento Airport, Claudia took a deep breath.

Through the window, she saw Italy's sun-kissed coastline unfolding below—a stretch of golden beaches, deep blue sea, and historic towns that looked like something out of a painting.

The jet touched down smoothly, and, as the aircraft slowed, Claudia knew one thing for sure. She had no idea what awaited her in Puglia.

But she was ready for whatever came next.

* * *

The moment Claudia stepped off the private jet, the warmth of the Italian sun wrapped itself around her, a stark contrast to the cool, controlled air inside the aircraft. There was a light breeze carrying the scent of citrus and olive trees, mingled with the faint salinity of the nearby sea.

She had barely adjusted to her surroundings when she spotted Antony.

He was standing next to two luxury cars parked just outside the private hangar—an Aston Martin DB11, with its sleek deep-blue paint glistening under the morning sun, and a Bentley Bentayga, which looked dark and commanding.

He wasn't alone.

Standing beside him were four other people, two men and two women—the same ones she had seen in his office. They carried themselves with the same polished confidence, speaking to one another in hushed tones, but there was an ease between them, a familiarity that told her they weren't just colleagues.

Antony's gaze found hers almost immediately.

He was dressed in a crisp white linen shirt with the sleeves casually rolled up, dark tailored trousers, and a watch that looked like it probably cost more than her rent. His sunglasses were tucked into the neckline of his shirt, and his expression was unreadable—except for the faint composed smile that tugged at the corner of his lips when he saw her.

"Welcome to Italy," he said smoothly as she approached.

Claudia let out a short breath. "Quite an entrance, wasn't it?"

"It suited you."

Before she could reply, one of the women stepped forward—the same one who had been looking at Antony a little too intently the last time Claudia saw her.

"Claudia," the woman greeted, her tone polite but distant. "Nice to see you again."

Claudia offered a small smile in return.

The introductions were brief—she still wasn't entirely sure what their roles were in Antony's life, but there was no time to dwell on it.

Antony moved toward the Aston Martin, pulling open the driver's side door without hesitation.

"You're with me," he said, his voice even but leaving no room for argument.

Sliding into the passenger seat, Claudia sank into the soft leather of the Aston Martin, inhaling a mix of cedarwood, leather, and something distinctly Antony. The car hummed to life, a low, smooth purr as he eased them onto the road, merging seamlessly into the quiet rhythm of Puglia's countryside.

As they left the airport behind, the scenery unfolded like a painting—rolling vineyards stretching out endlessly, sun-drenched olive groves, and clusters of whitewashed buildings nestled into the hills. The sky was a crisp blue, with wisps of clouds drifting lazily across it. Everything here felt untouched by urgency.

Claudia let out a small breath, her fingers absently tracing the edge of the car door. "This doesn't even feel real."

Antony glanced at her briefly before turning his focus back to the road. "It is."

She turned toward him, arching a brow. "Do you ever just give a straightforward answer?"

The corner of his lips twitched. "You don't ask straightforward questions."

She shook her head, but there was amusement behind it. He always had a way of flipping things back onto her.

For a while, they drove in silence, with the low hum of the engine blending with the distant chirping of birds and the occasional rustling of trees as the wind swept through the vineyards. Claudia let herself soak in the stillness, and the way the golden sunlight danced across the endless rows of grapevines.

"I've been to Italy before," she said after a while. "Twice. When I was young."

Antony didn't take his eyes off the road. "Where?"

"Milan," she said, "but I don't really remember much."

He nodded slightly, as if filing the information away.

Ahead, the road curved gently around a vineyard, where the neat rows of grapevines created perfect patterns against the rolling hills.

"Puglia's famous for its wine, right?" she asked.

"Primitivo and Negroamaro," Antony confirmed. "Some of the best reds in Italy."

Claudia smirked. "Do you drink?"

"No."

She waited, expecting him to elaborate. He didn't.

That was it. Just a simple, definitive no.

Her curiosity buzzed, but something about the certainty in his tone made her hold back from pressing further.

Instead, she turned her attention back to the scenery, letting the sun warm her skin through the open window. The world outside moved slowly—it was quieter and simpler than the city she had left. She watched as they passed a small roadside café, where a few locals sat outside, sipping espresso from tiny porcelain cups, seeming completely unbothered by time.

She sighed, a little envious. "People live so slowly here."

Antony glanced at her. "Would you rather be stuck in traffic back home?"

She let out a soft laugh. "Not exactly."

Another stretch of silence followed, but it wasn't uncomfortable. Claudia let herself sink into it, appreciating the unfamiliar feeling of having nowhere to be, and nothing urgent pulling her away.

After a few more minutes, she turned to him again. "So... where exactly are we going?"

Antony's fingers tapped lightly against the steering wheel as he took another smooth turn.

"Puglia."

She rolled her eyes. "That's not an answer."

He glanced at her. "You'll see."

Claudia exhaled, shaking her head with a small laugh before leaning back in her seat.

She realized wasn't worried about what was coming next. Whatever awaited her, she'd find out soon enough.

27

UNCHARTED WATERS

A s they arrived at a marina, the view was breath-taking. The clear turquoise waters stretched out, meeting the golden glow of the morning sun. Several luxurious yachts were docked, but the one they were headed for stood out—a sleek, white hydrofoil yacht with polished wood decks, exuding pure elegance.

Claudia followed the group aboard, her bare feet touching the smooth wooden deck as the light sea breeze kissed her skin. Once inside, she stepped into the yacht's changing room and slipped out of her travel clothes, switching into a black bikini. She threw on a sheer white cover-up, loosely draping it over her shoulders before heading back out.

As the crew prepared the yacht for departure, Claudia noticed how effortlessly everyone eased into the luxurious setting—champagne glasses were already in hand, music played softly from hidden speakers, and laughter floated in the salty air.

But what caught her attention was Antony.

Unlike the others, who lounged and drank, he had taken the wheel. His white linen shirt hung loosely, with his sleeves rolled up to his elbows, exposing his forearms as he steered the yacht out into the open sea. His face, always composed, was different here—he looked relaxed, absorbed, and... happy.

Claudia found herself watching him, the way his hands moved over the controls, and his gaze never wavered from the horizon. He wasn't just sailing; he was enjoying it.

Even as the others clinked glasses, sipping on crisp white wine and champagne, Antony remained at the helm, with the wind ruffling through his dark hair, a small yet unmistakable smile playing on his lips as he navigated through the waves.

Claudia tore her gaze away when one of the women handed her a drink.

"You look like you're thinking too much," the woman said, taking a sip of her wine.

Claudia let out a soft chuckle, raising her glass. "Not at all. Just... enjoying the view."

The yacht picked up speed, smoothly slicing through the waves, lifting slightly above the water's surface due to its hydrofoil. It was exhilarating—like nothing like she had ever experienced before. The open sea, the sun warming her skin, the salty breeze—it felt surreal.

After spending hours sailing, laughing, and soaking up the sun, they anchored near a secluded cove. The water below was impossibly clear, shimmering in the late afternoon light.

The crew brought out diving gear—sleek wetsuits, oxygen tanks, and masks. As everyone changed into their diving suits, Claudia felt a nervous excitement settle in her stomach. One of the crew members, walked over and began explaining the safety procedures to her—how to check the pressure gauge, signal underwater, and what to do if she felt uncomfortable. His calm, patient tone helped steady her nerves, even as adrenaline hummed beneath her skin.

Antony, now dressed in a black diving suit, walked past her and adjusted his gear. "Have you ever done this before?" he asked.

Claudia shook her head. "No, first time."

He smiled. "You'll like it."

And she did.

The moment she descended beneath the surface, an entirely new world opened up before her.

Schools of vibrant fish darted past, with their scales catching the filtered sunlight. The ocean floor was alive with coral reefs, swaying with the rhythm of the sea. A sea turtle glided gracefully, unfazed by their presence. Tiny bubbles escaped from her regulator as she took in the vast beauty of the underwater world.

She turned, spotting Antony nearby. Even underwater, he looked perfectly at ease, moving effortlessly, with his eyes scanning the marine life with quiet interest.

Claudia reached out, brushing her fingers against a passing school of fish, watching in awe as they shimmered and dispersed. The sensation was beyond anything she had imagined—peaceful, freeing, and almost meditative, as though time no longer mattered.

By the time they resurfaced and climbed back onto the yacht, the sun was beginning its descent, casting the sky in hues of gold, pink, and orange. Wrapped in plush towels, Claudia sat on the deck, feeling the warmth of the sun still lingering on her skin.

The group gathered around, sipping on warm drinks as the yacht drifted lazily across the sea.

Claudia leaned back against the cushioned seating, her damp hair tousled by the breeze. She turned her head slightly, catching sight of Antony. He was at the helm again, with his gaze fixed on the horizon, looking completely at peace.

Claudia felt something she couldn't quite explain.

She wanted this day to last forever.

* * *

By the time they had made their way back and reached the hotel, the warm evening air was carrying a soft breeze from the sea. The entrance was grand, with marble floors that reflected the golden glow of chandeliers hanging high above. A concierge stood ready at the door, offering polite smiles as the group made their way inside.

Claudia followed the others to the reception, feeling the exhaustion from the day's adventure settling into her muscles, though she didn't mind. If anything, she felt content, with the kind of tiredness that came from a day well spent.

One by one, the staff handed over the room keys to Antony's colleagues. When it was finally Claudia's turn, Antony hesitated, patting his pocket before turning toward the receptionist.

"I forgot to book a room for her," he said casually, placing his card on the counter. "Give her the best available one."

Claudia wanted to say she didn't mind sharing a room with Antony, but she worried he might misunderstand her intentions, so she decided to stay quiet.

Without another word, he booked a separate room for her. She watched as he signed the paperwork, with his posture relaxed but decisive.

Just as they were about to head toward the elevators, Antony gestured toward his colleagues, who had already started discussing their plans for the night.

"They're going clubbing tonight," he said, glancing at Claudia. "Would you like to go with them?"

Claudia looked at the group, who were laughing among themselves, and clearly already in the mood for a party. She hesitated before turning back to Antony. "What about you? What are you doing tonight?"

He rolled his shoulders slightly. "Having dinner. Then sleeping."

She thought for a second, then asked, "Can I join you?"

He didn't answer immediately, just studied her as if considering something. Then, with a small nod, he said, "Yes."

Claudia exhaled, relieved.

Antony glanced down at her before casually adding, "I'll try to get you a dress."

Without giving her a chance to respond, he turned and walked toward the concierge desk, presumably to make arrangements.

Claudia lingered for a moment before heading to her room, feeling a strange mix of anticipation and curiosity settle in her chest.

28

TRUTH IN CANDLELIGHT

Antony sat at a table near the floor-to-ceiling glass wall, separated from the sea only by the transparent pane that framed the view like a painting. The waves glistened under the moonlight, rolling in soft, rhythmic movements against the shore. The distant glow of lights from small fishing boats flickered in the distance, creating an almost dreamlike atmosphere.

When Claudia walked into the restaurant, for the first time that day, something in Antony's composed demeanor shifted.

She wore a black spaghetti-strap dress, simple yet striking, the kind of elegance that didn't need embellishment. The fabric was just flowing to carry an air of understated grace. Her hair was styled naturally, with loose strands framing her face. She wasn't just beautiful—she was captivating, even in the slight hesitation of her steps as she approached the table.

Antony watched her, his gaze steady and unreadable.

She reached the table and, just for a second, hesitated before sitting across from him.

Antony leaned back slightly, his fingers resting lightly on the edge of the table. "You look…" he paused briefly, as if considering his words. Then, with the faintest trace of a smile, he said, "Beautiful."

Claudia's lips curved into a small, amused smile. "Mr. Nobody gives compliments now?"

Antony shrugged slightly. "I just said the truth. How I felt."

Her smile lingered, but she only nodded. "Well… thank you."

The waiter approached with polished efficiency, handing them menus. Claudia opened hers, scanning the list, but it didn't take long for her to realize that she didn't recognize half of the dishes. The names were elegant, foreign—some in Italian, some in French—nothing like the casual restaurant menus she was used to.

Antony, noticing the slight crease in her brow, set his own menu down. "What do you like?" he asked simply.

She glanced up. "Seafood."

He nodded, flipping a page. "Then I'd recommend the branzino. It's grilled, simple, but done perfectly. Or if you want something richer, the seafood risotto here is excellent."

Claudia considered it for a second before nodding. "Branzino sounds good."

Antony turned to the waiter and ordered for both of them, seamlessly switching between Italian and English. The waiter gave a subtle nod of approval before jotting it down.

When it was time for drinks, Claudia asked for a cocktail, something light and fruity. Antony simply ordered sparkling water.

The moment the waiter walked away, Claudia leaned in slightly, tilting her head. "I know you said you don't drink, but… I saw you drinking that night on the bridge. Remember?"

Antony met her gaze without hesitation. "You saw me drinking Lucozade and assumed it was alcohol."

She blinked, caught off guard. "What?"

He smiled slightly. "It wasn't alcohol. It was an energy drink. You thought it was something else because the bottle was wrapped in a cover."

Claudia frowned slightly, thinking back to that night. The way he had been standing there, looking out at the water, the bottle in his hand. She had been so sure...

"It was a long day," Antony continued, his voice calm, as if explaining something simple. "I needed something to keep me going, not something that would slow me down."

Claudia leaned back in her chair, feeling a little ridiculous for having made assumptions. "Huh."

Antony raised an eyebrow. "You don't believe me?"

She shook her head, letting out a small chuckle. "No, I just... I guess I expected something different."

A brief silence settled between them, as the soft murmur of the restaurant blended with the rhythmic sound of the waves outside.

Then, before she could stop herself, Claudia asked, "But what had made you feel so drained that day?"

Antony's gaze flickered toward her, his expression unreadable—like he was silently asking, Do you really think I'm going to tell you that? But there was no hostility in it, just a quiet, amused patience.

Before he could say anything, Claudia exhaled and quickly shook her head. "I know. I should mind my own business. Sometimes I forget—you don't need to remind me." She smiled to herself, pressing her fingers against her temple. "I'm sorry. I can't help myself—I ask too many questions. I like knowing things."

Antony didn't comment, but something in his expression shifted

Just then, the waiter arrived, placing their drinks down with smooth precision before giving a polite nod and stepping away.

Claudia picked up her glass but hesitated before taking a sip. Instead, she glanced at Antony, studying him. "I believe you don't smoke either."

Antony took a sip of his water, setting the glass down before answering simply, "No, I don't."

As Claudia swirled the drink in her glass, she glanced at Antony, with lingering curiosity. "Mostly everyone I know either drinks or smokes. It's almost impossible to come across people who don't, at least socially."

Antony remained unfazed, his expression steady.

She leaned forward slightly. "So, you're saying you've never had a drink or smoked a cigarette in your life?"

He gave a small shake of his head. "I never said that. I've had alcohol twice in my life. That was enough."

Claudia raised an eyebrow. "Only twice?"

Antony nodded. "And never tried smoking."

That caught her off guard. "Not even once?"

"No."

Claudia studied him for a moment. "Okay... so at least tell me why. Why don't you drink or smoke?"

Antony didn't answer immediately. Instead, he just looked at her, calm and unreadable.

Then, instead of answering, he turned the question back to her. "Why do you drink?"

Claudia blinked. She leaned back in her chair and let out a small breath, considering the question.

"Well... I don't smoke, but drinking—" she hesitated before continuing, "It makes me feel happy. Relaxed. Sometimes, it helps me forget about things. If I'm feeling alone, or stressed... it takes the edge off. At least for a while."

Antony nodded slowly, as if weighing her words.

"Now tell me yours," Claudia prompted, tilting her head.

Antony exhaled slightly, giving a small, almost amused smile. "My answer might not be short or interesting, so we can skip it if you want."

Claudia shook her head. "No, no. You can't throw something like that out there and expect me to let it go. I want to know."

He leaned back in his chair, fingers lightly tapping against the table. "Alright," he said finally. "You said you drink because it makes you happy and relaxed."

She nodded.

Antony looked at her, his tone even. "I don't believe happiness is something you find in a drink or in another person. It has to come from inside."

Claudia tilted her head, with a skeptical expression. "That sounds nice in theory, but what does that actually mean?"

With a slight smile, he asked, "Do you remember when I told you to start running?"

She nodded. "Yeah, and I actually do run now. Every day."

"Even on the days you don't feel like it?"

Claudia hesitated. "…Yeah."

Antony gave a small nod. "And after you finish a run, how do you feel?"

She thought about it for a moment. "Accomplished. Like I did something good for myself."

He leaned forward slightly. "That feeling—that quiet sense of achievement, of strength—that's happiness from inside. It's not something given to you. It's something you built."

Claudia tapped her fingers against the table, mulling over his words.

Antony continued, his voice calm but steady. "Now, compare that feeling to how you'd feel looking at your sweaty t-shirt after a run, to how you'd feel looking at the same t-shirt after a long night of drinking."

Claudia raised an eyebrow. "That's an oddly specific example."

His expression didn't change. "One makes you feel proud of what you've done. The other…" he lifted his brows slightly, "…usually leaves you regretting it."

She scoffed, shaking her head. "That's not always true."

"No?"

"Well… okay, fine, sometimes I wake up regretting it," she admitted. "But that doesn't mean it's all bad."

Antony didn't argue, just watched her with quiet amusement.

She narrowed her eyes slightly. "You're really good at this, you know?"

"At what?"

"Making me overthink my life choices," she muttered, taking a sip of her drink.

Antony's lips twitched.

Claudia set her glass down. "Fine. But the thing is, drinking helps me relax. And running, or exercising, or whatever—it's not the same."

He tilted his head. "It's better."

She let out a short laugh. "You're unbelievable."

Antony remained unfazed. "You said alcohol helps you forget your problems, at least for a while. But the problems are still there when you sober up, aren't they?"

Claudia exhaled, looking away for a moment. "Yeah… they are."

"Then it's not a solution," Antony said simply. "It's a distraction."

She didn't respond right away, just stared at the condensation forming on her glass.

Antony leaned back again, his tone softer now. "Being alone doesn't have to be something you escape from. It can be the best time to find yourself. To create something. Like music, in your case."

Claudia looked up at him, with something shifting in her expression.

The conversation had started as a casual question, something she had thrown at him out of curiosity. But now, as she sat there, she realized she wasn't just listening—she was thinking.

Really thinking.

For once, she didn't feel the need to challenge him.

Instead, she just sat with his words, letting them settle inside her in a way she hadn't expected.

Claudia sat back for a moment. She traced the rim of her glass with her fingertip, thinking. Then she looked up.

"Is this why you told me to start running that day?" she asked, with her voice softer now. "I didn't understand it at the time."

Antony held her gaze, a knowing glint in his eyes. "I believe you do now."

Claudia exhaled, glancing down for a second before nodding slightly. She did understand—more than she had realized before.

"And I bet you felt the same," Antony continued, "when you were shooting, flying, sailing... and even scuba diving." He leaned back slightly, his tone casual but firm. "It's a different level of confidence, a different kind of satisfaction."

Claudia thought back to those moments—standing on the shooting range, gripping the yoke of the aircraft, diving beneath the surface of the sea. There had been fear, but also a quiet thrill, a sense of achievement.

She tilted her head, watching him. "Is that why you're always into sports?"

"You could say that," he admitted. "It gives me happiness. It keeps me positive about myself." He paused, then added, "But this? This is the bare minimum. The least anyone can do."

Claudia furrowed her brows slightly. "What do you mean?"

Antony met her eyes, his voice steady but certain. "I don't have a skill like you. I don't create music. But you?" He gestured subtly toward her. "You have something that most people don't."

She blinked.

"Just imagine," he continued, "creating music like you once dreamed of doing as a child. Imagine the world listening to it, celebrating it." He leaned forward slightly, his expression unwavering. "There's no feeling in the world that can compare to that."

Claudia's lips parted slightly, but no words came out. It felt so different—someone wasn't just acknowledging her talent—they were challenging her to see its worth.

Before she could respond, the waiter arrived with their food, elegantly placing the plates in front of them. The conversation naturally shifted as they started eating, but something lingered between them—an unspoken understanding, a quiet shift in how Claudia saw herself.

NOW, she wasn't just thinking about the past.

She was wondering about the future.

Claudia twirled her fork between her fingers, staring at Antony across the table. The glow of the candlelight flickered against his composed features, casting shadows across his face. He ate calmly, unbothered, as if they weren't in the middle of the kind of conversation that was leaving her mind in tangles.

Claudia hesitated for a moment, debating whether to ask what was on her mind, but then curiosity won over.

"Can I ask you something?"

Antony looked up from his plate, chewing thoughtfully before setting his knife down. "Go ahead."

Claudia exhaled, keeping her tone casual. "Why are you telling me all this?"

He didn't react.

"I mean…" she continued, tapping her fingers against the stem of her glass. "Who am I to you? Why are you spending time with me?"

For the first time that evening, Antony didn't answer immediately. Instead, he studied her, with an unreadable expression. Then, with a slight tilt of his head, he gave her a small, knowing smile.

"You think you're not worth my company?"

She let out a quiet laugh, shaking her head. "There it is. The clever answer."

Antony simply picked up his glass, taking a slow sip before responding. "It's not clever. It's a question."

Claudia sighed, leaning forward. "I don't want a riddle. I want a normal, straightforward answer—like how regular people talk."

His smirk deepened slightly. He took another bite of his food, chewing slowly, deliberately. It was clear he wasn't in a rush to answer, and for a second, she wondered if he would at all.

Just as she was about to push him again, he finally spoke.

"I'll tell you," he said simply.

Claudia narrowed her eyes. "When?"

Antony met her gaze, with his expression calm, and steady. "When it's the right time."

She tilted her head slightly, searching his face for something—anything—that would give her a clue as to what he meant. "And when will that be?"

Antony didn't waver. "Not now."

A small, frustrated laugh escaped her lips as she leaned back into her chair, crossing her arms. "You really enjoy doing this, don't you?"

He arched an eyebrow. "Doing what?"

"Giving half-answers," she said, shaking her head. "Saying just enough to make me think, but never enough to actually answer the question."

Antony took another sip of his drink. "And yet, you keep asking."

Claudia exhaled, watching him for a long moment before finally picking up her fork again.

Whatever the answer was, it was something worth waiting for

Claudia set her fork down, letting her fingers rest lightly on the edge of her plate. The conversation had taken a turn, one she hadn't entirely expected, but it felt natural—like something that had been waiting to surface.

She looked at Antony, studying him for a moment before shaking her head with a small, almost disbelieving smile.

"I've never met anyone like you," she admitted. Her voice wasn't overly sentimental, just honest. "You're... different."

Antony's gaze remained steady on her, unreadable as always, but something flickered in his eyes—just for a moment.

She hesitated before adding, "I don't want to be dramatic, and I know you're well aware of yourself, so I won't say more than that."

A quiet chuckle escaped him, low and effortless. He picked up his glass, taking a small sip before setting it down.

"I don't think I'm special," with he said, his voice calm, even. "You just haven't met anyone like me before. That's all."

Claudia exhaled, letting out a soft laugh. It was such an Antony answer—simple, and matter-of-fact, without a hint of arrogance.

She tilted her head slightly, watching him as he returned to his food, eating with the same deliberate ease with which he did everything else.

As they ate, the waiter approached their table again, this time with a polite inquiry.

"Would you like to order any dessert?" he asked smoothly, standing with practiced patience.

Antony, without a second thought, shook his head. "None for me."

Claudia glanced up briefly before turning back to the waiter. "I'm good too, thank you."

Antony's eyes flicked to her, studying her for a beat. He leaned back slightly in his chair, tilting his head. "You're not ordering because I didn't, aren't you?"

Claudia smirked at the assumption. "No," she said, shaking her head. "I genuinely don't want any."

Still, he watched her, as if deciding whether or not to believe her. After a moment, he gave a slight nod, letting it go.

As they finished their meal, Claudia took a sip of her drink and set it down, exhaling lightly. "So... what's next?"

Antony wiped his hands with the napkin, then leaned back in his chair, his expression as calm as ever. "We'll go to sleep."

She blinked. "That's it?"

A small smile pulled at the corner of his lips. "We have to wake up early."

Claudia raised an eyebrow. "For what?"

He took a sip of water before replying. "Mountain climbing. On the cliffs in Salento."

She froze mid-reach for her glass. "Mountain climbing?"

He nodded, completely unfazed.

She stared at him, unsure whether to be amused, impressed, or slightly horrified. But instead of showing any hesitation, she straightened up and nodded with confidence. "Alright."

Antony's expression didn't change, but she caught the way his eyes briefly lingered on her face, like he was reading something beyond her words.

After they finished dinner, Antony settled the bill without hesitation, his movements as seamless as ever. Then, they made their way out of the restaurant, with the warm sea breeze meeting them as they stepped outside.

Their footsteps were quiet against the marble flooring of the hallway leading to their rooms.

Just before entering his, Antony turned slightly. "Good night."

Claudia met his gaze, offering a small smile. "Good night."

She lingered in the hallway for a second longer than necessary, watching as he disappeared behind his door.

There was still so much she wanted to talk about. So much she wanted to ask.

But instead, she sighed, turned, and walked toward her own room.

29

CLIMBING INTO CLARITY

The morning breeze carried the scent of fresh pastries and brewed coffee as the six of them gathered on the hotel's terrace for breakfast. The sun was warm but not overbearing, casting a golden hue over the sea—one of those mornings that promised adventure.

Claudia sat between Antony and Sophie, slowly sipping her cappuccino.

"So... mountain climbing," she said, lazily stirring the foam.

Marco leaned forward, a playful glint in his eyes. "Yeah. You scared?"

Claudia shook her head. "Not scared. Just... excited."

Anna, sitting opposite, raised a brow. "Excited? Have you done this before?"

"No," Claudia admitted. "But I've got a feeling it's going to be fun."

James, next to Anna, grinned. "You sound like someone who actually likes challenges."

Claudia mugged like a comic book villain. "What sort of life is it if there aren't any?"

Antony, cutting into his omelette, looked at her then—his lips curling into a quiet smile. Their eyes met for a moment, something unspoken passing between them. Claudia returned the smile and gave him a subtle wink.

Sophie groaned in mock dismay. "Oh my God. Who am I sitting next to?"

Anna looked around the table. "Has anyone actually done this before?"

"Antony and I have," Marco said, reaching for his espresso. "Not here, but yeah—climbing."

Sophie suddenly paused. "Should I be worried?"

Marco smirked over the rim of his cup. "Don't worry. Just a little physical and mental torture halfway up."

Sophie blinked. "Oh great. Incredibly reassuring."

* * *

After breakfast, they packed their gear and set off. Their destination: Settore Mannuta, one of the popular climbing spots along the cliffs of Salento. The drive was scenic, winding along coastal roads where the Adriatic Sea stretched endlessly on one side, while olive groves and rolling hills lined the other.

When they arrived, Claudia stepped out of the van and craned her neck to look up at the limestone wall towering above them.

"Is this the one?" she asked, eyes wide.

Antony, already adjusting his harness, glanced over. "You'll be fine."

She gave him a dry look. "I never said I was worried."

He smiled, clearly impressed. "Noted."

Sophie clapped her on the back. "If anyone gets stuck, just scream—so we know which route not to take."

Laughter rippled through the group.

"Great. Just the supportive team I need," Anna muttered with a smirk.

As they sorted into groups, Antony and Marco opted for a steeper, more advanced climb, while Claudia, Sophie, and the others chose a more manageable path.

Antony looked over as he tightened the last strap on his harness. "You sure you don't want to join us? It's only terrifying if you look down."

Claudia hesitated, then nodded. "Okay. I'll follow you."

Sophie shot her a sideways glance. "Don't try to show off. You'll regret it."

As they began the ascent, Claudia watched Antony move up the rock face with effortless precision—fluid and controlled, like he'd done it a thousand times.

She took a deep breath, placed her hands on the rock, and focused on one movement at a time.

Halfway up, Claudia made the mistake of looking down.

"Oh. Nope. Nope, nope, nope," she muttered, squeezing her eyes shut and pressing her forehead against the stone.

From the other side of the cliff, Marco called out, "You alright over there, Claudia?"

"Not really," she shouted back. "But do I have a choice?"

"Want me to come down and help you?"

Claudia shook her head, still clinging to the rock. "No, no—thank you. I need to finish this myself."

It felt like an eternity—but probably only a few more minutes— before she finally hauled herself over the last ledge. She collapsed on the flat surface at the top, gasping and dramatically sprawled out like she'd just conquered Everest.

Antony and Marco were already there, completely unfazed, taking in the sweeping view like they were on a casual stroll.

Marco gave her a thumbs-up. "Not bad, Claudia. You survived."

Claudia sat up, brushing the hair from her face. "Survived? Please. I crushed it."

Antony glanced over, a flicker of amusement in his eyes. "How are your fingers? Hurting?"

She flexed them and winced slightly. "Yeah… but nothing I can't handle."

He smiled. "Either way, you did well."

By then, the rest of the group had reached the top. One by one, they dropped their gear and sank onto the rocky ground, catching their breath. The cliffs towered above the Adriatic, the sea below shimmering in the golden sunlight. A cool breeze drifted past, carrying the scent of salt and wild herbs from the slopes below.

A short distance away, Antony wandered toward the edge and sat down alone, his gaze fixed on the horizon. After a moment, Claudia stood and followed. She lowered herself beside him without a word.

For a while, they sat there—side by side—quiet, content, the wind in their hair and the world stretching endlessly below.

Claudia exhaled slowly, letting the stillness settle around her. "Okay," she said softly. "I'll admit… this was worth the suffering."

Antony beside her, with his arms crossed, and eyes fixed on the horizon. "I told you."

Claudia glanced at him, then back at the view. Something about this moment—the climb, the effort, the sense of accomplishment—felt different from anything she had ever experienced before.

"I think now… I can feel the happiness you were talking about. From the inside."

Antony turned slightly, his gaze landing on her. He didn't say anything, but the small knowing smile on his face told her he understood.

She continued, with her voice softer, more thoughtful. "Now, I

247

think I have an idea of what's worth living for."

Antony's expression didn't change, but there was something in his eyes—something deeper.

Claudia let out a small, breathy laugh. "You know... I never did anything like this before. Any of it. Flying, shooting, sailing, scuba diving... how was I supposed to know what I was missing?"

Antony gave a small nod. "Now you know. There's another side of life you hadn't seen before."

She nodded, staring out at the sea. "I do. But..." she hesitated, then added, "everything you do is expensive. For people like me, this kind of life isn't even an option. Don't you think that's unfair? That the rich get to experience life so differently from everyone else?"

The second the words left her mouth, she sensed a shift in Antony's demeanour.

His jaw tightened ever so slightly, and, while he kept his gaze on the sea, his silence carried weight.

After a long moment, he finally spoke. But his voice—usually so steady—was colder, more measured. "So you think rich people are just lucky to have a life like this?"

Claudia instantly picked up on the change in his tone. She could almost feel the tension in the air. But she had already said it—there was no taking it back.

She swallowed, carefully choosing her words. "I'm not saying they're just lucky. But in a way... yes. They get to live differently, experience more."

Another pause.

Then, Antony let out a quiet, humourless laugh, shaking his head slightly. When he finally spoke again, his voice was calm, but it held something undeniably sharp beneath the surface.

"When I was growing up in a foster home, I never had the luxury of love. Or family. Or even a place that felt like home. My childhood

248

wasn't colourful like yours."

Claudia stiffened slightly; she hadn't been expecting this.

"Disrespect. Rejection. Being ignored on purpose—those were my childhood friends."

She looked at him, but he didn't meet her gaze. His eyes were still on the sea, but his expression was distant, as if he were looking at something far beyond the horizon.

"But I didn't give in. I fought. I built everything I have from nothing. Do you know where I slept when I was developing my first mobile app?" He let the words hang in the air for a second before answering himself. "In Marco's old car. And I was grateful for it. Because at least I wasn't sleeping on the street."

Claudia felt a lump form in her throat. She had no idea.

The air around them felt thicker, heavier.

She didn't know what to say.

Did anything she had said before even make sense now?

Antony finally turned to look at her; his expression was cold and unreadable.

"And yet, you sit here, blaming rich people for your pain."

Claudia's breath caught in her throat.

"Tell me something—" Antony continued, in the same disturbingly calm tone. "What have you done to change your life? Other than looking for sympathy? Other than standing on that bridge, ready to jump?"

The words hit her like a punch to the stomach.

There was a silence.

She could feel her eyes burning, but she blinked fast, not letting any tears fall.

Antony didn't stop.

"You haven't done anything to make your life better. And yet you sit here, blaming people you don't even know—assuming they've had it easy, that life just handed them something." His voice stayed controlled, but there was an undeniable edge to it now. "Take responsibility, Claudia. Stop blaming others. Stop blaming circumstances. Stop acting like you had no choice."

Claudia felt her throat tighten, as the weight of his words pushed down on her.

Her fingers curled slightly on the fabric of her pants, her nails digging into her palms. She wanted to argue. To say something. But the truth was, he wasn't wrong. And that was the part that hurt the most.

She had spent so much time resenting her life, resenting what she didn't have, that she never actually thought about what she had done to change it. Or more accurately... what she hadn't done.

She swallowed hard, staring out at the sea.

Antony didn't say anything else. Instead, he simply turned back to the horizon, letting the silence linger between them.

For once, Claudia didn't break it.

Marco clapped his hands together from the back, breaking the silence. "Alright, we survived. Can we eat now?"

Sophie groaned dramatically, stretching her arms. "Yes. I need carbs—immediately. Preferably something fried and totally unhealthy."

The group laughed, but Claudia wasn't fully present. She was still processing everything Antony had said.

Her eyes stayed fixed on the horizon, her chest tight, thoughts looping in quiet chaos. *Was he right? Had she really never done anything to change her life?*

When she finally stood and turned around, Marco—still grinning—caught a glimpse of her face. His expression changed instantly.

"Claudia? What happened?"

She blinked quickly, realizing her eyes were glossy with unshed tears. She looked away, brushing it off with a shake of her head. "Nothing. Something got in my eye."

Anna stepped closer, frowning slightly. "Wait, let me see." She gently cupped Claudia's chin, leaning in to blow softly into her eye—like you would for a child with dust in their lashes.

"Better?"

Claudia forced a small smile, blinking rapidly to push back the emotion still stinging behind her eyes. "Yeah. I think it's gone."

Anna nodded, satisfied. "Good. Because I was about to rinse it out with a water bottle—and that would've been much less graceful."

The others chuckled.

Antony was the first to turn and walk away.

One by one, the group followed, heading down the trail toward the cars, already chatting about food and debating which restaurant to stop at next.

Claudia lingered for a moment, watching Antony walk ahead—silent, thoughtful.

He hadn't pushed her to say anything, hadn't demanded a reaction, and hadn't tried to soften what he had said.

And maybe that was what hit her the hardest.

He wasn't expecting her to defend herself. He had left her with a choice—to sit with the truth of his words, or to keep running from it. She swallowed hard before moving toward the cars.

Then she hesitated. For the first time since arriving, she wasn't sure if she should get into Antony's car.

But she did.

Quietly, without saying a word, she pulled the door open and slipped into the passenger seat.

The car hummed softly as Antony started the engine. For a long moment, neither of them spoke. The others were still chatting outside, finishing up their gear before getting in their own cars.

Antony didn't turn to look at her. And Claudia didn't look at him. She just sat there.

Thinking.

Feeling.

She was trying to decide whether this moment—the depth of everything she had just realized—was something she was finally ready to face. Or if she would keep pretending it wasn't there.

The hum of the car engine filled the space between them. Claudia shifted slightly in her seat, with her hands clasped together in her lap. Her throat felt tight, but she forced herself to speak.

"I'm really sorry," she said quietly, her voice uncertain. "I didn't mean to upset you. You know I don't know much about you, so I was just talking casually. Please don't be mad."

Antony's gaze stayed fixed on the road. After a moment, he said evenly, "That's exactly my point. You don't know other people's stories." He let the words sink in before adding, "I'm not angry. Just disappointed. That's all."

Somehow, that felt worse.

Claudia swallowed, and her fingers tightened around each other. "I'll own that," she admitted. "I'm sorry. It's not like I had anyone growing up to teach me things that would change my perspective. Everyone around me thought the same way, so I thought that was normal. That was my knowledge." She exhaled slowly. "I wasn't trying to be ignorant. Please... forgive me."

Antony let out a slow breath. "It was irritating," he admitted, "but now you know."

Claudia nodded. "Yeah."

A long silence stretched between them. The coastline blurred past outside, endless and golden in the fading sunlight. After a while, Claudia spoke again.

"I don't know if this is the right time to ask, but I'm still going to ask."

Antony flicked a glance in her direction, waiting.

She continued, "You know I wanted to be a musician."

Antony smiled slightly. "I thought that was just a childhood dream. Not anymore?"

"Please listen to me, I'm serious," Claudia insisted. "I want to create music, but not just any music. I don't want to copy what already exists—I want to create something special, something unforgettable. I want my music to matter." She hesitated, then asked, "How do I turn myself into that kind of person? Do you have any suggestions?"

For the first time since their argument, Antony's expression shifted. He crinkled the corner of his mouth.

"Go to India and live there for a while."

Claudia blinked, caught off guard.

Of all the answers she had expected, that wasn't one of them.

She noticed that Antony had started to relax again, and his posture was a bit less rigid. Wanting to lighten the mood further, she joked,

"Why do you want me to go to India? After a climb, do I smell like curry?"

But the second the words left her mouth, she knew she had miscalculated.

Antony's entire demeanour changed. His expression shut down. His jaw clenched, and the easy relaxation he had started to show disappeared instantly.

Claudia immediately backtracked. "I was just joking..."

Antony's voice was cold. "A joke?"

"I..." She hesitated, suddenly feeling very small. "I didn't mean it like that. I was just messing around. It wasn't serious."

His voice remained level, but there was a sharp edge to it. "I lived in India, in Kerala. For six months."

Claudia blinked, startled. "Oh."

"Not the India you see in 'Slumdog Millionaire.' Not the one the internet turns into a stereotype. The real India." He exhaled slowly, gripping the wheel a little tighter. "Do you know what I learned?"

She shook her head. "No…"

He let the silence hang before adding, "Anyway, you wouldn't understand. So why waste my time?"

A wave of guilt crashed over Claudia. "I didn't mean to offend you." She tried to lighten the mood, grasping at words. "It's just… something people say. It's like a thing on Twitter, you know?"

Antony let out a sharp breath, shaking his head slightly. His tone was controlled, measured—but firm.

"Says the same person who was exhausted from other people saying that bullying is just 'a thing.'"

Claudia froze.

Her lips parted, but nothing came out.

Antony leaned back slightly, still focused on the road. "So tell me, is the internet the reality now?"

"No, I didn't mean…"

"Because if that's the case, then based on content creators on OnlyFans, the rest of the world should assume all Western women are whores."

Claudia's eyes widened. "That's… an extreme comparison."

Antony raised an eyebrow. "Oh? But when it applies to others, it's just 'a thing.' And when it applies to you, it's suddenly extreme?"

Claudia exhaled, shaking her head. "No, I mean—calling them whores is extreme."

Antony's expression didn't change. "What would you prefer? Slut?"

Claudia's stomach twisted. "Come on, Antony. They're not that."

Antony didn't blink. "Back in the day, women who sold their bodies for money were called prostitutes. What do you call it now?"

Claudia hesitated. "I mean… I get what you're saying, but OnlyFans isn't the same as that."

Antony's voice remained eerily calm. "Then tell me—what exactly are they selling?"

Claudia fell silent.

She didn't have an answer that wouldn't prove his point. Antony continued. "At least back then, they did it in private. Now, they sell themselves for the whole world to see. Just because something is normalized doesn't make it respectable."

Claudia didn't say another word.

She turned toward the window, with her stomach churning.

She wasn't angry.

She wasn't frustrated.

She just felt exposed.

Not because of what he said. But because deep down, she knew he wasn't wrong.

The rest of the drive passed in silence.

When they arrived back at the hotel, neither of them spoke as they went their separate ways to their rooms.

* * *

Claudia lay on the bed, staring at the ceiling, with her mind still replaying the day's events. The climb, the breath-taking view, and the sharp conversation in the car—Antony's words lingered in her thoughts, both challenging and thought-provoking.

She sighed, shifting onto her side, with her fingers absently tracing the fabric of the duvet. The room was quiet, but inside her head, everything felt loud.

Then, her phone buzzed beside her. It was Antony.

She hesitated for a brief moment before answering. "Hello?"

His voice was steady, as usual. "Would you like to eat something?"

Claudia frowned slightly, caught off guard by the question. She wasn't particularly hungry, but she could tell he wasn't asking just to be polite. Still, she answered, "No, I'm fine."

There was a small pause. Then, his tone was as direct as ever: "We're leaving in an hour. Heading back home."

She sat up a little, blinking. "Already?"

"Yes. Tomorrow is Monday. You have school. I have work."

Claudia hadn't even thought about that. It had been easy to lose track of time here, to forget that normal life still existed outside of this trip.

She exhaled. "Right. That makes sense."

There was no unnecessary explanation from him, no drawn-out farewell. Just a simple statement of fact. Before she could say anything else, the call ended.

She stared at her phone for a second before tossing it onto the bed. Just like that, the trip was over.

Pushing herself off the mattress, she stretched before heading to the bathroom to freshen up. Something about this trip had shifted something in her. It wasn't just about the things she had done—it was the way she had started seeing things differently.

And whether she was ready or not, it was time to go back to reality.

* * *

By the time they reached the airport, night had settled in, and exhaustion was visible on everyone's faces. The private jet was waiting for them, and, as soon as they boarded, the quiet hum of luxury wrapped around them once again.

Dinner was served shortly after take-off, but the energy was different now. Everyone was drained from the long day—between the climb, the intense conversations, and the overwhelming beauty of the place, it felt like a trip that had lasted longer than it actually had.

After eating, most of them reclined their seats and drifted off into sleep, letting the gentle hum of the jet soothe their tired bodies. Everyone except Antony.

Claudia, nestled in her seat, glanced in his direction. He was sitting across the cabin, with his laptop open, and his fingers moving over the keyboard with quiet efficiency. His expression was calm, composed, and focused.

It was as if nothing from the trip had affected him at all.

She wanted to go over and talk to him, to clear the air somehow, but an odd sense of shame held her back. She had pushed too far—spoken too much without thinking, and assumed too much without understanding. And now, she wasn't sure how to undo that.

Instead, she remained in her seat, shifting slightly, watching him out of the corner of her eye.

He didn't even glance up.

Eventually, fatigue took over, and Claudia let herself fall asleep, though it wasn't the most restful one.

Eventually, the jet landed smoothly; the moment they stepped off, a line of luxury cars was already waiting for them. The cool night air hit Claudia's skin as she descended the stairs, still groggy from sleep.

She noticed Antony speaking to the drivers, instructing them, with his usual composed demeanor in place.

A Mercedes GLE pulled up in front of her, sleek and polished.

"Your car is ready," Antony said, turning to her with the same polite, unreadable smile he always wore.

Claudia hesitated for a second, searching his face, but there was nothing there—no lingering tension, no sign that the day's conversations had affected him in any way. He was treating her as if nothing had happened. As if none of it mattered.

257

It unsettled her.

She forced a small nod. "Thanks."

He gestured toward the car. "Get home safely."

That was it. No further conversation, no hint of anything beneath the surface.

Claudia slid into the back seat, and the door closed behind her with a soft click. As the car pulled away, she found herself glancing back through the window. Antony was already walking towards his own car, with his back straight, and movements smooth, as if it had just been another ordinary day.

As Claudia settled into the back seat of the Mercedes GLE, the soft hum of the engine filled the space around her. The leather felt cool beneath her fingertips, but her mind was anything but calm. She stared out the tinted window, watching the city lights slide past as the car moved through the quiet streets.

She had wanted to talk to him on the flight back, to say something—anything—to clear the air. But shame had kept her rooted in place.

She exhaled, running a hand through her hair.

A part of her felt stupid. She hadn't meant to offend him. She hadn't thought twice before making that joke. But the way Antony had reacted—the coldness, and the sharpness of his words—had shaken her.

And yet, he had sent her home with the same steady presence as always. No anger. No awkwardness.

This meant one thing. It was only her who felt uneasy now.

She sighed, leaning her head against the window, the cool glass grounding her.

Why was she like this?

Why did she care so much about what he thought?

Maybe it was because Antony wasn't like anyone she had met before. He wasn't someone she could predict, charm or push into reacting how she wanted.

And that unsettled her.

The car slowed as they turned into her street. The familiar sight of her house—small, warm, and simple—came into view.

The driver stopped smoothly by the curb. "Miss Claudia, we're here," he said gently.

She blinked, snapping out of her thoughts. "Oh... thanks." Reaching for her bag, she hesitated for a second.

Should she text Antony? Apologize again? Try to fix whatever it was that had shifted?

No.

Not tonight.

She sighed and stepped out of the car, into the crisp night air. The driver waited until she was inside before pulling away.

Claudia locked the door behind her, standing in the silent house for a moment.

The trip had been unforgettable. But something told her—this was just the beginning.

She exhaled, shaking her head as she made her way to her room.

Tomorrow, she'd have to return to her routine, to school, and to everything she had put on pause.

But tonight, she just needed to sleep.

And maybe—just maybe—she would wake up with some clarity.

30

RUNNING TOWARD BETTER

Claudia woke before the sun had fully risen. She laced up her running shoes and stepped outside, feeling the cool morning air hit her skin.

As she started running, with her feet hitting the pavement in rhythm, something strange happened. For the first time, she fully understood what Antony had been saying.

The feeling of achievement, the happiness that didn't come from anything external—just from her, from her own effort.

She pushed herself harder, feeling the burn in her legs, the tightening of her chest, and the sweat trickling down her back. By the time she reached home, her T-shirt was completely soaked, clinging to her body. But she felt amazing.

As she entered the house, Janet was already at the kitchen table, sipping her morning coffee. She looked up the moment Claudia walked in and smiled. "Looks like you had a good session," she said, raising an eyebrow.

Claudia, still catching her breath, managed a small smile. "Yeah... I think I did."

Janet gave her an approving nod before going back to her coffee.

Claudia made her way to her room, peeling off her drenched shirt. The shower felt refreshing, as the hot water washed away the exhaustion.

She dressed and headed out for work, but something felt... different.

Walking into the school, Claudia immediately sensed the contrast. It was nothing like the world she had lived in for the past two days. Everything felt loud, rushed, and chaotic—but not in a way that was exciting or inspiring.

Just... noisy.

People were talking over each other, students rushed through the halls, and teachers moved around with coffee cups in hand, exhausted before the day had even started.

Claudia made her way to the staff room and settled into a chair, half-listening to the conversations around her.

It wasn't that these were bad conversations. They just suddenly seemed pointless.

Someone was gossiping about a colleague's weekend. Another was talking about cleaning the house, shopping for groceries, organizing a birthday party. One of the teachers was going on about how her husband had bought her designer clothes, showing off a new handbag as if it were an achievement.

Claudia sat there, staring at them, and she felt alienated; it wasn't like the old alienation, when she had felt shunned and taken for granted. But she still felt it.

This had seemed normal.

She had enjoyed these conversations.

She had contributed to them.

Now? She just felt... bored.

She exhaled, leaning back in her chair, suddenly aware of how different she felt from the people around her.

She didn't look different. She hadn't changed on the outside.

But inside, it wasn't the same anymore.

And she couldn't unsee it.

Then, a conversation caught her attention.

A group of teachers were discussing a retirement gift for one of their colleagues.

"I think we should all chip in £20," someone suggested.

"£20? That's a bit much," another replied, shaking their head. "We already contribute for birthdays, baby showers, Christmas gifts…"

"I think £10 is enough," someone else chimed in. "It's just a gift, not a huge farewell party."

One of the teachers sighed, rubbing their temple. "Honestly, if this keeps up, I might need to pick up more hours just to be able to afford all these fundraisers."

A few laughed, but Claudia just sat there, silent. In the last two days, she hadn't heard a single conversation about money.

Not when they stayed in a luxury hotel.

Not when they went sailing.

Not when they had expensive meals.

Not when they flew on a private jet.

And it wasn't that Antony and the others didn't care about money— she wasn't naïve enough to think that. But it just wasn't a factor in their conversations. It wasn't something they debated or stressed over. They didn't act like they had endless amounts of it.

They just lived like it wasn't something that controlled them.

And now, sitting here, listening to her colleagues go back and forth over £10 or £20, it felt like she had stepped into a different world.

Not better. Not worse.

Just… different.

And for the first time, she wasn't sure where she fit anymore.

* * *

That night, Claudia lay in bed, staring at the ceiling, her thoughts tangled in her realizations of the day. The way people spoke about money at school. The way Antony and his group never even mentioned it. The contrast between these two worlds kept her mind restless.

Finally, unable to shake the thoughts, she got up and walked to the lounge, where Janet was sitting on the couch, watching television with a cup of tea in her hand.

Without a word, Claudia sat down next to her.

Janet glanced at her. "You look like someone with a lot on her mind."

Claudia hesitated for a second, then asked, "Janet, what do you think is the importance of money in a person's life?"

Janet turned to her, raising an eyebrow. "What's with the sudden question?"

Claudia shrugged, trying to sound casual. "You have more life experience than me, so I'd like to know your take on it."

Janet took a sip of her tea, considering the question. "People approach money in different ways. It depends on what you're really asking."

Claudia frowned slightly. "Different how?"

Janet leaned back against the couch. "Some people don't care about money at all. Some care about it too much. Some live with what they have and are content, while others constantly chase more. It depends on the person."

Claudia thought about that for a moment, then said, "Someone told me that money is very important for happiness. Do you agree?"

Janet let out a small chuckle. "I do. I've met plenty of people who say, 'Money can't buy happiness,' yet they spend their whole lives working for it. Funny, isn't it?" She shook her head. "The truth is, money is important—for respect, freedom, comfort, and everything in between."

Claudia tilted her head. "Freedom? But aren't we all free?"

Janet smiled. "Alright then, can you change your morning run to 11 a.m. every day instead of your usual time?"

Claudia blinked, caught off guard. "Well, no... I have to be at school."

Janet gave her a knowing look. "See? You're not as free as you think. You need money to live, which means your time isn't entirely yours."

Claudia sat back, absorbing that. She had never thought about it like that before.

Janet continued, "Look at me. With my little financial knowledge, I managed to buy four properties while I was working. Now, I have a stress-free life in my old age. If I ever need more money, I don't have to depend on anyone—not even my daughter." She paused for a moment, then smirked. "Not that she'd help me anyway."

Claudia gave her a sympathetic smile, but inside, her mind was still racing.

Janet studied her for a second before asking, "Why are you suddenly asking all this?"

Claudia hesitated, then admitted, "I grew up believing that money couldn't buy happiness. My mother used to point at a rich man who lived near us. His daughter had been sick since childhood, and she'd tell me, 'Look, he has all that money, but he's still not happy.'"

Janet exhaled, shaking her head. "That's fate, Claudia. Even if he were poor, his daughter would have had the same illness. The only difference? She got the best medical care money could buy. Now imagine if she had been born into a poor family. What could they have done for her? Pray and hope for a miracle."

Claudia stared at her, speechless. For years, she had carried that belief without ever questioning it. But in that moment, something shifted.

Everything she had thought she knew about happiness, success, and money suddenly felt wrong.

Janet watched her carefully before adding, "And one more thing, Claudia. Money allows you to be yourself. When you're financially independent, you don't have to fear expressing how you feel. You don't have to stay silent or tolerate things just because you are relying on someone else to support you."

Claudia sat with that thought for a moment. She had never looked at money that way before. She stood up, still lost in thought. As she reached the hallway leading to her room, she turned back.

"Good night, Janet."

Janet gave her a thoughtful smile. "Good night, Claudia."

With that, Claudia walked into her room, shutting the door softly behind her, with her mind still turning over everything she had just heard.

Lying in bed, she stared at the ceiling; her mind was restless. The past few days had been a whirlwind of experiences, realizations, and contrasts she couldn't ignore. Everything she had known, the world she had comfortably existed in, suddenly felt small.

As the rest of the week unfolded, that feeling only grew stronger.

She watched people go about their daily lives—conversations in the staff room, the routines, the little complaints, the predictable weekend plans. It all felt like an endless loop, a cycle she no longer wanted to be a part of.

For the first time, she saw the deeper difference between the life she had and the life she had glimpsed. It was not just in wealth, and not just in material things, but in mind-set, in possibility, and in quality.

And now, she couldn't forget that.

The dissatisfaction settled deep within her. She didn't just want small changes—she wanted out—out of the life she had built, and out of the limitations she had unthinkingly accepted.

She wanted more. More than routines, more than survival, more than just "getting through" life. She had felt what it was like to truly live, and nothing else seemed enough anymore.

And then there was Antony.

She thought about him every day—his presence, his way of thinking, the way he carried himself like he had already unlocked the secrets of life. She wasn't sure what this feeling was, but she knew she missed him.

It wasn't about grand gestures or dramatic emotions—she just wanted to be around him again, to listen, and to see what new experiences would unfold in his presence.

But she hesitated to call.

She told herself he was busy, that Friday would be soon enough. Still, every night, she checked her phone, half-expecting a message from him.

And every night, when there was nothing, she told herself to wait just a little longer.

* * *

Friday felt endless. Claudia found herself checking her phone every few minutes, hoping—expecting—to see a message from Antony. But each time she looked, the screen remained blank. No notifications. No missed calls.

At school, she was barely present. Conversations blurred around her, lessons felt like background noise. Her mind was completely elsewhere. By the time she got home, the anticipation had turned into anxiety.

That night, sitting in her room, she couldn't contain the emotions churning inside her any longer. She hated this uncertainty. Had she ruined everything with Antony? Was he really upset with her? She stared at her phone, debating whether to call. She picked it up, then set it down. Then picked it up again.

Her heart pounded as she opened WhatsApp and hovered over his name.

What if he ignores me?

What if he doesn't want to see me again?

She exhaled sharply and started practicing.

"Hey, I just wanted to say I'm sorry."

"I know what I said was wrong, and I regret it."

"I just... I want to see you."

She tried different variations, speaking them out loud, trying to sound casual, and to sound sincere. But no matter how she said it, she felt ridiculous.

By 8 p.m., the fear of him not calling, or not responding at all, became unbearable. Her hands were clammy as she tapped his name and hit the call button.

The phone rang.

Once.

Twice.

Three times.

She swallowed, gripping the phone tighter.

Then—click. "Hello," Antony's voice came through, calm as always.

Claudia felt her breath hitch. She had spent so much time preparing, but now, hearing his voice, her mind went blank. "I..." she stammered. Then, quickly, "I know you might be angry with me because of what happened, but I just wanted to say I'm sorry... and I'd really like to meet you again."

There was a brief pause on the other end. Then Antony said, "I'm not angry with you."

Claudia blinked. "You're not?"

"No. You said what you knew, and I corrected you. That's it. There was nothing wrong with it."

Her grip on the phone tightened. "So... you're really not upset with me?"

Antony sounded almost amused. "Why should I be?" Relief flooded her. She hadn't realized just how much she needed to hear those words until now.

"So..." she hesitated. "I know you don't owe me anything, but still... can I meet you this weekend?"

There was a pause before Antony responded, "I'm not in the UK at the moment."

Claudia frowned slightly, caught off guard. "Oh. Where are you?"

"I'll be back in a week. We'll meet when I return."

In the background, she heard the faint hum of voices—people speaking in Arabic. It sounded like he was in the Middle East.

Claudia didn't know why, but something about that made her feel relieved. Maybe it was just knowing he wasn't avoiding her. Maybe it was because, despite the distance, he had still picked up her call. A small smile formed on her lips.

"Okay," she said softly. "I'll wait."

The moment Claudia ended the call, something inside her shifted. The weight that had been pressing down on her all week suddenly lifted. The uncertainty, and the self-doubt—it was all gone.

She felt alive.

Without thinking, she walked over to her piano, lifted the lid, and placed her fingers on the keys. A smile tugged at her lips as she began to play, with her emotions spilling into the melody. Unlike before, she wasn't playing out of frustration or sadness. This time, it was pure joy. The notes flowed effortlessly, echoing through the room. She wasn't lost in overthinking, in wondering where she stood in Antony's world. She wasn't dwelling on what had been said, or what could go wrong.

She just felt good. That feeling carried through the rest of the week. She wasn't lost in her routine anymore. Instead, she felt like she was moving toward something.

Claudia started seeing things differently. She stopped worrying about what others thought of her. She stopped giving energy to meaningless conversations and distractions.

Instead, she started focusing on her life.

How to change it.

How to build it.

How to get out of the life she had settled into.

She thought about it while running—feeling the power in her own legs, and the way her body responded when she pushed herself.

She thought about it at school—realizing how little the conversations around her mattered, and how people spent their time stuck in cycles they didn't even notice.

She thought about it at home—seeing how much of life was dictated by habits, expectations, and limitations people placed on themselves.

For the first time ever, she was truly investing in herself. And it felt good.

Everything around her continued as usual—people still gossiped, and still worried about things that didn't matter. But it didn't bother her anymore.

Because she was walking toward something better.

The Unexpected Invitation

The weeks flew by so fast that Claudia barely realized it was Friday again.

Sitting in the staff room, she kept checking her phone, hoping for a text or call from Antony. She tried to stay focused on the conversations around her, but nothing could hold her attention. Then, finally—her phone rang.

She grabbed it quickly, and saw the name flashing on the screen. It was Luca. She exhaled, slightly disappointed, but picked up anyway. "Hello?"

"Hey," Luca's voice came through the speaker. "So… last time, you bailed on us. Are you coming this time?" Claudia sighed, already knowing where this was going. "No, I can't."

"Come on," Luca insisted. "Don't worry about the money. I got paid, so you don't have to cover anything."

"It's not about that," she said quickly. "I just have plans."

Before Luca could say anything else, another call beeped in.

Antony.

Claudia sat up straighter, suddenly more alert. "I'll call you later, Luca." She didn't wait for his response before switching to the other call.

"Hello?"

"Are you busy?" Antony's voice came through, calm as always.

"No, just on my break," she said, suddenly feeling more awake. "Tell me—how are you? When did you get back?"

"I'm good. I got back on Wednesday."

Claudia froze.

Wednesday?

She frowned slightly, feeling a strange twinge of disappointment. "Wednesday? And you didn't call me?"

There was a brief silence before Antony spoke again—this time, with amusement laced in his tone. "What do you mean?"

"I mean…" Claudia hesitated, suddenly realizing how needy that sounded. "You said when you came back, you'd call me."

He let out a soft chuckle before replying. "Yeah… I came back. And now I'm calling you."

Claudia pressed her lips together, at a loss for words.

There was a brief pause before Antony continued. "So… tomorrow morning, we're planning a trip to Peak District for hiking. We'll stay in tents overnight."

Claudia blinked, caught off guard by the invitation.

"Would you like to join us?"

Her heart skipped a beat—not just because of the trip, but because he had said we. Which meant she'd be spending the weekend with him.

"Yes," she said without hesitation. "I'd love to."

"Great," Antony said. "I'll send you the details later."

Before she could say anything else, he ended the call.

Claudia stared at her phone, with a slow smile creeping onto her lips.

A few moments later, her phone buzzed with a new message.

She picked it up, with heart still beating a little faster .

Antony: Don't worry about the tent. I got you. Be ready by 6:30 am.

Claudia smiled at the screen, reading the message twice. It wasn't long or overly detailed, but it was so Antony—straight to the point, no unnecessary words, yet thoughtful in his own way.

* * *

31

THE SPACE BETWEEN US

A t 6:30 am sharp, Claudia heard the familiar rumble of the Ferrari's engine pulling up outside. She stepped out, dressed in comfortable hiking gear, with her backpack slung over one shoulder. The passenger window rolled down, and Sophie leaned out with a sleepy grin.

"Morning," she murmured, her voice still groggy. "Ready for the adventure?"

"Not sure if I'm ready, but I'm here."

Sophie reached over and pushed the door open for her, and Claudia slid into the back seat beside her. Marco was already in the front passenger seat, chatting casually with Antony.

As the car pulled away, the city lights faded behind them, giving way to the open road. The sky was still a soft shade of blue-gray, with the first hints of sunlight stretching across the horizon.

The interior of the Ferrari was warm compared to the crisp morning air outside. Claudia adjusted her sleeves, pulling them over her fingers, feeling the cold still lingering on her skin.

Sophie, sitting beside her, let out a quiet sigh and shifted in her seat, wrapping her arms around herself for warmth. "Wake me up when we get there," she mumbled, already closing her eyes and resting her head against the window.

Claudia chuckled lightly, watching as Sophie curled up, and her breathing evened out.

Up front, Marco and Antony were speaking in a low, easy tone, their voices blending with the soft music playing through the car's speakers. It was some kind of chill instrumental playlist, not overpowering, just enough to fill the quiet gaps.

Antony, as usual, drove with calm precision, with one hand resting lightly on the steering wheel. He seemed completely at ease, navigating the open road, as if he had done this 1,000 times before.

"Did you sleep well?" Marco asked, turning slightly in his seat to glance at Claudia.

Claudia stretched slightly, leaning her head back against the seat. "Yeah... well, kind of. You know when you wake up every hour because you're scared you'll oversleep?"

Marco laughed. "Oh, definitely. Every time we have an early start, I feel like my alarm is judging me."

Antony, eyes still on the road, smirked. "That's because you set 15 alarms and ignore the first 14."

Claudia chuckled at that, watching as Marco rolled his eyes dramatically.

"Hey, those alarms are strategically planned," Marco defended. "They work."

Antony raised an eyebrow but didn't argue.

Claudia, meanwhile, turned her attention to the passing scenery.

Outside, the landscape slowly transformed, from quiet residential streets to long stretches of countryside. The rising sun cast golden streaks across the sky, illuminating the rolling fields and early morning mist lingering over the hills. It was beautiful.

She pressed her forehead lightly against the window, watching as the road stretched ahead, disappearing into the morning light.

She could hear Marco still chatting with Antony, throwing in the occasional joke or comment.

But her thoughts kept drifting to the front seat.

She missed being beside Antony—hearing the subtle shifts in his voice, watching his hands on the wheel, catching the occasional side glance when he spoke to her. It wasn't something she could explain, and she wasn't sure why it even bothered her. But she felt the distance more than she expected.

Of course, she didn't say a word.

Instead, she forced herself to enjoy the ride, pushing the thought away as they continued toward Peak District.

* * *

By 10 am, they had arrived at Ashbourne-Ilam, the group took a short break, enjoying breakfast at a cozy countryside café. The smell of fresh coffee filled the air, mixing with the crisp morning breeze.

The hike began easily enough, with the cool air refreshing as they walked through winding trails. The early morning mist still clung to the valleys, and the earthy scent of damp soil and wildflowers made the whole experience feel like as if nature had composed it just for her

As they climbed higher, the hills stretched ever further before them, rolling green against the sky. The group's chatter and light-hearted banter filled the quiet spaces, making the uphill trek seem less strenuous than it actually was.

Even though Claudia was having fun, she couldn't shake the feeling that she was missing something—or someone.

She missed the private moments she had often had with Antony, the way he gave her his full attention when they talked. But with Marco and Sophie around, those moments felt fewer and farther between.

Not that she let it show. Instead, she laughed along with them, letting herself enjoy the camaraderie.

At some point, Antony casually mentioned, "Shall we cook our food ourselves at the camp tonight?"

Marco raised an eyebrow. "Who's gonna be the chef?"

Antony glanced at Sophie with an amused look.

Sophie scoffed. "Don't look at me—I left my chef hat at home. No hat, no cooking."

Claudia smirked. "I'm not much of a cook either. What about you?"

Antony's lips twitched. "I guess you'll find out tonight."

Sophie rubbed her hands together, grinning. "This is either going to be great... or a disaster. Either way, it'll be fun."

The group laughed, continuing their hike as the terrain grew steeper.

As they reached a particularly steep incline, Claudia sighed dramatically and leaned against Antony, resting her full weight on him.

"I'm tired," she announced, tilting her head against his shoulder. "Please carry me."

Antony didn't move.

He simply stood there, letting her lean against him while a small, knowing smile played on his lips.

"You're not that tired," he murmured, amusement lacing his voice.

Claudia peeked up at him. "You don't know that."

Antony smirked. "I do."

Marco, overhearing, chuckled. "Nice try, Claudia. If you get carried, I'm next in line."

Sophie snorted. "Yeah, keep dreaming."

Claudia rolled her eyes playfully before pushing herself upright again. The warmth from where she had leaned against Antony lingered, but she brushed the thought away and continued walking.

As they made their way up the hill, Sophie glanced over at Claudia. "Ever slept in a tent before?" she asked.

Claudia shook her head. "Nope. Never."

Marco grinned. "Then you're in for a fun night."

Almost absent-mindedly, Claudia murmured, "I'm kind of scared of sleeping alone in a tent."

Sophie's eyes immediately lit up. "Oh?" She smirked. "So you'd be comfortable sharing with... someone else?"

She didn't say the name, but she didn't have to—her pointed glance in Antony's direction said enough.

Claudia let out a laugh, shaking her head. "I didn't mean it like that."

Sophie wasn't convinced. "I've been watching you," she said with a teasing grin.

Claudia raised an eyebrow. "Watching me?"

Sophie folded her arms, looking entirely too pleased with herself. "You're trying. Hard."

Claudia scoffed. "Trying what?"

Sophie folded her arms, smirking. "Let me save you some time—so many girls have tried, but failed. You're just going to be another name on the list."

Claudia forced a laugh. "Wow, thanks for the encouragement."

Marco, shaking his head with a grin, added, "He only dates women from rich families anyway—less chance of them being gold diggers."

Then, he laughed at his own comment.

Claudia grinned, pretending to be unbothered. "Good to know. I'll make sure to include my bank statements on my next date application."

The group burst into laughter; even Antony smiled at her response.

But as the laughter around her faded, Claudia found herself caught in her own thoughts.

Marco's words lingered, sinking deeper than she wanted to admit.

"He only dates women from rich families anyway—less chance of them being gold diggers." She replayed the statement over and over in her head.

Was he right?

Her gaze flickered toward Antony, watching as he walked ahead, with his posture relaxed, and his movements effortless. He felt like a world apart from her.

It was not just because of money, but because of everything—the way he carried himself, the way he thought, and the way he lived.

"Look at him. Look at me. We don't even match in any dimension." A small, unsettling feeling crept into her chest. She had been avoiding this question for a while, but now, she couldn't push it away any longer.

"Do I love him?"

The thought startled her.

She wasn't sure what she felt, but she knew that Antony's presence had changed something in her. She wanted to be better—not for him, but because of him. But even if she did feel something deeper for him...

"What about Antony? What does he think of me?"

Marco's words echoed again.

"What quality do I have—why would I be with him?"

For the first time, Claudia felt small—not because of who she was, but because of who she wasn't. The weight of those thoughts sat heavy in her chest, but she kept walking, pretending nothing was wrong.

No one could see the storm inside her.

Not even Antony.

By 2 pm, the group arrived at the site where they had planned to camp for the night. The open landscape stretched before them, with the green hills blending seamlessly into the horizon. The afternoon sun cast a warm glow, and a soft breeze rustled through the trees, making the place feel peaceful—almost untouched.

They dropped their backpacks and took a moment to soak in the view. Marco, always prepared, pulled out snacks from his bag and passed it around. Everyone settled in, eating as they admired the vast beauty of their surroundings.

After a few bites, Claudia got up and walked over to where Antony was sitting. Without a word, she sank down beside him, holding out her water bottle. "Do you want some?" she asked.

Antony had his own bottle sitting right next to him, but without hesitation, he reached for hers instead. "Thanks," he said, taking a sip.

Across from them, Marco and Sophie exchanged a knowing glance, sharing a small, amused smile before continuing their meal.

Claudia hesitated for a moment before speaking. "Can I ask you something?"

Antony wiped his fingers on a napkin and glanced at her. "Go ahead."

She shifted slightly, looking out over the hills. "Music is the only thing I know. I teach it at school, but I was thinking... maybe I could start something on YouTube too—teaching instruments, breaking down techniques, that sort of thing. What do you think?"

Antony looked at her thoughtfully before replying. "At least you're starting somewhere. That's a good idea."

Claudia nodded. "I know there are already a lot of channels teaching music, but I still feel like I should start somewhere."

Antony leaned back slightly, with a calm expression. "It doesn't matter how many people are already doing it. What matters is whether people feel your channel is worth their time. If you can make them feel that, you'll be successful."

Claudia smiled, taking in his words. "I was also thinking about not showing my face in the videos."

Antony nodded. "That's fine. Your content is what matters. If it's good, people will follow."

Claudia let out a small breath. "But I don't want to just be a YouTuber. I want to be a musician. You told me last time I should go to India, but I ruined the moment, and you never told me why."

Antony was silent for a second, then said, "Explaining what India has to offer won't make a difference. You have to go and experience it."

Claudia frowned slightly. "Why India, though?"

Antony reached into his bag, searching for something as he continued speaking. "If you do go, don't go with a judgmental mind-set. Try to get to know the real people, not just the ones catering to tourists."

Claudia thought for a moment. "So, you're suggesting Kerala?"

Antony nodded. "I've only been to Kerala and Tamil Nadu. But Kerala is a good place to start."

Claudia absorbed his words, rolling them over in her mind. But before she could ask anything else, Antony suddenly stood up. His expression had shifted—his usual composed demeanor now replaced with something unreadable.

He walked over to Marco. "I think we need to cancel the overnight stay."

Everyone stopped eating. Sophie and Marco exchanged a confused glance.

"What?" Marco asked, his brows furrowing.

Antony sighed, rubbing the back of his neck. "I forgot—I have something important to do before I leave tomorrow."

Claudia frowned. "Wait... we're leaving? Now?"

Marco gave Antony a skeptical look. "You serious?"

Antony's tone was calm but firm. "Before I travel, I was supposed to take care of something. I completely forgot, and I don't have a choice. I need to handle it before I go."

Sophie folded her arms. "Are you sure we can't stay? I mean, we have everything set up."

Antony nodded. "I'm sure."

Marco let out a sigh and shook his head, clearly not thrilled but not arguing either. "Fine."

Claudia still felt thrown off. "Wait, travel? Where are you going?"

Antony glanced at her. "I leave for the U.S. tomorrow at 3 pm. I'll be gone for three weeks."

Three weeks.

Claudia felt the words sink in.

Antony continued, "We're selling one of our apps to a U.S.-based company, so I need to be there."

Claudia nodded slowly, not knowing what to say.

He turned back to the group. "I'm really sorry for the inconvenience, but we need to start heading back."

With that, everyone began gathering their things, the excitement from earlier fading into a quiet acceptance.

As they started the descent, Claudia couldn't stop thinking that three weeks felt like a long time. She also couldn't help but notice how quickly everyone else had moved on from the sudden change of plans. The initial surprise had faded, and now, apart from her, everyone seemed relaxed.

Sophie was already joking with Marco, and Antony walked ahead, seemingly unfazed by the shift in plans.

By contrast, Claudia still felt that slight sting of disappointment.

She had looked forward to staying overnight, to spending more time here... to spending more time with him.

As if sensing her mood, Marco turned around, catching the look on her face.

With an easy grin, he said, "Don't waste your time sulking over a disappointment. We're all still here together—that's what matters. The place isn't going anywhere. We can always come back."

Claudia blinked, then let out a small, reluctant smile.

He was right. She was too caught up in what didn't happen instead of just enjoying what was still happening. As they continued down the trail, the mood lightened again.

Jokes were exchanged, laughter filled the air, and just like that, the group was back to normal.

Even Claudia found herself letting go, and laughing along. Yet, in the back of her mind, one thought lingered—

Why are they so different from me?

Why is it so easy for them to adapt, to move forward without dwelling?

And more than that...

Why did she feel like she wanted to be more like them?

* * *

By the time they reached the car around 3:30 PM, Antony stretched his arm out, casually tossing his car keys to Marco.

"I don't feel like driving," he said simply.

Marco caught the keys with a grin. "Guess I'm the chauffeur today," he said before sliding into the driver's seat.

Sophie, Claudia, and Antony got into the car. The drive started off light-hearted, with music playing softly in the background.

Claudia, Sophie, and Marco were chatting and laughing, reminiscing about the hike, and throwing playful jabs at each other.

However, Antony was quiet. He wasn't asleep, nor did he seem tired—he just seemed to be somewhere else entirely. His gaze was fixed out the window, his fingers absently tapping against his knee.

Claudia kept stealing glances at him. It wasn't like him to zone out this much.

It wasn't until the sky darkened, and the car naturally fell into a more peaceful silence, that she finally asked,

"Are you okay? You look... different."

Antony blinked, as if he had just been pulled back into the present. He exhaled through his nose. "I'm fine," he said. Then, with a small, apologetic glance at her, he added, "I'm just... working in my mind."

Claudia frowned slightly. Working in his mind?

Before she could ask what that meant, Marco let out a knowing chuckle.

"Oh, Claudia," he sighed, shaking his head. "You have no idea how bad it gets when he's in work mode."

Sophie nodded in agreement. "I suggest staying away from him," she added, half-joking.

Claudia looked between them. "Why?"

Marco smirked. "You know why I'm flying out in a week?"

Claudia raised an eyebrow. "Why?"

Marco stretched his arms. "Because when he's like this, you don't want to be anywhere near him."

Sophie laughed. "Yeah, trust me, he turns into a different person. I mean, you think he's intense now? Just wait."

Claudia turned to Antony, expecting him to deny it, but instead, he just let out a low sigh.

"Guys," he muttered, rubbing his temple, "just let me think."

Sophie snickered. "See?"

Marco chuckled, shaking his head as he focused on the road.

Claudia, meanwhile, sat back, watching Antony. She had seen different sides of him, but this one was new. And she wasn't sure whether it intrigued her... or unnerved her.

The rest of the drive continued in silence, with the city lights glowing in the distance as they headed towards Antony's home.

At around 7:30 pm, they finally pulled into Antony's driveway in Kent. As the car slowed to a stop, Antony glanced at the time and turned to Claudia.

"I know you're tired," he said, his voice calm as always. "So you have two choices—one, you can wait half an hour, and I'll arrange for someone to take you home. Or two, you can stay here and leave tomorrow."

The moment those words left his mouth, Claudia felt a rush of happiness. She tried to hide her excitement, but Sophie caught it immediately. Without saying a word, she gave Claudia a knowing look, raising an eyebrow that silently screamed: You did it, girl.

Claudia fought the urge to roll her eyes.

Meanwhile, Marco handed Antony back his car keys before casually walking over to his own Bentley Bentayga. Without much fuss, he got in, started the engine, and drove away.

Sophie, still smirking, tossed her bag into her Jaguar F-Pace and called out, "Don't have too much fun, Claudia," before pulling out of the driveway.

Claudia shook her head, watching her go.

32

BETWEEN US

N ow that they were alone, Claudia finally took in her surroundings.

The house was huge—a mansion, but not the modern glass-and-marble kind she had expected. From the outside, it had an old-world charm, surrounded by a well-maintained garden, the kind of place that spoke of history rather than just wealth.

As they stepped inside, however, it was a different story.

The moment the doors closed behind them, the house lit up automatically, with subtle ambient lighting illuminating the sleek, technology-driven interior.

Everything was automated. The temperature adjusted on its own. The lights dimmed just right. A faint, clean scent filled the air, like expensive wood and fresh linen. Claudia barely had time to take it all in before Antony gestured toward the lounge area.

"Please sit down," he said, in a neutral tone. "I'll be back."

And just like that, he disappeared deeper into the house.

Claudia lowered herself into one of the plush lounge chairs, sinking into the comfort as she took a deep breath and looked around. The room was a perfect mix of minimalism and warmth—elegant but not overly flashy.

But what really caught her eye were the pictures.

Lining one side of the room were framed photographs—some casual, and some clearly taken at high-profile events.

Famous faces.

Actors. Musicians. CEOs.

People she had only seen on TV and in magazines.

And then...

Her eyes landed on a particular photo frame.

It held two pictures side by side.

The first one was an old photo—a young Antony, maybe seven or eight years old, standing next to a man who was smiling at the camera.

The second was the same, as though they had recreated it recently.

Antony—now grown—stood in the exact same position. And the man was also there—older now, but wearing the same smile.

Claudia leaned in slightly, with curiosity stirring in her chest.

Who is that man?

And more importantly, why had Antony chosen to recreate that exact moment.

An Unexpected Moment

When Antony returned to the lounge, Claudia noticed he looked more relaxed, as if whatever had been unsettling him earlier had faded away. He approached her with a calm smile.

"Feeling more comfortable now?" he asked, his voice gentle again.

Claudia returned the smile. "Yeah. Your house...it suits you."

He tilted his head slightly, intrigued. "How's that?"

She glanced around, smiling softly. "The more you get to know it, the more interesting it becomes—and the more you feel like making it your own."

Antony's lips curled up at the edges. "Interesting observation."

He gestured down the hallway. "Come, let me show you your room."

As Claudia followed Antony through the quiet corridor, she took in every detail—the soft lighting that illuminated their path as they walked, the subtle scent of cedar and something else uniquely comforting that lingered in the air. It felt strangely calming, and familiar despite its luxurious elegance.

When they reached the guest room, Antony opened the door, stepping aside so she could enter. The room was spacious, warmly lit, and tastefully decorated, matching Antony's sophisticated simplicity.

He pointed out everything casually: the neatly made bed, the small desk, and the closet. He moved toward the bathroom, stopping at the doorway as he continued explaining the facilities.

Claudia listened, but her thoughts were elsewhere. Her heart beat faster as she watched him standing there, so close yet somehow distant. She could feel her pulse quicken, and emotions bubbling up within her, impossible to contain.

As Antony finished explaining something about the bathroom, Claudia took a step closer. The words faded from her mind as she watched him.

He paused, noticing the shift in her expression. "Are you alright?"

She didn't answer right away. Instead, she stepped even closer, hesitating for only a moment before gently placing her hands around his neck.

Antony went still.

"I don't know how you see me," Claudia said softly, her voice barely above a whisper. She rose slightly onto her toes, bringing her face closer to his. "But—"

She leaned in, heart racing, feeling the warmth radiating off his skin. She could sense him tensing under her touch, but she kept moving forward, desperately hoping he felt what she was feeling.

Just before their lips could meet, Antony firmly grasped her shoulders and gently pushed her away.

"Not now—I can't... I am sorry ," he said quietly; his voice was controlled but strained. Without another word, he turned and walked swiftly out of the room, leaving Claudia standing alone, with her heart hammering in her chest.

For a moment, Claudia stood frozen, staring at the empty space where he had just been.

What had she done?

She stood there alone, with heat rising to her cheeks. Her stomach twisted painfully with embarrassment as Antony's words echoed clearly in her head:

"Please don't invest your emotions in me."

She closed her eyes briefly, mortified. How could she have forgotten that lesson so easily?

Marco's comment earlier in the day also replayed in her mind: "He only dates women from rich families anyway."

How could she have been foolish enough to assume things would be different for her?

Shame filled her chest, heavy and suffocating. She felt exposed and foolish. Unable to bear the embarrassment any longer, Claudia hurriedly grabbed her belongings. Without another thought, she quickly gathered her things—her jacket, her phone, and bag—and quietly left the room.

She walked down the hallway, not daring to look back. Her footsteps echoed softly against the polished floor, and she slipped out of the front door without looking behind.

The cold night air hit her immediately, but it was nothing compared to the icy feeling in her heart. Pulling her coat tightly around herself, Claudia hurried down the driveway, with the gravel crunching sharply beneath her boots.

Inside the house, Antony emerged from his room a few minutes later. His face was fresh, his hair damp from a recent face wash. He glanced around casually at first, but quickly noticed the eerie silence. He frowned, calling softly, "Claudia?"

There was no response.

He stepped toward her room, pushing the door open wider. It was empty. Claudia's belongings were gone.

Something unreadable flickered across his face—a mixture of confusion and concern.

He quickly headed toward the front door, opening it to see only the dark, empty driveway stretching ahead of him.

She was already gone.

As Antony dialed Claudia's number, the soft ringing tone echoed quietly in his ear. He paced slowly around the living room, with one hand tucked into his pocket, waiting for her to pick up.

But the call went unanswered.

He paused, glancing down at his phone. For the first time in a long time, a small crease of worry formed on his brow.

Meanwhile, Claudia was sitting in the back seat of an Uber, with her gaze fixed on the illuminated screen. Antony's name flashed silently on her phone, but she couldn't bring herself to answer it. Her thumb hovered shakily over the screen, her vision blurring slightly with unshed tears.

She felt humiliated, and embarrassed at her impulsive attempt. Her cheeks burned as the scene replayed in her mind—the way he had gently but firmly pushed her away. Claudia leaned her head against the window, with tears finally slipping down her cheeks. The phone kept buzzing softly in her hand, lighting up the dark interior of the car. She drew a shaky breath, pressing her forehead against the cool glass.

After several long moments, the ringing stopped.

Silence.

She stared at the screen, Antony's name lingering for a second longer before fading into darkness.

Closing her eyes, Claudia took a deep breath, with the phone still clutched tightly in her trembling fingers.

Claudia was leaning back against the headrest as the car pulled up in front of her house. Her eyes felt swollen and raw from crying, and exhaustion had settled heavily into her body. She stepped out silently, barely registering the driver's polite "good night" as she walked slowly toward the front door.

Inside, the house was quiet and dimly lit, with only the soft glow of a distant lamp illuminating the hallway. Claudia moved through the silence and went into her room, shutting the door softly behind her. She slumped onto her bed, staring blankly at the ceiling for a long moment before pulling out her phone again.

Her heart tightened as she saw several missed calls from Antony, each one like a gentle knock at a door she wasn't ready to open. The screen blurred as fresh tears welled up, but she quickly wiped them away.

Claudia stared at her phone screen, with her fingers trembling slightly as she typed out the message. She took a shaky breath, rereading her words before hitting Send.

"I'm really sorry about earlier. I don't know what got into me. I didn't mean to ruin things. Please forgive me. Thanks for everything. Goodnight."

The small blue checkmarks, indicating he had read it appeared immediately. Claudia stared at the screen for a long moment, with her heart pounding painfully in her chest, waiting for a response. But none came.

She put the phone down again, rolled over and pulled the covers tighter around her. The silence in the room felt louder than usual, echoing her discomfort and embarrassment.

Eventually, sleep came—but it was restless, and filled with uncertainty about what the next day might bring.

* * *

33

THE WOMAN I'VE BECOME

The next morning, Claudia woke up late, with her body heavy, and mind clouded with memories of the night before. She lay still for a long moment, staring blankly at the ceiling, feeling both embarrassment and exhaustion pulling at her. Taking a deep breath, she finally reached for her phone. But Antony hadn't replied. Not even a single word. Her heart sank a little more, even though she'd expected it.

She sat up slowly, feeling drained. Needing to break the suffocating silence around her, she dialed Luca's number, biting her lip nervously as she waited.

Luca picked up after a few rings, sounding distracted. "Hello?"

"Hey, Luca," Claudia began quietly, trying to sound casual. "Are you still going out today?"

There was a pause, and some muffled voices in the background, then Luca answered, "Yeah, we're just about ready to leave."

Claudia hesitated. "Would it be okay if I join you?"

Another brief silence, then Luca cleared his throat. "Rosie's coming with us today, so if you're okay with that, then sure, you can join."

Claudia's heart sank slightly at the mention of Rosie. After a moment, she forced herself to say, "Oh... actually, never mind. Maybe another time."

"Okay," Luca replied, sounding a bit confused. "Next time, then."

She hung up, feeling a fresh wave of disappointment wash over her. Pushing the covers aside, Claudia slowly got out of bed and stepped toward the kitchen, deciding she needed coffee to clear her mind.

As she entered, Janet glanced up from the sofa, with fresh coffee in hand; she looked as if she had been awake for hours. Her eyes immediately took in Claudia's tired expression.

"Are you alright?" she asked gently.

Claudia gave a weak smile. "Just tired."

Janet didn't look convinced but didn't push further. Instead, she took a sip of coffee and said, "I thought I'd go shopping this afternoon. Maybe grab some lunch in town. Want to join?"

Claudia hesitated, then nodded gratefully. "Yes, actually—I'd like that."

"Good," Janet said warmly. "It'll do you good to get out of the house."

Claudia nodded, grateful for the distraction, and headed to the bathroom for a much-needed hot shower, hoping the day would offer her a chance to clear her head.

* * *

Claudia and Janet wandered through the high street, the afternoon sun warm against their backs. The air carried the subtle scent of freshly brewed coffee and baked pastries from the cafés lining the street. Claudia felt lighter, as her thoughts were momentarily distracted by Janet's easy conversation about what they should have for lunch.

As they neared the bank, Janet slowed her pace.

"I need to stop in here for a moment," she said, nodding toward the entrance.

Claudia raised an eyebrow, amused. "Why do you still go into the bank? You know you can do everything on your phone now, right?"

Janet let out a soft chuckle, waving a dismissive hand. "You know me, love. Older generation. These new online things just complicate everything. The bank feels easier."

Claudia smiled. "Right. Because standing in a queue is way simpler."

Janet laughed, shaking her head. "Go on, then. Wait in that café over there. I won't be long."

Claudia nodded and headed toward the café across the street. She stepped inside, ordered a coffee, and settled by a window, watching the people pass by as she waited for Janet. The café was quiet, with the gentle hum of conversation blending with the soft clinking of cups.

Just as she was starting to relax, a chair scraped across the floor, pulled out abruptly in front of her. Before she could look up, someone slid into the seat opposite her.

Andrew.

He leaned back casually, with a smile, as if nothing had ever changed between them.

"Hi, Claudia."

Her posture stiffened slightly, but she remained composed. "Andrew?"

His gaze swept over her, lingering for a moment. "You look… different."

Claudia arched an eyebrow. "Do I? Not that I asked."

He let out a short laugh. "Relax. I just wanted to talk."

She exhaled through her nose, unimpressed. "About what?"

Andrew hesitated for a moment before leaning forward slightly. "About us."

Claudia barely suppressed an eye-roll. "There is no 'us' anymore, Andrew."

He tilted his head, smirking. "Come on. You're still holding onto that? I know you missed me."

Claudia blinked, then let out a quiet laugh. "No, Andrew. I really didn't." She reached for her phone and stood up, shaking her head. "I'm here with someone. I don't have time for this."

Andrew's smirk faltered. "Wait…"

There was something different in his voice now. Less cocky, more hesitant.

"I just wanted to apologize," he said, lowering his tone. "Seriously. I messed up big time, and I regret it."

Claudia met his gaze, unreadable. "Okay. You're sorry. I understand. But that doesn't change anything."

Andrew let out a slow breath, rubbing his temple. "I know." He hesitated, then leaned in slightly. "Look, I wouldn't be asking if I had any other choice. I'm in trouble, Claudia. I just need a little help."

Her expression remained blank. "Help?"

He swallowed hard. "Four hundred pounds. Just to get me through something. You know I've helped you before. Think of it as a favour between friends."

Claudia let the silence stretch for a moment, studying him. Then, calmly, she asked, "That's why you're here?"

Andrew nodded. "Yeah. Just this once."

She exhaled through her nose, shaking her head slightly. "Fine. I'll help you."

His face lit up with relief. "Claudia, thank you, really—"

She held up a hand, stopping him. "I'm not finished." Her voice was firm but quiet. "I'll give you the money on one condition—after today, you never contact me again."

Andrew's expression faltered, the humiliation evident in his eyes.

"It's like that, huh?"

Claudia gave a small, indifferent shrug. "Yes. Exactly like that."

He clenched his jaw, his pride visibly wounded. "I thought we were past this bitterness."

She shook her head, sipping her coffee. "It's not bitterness. Actually, I should probably thank you."

Andrew frowned. "Thank me? For what?"

Claudia set her cup down and looked at him, her voice steady. "Because if you hadn't done what you did, I'd probably still be stuck with someone pathetic. So, in a way, you saved me."

His face darkened, his fingers curling slightly into his lap. "You don't have to insult me."

He drew a breath, ready to fire back, anger flaring briefly, but Claudia raised her hand again, stopping him. "Careful. One wrong word, and you won't see a penny."

Andrew gritted his teeth, swallowing back his pride. He nodded stiffly. "Alright. I get it."

She smiled, almost sympathetically. "I'm just stating the truth. And look at you—even after everything I said, you're still sitting here, waiting for money. Tell me, what kind of person does that?"

Andrew's face flushed; his mouth opened as if to argue, but no words came.

Without another word, Claudia tapped her phone, transferring the money. Then, without a second glance, she rose smoothly from her seat, picked up her coffee, and walked out.

She didn't even bother looking back.

* * *

Later that night, Claudia lay in bed, staring at the ceiling, with her mind restless. The room was dim, bathed in the soft glow of her bedside lamp, casting long shadows against the walls. Outside, the world hummed faintly—cars in the distance, the occasional rustling of wind—but it all felt far away, drowned out by the thoughts swirling inside her.

She thought about Andrew

When she had been with Andrew, she had been stagnant, drifting through life without real purpose, and without ambition. She had accepted mediocrity, convinced herself that she was fine with the way things were. That she was happy.

But now... now, everything was different.

She wasn't the same person she had been before. And the thought of going back—of slipping into her old patterns, of surrounding herself with people like Andrew again—felt unbearable.

Then there was Antony.

Antony, who had never asked her for anything. Antony, who had challenged her, and made her question everything she once believed. He had had no reason to guide her, no obligation to push her toward something better, and yet, he had. Even when they disagreed—even when she upset him—he never demanded, never manipulated, and never made her feel small.

How different people could be.

People could influence each other in ways she had never realized before. Some could drain you, keep you stuck, and make you doubt yourself. Others could push you, challenge you, and open doors you never even knew existed.

And that thought unsettled her. Because she realized how much she wanted to keep growing. How much she didn't want to lose the path she had started walking on.

And, most of all... how much she wanted Antony to be there as she did.

Claudia closed her eyes, with her thoughts still racing, but now, there was something else mixed in with them—a quiet determination.

She wasn't going back.

Not now. Not ever.

Abruptly, she made a decision.

She would meet Antony once he returned from the U.S.

Three weeks. That gave her time. Time to let the sting of embarrassment fade, time to collect herself, and time to figure out exactly what she wanted to say. She wouldn't let what had happened at his house be the last moment between them.

But more than anything, she needed answers.

Why had Antony done all of this for her? Why had he pushed her, guided her, and changed the course of her life without asking for anything in return? It was a question that had been lingering in her mind for weeks, but now, she couldn't ignore it any longer.

And then there was her own truth—the one she could no longer deny. She was in love with him.

It wasn't just admiration, or gratitude, or fascination. It was deeper than that. She wanted to stand beside him, not just for now, but for the rest of her life.

She exhaled slowly, staring at the ceiling.

She had never felt this certain about anything before.

Three weeks.

When he returned, she would finally tell him.

* * *

For the next three weeks, Claudia was fully focused on herself.

She didn't let anything distract her—not emotions, not doubts, and not the past. She poured all her energy into building something real, something that belonged entirely to her.

Every morning, she ran. Every evening, she hit the gym. She pushed herself harder than ever before, feeling her body grow stronger, more capable with each passing day.

But it wasn't just a physical transformation—her mind had shifted too.

She finally launched her YouTube channel, dedicated to teaching musical instruments. Without hesitation, she committed to uploading three videos a day. No overthinking, no self-doubt. Just her hands, the instruments, and her voice—clear, confident, and precise.

And as time passed, something unexpected happened.

People started watching.

Views grew steadily, then rapidly. Subscriptions increased. Comments poured in—people appreciating her lessons, thanking her for making learning easy, for sharing her knowledge. Encouraged by the response, she expanded, creating separate courses for more in-depth teaching.

She was too busy building something real to worry about anything else.

Then, on a Monday morning, while sitting in the staff room, sipping her usual cup of coffee, a notification popped up on her phone.

Payment Received: £5.00

Her heart skipped a beat.

She clicked on the notification, staring at the message. Someone had bought her teaching course.

It was only five pounds.

But it wasn't about the amount.

Someone had found her work valuable enough to pay for it.

A quiet, unexpected joy filled her chest. It wasn't a massive breakthrough, but it was proof. Proof that she wasn't just trying—she was actually doing something that mattered.

She exhaled, setting her phone down, resisting the urge to grin like an idiot.

For the first time, she wasn't just chasing something—she was creating something.

She wasn't waiting for motivation. She wasn't looking for validation.

She was building.

And the best part?

She was proud of herself.

Not just for what she was achieving, but for proving to herself that she could—that she was capable of more than she had ever imagined. It was also proof that she was no longer the same Claudia from before.

She sat in the staff room, with her fingers lightly tracing the edge of her phone. She wanted to tell someone—someone who would understand just how much this meant to her. And there was only one person who came to mind.

Antony.

For three weeks and a day, she had kept herself busy, focused, and determined—but something still felt unfinished.

She hesitated.

Would he even want to see her after everything?

A part of her feared that maybe things had changed. That maybe, this gap between them had become more than just time. But then— what if it hadn't?

Before she could overthink it, she pressed dial.

The phone rang.

Once.

Twice.

Then—

"Hello, Claudia."

The sound of his voice made her exhale, as a quiet relief settled over her.

"Hey... You're back?"

"Yeah," Antony said, his voice calm but slightly tired. "Landed this morning. I was just about to sleep."

She hesitated, but the words left her lips before she could second-guess them.

"Is there any chance we can meet?"

A pause.

"Today?"

"Yeah. If possible."

"What time?"

Without thinking, she blurted out, "Anytime. I can cancel the rest of the day from school and come right now."

A soft chuckle. "No, that's not nice. Finish your day. We'll meet after school—if that works for you?"

Claudia nodded quickly, then realized he couldn't see her.

"Yes! Of course."

"Alright. I'll send you the location."

The call ended, and within seconds, a message appeared on her screen.

Almost immediately, a message popped up with a location pin. Claudia clicked on it, her curiosity piqued.

It was somewhere Kent.

She switched to the satellite view, zooming in. The place was a vast open field with a small hill, surrounded by greenery, untouched and peaceful.

Her lips curled into a smile. Something about it felt... different.

Not a restaurant. Not a fancy meeting spot. A quiet, secluded place.

Claudia could hardly sit still. She tapped her fingers against the table, glancing at the clock. She still had a few hours of school left, but her mind was already gone. All she could think about was seeing

Antony again.

34

BEFORE THE SUN SET

Claudia arrived at the location in an Uber, stepping out onto the quiet roadside.

She glanced around, taking in the view. It wasn't a park—just an open field, stretching out toward the horizon, with a small footpath winding through the tall grass. It was the kind of place where people came for evening walks, to clear their minds, to just be. The air smelled fresh, untouched by the rush of city life.

But Antony wasn't there.

Claudia frowned, checking the time. He was 15 minutes late. That wasn't like him.

He wasn't the type to keep someone waiting.

She pulled out her phone, ready to call him—just as a black Uber slowed to a stop in front of her.

The back door opened.

And Antony stepped out.

Claudia's breath hitched in surprise. She had never seen him take an Uber before.

As he approached, his usual easy smile was there, but something was different.

She took him in—his face looked leaner, sharper, his eyes slightly sunken with exhaustion. He looked tired. And that was when she realized what it was—he had lost weight.

For a second, she wasn't sure what to say. Then, as he reached her, he spoke first.

"I'm sorry for being late." His voice was steady but had a slight roughness to it.

Claudia studied him for a second before blurting out, "I've never seen you in an Uber before." Antony exhaled lightly, running a hand through his hair. "I'm tired, so I knew I shouldn't drive."

She didn't say anything right away, but her mind was racing. It was the first time she had ever heard Antony admit something like that.

They started walking along the path, with the soft rustling of grass beneath their feet the only sound between them for a moment.

Claudia glanced at him again. "You look like you've lost weight."

Antony gave her a small, tired smile. "It was a hard three weeks. Stressful. Maybe that's why."

She wanted to ask more. But she held back.

Instead, they continued walking, following the small footpath as it led them toward the hill.

When they reached the top, they sat down on the grass, looking out at the breath-taking view in front of them.

The sun was setting, casting the sky in a breath-taking blend of deep orange, pink, and gold. The clouds glowed softly in the fading light, and the gentle whisper of the wind filled the silence between them.

For a long moment, neither of them spoke. Then, Antony broke the stillness. "I have something to tell you."

Claudia's heart clenched.

A sudden wave of panic crashed over her. Was he going to tell her they should stop seeing each other? That things had gone too far?

That after everything, they should go their separate ways?

She couldn't let him say it.

"Stop! Stop, stop, stop!" she blurted out, holding up a hand as if physically stopping his words. "I called you to meet, so I should go first."

Antony blinked in surprise, his lips twitching into a small, amused smile. "Okay," he said smoothly. "You first."

Claudia exhaled, steadying herself. Then, she really looked at him. The sun sat just behind his head, casting a golden glow around him, making him look almost ethereal—like an angel with a halo.

She swallowed, suddenly overwhelmed.

"You know…" she started, her voice soft but steady. "You are one of the best things that ever happened in my life."

Antony didn't say anything, but he was listening—truly listening.

"You changed my life," she continued, feeling each word leave her lips with a weight she couldn't ignore. "You made me understand who I am, what life actually means—things I never had a clue about before I met you."

She glanced down for a moment, gathering herself before looking back up at him.

"I will never, ever do something as stupid as what I did that night on the bridge. No matter what life throws at me, I know I can handle it now." She hesitated, then pushed onward. "I know what I did that night in the bathroom was wrong, but…" She trailed off, staring at him again. The sunlight framed him perfectly, casting his face in golden hues, making him look almost too perfect.

I love him.

The realization hit her fully, sinking into her bones.

"I don't know why you chose me or what I am to you," she whispered. "But one thing I do know for sure—I'm in love with you. Completely."

Antony's expression softened, with a glint of something unreadable in his eyes.

"I want to have kids with you," she admitted, her voice barely above a whisper. "I want to grow old with you. I want to love you with my whole heart."

For a moment, Antony looked like he was soaking in every word—and he was truly savouring them.

She took a shaky breath.

"Will you marry me?"

For the first time, Antony hesitated. His expression wavered, and Claudia felt her heart pound in the silence between them.

But before he could speak, she saw a drop of blood. Claudia's eyes widened as she saw it trickling from Antony's nose.

She said "You're bleeding."

Antony lifted a hand and wiped the blood casually, glancing at it as if it were nothing.

"It's okay," he said, brushing it off. "You continue. I'm listening."

But Claudia couldn't continue.

More blood poured from his nose.

"No—you're bleeding a lot," she said, panic creeping into her voice.

She reached into her pocket, pulling out a handkerchief and pressing it against his nose, but the bleeding wouldn't stop. The crimson soaked through the fabric too quickly, seeping between her fingers.

Antony exhaled, shaking his head. "I know how to manage it," he muttered, pushing himself up from where he was sitting.

And then—

His body jerked violently.

His legs buckled.

His arms seized up.

And then, he collapsed.

Claudia's breath caught in her throat. A scream built in her chest, but no sound came out—only a choked, panicked gasp.

Her hands trembled as she grabbed his shoulders, trying to shake him awake. His body convulsed, his limbs rigid, his eyes fluttering uncontrollably. Then she managed to scream for help.

A couple of people walking across the field turned at the sound of her panicked cries and rushed toward them. A man pulled out his phone, quickly dialling emergency services.

Claudia was frozen in place.

She barely heard the distant voice on the phone, the panicked murmurs of the strangers around her.

Her world had shrunk to just Antony.

His face was pale.

His breathing was shallow.

By the time the ambulance arrived, Antony was unconscious.

The paramedics moved fast, checking his vitals. One of them looked up, with the urgency clear in his voice. "His oxygen levels are dangerously low. We need to get him to the hospital now."

Claudia tried to explain what had happened, but her words wouldn't come out.

She was shaking. Her mind was spinning.

They placed Antony on the stretcher, securing an oxygen mask over his face.

Then—

His fingers twitched.

His eyelids fluttered.

And with weak, trembling hands, he reached up and pulled off the oxygen mask.

"Wait," he murmured.

The paramedics hesitated for just a second.

His gaze found Claudia's, and despite the pain, he smiled.

"I'll give you the answer to your question..." he said, voice hoarse. "If I come out of this."

Claudia stopped breathing.

Her heart felt like it had stalled.

"Even if you never called me that, I know you knew," Antony said softly. "But still—let me introduce myself." His eyes locked onto hers. "My name is Antony Sewell."

He let out a small, smile before adding, "No more Mr. Nobody."

Then—his body seized again.

The paramedics rushed him into the ambulance.

Claudia followed.

The doors slammed shut.

The sirens wailed.

As they raced toward the hospital, Claudia sat there, with her hands trembling, and her chest tight, feeling like the ground had just been ripped out from under her.

* * *

The ambulance pulled up to the hospital, with its sirens fading into a distant hum as the paramedics rushed Antony inside. Claudia followed closely, with her heart pounding with every step. But just as she was about to enter through the doors behind them, a nurse gently stopped her.

"I'm sorry, Miss, but you'll have to wait here."

Claudia's breath caught. She watched helplessly as Antony was wheeled away, disappearing behind the emergency room doors. She stood frozen for a moment, not knowing what to do. She gave her details to the reception desk. Then, she numbly walked to one of the chairs in the waiting area and sat down.

Minutes passed. Maybe hours. She had lost all sense of time.

Her fingers clenched around the hem of her jacket, as her mind replayed everything that had just happened—the blood, the seizure, and Antony's last words before he collapsed.

She stared at the hospital floor, almost not noticing when a doctor finally approached her.

"Miss?"

She snapped her head up, and her stomach twisted at the sight of his white coat.

The doctor gave her a neutral, professional look. "Are you with the patient?"

Claudia quickly nodded. "Yes."

"We need some details about him."

Claudia sat up straighter. "Okay... what do you need to know?"

"His name?"

"Antony," she said immediately. "Antony Sewell."

The doctor scribbled on his clipboard. "Date of birth?"

Claudia's stomach dropped.

"I... I don't know," she admitted, feeling embarrassed.

The doctor glanced up. "Do you know which GP he's registered with?"

Claudia shook her head. "No... I don't know that either."

A flicker of concern crossed the doctor's face. "His emergency contact?"

She swallowed hard. I don't know that either.

Marco. Sophie. Someone. But she had never saved their numbers, as she had never needed to.

Her chest tightened. How can I be this close to someone... and still know so little about him?

"I have his phone number," she said quickly. "I can give you that."

The doctor hesitated, then nodded. "That might help."

Claudia quickly recited Antony's number from memory. The doctor jotted it down, gave her a polite nod, and disappeared through the same doors Antony had been taken through.

And then, the waiting began.

She sat still, staring at nothing, as her hands gripping her knees so tightly her knuckles turned white.

Then, after what felt like an eternity, the doctor returned.

Claudia jumped to her feet. "How is he?"

The doctor hesitated. "I can't say much at the moment. We're running tests."

Claudia's stomach twisted.

"But..." the doctor continued, flipping through his notes, "we managed to track down his emergency contact from his medical records."

Claudia's breath caught.

Emergency contact?

The doctor glanced at her. "A Mr. Sewell."

Claudia's mind reeled.

Mr. Sewell?

Her lips parted, but no words came out.

Who was Mr. Sewell? And why had Antony never mentioned him?

* * *

Claudia sat in the quiet hum of the hospital corridor, with her hands cold and numb on her lap. Her mind kept circling back to the doctor's words.

Mr. Sewell.

She could still hear Antony's voice in her head.

"My name is Antony Sewell. No more Mr. Nobody."

Her thoughts were interrupted by the sound of slow, deliberate footsteps approaching. She looked up.

A man, probably in his late sixties, walked down the corridor. His face was worn, his expression unreadable, but there was something about him—something familiar.

Claudia's eyes narrowed slightly, with her mind racing.

Then it clicked.

The picture.

The framed photo in Antony's house—the one with a younger version of Antony standing beside a smiling man.

This was him.

The man finally reached her and sat down beside her. His presence carried a quiet weight, a sadness that needed no words.

After a moment, he turned to her.

"Claudia?"

His voice was deep but gentle.

She swallowed. "Yes."

He nodded slightly, as if confirming something to himself. Then he said, "He told me a lot about you."

Claudia's throat tightened.

After a moment, he exhaled and extended his hand. "I'm Mr. Sewell."

Claudia's eyes widened slightly.

Before she could even ask, he continued, "Antony grew up in my house as a foster child."

Claudia blinked. "I've seen you before," she murmured. "In his house. In the picture."

A ghost of a smile flickered across Mr. Sewell's face, but it didn't reach his eyes.

"Was he in a lot of pain?" he asked quietly.

Claudia hesitated, as her mind flashed back to the way Antony had smiled at her, even as blood ran down his face.

"I don't know," she admitted. "He was smiling even when he was bleeding."

Mr. Sewell's lips pressed together in a bittersweet expression.

"That sounds like him," he murmured. Then, with a deep breath, he said, "Our house was his fourth foster home. He was eight when he came to us."

Claudia's chest ached at the thought of a young Antony, shuffled from home to home.

Mr. Sewell continued, with a distant gaze. "By that time, he had been through a lot. But he never complained. Never showed anger. He always had that smile on his face."

Claudia could picture it—the quiet, composed boy who had learned too early how to carry his pain without letting it show.

"One day," Mr. Sewell continued, his voice quieter now, "I asked him, 'I've never seen you without a smile, even though life hasn't been fair to you. How do you do it?'"

Claudia watched as a sad smile formed on Mr. Sewell's face.

"He looked at me and asked, 'How do you face your friends when they come to visit you?'"

Mr. Sewell let out a soft breath. "I told him, 'With a smile.'"

There was a long pause before he said, "And then Antony told me, 'That's exactly what I do. But problems are the only visitors I have, so I smile at them too.'"

Claudia felt her throat tighten. She turned her gaze to Mr. Sewell. "The picture," she said softly. "Why did you recreate it?"

Mr. Sewell looked at her for a moment, then asked, "Do you know what Sewell means?"

Claudia shook her head.

"It means 'Sea Strong,'" he said. "The ability to hold everything inside. To be strong enough to contain any storm."

Claudia held her breath.

Mr. Sewell looked down at his hands. "I gave him my surname

because, more than anyone I've ever known, he was the one who deserved it. Antony wasn't just strong—he was sea strong. He carried everything, all the pain, and all the weight—and never let it spill over."

Claudia swallowed hard, suddenly understanding the depth of it all.

Mr. Sewell exhaled. "That was the day we took the picture again. To mark the day he became my son in every way that mattered."

Just then, the sound of footsteps echoed down the hallway.

A doctor approached them, with his face unreadable.

Claudia's heartbeat quickened.

Mr. Sewell stood up.

The doctor took a breath before speaking. "I'm very sorry," he said quietly.

Silence.

Claudia felt her world tilt, as the weight of those words crushed her chest.

"He didn't make it."

The air in the hallway seemed to vanish.

Claudia couldn't move. Couldn't breathe.

Mr. Sewell clenched his jaw, his expression unreadable.

Claudia tried to speak, but no words came out.

No.

No, this wasn't how it was supposed to happen.

She had just told him she loved him.

She had just asked him to marry her.

And he had promised to give her an answer.

But now...

Now, there would be none.

A sound finally escaped her—a soft, broken breath.

Her hands trembled as she gripped the sides of her chair, but she felt like she was falling.

Falling into a void where Antony no longer existed.

35

A LIFE WORTH REMEMBERING

The rain fell in heavy sheets, soaking the earth, drumming softly against the rows of umbrellas that lined the cemetery. The sky was a deep, endless gray, as if mourning along with them.

Claudia stood among them—Mr. Sewell, Marco, Sophie, Anna, Luca, and others she didn't recognize. Important people. People who had known Antony in different ways. People who had come to say goodbye.

Yet, even in the presence of so many people, Claudia had never felt more alone.

The priest's voice blended into the sound of the rain, soft words of farewell carried away by the wind. The casket, dark and polished, was lowered into the ground, disappearing inch by inch beneath the weight of the world.

Marco stood still, with his face serious, and his usual light-hearted nature nowhere to be found. Sophie sniffled beside him, trying but failing to hide her tears. Mr. Sewell watched in silence, with his expression unreadable.

Claudia didn't cry.

She just stood there, staring at the grave, with her body still, and her mind an empty void.

Then, it was over.

People slowly began to disperse, stepping away in pairs or small groups, with umbrellas shielding them as they walked toward their cars.

Claudia did not move.

She drifted toward the church, seeking shelter from the rain, with her steps slow, detached, and almost mechanical.

Inside, the air was warmer, but it didn't reach her.

She sat in one of the wooden pews, facing the altar, with her hands clasped together in her lap.

She looked up at the statue of Jesus at the front of the church, but her face held no expression.

No tears.

No sadness.

No prayer.

Just silence.

The sound of rain echoed through the empty church, a soft, endless hum.

And Claudia sat there, unmoving.

Lost in a grief too deep to name.

Mr. Sewell approached quietly, his footsteps echoing slightly against the stone floor of the empty church. He walked with a weight beyond his years, with his face lined with sorrow but composed.

Without a word, he sat down beside Claudia; his presence was grounding.

For a moment, neither of them spoke. Then, he reached into his coat pocket and pulled out a slightly worn envelope.

With a deep breath, he held it out to her.

"He left this with me before he went to America," Mr. Sewell said, his voice low and steady. "In case he didn't make it back."

Claudia looked at the envelope in his hand but didn't take it right away. Her fingers twitched slightly, as hesitation crept in.

Her heart pounded against her ribs, as if it was bracing her for what lay inside.

She forced herself to reach out and take it.

Mr. Sewell gave her shoulder a light squeeze before standing up. He didn't say anything else. He just walked away, leaving her alone in the dim, quiet church.

Claudia stared at the envelope for a long moment.

Then, slowly, she slid her finger under the seal and opened it.

The world outside was moving, but Claudia was frozen.

She traced her fingers over the edge of the envelope, hesitating. Then, slowly, she broke the seal and unfolded the letter.

Hi, Claudia.

I know how you're feeling right now, but before you read any further, I want you to smile.

Just a little one. Come on, you can do it.

She stared at the words.

And suddenly, for the first time since the funeral began, the corners of her lips twitched.

Just for a moment—she felt like he was right there beside her, saying it in his voice, teasing her like he always did.

She swallowed the lump in her throat and kept reading.

I know you still remember New Year's Eve—the day that changed everything for me.

That day, I had been diagnosed with a brain tumor. The doctors told me I had a maximum of six months and that there was nothing they could do. I was shattered.

That night, I had been sitting on the bridge, looking out at the water, asking God, Why me? Why now, when there was still so much I wanted to do?

And then, on the other side of that same bridge, I saw someone tired of living.

You.

It felt like a cruel joke from the universe—on one side, someone begging for more time, and on the other, someone ready to throw it all away.

When I saw you, I saw innocence. When I spoke to you, I saw something even deeper. And the more we talked, the more I liked you.

But I knew I didn't have time.

I knew there could never be an us.

So I walked away. I left without giving you a chance to find me.

But you did.

And that amazed me, Claudia.

If there's one thing I learned about you, it's that when you set your mind to something, you find a way.

And from that moment, I knew—you weren't meant to give up on life.

As we spent more time together, I found myself falling for you in ways I never expected. I tried to resist it—I told myself it wasn't fair to you. But the truth is, I had already lost that battle long before I even realized it. That's why I told you not to invest any emotions in me—because I knew I had already invested mine in you.

But the night after the scuba diving, when we had dinner together...

That was the night I knew I was in love with you.

I didn't tell you. I couldn't. Because love, for me, would only end in pain.

Then, on the day in the Peak District, when Marco said "The place isn't going anywhere. We can always come back."—I knew.

I would never get another chance.

The real reason I cancelled our overnight stay? It wasn't just because of work.

I had forgotten to take my medication. I started getting headaches. The double vision returned. And I knew I had to go back before you noticed something was wrong.

That night, when you tried to kiss me... I wanted to kiss you back. God, I wanted to.

But I could feel the blood coming. My head was pounding.

So I walked away.

By the time I returned, you were gone.

I almost ran after you. Almost told you everything. But I stopped myself. Because I knew it wouldn't change anything.

Claudia, you once asked me why I chose you—why I helped you.

It was never about saving you.

I wanted you to see that the most luxurious thing a human can have is time.

If you don't believe me, just ask someone who doesn't have any left.

Now, I need you to know one last thing.

I left you £400,000.

I know—it's not much in the grand scheme of things. But it's a start.

Because anything that comes too easily has no real value.

Just like time.

And just like love.

So find yourself, Claudia.

And live a life worth remembering.

With love,

Mr. Nobody.

Claudia's hands trembled as she clutched the letter, with her breath uneven, and her chest tightening.

Tears welled up in her eyes, but she didn't cry.

Not yet.

Instead, she looked up at the statue of Jesus, with her expression unreadable.

Then, she did the only thing she could do.

She smiled.

* * *

Antony's house was quieter than it had ever been. The vast mansion, once filled with purpose and presence, now carried a weighty stillness. It wasn't just empty—it felt like something was missing.

In the lounge, Claudia sat with Marco, Sophie, and Mr. Sewell. No one spoke much. The air was thick, not with grief exactly, but with the strange hollowness that comes when reality fully sets in.

Mr. Sewell took a slow sip from his glass, with his eyes lost in thought. Then, he set it down with a quiet clink against the table and spoke, his voice steady but filled with quiet emotion.

"He grew up with nothing," he murmured. "An orphan with no money, and no family to call his own. But in the end, he didn't die poor. He died rich—not because of his wealth, but because of the people who loved him."Claudia stayed quiet, her hands clasped together, her thoughts distant. She hadn't touched a drop of alcohol, though the others were drinking in quiet reflection.

After a while, Mr. Sewell stood up and gestured for Claudia to follow him.

They walked through the long corridor, past the elegant yet minimalistic interiors that Antony had built—everything in this house had a purpose, much like the man himself.

Finally, Mr. Sewell stopped outside a door and pushed it open.

Antony's room.

The air inside was untouched, still carrying the faintest trace of him. It wasn't lavish, but it was full of depth—just like Antony. The shelves were filled with books, a few old photos remained on the desk, and a neatly made bed stood in the center, as if waiting for its owner to return.

"You can sleep here tonight," Mr. Sewell said gently.

Claudia's feet stopped at the doorway.

She looked inside but didn't step forward.

A deep ache spread through her chest, but it wasn't just grief—it was something else.

"I can't," she whispered.

Mr. Sewell turned to her, puzzled.

Claudia swallowed hard, her voice firm but quiet. "I'm not qualified to be in that space yet."

She didn't even glance inside again.

"I'll come back when I feel like I've earned it."

Mr. Sewell watched her for a moment, then said softly,

"Take all the time you need. you're always welcome here."

Claudia gave a faint nod, then turned away, walking toward the guest room.

Once she was alone, she lay on the bed, staring at the ceiling. The past few weeks, the past few months—it all blurred together in her mind.

Antony had shaped her in ways she hadn't even fully understood yet.

She took a deep breath.

Then, in the quiet of the room, she whispered to herself—

"What's next?"

She already knew the answer.

36

A PLACE CALLED IDUKKI

Three weeks later, Claudia found herself in Kerala, India—the exact place Antony had once told her .

She had travelled across the region, exploring Kochi, Alappuzha, and Kottayam, trying to experience the essence of the place. But something felt off.

Even though she remembered Antony's words—"Don't stick with the tourist people, find the real ones"—she had struggled to do so. No matter where she went, she mostly encountered people working in the tourism industry, and it all felt transactional. Everywhere, there were guides, shop owners, and vendors eager to make money from travellers like her.

She wasn't sure what she had expected, but this wasn't it.

Two and a half weeks into the trip, and she felt no different. There had been no change, and no revelation.

She had hoped to see something, to feel something—but instead, she found herself growing frustrated.

Maybe Antony was wrong.

Maybe there was nothing special about this place.

Determined not to leave without trying harder, Claudia decided to escape the tourist areas.

She travelled deep into the countryside—to Idukki, a rural region of Kerala, where the hills curled into the distance, the forests whispered with life, and the air smelled of fresh rain and earth.

She checked into a small resort, a modest place tucked away in the greenery. Every day, she walked through the village, trying to observe, trying to understand.

But there was a problem.

She stood out.

Her fair skin, her foreign features—she was different, and everyone knew it. No matter how much she wanted to blend in, she couldn't.

And it frustrated her.

She felt like an outsider, watching from the edges, unable to break into the world Antony had told her about.

But there was one thing she had started to notice.

Unlike the people in tourist-heavy areas, the villagers weren't interested in making money from her.

Instead, they treated her like a guest.

They smiled warmly, offered her food without asking for payment, and asked her questions—not to sell her something, but simply out of curiosity.

It was unfamiliar.

And, slowly, it started to make her wonder—maybe Antony had been right, and she just hadn't found what she was looking for yet.

Claudia was walking along a winding hill road in the early evening, savouring the cool breeze and the quiet hush of the countryside. The sky was tinged with the soft hues of dusk; the rhythmic crunch of her footsteps on gravel was the only sound.

She had just rounded a bend when—bam!

Something slammed into her from the side.

She lost her balance and hit the ground hard, her elbow scraping against the rough asphalt. A sharp pain shot through her arm. When she looked down, she saw the skin torn open and blood beginning to pool.

A few feet away, a motorbike lay on its side, with milk spilling from the metal containers strapped to the back, forming a pale puddle on the road.

The rider—a teenage boy with curly hair—scrambled to his feet. He wore an Indian cricket team T-shirt, now streaked with mud, and a pair of shorts. One of his slippers had come off in the fall. His knees were bloodied and scraped raw, patches of skin peeled away by the impact.

His wide eyes were filled with panic as he looked at Claudia, who was frozen in place, unsure whether to run or rush to help.

"Madam! Madam! I am sorry!" he said in a thick Indian accent, rushing toward her.

Claudia winced, clutching her arm. The pain was sharp, but her frustration was sharper.

"Where the hell were you looking?!" she snapped.

The boy kept apologizing, looking genuinely distressed. "Madam, sorry, madam! I didn't see! I am sorry!"

Claudia glared at him. "What am I supposed to do with your sorry?!" she spat out. "I need to go to a hospital. Take me to the nearest one!"

The boy's face turned pale.

"Madam... I can't take you to hospital."

Claudia's jaw clenched. "What? You hit me, and now you won't even help me?"

"No, no, not like that, madam!" he said quickly, shaking his head. "I don't have license. Police checking will be there."

Claudia let out a frustrated sigh, still holding her injured elbow. "Fine. I'll wait here for a vehicle and go by myself."

The boy, still looking panicked, shook his head quickly. "No, no, madam! Please don't go! If you go to hospital, they will ask how it happened, and I don't have a license. They will take my bike, madam."

Claudia shot him a sharp look. "Then maybe you should have thought about that before you ran into me!"

The boy stood there awkwardly, shifting from foot to foot as Claudia scanned the road. But after ten minutes, not a single vehicle had passed.

"Great."

The boy looked genuinely distressed now; he had his hands pressed together in a pleading gesture. "I am really sorry, madam. Please, don't go."

Claudia rolled her eyes. "And stop calling me madam. It's so annoying."

"Okay, madam."

She exhaled sharply. "I just told you to stop! My name is Claudia. Call me Claudia."

The boy hesitated, then nodded quickly. "Okay, Claudia."

She sighed, still irritated but slightly amused by his nervousness. "Now what? You expect me to sit here and bleed?"

He straightened up suddenly, as if remembering something. "My mother is a nurse. If you come home, she can help. It's very rare to get a vehicle here at this time."

Claudia stared at him, debating whether to trust him or not.

The road was completely empty. Her arm was still bleeding, and the dull pain was becoming sharper.

"How far is your house?" she finally asked.

"Just five minutes' walk."

She exhaled heavily. "Fine. Lead the way."

As they started walking, Claudia winced slightly at the throbbing pain in her elbow. She looked at the boy walking beside her, still flustered from the accident.

"Where were you going in such a hurry?" she asked.

The boy, still looking guilty, replied, "To the 'Paal Society.'"

Claudia frowned. "The what?"

"Paal Society," he repeated, as if it made perfect sense.

She gave him a confused look. "I have no idea what that is."

The boy glanced at her and then said, "The place where they collect milk. I was going to sell it."

Claudia finally understood and smirked. "Oh, the milk society? You could've just said that."

The boy gave a nervous laugh. "Sorry... I thought you'd know."

Claudia shook her head, amused despite her injury. "Well, now I do." She then added, "And what's your name?"

"Roshan ," he said simply.

She nodded, giving him a teasing smile. "At least now I know the name of the guy who almost ran me over."

Roshan scratched the back of his head, looking even more embarrassed. "I said sorry, no?"

Claudia sighed. "Yeah, yeah. I've heard it enough times."

Roshan smiled, seemingly relieved that she wasn't as angry anymore.

"Where are you from, Claudia?"

Claudia glanced at him, her voice casual.

"England."

As they walked, Claudia took in her surroundings. The scenery was breath-taking—lush green hills stretching into the horizon, the scent of fresh earth and spices in the air. Birds flitted between the trees, and somewhere in the distance, she heard the faint ringing of a cowbell.

The narrow road was uneven, winding slightly uphill. She carefully stepped over a patch of loose stones, wincing again at the pain in her elbow.

"How far is your house?" she asked.

"Just a little ahead. Five minutes," Roshan assured her.

Claudia raised an eyebrow. "Five minutes? You sure?" She had heard enough people say "five minutes" when they really meant 20.

Roshan grinned. "I promise, it's close."

True to his word, they soon reached his home—a modest white house nestled in the middle of farmland. Three cows stood lazily in a shed beside the house, a few chickens pecked at the ground nearby, and Claudia could see rows of what looked like cardamom plants.

Roshan ran ahead as they reached the house, calling out, "Amma!" His voice echoed as he disappeared toward the front door.

A woman rushed out of the house, her face etched with worry. She was dressed in a simple saree, with her hair tied back neatly. She looked at Roshan, then at Claudia, then back at Roshan—her eyes narrowing as she spoke rapidly in Malayalam.

Claudia stood there, watching them go back and forth in a language she didn't understand.

Roshan was gesturing toward his bike, then pointing at Claudia's arm, in a slightly panicked voice. His mother's expression shifted from anger to concern as she looked at Claudia properly.

Claudia didn't need to know Malayalam to figure out what was happening.

It was a very typical "Mom-scolding-son" moment.

Trying not to laugh at Roshan's obvious discomfort, Claudia simply stood there, waiting for whatever would happen next.

Roshan's mother stepped closer, her eyes scanning Claudia's injured elbow with concern. She motioned toward the house and spoke in broken English.

"Come... inside. Sit down."

Claudia hesitated for a moment before nodding and following her inside. The house was simple but warm, with a homely feel. A wooden table sat in the centre of the room, and a dim yellow bulb lit up the space.

As Claudia sat down, the woman gave her a small, reassuring smile. "I... nurse," she said, pointing to herself. "Come... with medicine."

Claudia smiled despite herself and nodded. "Okay."

Roshan stood nearby, looking at her awkwardly. "Do you have pain?" he asked hesitantly.

Claudia raised an eyebrow at him. "What do you think?"

Roshan wisely kept quiet.

His mother returned with a small box of medicine and a glass of water. She handed Claudia the water first, gesturing for her to drink, before carefully tending to her wound. She cleaned the scrape gently but efficiently, dabbing it with antiseptic before wrapping it in a bandage.

Claudia winced slightly at the sting but remained still. The woman worked with skilled hands, and within minutes, the dressing was done.

When she finished, she stepped back and smiled. "Good."

Roshan translated, "She's saying you're all fixed up."

Claudia smiled, flexing her arm lightly. "Tell her thank you."

Before Roshan could translate, his mother had already disappeared into the kitchen. A moment later, she returned, gesturing toward the table.

"Eat."

Roshan turned to Claudia. "She's asking you to have something to eat."

Claudia shook her head politely. "Oh, no, really, I'm fine..."

But the woman insisted, gently nudging the plate toward her. Claudia glanced at Roshan, who simply shrugged.

"Trust me, you won't win this argument."

With a small chuckle, Claudia gave in and sat down. Soon, a plate of warm chapati and fragrant chicken curry was placed in front of her. The aroma hit her instantly, making her realize just how hungry she was.

Taking a bite, she was pleasantly surprised—it was delicious. The spices, the warmth, the depth of flavor—it was unlike anything she had eaten in the tourist areas.

She ate in comfortable silence, while Roshan's mother watched with a satisfied smile, seeming happy to see a guest enjoying the food.

Once she finished, Claudia washed her hands and stepped outside. The night had fully set in, and the air was cooler now, as the distant sounds of crickets filled the quiet.

Roshan's mother followed her to the doorway and spoke again.

"Don't go... stay here. Sleep here. Go morning."

Claudia blinked in surprise. "Oh, no, I have a room at the resort. I should head back."

Roshan, who had been listening, stepped in. "I think you should stay."

Claudia turned to him. "Why?"

He gestured toward the hills. "It's dark, and this is a forested area. It's not safe to walk alone at night."

Claudia hesitated, looking out at the path she had walked earlier. The trees faded into darkness; she had no flashlight, and no idea what animals might be lurking in the woods.

With a sigh, she finally nodded. "Alright... I'll stay."

Roshan's mother smiled warmly and guided her back inside, already preparing a place for her to rest.

Later that night, Claudia took a shower in the small bathroom attached to the house. Everything was simple—different from what she was used to—but there was a comforting warmth in that simplicity.

Roshan's mother handed her a nightdress, a soft cotton nighty that felt unfamiliar against her skin. At first, Claudia hesitated, but seeing the woman's kind, expectant smile, she accepted it with a small nod.

As the night deepened, Claudia sat outside on the veranda with Roshan, both gazing up at the sky. The stars were brighter here, scattered like tiny lanterns in the darkness.

"You don't have anything to study?" Claudia asked, breaking the silence.

Roshan shook his head. "It's summer holidays till June."

He turned toward her. "What about you? No phone?"

Claudia smiled faintly. "I just don't feel like using it right now. What about you?"

Roshan sighed dramatically. "I wish! But Amma took it away today. She told me to give you company since you're our guest."

Claudia chuckled. "So, what do you think about that?"

Roshan tilted his head, pretending to think. "I'm thinking... if I had driven a little slower, I could have avoided counting stars tonight."

As Claudia and Roshan sat in comfortable silence, gazing at the endless night sky, the wooden door behind them creaked open. Roshan's mother stepped out, her presence gentle but warm. In her hands, she carried a small cup.

"Tea? Coffee?" she asked in her broken English, her voice kind but uncertain.

Claudia turned to her, offering a small smile. "No, thank you," she said softly, shaking her head.

Roshan's mother didn't say anything else. She simply nodded and stood near the doorway, not going back inside.

Even though they couldn't communicate in the same language, Claudia understood what she was doing. The woman didn't want her to feel alone or uneasy in a new place. This was her way of providing silent company, of making sure Claudia felt safe and welcomed in their home.

Claudia glanced at Roshan, who rolled his eyes slightly but didn't comment. Instead, he went back to looking at the stars.

Eventually, exhaustion from the long day settled in. Claudia stretched her arms, letting out a quiet yawn. "I think I should sleep now."

Roshan nodded. "Yeah, me too. Amma will get mad if I stay up too late."

Claudia smiled as she stepped inside, settling into the small but cozy guest room. As she lay down, listening to the distant sounds of crickets and the occasional rustling of the trees outside, she realized how different this night was from anything she had ever known.

And yet... it felt peaceful.

* * *

Around 6:45 am, Claudia stirred awake to a mix of unfamiliar yet soothing sounds—the rhythmic chanting from a distant temple, the occasional crowing of chickens, and birds calling out to the sunrise.

The sky was painted in soft shades of pink and orange, as the sun was barely peeking over the horizon. The air was cool and fresh, carrying the faint scent of earth and morning dew.

Still half-asleep, Claudia stretched before sitting up, momentarily disoriented. It took her a second to remember where she was.

Roshan's home.

A content smile played on her lips as she got out of bed. Everything around her was simple, yet it felt peaceful.

She walked around the house, expecting to see Roshan or his mother—but the house was empty.

"Where are they?" she mumbled to herself, peeking into different rooms.

Still no one.

Confused, she stepped outside, glancing around. The early morning mist still hung in the air, covering the hills in a soft haze. Just as she was about to call out for Roshan, his mother appeared from behind the small cattle shed, holding a steel container of fresh milk.

She greeted Claudia with a warm smile. "Good morning."

Relieved, Claudia smiled back. "Good morning."

Roshan's mother lifted the milk can in her hand slightly, then pointed at Claudia. "Brush?"

Claudia blinked for a second before realizing what she meant. She grinned and flipped her hand the same way, mimicking her simple English. "No brush."

Roshan's mother chuckled, walking inside with the milk. Claudia stood outside, still looking around for Roshan but not spotting him anywhere.

A few moments later, his mother walked back out, this time holding a tube of toothpaste. She gestured for Claudia to come closer.

Curious, Claudia approached, about to tell her again that she didn't have a toothbrush—when Roshan's mother suddenly grabbed Claudia's hand and squeezed some toothpaste onto her index finger.

Then, with a playful smile, she demonstrated brushing her teeth with her finger.

Claudia laughed, shaking her head in amusement.

"Oh, this is new," she muttered, but decided to go along with it. She started brushing with her finger just as she was shown.

After finishing up and washing her face in the small outdoor sink, Claudia stepped back inside. Roshan's mother handed her a steaming cup of tea.

The rich aroma of fresh milk filled her senses as she took her first sip. It was incredible.

"Wow," she murmured, savouring the warmth.

As she sat on the veranda, enjoying her tea, Claudia gestured toward

Roshan's mother, pointing around. "Roshan?"

The older woman smiled and responded. "Tapping... will come soon."

Claudia had no idea what that meant, but she simply nodded and smiled back.

For now, she just enjoyed the moment.

Sitting there on the veranda, the world felt so different from the one she knew—slower, simpler, yet full of warmth.

A few moments later, Roshan appeared, with his once-white shirt now streaked with brown, and his trousers just as dirty. His hair was damp with sweat, and in his hand, he held a long, curved knife.

Claudia, now changed back into her own clothes, frowned at the sight. "What is that? And where have you been this early in the morning?"

Roshan smiled, wiping his forehead with the back of his hand. "Went for rubber tapping."

She narrowed her eyes. "Rubber... what?"

He gestured for her to follow him a few steps to the edge of the property, pointing at a small grove of trees. "Rubber tapping. It's how we collect latex from rubber trees. We make cuts in the bark, and the latex drips out."

Claudia processed this, tilting her head slightly. "Oh... got it." She made an exaggerated gesture of understanding, making Roshan chuckle.

Without another word, he disappeared into the house, reappearing within minutes in clean clothes.

"You're ready?" he asked, glancing at Claudia, who was now dressed in her jeans and top from the day before.

She nodded. "Yeah, I just wanted to say thank you to your mom first."

Roshan nodded, stepping back inside and calling out to his mother in Malayalam. She responded from inside, and he turned back to Claudia.

"She said she's getting ready for work at the hospital. Just a minute."

A moment later, Roshan's mother stepped out, still brushing her hair. She smiled warmly at Claudia and spoke again in Malayalam. Roshan translated. "Amma said she's really happy you stayed here. She hopes you slept well."

Claudia smiled genuinely. "Thank you. I really did."

She reached into her pocket and pulled out some money, extending it toward the woman. "And for last night, for the food, the medicine—"

Roshan's mother's expression immediately shifted. She stepped back, her face a mix of offense and disappointment.

Roshan's tone turned serious. "Please don't insult us."

Claudia froze.

"Amma said she loved having you here. You were a guest, not a customer."

Claudia felt something stir deep inside her.

Most of the people she had encountered in India so far had treated her like a walking wallet. Every experience had come with a price tag.

But not this.

She looked at Roshan's mother, her throat suddenly tight.

"Thank you," she said, her voice softer now, tucking the money away.

The woman smiled, then turned and walked back inside to finish getting ready for work.

Claudia exhaled, taking a final glance at the small house—the chickens pecking in the yard, the cows lazily chewing nearby, and the mist that still hung over the hills.

Roshan walked over to his bike, strapping the steel milk container onto the back. "I have to take this to the collection point before it gets too late. I'll drop you at your resort on the way."

Claudia climbed onto the back of the bike, and Roshan started the engine.

As they pulled onto the winding dirt road, Claudia held onto the sides of the seat—not Roshan.

But as the cool morning air rushed past her face, she couldn't help but smile.

For the first time since arriving in India, she felt like she had truly been somewhere real.

37

THE LIGHT NAMED ROSHAN

As the bike rumbled along the winding countryside road, Claudia held onto the seat, letting the cool air whip past her face.

She glanced at Roshan, as he maneuvered the bike with ease, his posture relaxed yet focused.

"So, what are you going to do when you get back home today?" she asked, curious about his routine.

Roshan didn't hesitate. "First thing, I have to cut grass for the cows, then feed the chickens. After that, I'll work in the cardamom field for a while. In the evening, I need to milk the cows and bring the milk back here to sell. By the time I'm done, Amma will be home, and we'll do our usual things—like what you saw yesterday."

Claudia raised an eyebrow. "I thought you said it's summer holidays? Shouldn't you be playing or doing something fun?"

Roshan let out a small chuckle, shaking his head. "Play?" He glanced at her briefly before returning his focus to the road. "I play when I get a chance. But right now, I don't have time for that. You won't be able to understand it."

Claudia fell silent for a moment, absorbing his words. His life was so different from anything she had ever known.

Before she knew it, they had reached the resort.

She got down from the bike and was about to thank him when, suddenly, a thought struck her.

"Wait." She placed her hand on the bike's handlebar, stopping him before he could ride off.

Roshan looked at her, puzzled. "What?"

Claudia hesitated for a brief second, then said, "Can I stay one more night at your house?"

His eyebrows shot up in surprise. "What? Why?"

She smiled, tilting her head. "I didn't come here for comfort—I can do that back in my country. I want to stay one more day at your house. Can I?"

Roshan looked genuinely confused. "But why? You have a better place to sleep here."

Claudia shook her head. "Like I said, I didn't come here just to sleep."

Roshan exhaled, thinking for a moment before pulling out his phone. He dialled his mother and spoke quickly in Malayalam. Claudia watched as his face remained neutral, but after a few seconds, his posture relaxed.

He hung up and turned to her. "She said yes."

Claudia's face lit up with a smile. "Great! I'll go inside, get changed, and in the meantime you go to the milk collection point. When you're done, come back for me."

Roshan gave her a half-smile, shaking his head as if he still couldn't believe what was happening.

"Alright, do what you want."

With that, Claudia hurried inside the resort, feeling more excited.

* * *

On the way back, as the bike rumbled along the winding road, Roshan glanced over his shoulder and asked, "Why did you come to India? And why do you want to stay again tonight with us

Claudia, holding onto the side of the seat, let the question settle for a moment before answering.

"I came to India to experience the real India, and learn Indian music " she said, in a thoughtful voice. "But for the first few weeks, all I met were people who were just after my money. It felt like no one saw me as a person—just a tourist, an opportunity to make a few extra rupees."

Roshan let out a small chuckle. "Claudia," he said simply. "This is how anyone who lives off tourists would have behaved with you."

She frowned slightly, confused. "You say they are not wrong?"

"What did you expect from them? They don't have the luxury to be anything else. They see thousands of foreigners like you passing through, spending money like it's nothing. To them, survival is about making sure they get their share of it."

Claudia listened carefully.

"But here, with you and your mom... it was different," she said. "You treated me like... like a guest, not a customer."

Roshan nodded. "That's because, to us, a guest is not a transaction. It's a responsibility."

Claudia fell quiet. She thought about all the moments over the past day—the way Roshan's mother had taken care of her without expecting anything in return, the way Roshan had worried more about her wound than the spilled milk, the way he had given up his phone just to keep her company.

It was a different kind of wealth.

And for the first time, she started to see what Antony might have wanted her to understand.

Claudia spent the entire day following Roshan, doing whatever he did. She helped him gather grass for the cows, watched as he fed the chickens, and even walked with him to the cardamom fields. Though she wasn't much help, Roshan didn't seem to mind.

It was a simple day, filled with small tasks, but it felt peaceful.

Later that evening, as they sat outside, with the sun slowly dipping behind the hills, Roshan mother returned home. Claudia noticed her beaming smile first, then the bags in her hands—so many of them.

She spoke excitedly in Malayalam as she walked towards them, and Roshan turned to Claudia with a grin.

"She said she bought something special from the market so she can cook our traditional food for you tonight."

Claudia blinked in surprise. "For me?"

Roshan nodded. "She's excited to have you here."

Claudia felt something unfamiliar stir in her chest. She had never experienced someone celebrating her presence like this. She was just a guest—a stranger, really—but they were going out of their way to make her feel special.

That night, as the scent of spices filled the air, Roshan and Claudia sat outside, under the dim glow of the hanging bulb, talking about small things—the weather, the hills, and the funny things he had seen in school.

Then, Roshan's mother walked out with two glasses filled with something white and handed one to Claudia and one to Roshan.

"Payasam," she said, smiling warmly.

Roshan translated, "Dessert."

Claudia took a sip, and the sweet, creamy taste of rice and milk filled her mouth. She let out a satisfied hum and smiled back at Roshan's mother.

"This is really good," she said, and though his mother didn't understand the words, she seemed to understand the sentiment.

They sat in quiet contentment, enjoying the peaceful night.

Then Claudia remembered something. "Wait... aren't you supposed to sell milk in the evenings too? Are you not late?"

Roshan gave her a small smile. "Not today."

"Why?" she asked.

He glanced at the glass in her hand. "Because that's what we're enjoying now."

Claudia froze, looking down at the payasam.

They had given her everything.

Milk, which they would normally sell for money, had been turned into something sweet just for her. They weren't rich. In fact, they had so little. But they chose to give, not because they had to, but because they wanted to.

Something inside her shifted.

Then, without thinking, she asked, "I haven't met your father yet. Where is he?"

The change was instant.

Roshan mother turned around and walked quietly back into the house without a word.

Claudia's stomach twisted. She had said something wrong.

Roshan lowered his gaze, his hands gripping his glass tighter. "He died three years ago," he said quietly.

She inhaled sharply. "Oh... I'm so sorry."

He nodded but didn't say anything for a while. His fingers traced the rim of his glass, and his eyes were distant.

"He was a bus driver," he finally continued. "He died in an accident."

There was no anger in his voice, nor bitterness—just a quiet grief that clearly hadn't faded with time.

He blinked a few times, as if trying to push back the emotion. But a single tear slipped out and rolled down his cheek.

Claudia didn't say anything. She didn't try to comfort him with empty words.

Instead, she simply sat there, letting the silence speak for them both.

After that long moment of silence, Claudia turned to Roshan. Her voice was soft, and she careful not to break the stillness that had settled between them.

"Do you have a dream?"

Roshan didn't flinch or hesitate.

"I really want to become rich," he said plainly.

Claudia blinked, caught off guard by the directness. There was no embarrassment in his tone, no shyness—just honesty.

"Why?" she asked.

Roshan looked down at the tumbler in his hand, then back up at her.

"Do you know the meaning of my name?"

Claudia shook her head. "No... what does it mean?"

He offered a faint smile, one touched with something deeper.

"Roshan means light," he said quietly. "My father gave me that name. He believed I would be the light of this house."

He turned slightly, glancing back at the doorway, where his mother's shadow moved behind the curtain of the kitchen.

"I want to build a better house for her. I want her to rest. I want her to smile without worry. That's why I want to be rich—. Just for us to live happily. Comfortably."

Claudia felt something catch in her chest—a gentle ache, warm and bittersweet.

"And how do you plan to do that?" she asked.

Roshan straightened his back slightly, as his eyes sharpened with a quiet fire.

"That's why we do everything we can. We sell milk, we work in the fields, and we take care of what we have. In two years, I'll go to engineering college. That's the plan."

He said it with such clarity, and such conviction, that Claudia was momentarily stunned. This boy—barely into his teens—had more purpose and direction than many adults she'd known.

Before she could say anything more, the curtain lifted and his mother stepped out, wiping her hands on her saree.

"Dinner is ready," she said warmly.

As they stepped inside, the house was filled with the scent of something rich and spiced. Claudia sat at the modest dining table, with a plate placed in front of her—chunks of something golden, tangled in a deep red gravy.

"What is this?" she asked, intrigued.

Roshan grinned. "Kappa biryani."

Claudia raised an eyebrow. "Biryani? It doesn't look like rice."

He laughed, already digging into his plate. "It's not. It's made of tapioca and meat."

Claudia took a bite, and her eyes widened at the burst of flavors—earthy, bold, a bit fiery.

"This is amazing," she said between breaths. "But... definitely hot."

Roshan's mother chuckled softly at her reaction, clearly pleased.

Feeling the warmth in the room, Claudia turned to her. "What's your name?"

The older woman's eyes softened. "Mary."

Claudia repeated it gently. "Mary."

It suited her. There was a quiet strength in her, a glow that came from giving without asking.

Later that night, Claudia stepped into the small room they had prepared for her. She paused in the doorway, with her heart tugging gently.

It was the best room in the house.

She could tell. The cleanest bedsheets, the softest blanket, the only window that looked out onto the hills. They had given it to her without question, without hesitation.

She lay down, staring up at the ceiling, with her thoughts slowly drifting back over the past two days.

There was no luxury here. No air conditioning, no crisp linen or modern lighting.

And yet, it felt more welcoming than any place she had stayed in weeks.

She turned on her side and pulled the thin blanket closer to her body, letting the quiet of the night settle around her like a lullaby.

This boy—this child, really—was living a life built on effort and responsibility. He had no complaints and no expectations. Just a simple, burning desire to take care of the one person who had raised him.

She thought of her own life. All the times she had crumbled under doubt, believing the world was unfair. All the comfort she had taken for granted. All the time she had wasted waiting for something to change.

And here was Roshan.

Changing his world one small act at a time.

A slow, steady breath escaped her lips. A knot in her chest began to loosen.

She was beginning to understand now.

* * *

Claudia woke before dawn, knowing that it was her last morning in the small house on the hill.

She dressed quietly and packed her belongings. Before leaving the room, she slipped a bundle of Indian currency—around five hundred pounds worth—under the pillow, with a note for the young engineer. She wished she could leave more, but it was all the cash she had left in that bag .

Nobody noticed.

As she stepped outside, the comforting sounds of the village waking filled her ears: distant temple bells, birds calling from the trees, and the gentle rustle of the breeze through cardamom fields.

Roshan was already on his bike, with the milk container tied securely to the back, ready for his morning deliveries. Nearby, his mother stood with folded hands, smiling warmly at Claudia.

Without hesitation, Claudia stepped forward and hugged her.

"Thank you, Mary," she whispered, feeling a sudden tightness in her chest. "I'll never forget this."

Though Mary didn't fully understand Claudia's words, she responded with a gentle pat on Claudia's back, and a deepening smile as she stepped away.

Claudia climbed onto the back of the bike, and Roshan glanced over his shoulder.

"Resort?" he asked casually.

She shook her head. "I checked out yesterday."

He frowned slightly. "Then where to?"

"The bus stop."

Roshan nodded without further questions, started the engine, and they rode in comfortable silence along the winding hill roads. The cool morning air brushed Claudia's face, carrying with it scents of damp earth and fresh greenery.

* * *

At the quiet roadside bus stop, Claudia stepped down from the bike as Roshan killed the engine. The early morning light had turned golden now, stretching long shadows across the cracked pavement.

He looked at her, with one foot still on the pedal, and the other planted in the dust.

"So," he asked, "what's next for you?"

Claudia took a breath, with her eyes scanning the hills one last time, before turning back to him.

"I'm meeting a few people... to learn more about Indian music," she said. "Then I'll fly back home. I have things I need to finish."

Roshan nodded, watching her closely.

"Hope you enjoyed your time here."

She smiled. "I did."

There was a brief pause. The wind rustled in some nearby trees, and a bird cried overhead. Then Claudia's voice dropped to something softer, more tentative.

"I want to say sorry to you."

Roshan raised an eyebrow. "For what?"

She hesitated, exhaling slowly.

"For who I was. For the way I thought about India before I came. I think... a lot of people outside don't really see India for what it is. I used to be one of them."

Roshan smirked. "So, you were one of those people who say India smells like curry?"

Claudia flinched a little—but didn't look away. "I used to. Not anymore."

She gave him a curious look. Roshan tilted his head. "You wonder how I know all this, don't you?" He shrugged, in a matter-of-fact way. "The internet is available everywhere in the world, not just the UK."

Claudia studied his face, unsure whether he was offended or just stating facts.

"You're not... angry at me? For thinking that way before?"

Roshan laughed, shaking his head.

"Why would I be? Just because someone calls us 'curry people,' do you think we'll stop eating curry?"

He paused, then added, "A person who keeps changing just to fit others' opinions will never be happy. Because they lose themselves. Twitter is not reality"

Claudia went quiet, letting his words settle deep.

Then Roshan looked at her with a more serious gaze.

"Tell me something… Have you ever wondered why Indians do well in other countries, but so many still struggle here?"

She nodded slowly. "I have. But I never really understood why."

Roshan leaned in slightly, with his voice low and firm.

"Because in countries like yours, the opportunities are already there. You just have to find them. Here… we have to create them."

His words hit like a slow, invisible wave.

"It's not just India," he added. "It's every developing country. We can survive here, sure. But if we want to compete with the rest of the world—we have to work five times harder. Because everything is stacked against us. Currency, perception, resources… all of it."

Claudia's throat tightened. She felt as though he'd peeled back a curtain she hadn't even known existed.

After a long moment, she asked, almost in a whisper, "How old are you?"

Roshan grinned, his boyishness returning for a flicker. "I'm 16."

She stared at him. A 16-year-old with the wisdom of someone twice his age.

"Why are you so different?" she asked.

His answer was soft but immediate. "Because there's a difference between a person who wishes for something—and a person who needs something."

Claudia didn't respond right away. She couldn't. That sentence held a truth she felt in her bones.

Then, almost involuntarily, she laughed—a soft, breathy laugh filled with disbelief and quiet admiration.

She shook her head, smiling as she looked at him.

"There's something about you, Roshan…"

There was something about this place. This family. This boy who had reminded her how small her problems really were—and how much she still had to learn.

The bus pulled into the station with a groan of brakes and a cloud of dust.

Claudia turned to him, with her bag slung over her shoulder. She offered him a genuine smile—the kind that only comes after something real has shifted inside.

"Thank you, Roshan."

He raised a brow. "For what?"

"For everything."

He didn't say much. Just a small nod, the kind that said I get it.

"Take care, Claudia."

She climbed onto the bus, and, as it pulled away, she looked back one last time.

Roshan stood there, one hand resting on his bike, watching the bus go—not with sadness, but with something steady. Solid. Sure. And Claudia realized that, in a quiet corner of Idukki, in just a few days, a stranger had helped her see the world—and herself—a little more clearly.

She found a seat by the window, and, as the vehicle pulled away, she watched Roshan standing there, with his bike beside him, in his world that was so different from hers, yet somehow, she felt like she understood it now.

As the hills of Idukki faded into the distance, she thought about all the things she had learned in just two days.

Claudia stayed in Kerala for two more months, fully immersing herself in learning Indian music, understanding rhythms and melodies that were completely new to her.

And then, with a heart full of lessons and a mind clearer than ever before, she set off on the return journey.

38

BECOMING CLAUDIA

E ight months later, The stage lights bathed Claudia in a soft golden glow as she stepped forward, her silhouette striking against the vast concert hall. The air was electric with anticipation, a quiet hum of breathless energy just before the storm.

The world had been watching.

Her journey—from a schoolteacher with a dream to a celebrated musician standing at the height of global acclaim—had unfolded in ways even she hadn't foreseen.

Tonight, she wasn't just an artist.

She was a voice.

A vessel of stories.

A testament to resilience, to grace, to growth.

She had just won multiple music awards—not for her technical brilliance, but for the soul she had poured into every note, every composition, and every silence between sounds.

An interviewer stood beside her, mic in hand, smiling. "Before we listen to the masterpiece you've created," he said, "do you have anything to say to your fans?"

Claudia took a deep, steady breath and looked out over the sea of faces before her.

She thought of Antony, and his quiet wisdom.

She thought of the days when she had doubted herself. The weeks of searching. The silence inside her that had once felt like failure—but that had only been waiting for music.

Her eyes scanned the audience, and amidst the thousands, she spotted them.

Luca stood tall with a proud smile on his face, his arm around his young son Pete, who clapped with uncontainable joy. Not far from them, Mr. Sewell stood in quiet admiration, his expression calm but full of pride.

Her lips curved into a small smile.

"Don't look for happiness anywhere," she said into the mic, in a voice gentle but sure. "Find your happiness inside you. And be happy from the inside."

For a heartbeat, the hall was silent.

Then, the applause erupted—wave after wave of thunderous appreciation crashing around her, rising like a tide.

And then—

The music began.

"Free Soul."

It was unlike anything the audience had ever heard.

The haunting, meditative melody of the sitar intertwined with a wistful, melancholic piano. Bagpipes hummed softly beneath, their breathy voice wrapping around a lush violin section that sang with ache and triumph. African drums beat in rhythm with Indian tablas, while orchestral strings carried it all forward—bold, sweeping, alive.

It wasn't just music.

It was a memory.

A map.

A mirror.

It was Antony's calm voice in the chaos.

Roshan's fire and steadiness.

Mary's quiet hospitality, and her hands that healed without asking for thanks.

It was pain and hope. Doubt and faith.

It was the voice of every person who had helped her find her own.

And it was breath-taking.

As the final chord faded into silence, Claudia lifted her hands from the piano, letting the stillness settle.

For a moment, there was utter stillness.

Then the audience rose as one, in a standing ovation—thunderous applause, tears, cheers, and joy.

Claudia sat quietly for a second longer, with her eyes closed, as the warmth of the room washed over her.

She had done it.

Not just as a musician.

As a human being.

She had created something that mattered.

And more than that—

She had become someone who mattered.

* * *

Back at Antony's house, the air felt different.

It no longer felt like she was visiting.

It felt like she had come home.

For the first time since his passing, Claudia walked up to the door that had remained shut all these months. The room she had not dared to enter.

Until now.

Her hand hesitated on the doorknob, then she turned it.

The door creaked softly as it opened, revealing a space suspended in time. The desk was still neat, a half-used notepad resting beside a worn-out pen. Books lined the shelves—some with the spines bent, some marked with yellowed post

His bed was still perfectly made, with the blanket tucked in carefully, untouched.

Claudia stepped inside slowly, not wanting to disturb the silence.

She ran her fingers gently across the edge of the desk, and over the blanket.

She sat on the edge of the bed and lowered herself back, letting her head rest on the pillow.

For a long moment, she stared up at the ceiling.

And then, quietly, she closed her eyes.

In that stillness, she could feel him.

A presence.

A warmth.

It was as if Antony had never really left—he had just stepped into another room.

Claudia smiled faintly, as the weight in her chest loosened with something like peace.

"Thank you, Antony," she whispered into the quiet.

"It's warm in here

39

A LETTER TO THE READER

D
ear Reader,
 Hi! I hope you had a wonderful journey with Claudia.
 Thank you for choosing to walk beside her—through her struggles, her growth, her heartbreak, and the quiet strength she found in unexpected places.

As a new writer, every story I write is a step forward, and every reader like you makes that journey meaningful. Your thoughts, reflections, and feedback mean the world to me. I kindly request you to leave your honest review—whether it's praise, critique, or suggestions. It will help me grow, improve, and evolve as a better storyteller.

Thank you so much for buying this book and investing your valuable time to time-travel with Claudia.

If you'd like to discuss anything related to the story, feel free to reach out to me on Instagram. I'll do my best to respond as promptly as possible.

With deep gratitude,

S. Sebastian

(A storyteller in progress)

@S.SEBASTIANOFFICIAL

About the Author

You can connect with me on:

🌐 https://www.goodreads.com/user/show/191573457-s-sebastian

🔗 https://www.instagram.com/s.sebastianofficial

Subscribe to my newsletter:

✉ https://knightswordpublication.com

Printed in Dunstable, United Kingdom